PRAISE FOR SONYA CHUNG'S DEBUT
Long for This World:

"An intricately structured and powerfully resonant portrait of lives lived at the crossroads of culture, and a family torn between the old world and the new, *Long for This World* marks a powerful debut from a young writer of great talent and promise."
—Kate Walbert, National Book Award finalist for *Our Kind* and author of *A Short History of Women*

"Chung presents each scene with confidence and trusts us to make the necessary connections, to see what the characters are saying by allowing themselves to be seen. And in fact, one of the joys in reading this debut is connecting the pieces, then stepping back for the big view: the intricate and nuanced family story that emerges . . . a portrait of the way the Hans are both fractured and then relinked in unexpected ways."
—Celeste Ng, *Fiction Writers Review* and author of *Everything I Never Told You*

"[A] beautiful book that focuses on the small but complicated negotiations of a family, and larger, global questions of identity, art, and happiness . . . I loved it. It's so gracefully told, and rich—not to mention riveting."
—Edan Lepucki, *The Millions* and author of *California*

". . . lyrical and insightful debut novel . . . Chung carefully describes the longing and loss felt by each of the characters she has flawlessly created . . . Alliances and allegiances are formed between East and West, male and female, young and old, parents and the childless. Chung juxtaposes the Hans in obvious and less obvious pairings, each of which shows them in a new light and highlights their complexity as they struggle with their roles in the family and the world in terms of gender, relationships, career goals, and cultural expectations."
—*The Boston Globe*

". . . elegant debut novel . . . Switching deftly between different characters' points of view, Chung portrays with precision and grace each character's struggle to find his or her place in the family and in the world."
—*Publishers Weekly*

the Loved Ones

A NOVEL BY

Sonya Chung

Relegation Books, USA

Book design by Zach Dodson
Cover lettering by Teo Tuominen

ISBN: 978-0-9847648-4-6

Library of Congress Control Number: 2015958933

the
loved ones

A NOVEL

SONYA CHUNG

RELEGATIONBOOKS
2016

For John

For a moment she seemed poised to resist, but then she followed without a word. They arrived, breathless, at the oak grove on the ridge behind the village. The brilliant moonlight was no longer welcome. They searched for a place that was shadier still.

—Hwang Sun-won, *Lost Souls*

There has also been some inconsistency regarding what the sankofa, thought to stand for a West African proverb, means. The 2006 [African Burial Ground project] reports render the proverb as, "It is not a taboo to return and fetch it when you forget," while the new interpretive display offers the easier-to-grasp phrase, "Look to the past to understand the present."

—Sewell Chan, "Coffin's Emblem Defies Certainty," The New York Times, January 26, 2010

Image courtesy of Mark McCoy.

BOOK ONE:
Les Proches

Kenyon Street, NW Washington, DC
1951

Was the little girl who pulled open the front door with two hands. Yellow dress, and yellow ribbons at the ends of her braids. He saw that the dress was too tight across her chest and riding up where her buttocks were rounding out; fraying at the hem. It looked sad, and poor. But she loved the dress, obviously. Wearing it in the middle of winter.

Her mother sent her to answer the door, he knew. The grandmother or uncle would have blocked his way. *He ain't come to the hospital; why he come now.* He wasn't sure he didn't want his way blocked.

He was late even. Said he'd come in the afternoon. Somehow couldn't come in the light of day. But now—porch light on, cold dark night giving off starlight, too—he felt blinded, and caught out.

The girl stepped aside, big eyes and silent. Always eyeing him like that. *You're not my daddy,* the eyes said. *Give us back our mama.*

He stood on the porch, unmoving. The girl held the door. Inside he heard the baby crying; its mother's muffled tired voice.

His own mother had warned him; his big brother, his friends, too. *Don't start something you can't follow it through. Widow with four children. Three wild boys, that homely girl. Can't have her and not them. Woman's eyes are heavy on you.*

He liked it, though. Her being older, her full hips, loving on him so heavy; how he could make her dark spirits light up. She was deep sad when he met her that night at the club, and sexy in low-cut electric blue. After that night, all he had to do was smile his easy smile, touch her where and how he wanted. He liked too making the rest of them shake their heads and purse their lips; he was after the disapproval, the satisfaction of it. Eventually—too many years later—he'd outgrow that.

Feet lead heavy. The girl waiting. Then, swollen slippered feet coming down the stairs, hem of her housedress; baby in her arm. Baby boy.

She saw who it was and lit up like she always did,

then stopped short on the landing. Saw him frozen there, outside. Saw how, at the sight of her and the dark bundle, his face drew blank and hard, eyebrows straight across like thick painted lines on a road.

The girl looked back and forth between them.

Essie raised the boy up onto her shoulder, turned its face toward the door. Scrunched brown face, fist up by its cheek. It kicked its legs and opened its black licorice eyes. And Frank saw—he saw everything then. The boy was his, for sure. If he'd doubted, now he knew. Charles, they were calling him, but he didn't know it—not then, not for a long time. There was an instant, if it was that long: the shoulds, the rights, the wrongs flitted in and out of his mind like dumb brown moths flapping at a light bulb. He shut the light. No. Don't want. Want other, want out, out there. Got plans. Not here, this, them.

Feet no longer lead. Feet flying down the steps, onto the black street. Flying, flying away, into the night—to life, unlived, calling.

SUMMER 1984

1.

The boy was six, the girl nine. Their father, Charles Frederick Douglass Lee, was himself one of five children; each had looked after the next while Charles's mother worked night shifts and his grandmother worked days at the same corner store owned by a cousin. He'd come up fine and didn't believe in babysitters. It was his wife, Alice, who insisted the girl was not old enough to be left alone with the boy. "What if there's an emergency," Alice Lee said to Charles. She often made statements in the form of questions. She said "emergency" in a near whisper.

"She's a smart girl, she knows how to dial a phone." Charles favored the girl, loved her more, even; but he was careful not to show it as much as he might. Veda was dark-skinned, almost as dark as him, darker than the boy, but had most of her mother's features—heart-shaped face, gray eyes, celestial nose. She did have his full lips and bright, large-toothed smile, everyone said so. She had his dark, purplish gums, too; though no one said so. Veda's hair was dark brown, soft and wavy, but her mother didn't understand as well as her father what this meant, how lucky she was.

The boy, Benny, was light-skinned, but he had his father's thick eyebrows and prominent forehead. He was a big boy for his age and barreled around like a fullback, shoulders squared, hands balled into fists. He couldn't yet read, or wouldn't. Sometimes, he still wet the bed. He'd bitten other children, more than once, and crashed full-force into anything in-progress that he hadn't himself started—a jigsaw puzzle, another boy's Lego house, his sister's My Little Ponies arranged for a pageant. Charles marveled at Alice's calm, even tones with both children. Sometimes he loved her for it, sometimes he hated her. Sometimes he wanted to slap the boy and shove his wife; sometimes the other way around.

Alice Lee was going back to work. She was a social worker and had found a job at a Korean nursing home in Silver Spring. She'd been home with the children all these years and was fortunate to get the job after being out of the workforce. Alice did have a nurse practitioner's degree—she'd gone to night school when Benny started pre-K—and the nursing home needed someone like her, who could communicate well enough with the Mexican service staff (Peace Corps in Chile), with the residents and doctors (DoD educational assistant, Yongsan Base in Seoul), and with the pharmaceutical and insurance people on the phone.

For weeks Charles and Alice argued over whether to hire a babysitter—"discussed," Alice would say—and in the end Charles gave in, mostly for the girl's sake. Why should she have to watch over the boy.

"There's a nurse at the home whose daughter could do it," Alice said. "The director put me in touch with her, and she sounds *perfect*. Polite, responsible. Her mother has been with the home for many years."

So she's already arranged it, Charles thought. Of course she has.

"Her name is Lee," Alice said, like an offering, and with a chuckle. "Hannah—the girl—Hannah Lee."

A Korean girl. Charles didn't like it. Just as he didn't like his wife working at that nursing home. Did the mother of the girl know about him? Charles didn't ask, because he knew the answer: no way she did. Not at first. Alice would wait to reveal it, her *gamman-saram* husband—to the mother, to all her coworkers—after she'd proven herself trustworthy and likeable. His wife was a smart girl, too. Lee was likely a useful name to have around there.

Charles wasn't surprised: so many of them were named Lee. He'd gotten used to it in Korea, the bitter irony. The KATUSAs had found it especially amusing: *Lee-san,* they'd called him, though he generally didn't take it as friendliness.

Hannah Lee came by herself on a Saturday afternoon in late May to meet the children and be shown around. Alice was in the backyard with the boy when the bell rang. Charles got up from his recliner—he'd been scanning the scores and listening to WJFK sports—to answer it.

Hannah wore a navy T-shirt dress with a braided belt hanging below the waist, jelly sandals, and shiny lip gloss (in fact it was just

Vaseline; her mother did not allow makeup). Her legs were long, her hair wavy and brown at the ends, her eyeglasses perfectly round. She was taller and looked older than Charles had expected. Though come to think of it, Alice had never said how old she was. He guessed about thirteen. Maybe it was her handbag, a square Gucci that was slung across her body and reminded Charles instantly of the fakes sold in Itaewon by the dozens to officers' wives. Or maybe it was some other quality—the solemnity of her pale, rectangular face. When she smiled and introduced herself, it seemed to require much effort, an awkward exertion. But she was not surprised to see his black face. Charles knew this, because he knew that look well enough, had borne it over and over again from Alice's friends and family. No, it wasn't that. It was the nicety, a learned affect of cheerfulness, that seemed to cause the girl strain. Alice had apparently not detected it on the phone when she spoke to her the day before—*She sounds perfect,* she had said—and this knowledge gave Charles Lee a small burst of pleasure.

2.

The phone rang just as Soon-mi squatted by the flowerbed with her trowel and kitchen knife. She could hear it through the sliding screen door, and so could Chong-ho from across the small yard. The day was mild and still and overcast, and the deep ink-blue of the *Baptisia*—false indigo it was sometimes called—seemed to ring brightly, shockingly, along with the telephone.

It was late in the season to be dividing, but the forecast called for cooler weather and light rain tomorrow, Sunday, into Monday. There was space in the flowerbed that bordered the back of the house where a peony had been lost to an early spring storm (the gutter had come crashing down). Soon-mi thought she could divide and replant all three of the indigos, and finish the weeding she'd started earlier, before dinner.

Chong-ho looked to Soon-mi from the vegetable garden. Not with his eyes, but with his attention. The phone rang a second and third time.

Soon-mi stood and removed her gloves, laying them down, along with her tools, on the patio table; she slid the screen door open and stepped through.

Just before the door shut, Chong-ho looked up: he saw Soon-mi's blue rubber slipper dangling from her foot. The slipper dropped to the doormat, as Soon-mi disappeared into the house. Who could be calling, Chong-ho wondered. It was strange that the phone would ring at this time on a Saturday. Probably one of Hannah's school friends. That girl who was always calling, the fat one with the brown skin and short skirt who talked too fast. She'd come after school with Hannah once but then never again. Maybe Soon-mi had said something, though likely not; Hannah would not need to be told. Chong-ho grimaced and went back to transplanting the go-chu.

During the week sometimes there were sales calls, but never on weekends. Soon-mi thought it could only be one person, and she let out an audible sigh when she heard James's voice—as if her wishing had made it so.

"Hi, *Ummah*." There was an echo, along with yelling and laughing in the background.

"James?" Soon-mi said. She'd raised her voice, and it cracked. "Why so much noisy?"

"Those are just my suitemates. I'm in the bathroom with the phone. Remember when I switched the long cord from your phone last time? It's the only way to have any privacy around here."

"Sweet? Mate?"

"Roommates, Ummah. I have two, I told you. They're okay. Just blowing off steam before exams."

"Unh. Exam. You have exam now."

"Next week," he said. There was a muffled bang, then the crash of aluminum cans hitting the floor. James covered the mouthpiece and hissed, "Hey, dickheads, knock it off."

Soon-mi waited.

"Sorry, they're just horsing around. Anyway. Um . . ."

They spoke for just a few minutes, as always. His parents wanted to hear that James was doing all right and studying hard; and that's what he told them, every month. Usually he called on Sundays. This week he had study group all day Sunday, and an end-of-semester party at the home of one of his professors Sunday night. He explained all this, which didn't take long. When they finished speaking, he asked for Hannah. Soon-mi said she'd gone out. She didn't tell James about the babysitting job. It was a long story, and she didn't care to get into it; Hannah could tell him herself next time. And who knew how long it would last anyway. The American woman, Alice Lee—her children were old enough to be home alone, really.

"Tell her to call me sometime," James said. "Just, you know. Whenever."

"Unh, okay," Soon-mi said. Then quickly she told him to make sure he ate well, not just ramen noodles, and he laughed, even though she wasn't making a joke. Then they hung up.

Soon-mi stepped back out onto the patio and retrieved her trowel and knife. As she pulled on her gloves, she became thoughtful and laid the tools again on the patio table, then walked toward the far end of the yard, the sunny corner, where Chong-ho was putting the last of the go-chu seedlings in the ground.

"*Moh han-eun goon-yo?* What is it?" Chong-ho handed her a seedling, then proceeded to mix in the fertilizer he'd just sprinkled over the hole. Soon-mi cupped the ball of spindly roots in her orange gloves. She told her husband that James was fine and conveyed his reasons for calling on a Saturday. Chong-ho clawed at the dirt in the bottom of the hole with both hands—he never wore gloves—making sure the plant food was deeply and evenly mixed.

When he was done, Chong-ho held out his right hand, which was dark with earth, and Soon-mi placed the seedling in his palm. "Hannah missed talking to him." The words formed themselves, and multiple meanings, from an uneasy place that Soon-mi knew well; though only as a kind of bodily thrumming. She couldn't have named it, not even to herself.

"Where did she go?"

Soon-mi was silent for a moment. She had not anticipated this question; that is, she had not considered how she would answer it. She had been distracted by sending Hannah off. Of course Hannah's father would question the purpose of her having a job: they provided for her, she should be studying. "Out with a friend," Soon-mi said, and their eyes met briefly as Chong-ho stood to stretch his back. In that glance, Chong-ho was saying, *What you tell me is always truth enough*, and Soon-mi was saying, *I understand the nature of your trust.*

Chong-ho squatted again, and Soon-mi knelt next to him. He mixed in the plant food and set the seedlings in the holes; she scooped dirt and filled the gaps, then patted the soil lightly. When they got to the last hole, Soon-mi said, "Hannah should call him. He has good advice for her, I think. He is becoming more responsible, concerned for the younger one."

Chong-ho said nothing. Soon-mi shifted her weight slowly to achy ankles and hips, and brushed off her knees. As she turned to go work on the *Baptisias*, Chong-ho raised his head and said, "She will be home for dinner?"

"Unh," Soon-mi said.

Chong-ho lowered his eyes, and with that, it was agreed: he would encourage Hannah to call her brother.

Soon-mi's slippers made a muted slapping noise against her socks as she walked toward the house. She would have time to divide and transplant only one of the false indigos. She worked from a squat, and when she plunged her trowel into the ground, loosening the root ball on all sides and then pulling up from the base of the stalks, she felt how deep and intricate the roots were; how they clung to the earth that fed them. She dug deeper, pulled firmly and evenly from the top, wiggling the plant from side to side. The roots loosened, and Soon-mi thought, Why *should* Hannah work for the American family? Soon-mi had made the offering to Alice Lee without thinking, though it seemed right at the time. She'd felt relief when the woman wrote down their phone number. Hannah would be occupied, looking after children. Soon-mi was not convinced this was a bad idea; nor a good one, exactly. The uneasy thrumming persisted.

The root ball came up, and Soon-mi fell back on her heels but maintained her squat. She laid the matted, gnarly thing in the dirt and eyed the knife, which she'd staked upright at the border where dirt met grass. She sighed. This was the part she didn't like. Always she had to remind herself, as she sliced through the bone-white roots and offshoots like baby hairs, that she was regenerating, propagating, and not destroying.

3.

It was the Saturday before Memorial Day, and Kenyon Street was lined with American flags. They shot out like saluting arms from the porch roofs of row houses. The flag on Charles and Alice Lee's four-bedroom brick was smaller than the neighbors'—colors dull and faded by comparison, material drab. In this way, the house stood out.

Hannah Lee walked east from the Columbia Heights Metro station along a sidewalk that was clean but badly cracked. Weeds and tree roots pushed up with a brute force that made Hannah think of her crooked front tooth—how the baby tooth had hung on stubbornly until the permanent one had to come breaking through at an angle. As she walked, Hannah scanned for the little peaks made by broken concrete, to keep from tripping.

There were people sitting on every porch or stoop along the block—black people, mostly old people, a few babies and toddlers in their laps. They stared at Hannah as she walked by. When she began to feel the stares, she looked up. She stared back. No one smiled. One little boy waved. Hannah was not frightened or nervous, though she had some awareness that perhaps she should be. She didn't mind—liked it even, a little, this being noticed.

The Lees' house was exactly mid-block. There was no one sitting on the porch or stoop, just a mess of bicycles and car/truck/train toys, and potted plants, flowers mostly, unkempt and clustered along the left end of the red-painted steps. Hannah liked the house right away, though she could not have said exactly why. She did think of how her father would have scoffed at the annuals in the pots—her parents grew only vegetables and hardy perennials, in large beds that they tended meticulously from March to November—and how her mother would have pursed her lips at the disorder.

Soon-mi had not asked to see the exact address; Alice Lee had told her, "a short walk from the Columbia Heights stop," but she had not said in which direction. Soon-mi had assumed west, toward the park. Alice Lee was a white woman with a master's degree, after all.

Hannah rang the bell and waited. A man came to the door. He looked surprised, and he stared at Hannah, though in a different way from the porch and stoop people. Hannah did not mind this man's staring either; though after a few moments of silence, she couldn't help but think of her brother, James, who—now that he was majoring in business instead of smoking pot behind the Burger King—had started calling her "spacey."

"I'm . . . Hannah. The babysitter." Something caught in Hannah's voice—a flatness swallowed her words. She had intended to be polite, and cheerful. She didn't know what had come over her: it was like when she had to read Ophelia's *Hey nonny, nonny* section in front of the class and she delivered it deadpan, even though she knew she was supposed to be dramatic.

The man was very dark, and big like an athlete. He had a broad, smooth forehead; wide Eskimo cheeks; a strong jaw, which hung slightly open. His eyes were round and shiny and black, like licorice jelly beans, and Hannah looked straight into the right one (his left), which she could just barely do without craning her neck. He was handsome, this man. She liked the word—much more than *cute* or *hot*—and enjoyed the pleasure of both beholding and thinking it. (*Pleasure*, on the other hand, was a word that Hannah would never have thought, or spoken.)

Charles blinked once. Hannah lowered her gaze to the many-colored flecks in his brown sweater vest, then to the crisp white of his T-shirt. Her eyes landed on Charles's collarbones, which pushed out just like the sidewalk's thick tree roots.

Another half-beat, then Hannah cleared her throat. "Mrs. Lee said . . . three o'clock." Her feet pressed hard into the concrete, her shoulders dropped from her ears. She looked up. Charles lowered his chin, put one hand on his head as if to rub it; then stepped back from the door. He said her name and got it wrong—*Come on in, Anna*—and Hannah corrected him: "No, it's *Haa*-nah." The voice that came out this time was strange, but also familiar—it was the one she normally heard and kept strictly inside her head. Not rude exactly, but absent the ubiquitous interrogative that all the girls had begun using.

The voice had raced out. Hannah was about to regret it, chase after the words and smash them with her hands like ants, when Charles's hand came off his head, licorice eyes rolling up and smiling bright. "Sorry, right. Come in, *Haa*-nah." Voice warm and deep. Not deep like a tuba, but lighter, and a little sad, like a clarinet. Hannah stepped past, two long strides, and into the house.

4.

Charles led Hannah through the kitchen to the back door. Hannah had both hands on her purse. In new places she felt loose and awkward with her hands dangling at her sides; she always wanted to touch things, like a blind person groping with her fingertips.

Charles opened the screen door and stepped out onto a square cement landing. "Alice," he called, and motioned for Hannah to descend the steps. His voice had changed: it was both heavier and more floaty. Hannah watched her feet as she took each steep and slanted step. Charles then disappeared into the house, the screen door falling shut behind him with a light crash.

"No slamming!" A boy stood up from a crouch, sausage finger pointing up in the air.

Alice Lee was kneeling in the grass. She raised herself up without using her hands, brushed dirt from her denim pedal pushers, then nudged a bouncy blonde lock from the corner of her eye with a knuckle. "And no shouting, mister," she said.

The boy was Bennett, after Alice's maternal great-grandfather. They called him Benny. He grinned, slapped a chubby brown hand over his mouth, then leaped a frog-leap to another corner of the sandbox, toward a yellow dump truck. Noisy, catastrophic collisions ensued. The boy was all hair, big and Brillo-y, the same burlap-sack color of his skin. He wore a T-shirt two sizes too big, shorts that went down to his calves. He was an ugly boy, and not a little frightening.

"You're Hannah," Alice said, smiling with her lips but frowning with her eyes.

It was an odd greeting; it made one feel caught out somehow. Charles leaned on the kitchen sink drinking a Pabst and looking out the window. He felt for the girl. He watched his wife amble toward Hannah in her cowgirlish way, reaching out her hand. The two were likely the same height, but Alice slouched slightly—or maybe it was just that she had sharp shoulders and a short neck, it was hard to tell. Charles did not care to watch the scene anymore. He went back to the scores, to his La-Z-Boy.

Out in the yard, Alice said, "So this is it," spreading her arms. "Did you have any trouble finding us?" Hannah shook her head no, said from Wheaton it was six stops and one transfer, and a short walk from the station, just as Alice had said. "Good, I'm glad it won't be a long commute for you. Makes everything simpler." Alice went on to describe the areas of the small yard and what each child liked to do there—Veda at the picnic table with her craft projects, Benny in the sandbox or on the climber. There was a trellis with thick brown vines growing all over it that looked like something out of a children's storybook. It was in fact a small fig tree whose branches had grown long and snakelike. "Hose play is fine, especially on hot days, but you should hold the hose for them, or else Benny gets a little wild."

"Should they be in swimsuits?" Hannah asked.

"Veda will want to change. Benny can just lose his shirt."

Hannah nodded.

"So Benny is six," Alice continued, as if pointing out yet another feature of the yard.

"Six and a quarter!" Benny shouted.

"Six and a *quarter*." Alice rolled her eyes, and Hannah pushed out a small laugh. "Veda is nine, ten in September. She's at a friend's house down the street. I'll show you the rest of the house and then you and I can walk over to the Mitchells' to pick up Veda. She's over there enough that you should meet them." Hannah nodded again. Alice Lee was clearly, thoroughly in charge.

After the tour, which was really just a walk around the first floor, Alice told Charles they'd be back in a few minutes. Benny continued to accelerate, crash, and explode things in back. "When you can't hear him, *that's* when he needs checking on." It was not clear for whom the statement was meant, Hannah or Charles.

The front gate closed behind them; Hannah and Alice headed west to the Mitchells'. With her mind, Hannah looked back toward the house; with her eyes, she noticed Alice Lee's bouncy blonde hair. It was just the style she herself had hoped for when she'd gone for a perm. On Alice Lee, though, with her pointed shoulders and skinny legs, it looked somehow not-right; like movie-star sunglasses on a cloudy afternoon.

They walked in the opposite direction from the station—just two streets over, but a different neighborhood altogether. The sidewalks were wider, and even; the faces mostly white, and relatively young. On one side of the street the houses were very tall and lean—like Olympic athletes, solid and erect—all brick, and without porches. Some of them looked like castles, with their bay windows and turrets. On the other side, the porch roofs were held up by beautiful white pillars. None of the houses on the Mitchells' street had chain-link fences.

Hannah thought how her father would consider all these houses—attached to one another, with their tiny yards—inferior. But Hannah liked them—the way she liked chess, which her friend Raj had taught her, and memorizing vocabulary and verb conjugations for Madame Glissant's French class. Anyway, she knew her father missed a lot of things; that he and her mother lived so much apart from others and did not see everything clearly.

Alice stopped in front of a fancy iron gate and let out a mysterious sigh. It was a tall porchless house with green double doors. Hannah and Alice ascended the steps, and Alice rang the bell. "Karen's a pediatrician, so I never worry when Veda is over here on the weekends." Alice spoke in tight, confident tones, like a receptionist for an important person. "Amy is Veda's best friend, and they're young for sleepovers, but I allow it. Amy's a very sweet girl."

On cue, they heard the pitter-patter of small feet running to the door, which opened slowly. A tiny, full-freckled girl pulled with both hands.

"Hello, Amy," Alice said, leaning down as if she might pet her.

"We knew it was you," Amy Mitchell giggled. Her bare feet were cross-stacked on top of each other, one knee bent, in the manner of children who have to go to the toilet. She chewed on a strand of frizzy brown hair, the rest of which was piled elaborately on top of her head with a fistful of bobby pins. Sparkly pink earrings hung from her lobes.

"Hi Alice, come in!" a voice called from within. Alice helped little Amy with the door, pushing her way inside.

"They're here!" Amy called.

"My, what pretty earrings," Alice said, reaching out with her fingertips.

The girl leaned forward with one ear, so they could be properly admired. "We're playing makeover." Amidst Amy's freckles were glitter stars, sparkling around her eyes and cheeks.

Amy turned and pattered back toward the kitchen. Alice and Hannah followed. Alice fell behind Hannah, lingering to notice the new bamboo floors. The lighting was different, too—modern half-moon sconces led them down the long hallway. Karen Mitchell had a busy practice and was highly sought-after among the government set; she also published articles and taught at Georgetown. Her husband, Rick, was an estate lawyer.

"Hi, Karen. I guess we're a little earlier than I said." It was not quite an apology.

In the kitchen they found Veda, sitting in a lacquer bar chair, legs crossed at the ankles. Her hair had been tightly French-braided and tied up in back; a rhinestone tiara circled her crown. Karen Mitchell leaned over her, applying blue eye shadow.

"Ta da!" The shadow was light and shimmery on Veda's dark skin. The girl sat perfectly upright, and with her hair pulled back so

tightly her face looked both calm and alert. Against the shimmer of
the blue shadow and the sparkle of the tiara, Veda's grey eyes turned
translucent, shifty and complex like a crystal.

Hannah nearly gaped. The sight of Veda took her breath away,
and for a moment, she saw not a made-up child in a stranger's
kitchen, but an African princess.

"My goodness." Alice's tone was somehow both airy and taut.
Amy giggled with her hand over her mouth.

"Oh, I hope you don't mind, Alice. I had a feeling this blue would
just be spectacular on V. Do you remember wearing this stuff? God,
the seventies!"

Alice smiled weakly. She'd never worn eye shadow in her life.
Karen's thin pink T-shirt was sliding off her bare shoulder, pale and
freckled like her daughter.

"These next, these next!" Amy was jumping up and down, holding
a small black container with a clear plastic top. False eyelashes.

"Put those down, honey. Those are for another time, maybe. In a
few years." Then Karen winked at Hannah. "Maybe when you're old
enough to babysit."

"Oh, gosh, sorry." Alice's voice was looser now, but too loud.
"This is Hannah, who I was telling you about. She'll be watching the
kids after school."

"We have a babysitter, too," Amy said, twirling around on the ball
of one foot. "She's sixteen, and she has big ones."

"Amy." Karen flashed her daughter a look, but she was smiling.

"Well, Hannah is thirteen, but she's very *responsible*."

Hannah flushed, and noted Alice's rounding up her age by a few
months.

Something had changed in the air. Karen Mitchell stepped back
from Veda, who thus far had not said a word.

Veda blinked her eyes and climbed down from the chair, her
head and neck held perfectly still. She reached out for Hannah's
hand and took it. "You have to help me wash this off now," she said,
as she led Hannah, her new responsible babysitter, to the bathroom.
Amy skipped along behind, and Alice stared after them.

Karen cleared her throat. "They had a nice time," she said.

"She always does," Alice said, remembering to smile.

"I thought I might have to run to the hospital and leave them with the sitter, but I'm so glad I was able to get someone to cover for me."

"Mm," Alice said.

"So Hannah seems nice," Karen said. "Very calm. How long has she been with you?"

"Oh, just today. It's her first day."

"Oh! My gosh. I didn't realize. I'm sure she'll be just great. And it's so terrific, Alice. You back to work. And using all of your . . . experiences, after all these years. I don't know if I could do it. If I'd stopped working when Amy was born. But you're so *brave*, and you've had so many interesting *adventures*. Remind me—you speak Korean, right?"

"Just a little."

"And is Hannah's English pretty good?"

Alice looked at Karen, whose linen miniskirt showed off her athletic thighs. Karen was turned away from Alice, gathering the makeup containers. Something hot and scratchy rose in Alice's throat. "Karen, Hannah speaks perfect English. Don't you have any colleagues at the hospital who are immigrants?" Alice laughed, a little too sweetly.

Karen turned to Alice, a quizzical look on her face. She might have been considering Alice's question; she might have been considering Alice.

Amy came skipping out from the bathroom to find the two women locked in silence. It was Alice who turned away first. "How's it going in there?"

"The soap," Amy said, "it's stinging her eyes."

"Oh, jeez, you need this," Karen said, reaching for a small blue bottle. "Here you go, pumpkin."

On the way home, Alice walked with her arm around Veda's shoulder and said to Hannah, "That Amy really is such a sweet girl."

5.

It was the first day of summer. The children's summer. School was out, but Hannah still took the Metro to Columbia Heights station in the afternoons, as she had for the previous three weeks. Alice worked the 3-to-11 shift at the nursing home, which meant she was home until 2:30. "So it will just be an hour earlier every day," she had said, and Hannah said that would be fine. Her only other plans for the summer were to read *Le Petit Prince*—which Madame Glissant had recommended to her—and to swim every day, which she did at the pool in Silver Spring. In the fall, Hannah would start high school and intended to be the number-one seed in backstroke. Raj's brother Ravi had said that the girls' team *sucked*, and this, Hannah thought, boded well for her.

Alice did not ask what else Hannah would be doing when she was not watching Veda and Benny. But she did raise Hannah's wage by fifty cents an hour. "It's the least we can do. There must be so many other things a girl your age wants to be doing with her summer afternoons." It was a funny thing to say, Hannah thought— as if Alice Lee had some completely different girl in mind when she said it. But Hannah was happy for the raise; it was the first time she'd had her own money, and she was saving up. For what, exactly, she didn't yet know.

In the evenings, Charles arrived punctually at six o'clock. Sometimes he carried bags of groceries, sometimes takeout Chinese or pizza. He wore short-sleeved collared shirts in light blue or yellow, or sometimes plaid, with a white undershirt that showed through; pleated slacks; and black rubber-soled shoes. He did not wear a jacket or tie. Hannah tried to guess where he was coming from, but she found she could only guess where he was not coming from: he was not a lawyer or a businessman, he did not work at a bank. He was probably not a doctor, either; though maybe he worked in a lab doing research like her father (who wore a pin-striped shirt and gray pants every single day). He was clearly not a plumber or construction worker: he had smooth, long-fingered hands; the half-moons of his fingernails were perfect and white. He looked like he could be a teacher, but then it didn't make sense that he would be going to work all day in the summertime. Hannah resorted to considering what sort of job the husband of Alice Lee would have, but that got her nowhere. In general, Hannah had trouble holding Alice Lee and Charles Lee as a pair in her mind; except for the first meeting, she never saw them together.

Hannah missed seeing Charles's licorice-bean eyes, as he always wore aviator sunglasses now, even inside as he unpacked food or handed Hannah her wages. When she left, Charles said, "Have a good evening," and he said it in an adult voice, as if Hannah were not a young girl but a restaurant hostess, or one of the grocery checkout ladies. When she looked into Charles's aviator lenses, Hannah tried to pretend she was looking straight into his left eye again, but all she saw was her own warped reflection, in which her forehead appeared huge, and her eyeglasses too round.

On the one hand, Hannah was glad about not having to make conversation. She was glad, for instance, that she did not have to be driven home by Charles Lee. She'd seen a movie once on TV where the husband pulled over on the side of the road, strangled the babysitter, and dumped her in the river. The scariest part, she thought, was that they didn't show the actual strangling, only the man (who looked like a teacher) reaching toward the girl with both hands; then the camera shifted to the outside of the silver Jeep with tinted windows, which sat still and silent in the dark night.

But then again, if Charles Lee drove her home, maybe he'd take off the sunglasses and not be scary at all. Maybe she'd find a way to surprise him again, to make his shiny black eyes go wide and a little confused. Maybe that voice—that strange, familiar, inside-her-head voice—would come back, and Hannah would say things she'd never said out loud before; wonderful, interesting things she only half-knew she'd thought. Maybe, too, she'd hear that sad woodwind warmth again in Charles's replies.

Before leaving, Hannah would tell Charles briefly what they'd done that afternoon, what they'd had for a snack; usually too some report on Benny's troublesome behavior. On that front, Hannah had found she had no trouble administering effective punishment: the boy hated two things above all else—silence and wearing shoes. And so Time Out meant putting on his sneakers and sitting in the Silence Chair. For his sixth birthday, Alice Lee's brother had given the boy a plastic digital watch, which he loved and wore every day; and so to keep him busy, Hannah would set the stopwatch for two minutes. The countdown, with its racing milliseconds, at least partially absorbed him; so while he whined and pouted all throughout the lace-up of the sneakers, he kept quiet for the two-minute period. Once, Hannah had offered Veda the chance to set the watch. The girl considered seriously for a moment, brow furrowed; then she raised her eyes and shook her head. *I'll have no part of it*, she seemed to be saying, and then went back to beading a bracelet.

One evening, Hannah described the shoes-and-Silence-Chair procedure to Charles. The children were off washing their hands. "You're a pro at this," Charles said. "You've figured it out pretty quickly." He'd raised his sunglasses off his nose to rub his eye, then dropped them back down.

Hannah had gone home that evening wondering what he'd meant by "it." She felt she knew even as she tried to understand. "It" had something to do with the girl's superiority, and the boy's stupidity. "It" was something she and Charles now shared, this understanding, and was something Hannah felt quite sure Alice Lee did not share, did not understand.

On the Metro ride home now, Hannah sometimes replayed the father-and-babysitter scene from the movie. She imagined herself as the babysitter, and Charles as the murderer, only in her version, when he pulled over to the side of the road, Charles reached for her with his hands and pulled her to him in an embrace. Once, while she was swimming backstroke at the pool, Charles's clarinet voice came into her ear, complimenting her on her long, smooth strokes and speed.

In early July, Hannah had a day off for the Fourth. She went to the mall with Teresa and Raj. After browsing rugby shirts at Britches Great Outdoors, they headed for the food court, in search of soft-serve. Suddenly Raj halted and grabbed Hannah's and Teresa's shirtsleeves. "Crap. Look." In a far corner, sitting alone, eating from a tray and reading a paperback, they saw Madame Glissant, their French teacher. Raj was in summer school with her—he'd gotten a C in French and his parents threatened to pull him out of chess club if he didn't improve. Teresa put her hand over her mouth. "That's so *sad*," she said. It *was* sad, Hannah thought. But maybe not in the same way Teresa meant. Raj had already turned to head back to the stores. Teresa was backing away with an uneasy smirk on her face.

Hannah didn't move. Monique Glissant hadn't looked up; she was deeply absorbed in whatever she was reading. She reached for her sandwich or her coffee every so often but never lifted her eyes. At the sight of her, something bloomed in Hannah's chest. *Madame* was a pretty woman with a full, hourglass figure; pale and dark-haired with black eyes and very pink lips. Hannah liked to see what she wore to class every day, because it was always similar to the day before but definitely different. For example, one day she would wear a charcoal sweater dress that hugged her hips, with zigzag tan tights, and the next day she would wear a two-piece charcoal sweater set, low-cut, with caramel-brown pumps. She had the same sheer silk blouse with a big-bow collar in black, red, and pink. Sometimes she wore miniskirts—stone-washed denim—with tall boots, which no other teacher ever did. It was hard to know how old she was: everyone knew Madame was divorced, yet she radiated a girlishness. Sometimes they saw her standing in the hallway with her head cocked, talking softly with Mr. Stevens, the history teacher.

"Hannah?" Teresa hissed. She was waving Hannah over with a sharp hand.

"Just a sec." Hannah crossed the seating area to the far corner and paid no mind to Teresa's bugging eyes.

"*Bonjour*, Madame," Hannah said.

Monique Glissant raised her eyes, slowly, and looked at Hannah over the top of her big cat-eye reading glasses. She set her book down on the table, spine up, then exhaled gently and sat back. Her pink lips smiled and showed just the top of her two front teeth, which were slightly yellowed, and her hair—usually tied back—flowed over her bare shoulders, bluish black and feathery light. She lowered her glasses, which hung from a colorful beaded chain, down to the low edge of her scoop-neck tank, against the skin of lightly tanned cleavage. "Well, hello there." She spoke English very prettily. Her students didn't get to hear her speak much English.

"How . . . are you?" Hannah asked. Her teacher said nothing and looked at her with bemused eyes. "*Comment . . . allez-vous?*"

"*Ah, bon. Maintenant, je comprends!*"

Hannah smiled. She liked being teased by Madame.

"*Je vais très bien, merci. Et toi, qu'est-ce que tu fais aujourd'hui? Tu vas faire du shopping?*"

Hannah was glad she used a word that was identical in both languages. She didn't know if she could think fast on her feet. "*Oui. Je vais faire du shopping. Avec . . . mes amis.*" Hannah turned and pointed at no one in particular.

"*C'est amusant, faire du shopping avec des amis!*" Hannah could tell that her teacher was turning the conversation into a French lesson. Her heart dropped; she wanted somehow to take advantage of being outside the classroom. She was sure there were . . . *autres choses* to talk about *avec jolie* Monique Glissant.

"*Oui,*" Hannah said, nodding. She bit her lower lip and was about to give up and say *au revoir*, when she noticed the book on the table. The cover was faded, the spine tattered; but the letters were curly and big and black: *Claudine à l'ecole*. "*Qu'est-ce que . . . vous lisez?*" Hannah asked.

Their eyes were now on the table, and Monique Glissant moved quickly to flip the book over. "Oh, it's nothing," she said, switching to English. She raked the fingers of her left hand through her hair, and Hannah thought she smelled lilac. "An old favorite. I like to reread things sometimes, just to relax. Have you been reading *Le Petit Prince*?"

Hannah nodded. "I've only just started." In fact she was finding it slow going. It was hard to grasp what was actually going on, what they were talking about—which was supposed to be, she knew, deep.

"If you have something else to recommend . . . I want to practice as much as I can," Hannah said.

Monique Glissant took the book from the table with both hands and placed it in her lap. She smiled her charming two-toothed smile all the while. "Let me . . . think about that," she said.

Hannah felt she'd spoken meaningfully, but she wasn't sure. Her teacher said nothing more, just replaced her pearly cat eyes, which seemed to cover most of her face. They said their *au revoirs,* and when Hannah peeked back over her shoulder from the tray station, she saw that Madame's nose was already between pages.

Once Hannah caught up with Teresa and Raj, they walked by a wall of movie posters at the Cineplex—Phoebe Cates in *Gremlins*; Kevin Bacon in *Footloose*; *Revenge of the Nerds*—and Hannah suddenly knew what she'd been saving up for: an appointment at Tease, the hair salon where Jessica Taft and Jami Eisenberg, two of the popular girls at school, got their hair done with their mothers. Also, a new pair of eyeglass frames.

6.

The boy was eating lo mein with his fingers and letting the noodles hang down from his mouth. "Raaahhhrrr!" he was saying, "I am the swamp monster!" Benny rolled his eyes up almost to complete whites. Charles sighed into the refrigerator, reached in for a Pabst, then closed the door extra slowly. He had had a long day at work; the East Gate cameras at the stadium were malfunctioning again. The boy was waiting for someone, his father or Veda, to react.

Charles turned to his son and beheld him: swamp monster, indeed. Hair like a tumbleweed on top of a cactus. "We're taking you to the barber shop on Saturday," he said.

The boy had told his mother that he liked his hair this way, and she'd said fine. Later, Charles and Alice had argued over— discussed—it, and Alice told Charles that children need freedom and a sense of self-determination. They also, Charles had said, need to learn how to sit still; this was the real reason, he knew, that the boy didn't like to have his hair cut. He was six years old, what did he know or care about liking his hair one way or another? You'd be surprised, Alice had said, how early it starts now. How early what starts? The importance of appearances, and self-image. Good god, Charles had said, though later on he couldn't remember if he'd said it out loud or only in his head. Regardless, he'd certainly expressed it one way or another, which was made clear by Alice's hard silence.

As a child, Charles had always himself had short hair. His grandmother made sure of it. By the time Afros were getting taller and fuller, he'd enlisted. Only once—when Benny was a toddler, just starting to walk on his own (and learning to make fists and throw tantrums), and life had become a constant chaos of noise and mess—during that time Charles went two months without a haircut. "You look like Bill Withers," Alice had said to him, and she sounded pleased about it. Charles remembered her saying that, because he remembered that they'd had sex that night—a rare occurrence in those days—and Alice had shocked him by giving fellatio. Charles always sensed Alice's semi-unwillingness to use her mouth in any sensual way—she never ate tomatoes because of the sliminess of the seeds, and she bit off bananas with her lips pulled back, teeth bared. That night, though, Charles hadn't cared. He'd pushed Alice to her knees. Had he pushed hard? What was "hard"? Where were his hands while she did it? Where were hers? Charles couldn't remember.

"Stop it, Benny. That's gross." Veda had spread pork and cabbage in a thin layer and was rolling her moo shu pancake into a narrow tube.

"Here," Charles said, reaching over from behind and gently unrolling it. He scooped another large spoonful into the pancake and re-rolled it. "You need to eat more, V. Skin and bones." He pinched Veda's upper arm playfully. She squirmed and giggled, then picked up her pancake with both hands. A strand of hair fell forward into her mouth as she got ready to take a bite; Charles hooked it with his finger and tucked it behind her ear.

On Saturday, Charles took Benny to the barber. He'd been going to the same barbershop on the corner of Georgia and Keefer Place since he was a boy. He'd known Vernon Mills for twenty-five years. In the end, this was how Charles had gotten Alice to agree: it would be a tradition, a father-son outing. Alice liked the historical notion of it, and she liked anything "special" that Charles did with the boy. As for Benny, *just like Daddy* was something to which he was generally responsive; it was how they'd potty-trained him (well, almost) at five and a half.

Vernon was not much of a talker. He let his customers do all the talking. Charles had always liked this about Vernon—not only was he comfortable in his silence, but also generous. After Nona had dropped him off, Charles would sit quietly in the chair, while Vernon clipped and sometimes hummed. Usually he had a cigarette going, the ashtray within reach of the chair. Charles would will himself not to cough, and he stared into the corners of the mirror, where he could see everyone else in the shop. The other men, most of whom were not there for haircuts or shaves, would talk and talk and talk. Charles didn't understand most of it, but what he perceived in the talk was a feeling that what they were saying, and what it really meant, were different things. For instance, the tone of the talk was often of complaint—taxes, mayors, wives, landlords—and yet the collective feeling among the men was one of joy, and pleasure. It was something that would come back to him, and ring familiar, in small moments, years later in the Army.

Charles vaguely dreaded bringing Benny to Vernon's shop. He considered taking him to a different barber, where no one knew him. His friend Dennis, who he came up with (and who'd talked him into enlisting when they were seventeen and no-count), had always gone to Van's on 11th and Kenyon. But Charles had already told the boy about Vernon, and whatever lie he might concoct to fool him now would need to be elaborate. Anyway, even if the boy believed it, his mother wouldn't.

"Well, well, what have we here?" Vernon spoke in almost a whisper now, his lungs and throat worn to reeds. He'd always slouched, but the slouch had curled into a stoop. He seemed ancient, though in fact he couldn't have been much older than sixty.

"Vern," Charles said, nodding. "My son. Bennett."

"Bennett Lee, Charlie's boy. And how are you, young man?"

"Fine." Benny was pulling at the hem of his long T-shirt with both hands, twisting back and forth.

"Fine, *what*, Benny." Charles put his hand on the boy's neck and pressed with two fingers.

"Fine . . . thank you," Benny mumbled.

"Fine, thank you, *sir*," Charles said. Benny looked up at his father with eyes that made Charles shudder. If the boy had the words, Charles thought, if he were smart, he'd be saying, *You fraudulent fuck, the word "sir" has never once been uttered in our household, and you know it.*

Vernon's nephew Mike interjected then, slapping his chair, which was opposite Vernon's. "Come right here, little man. I'll take care o' you today." Mike was a fat man, gregarious and cheeky, everything Vernon was not. Mike's cousin Lester was the serious one; he'd died in Vietnam.

Benny plopped into Mike's chair, staring up at him with a child's wonder. It took a moment for Charles to understand what exactly had captivated the boy. Charles saw it happening in slow motion. "I want *those*," Benny said, pointing at Mike's braids.

They were tight against his big skull, skinny rows, hanging down the back of his neck and beaded at the ends. On Fat Mike the Barber, pushing forty, they were fine, they said Cool Cat; he was an exuberant born-again, he led Bible studies for prison inmates, the braids were like plainclothes. On a young boy wearing too-big T-shirts, it was a different story.

"Something tells me your pops might have something to say about that," Mike said, eyeing Charles.

Benny was quiet. His face was radiant, excited. The boy, Charles saw, had a vision of himself—one that he was too young to fully understand, and yet, maybe, there was also a child's wisdom to it, something essential. *The importance of self-image*, Alice had said. Charles smiled and shook his head—not at Mike, nor at Benny, but somewhere inwardly.

"You know, why not?"

Vernon's eyes grew wide. Mike's narrowed. Charles shrugged his shoulders, which, for a blessed moment, felt looser, unburdened. Vernon shook his head too, but in his case it meant, Boy, you better know *what* you're doin. Vernon had had the occasion to meet Alice once, at a wedding.

Benny watched all of this, eyes big and waiting.

"The boy knows what he wants," Charles said.

Benny pumped his fist into his hip. "Yessss!"

Mike called in his cousin Yvonne from the back, where sometimes her girlfriends came in for manicures and extensions. "We need reinforcements; small, strong hands," he said to Charles. Then to Yvonne, "What's your sister doing today?"

"Maureen? Nothin."

"Get her over here. So these gentlemen don't have to be here all day."

It did take some time, and while the girls prepped for Benny, Charles sat back in Vernon's chair. "While we're at it, let's shave mine, all the way down. Gimme that baby's bottom special."

Vernon shook his head again, this time laughing from the gut. "You want a shave, too?"

"Nah. Let's grow that."

Everyone set to work. There was industrious joy in the shop, all around. Mike stood back and let the girls, and his uncle, work. If he wasn't already, Mike would be the new boss soon. They needed to bring in more young men to stay in business, maybe this was A New Day, fathers and their young sons coming in together, before they started losing the boys to the corners and all the rest. Mike didn't know that Benny would never again be back in the shop. Charles would not return for many years.

At one point, Benny did get restless, wiggling around in the chair. Charles reached over and set the boy's stopwatch, two minutes at a time. It worked like a charm.

At home that night, when Alice saw them, she said only, "Help your sister set the table." It was Veda who said it all, with her dropped jaw and hand cupped over her mouth. At dinner, no one spoke except for Benny, who told them Mike was the fattest man he'd ever seen. He said it admiringly. He also said Yvonne and Maureen smelled like strawberries and feet. Charles was the only one who laughed, while Veda was ever aware of her mother.

In bed that night, Alice hissed at her husband. "What's next, Charles—a switchblade? Hundred-dollar sneakers?"

"He asked for it. He was very clear about what he wanted. You're the one always saying—"

"Fuck you, Charles." Alice rolled over and faced the wall.

Charles thought, Yeah, fuck *me*. Or maybe he said it aloud, under his breath. He thought of a line from the movie he'd taken Veda to see for her birthday, Jeff Conaway to Stockard Channing: *With a cherry on top.*

7.

Hannah arrived thirty minutes early on a Monday. The previous Friday, Alice had asked her if she could begin staying an hour later to help with Benny's bath before dinner. "He just needs a little supervision. You'd be welcome to stay and eat with Charles and the kids afterward; though I'm sure your mother wants you home." In fact, Soon-mi worked the early shift at the nursing home; she and Chong-ho ate at 5:30 like clockwork. Hannah had been eating by herself all summer. Soon-mi would save her a foil-wrapped plate, and Hannah didn't mind, since dinner was typically a silent affair.

Hannah said yes, an hour later was fine, and they agreed she would come early on Monday so that Alice could show her the bath routine.

Alice came to the door in bare feet and a bathrobe, her hair still wet from the shower. The robe was the color of raw shrimp, and the half-moon puffs beneath her eyes matched. "Come in, Hannah," she said. Hannah stepped inside. Alice cocked her head slightly and said, eerily, as if reading some mirror image of Hannah's mind, "You look different."

Hannah had saved up enough for new glasses, which she'd just picked up over the weekend. Her round metal frames were still in her purse. The new ones were plastic—translucent purple—with tiny silver flowers at the temples that gave them a slight catty slant. Hannah had stared at herself in the window reflection on the Metro and decided she liked the new frames. They were different but not too different, and the little flowers were prettier the closer you looked. She liked that especially. But something in her reflection wasn't right: her forehead shone, long and wide like a loaf of bread. She had to start saving again for a hair appointment at Tease. She closed then opened her eyes, refocused, tried to imagine herself with Phoebe Cates pixie bangs, the rest feathered and flowing to her shoulders.

Alice uncocked her head. For a moment, Hannah was tongue-tied. She hadn't expected Alice to notice. Hannah didn't think Alice noticed her much at all. She said, "Um . . . so do you."

Alice made a face, then laughed. "Well. Just give me a second, I guess I should finish getting ready." She ascended the stairs and said over her shoulder, "Benny's watching a video. Veda's at Amy's."

Hannah wandered into the front room, what she'd heard Alice call the parlor. It was the most formal room in the house, off-limits to the children: everything was perfectly in order. The furniture was nicer and also, Hannah thought, more old-fashioned, as if it had been in the house forever, while everything else had come later. Hannah hadn't had much chance to be in this room, since she was always with the children.

Alice came back down the stairs just as Hannah stepped toward a wall of framed photographs. It was a relatively small frame amidst larger ones that caught her eye, the only one holding people she recognized.

"You picked us out," Alice said. Then, half-laughing, "Though I suppose it's not that hard." Alice's was the only white face amidst the black ones. "It's the only thing I changed in this room when we moved in, adding that photo. Charles's family cherished this room; it's basically a mausoleum." Alice laughed, but Hannah looked at her quizzically. "Like a . . . shrine. Honoring the family."

"Is everyone dead?" This bluntness surprised them both.

"Well," Alice said, closing her eyes tight, then looking up, as if to heaven. "Let's see. Charles's mother died just before he went into the Army. That's her, Esther, in the blue dress." Hannah followed Alice's eyes to a large family portrait, the dark woman with helmet-styled hair who wore shiny blue polyester and sat with her big hands in her lap, poised with a half-smile. The rest of the family stood around her like petals of a flower. A hand on her shoulder belonged to the man in the portrait—stocky with a baby-smooth face, and cheerful-looking. The three boys were all about the same age, although one of them, with a faint mustache and sleepy eyes, could be just a little older. The girl was younger—four or five, Hannah would guess, by her tiny front teeth—in a lemon-yellow dress and little bows at the ends of her braids. Hannah leaned in and squinted but couldn't make out which one was Charles Lee.

"Charles wasn't born yet," Alice said. "Not for a year or so. The other boys were close in age. Derrick and Carl are still with us, but we don't hear from them. It's almost like Charles is an only child. Except for his sister, Rhea. She took care of him most of the time." Hannah nodded, taking it all in. She studied the man and the woman in blue more closely. "That's Robert Lee; he died not long after. That portrait is the last photo they have of him. Stabbed by a junkie who wanted cash. Terrible." Alice shook her head. "Charles never knew either Robert or his own father, Frank, who came along . . . well, maybe he was already around by this time." Both Alice and Hannah stood very still for a moment. "He left suddenly. Frank. Just after Charles was born. Some men come around when the baby shows up—like it dawns on them, that they're a father. But Frank ran; he was one that ran and never showed his face again." Alice's voice had become light and thin. The parlor windows faced west, and the sun had begun filling the room like a floodlight, like white noise.

"Now that's Uncle Marvin," Alice continued, in a hard voice now. She pointed to a gilded frame on the end table. "This was his house. He passed three years after Essie—Charles's mother, that's what they called her. Grandma Nona was with us until, gosh, almost five years ago now. I never knew Marvin, but knowing Nona was almost like knowing Marvin. He was her favorite. There was a much-younger brother, Charles's Uncle Ernie, but he disappeared long ago, in his twenties, I think. They suppose he died, too. Drugs, alcohol, what have you."

Hannah's brow crinkled, she was figuring something in her mind. "So the mother lived longer than the children?"

Alice nodded, oddly animated, like a teacher being asked the question she'd hoped for. "It's something, isn't it. Unimaginable, really. Although, having known Nona, it's almost hard to imagine it any other way. She was something else." Alice enjoyed telling these family stories, despite their tragic content. And Hannah liked hearing them.

Hannah turned back to the small photo on the wall. "Where was this?"

Alice stepped over the threshold into the center of the room. "That was in Seoul. We'd just gotten engaged." She took another step forward, toward Hannah and the wall, squinting. Now she was like a tourist in a museum gallery, merely curious. And Hannah felt awkward, like an untrained docent, lacking the information she is expected to impart.

Alice laughed. "That uniform. It's strange: it's not the person wearing it who's acting or pretending; it's the uniform that has its own . . . personality. You never expect to be so impressed by it." Hannah listened to Alice while staring at the photograph. From her angle she could see Alice's reflection, from nose to neck; but not her own. Alice's face was thinner now than in the photo—her bones more prominent, lips drawn, eyes buggier. Charles's face had grown fuller. They both smiled wide, and their faces were joined at the ears. Hannah wondered if their arms were wrapped around each other; the photo showed them only just past their shoulders. Alice's brassy blonde hair fell beyond the bottom edge of the frame. Charles wore his private's cap.

"Sorry," Alice said, snapping herself out of her reverie. "I'm sure you've heard it before, *Beware of men in uniform*. It's not necessarily

true. Well, not any *more* true than anything else you might judge."
Hannah leaned on her right leg, just slightly, and tilted her head to
catch her own reflection in the frame. But the light was streaming
into the room now; the glass was all brightness and glare.

"Well," Alice said. She took a deep breath, as if about to turn and
walk out of the room.

"What was it like in Korea?" Hannah hadn't thought about her
question; the words seemed to come from elsewhere.

Alice rested her hand on the back of a velvet wingback. "What
was it like? Haven't you been?"

Hannah shook her head. "Well, once. When my grandfather
died. I don't remember, though. I was too young."

"I didn't know that. And they've never taken you since?" Hannah
shook her head. "That . . . I'm surprised to hear that. You seem very
Korean to me."

Hannah did not know what Alice meant by this, but she didn't
like the sound of it. "My brother says my parents wanted to stay,
but they left to get away from their families. I guess they wished
they could have kept Korea but not their families." She did not really
want to talk to Alice about Korea or her parents, but neither was she
ready to leave the room and the photos.

"So you never knew your grandparents?" Hannah shook her
head. "That's too bad." Alice said this flatly, but heat came on
suddenly between Hannah's eyes, a low but intense flame. Her
shoulders tightened. What did Alice Lee know about it? Or about
seeing very Korean?

They were real jerks, James had said about their father's parents.
*They were really against Dad marrying Mom. Wrong side of the tracks
or whatever. Dad was kind of a dark horse or something back then—
wrote poetry, rebelled against the Japanese. I guess our grandparents
were all about submitting to Japanese rule and following traditions:
Mom said Dad used to get the shit beat out of him.*

Something snapped inside Hannah, like a dry twig. "I don't
mind," Hannah said. "It doesn't mean anything, just to be related.
My parents are very close, like best friends. For like thirty years. And

their parents would have kept them from being together." Strictly speaking, all this was true. But Hannah's defense of her parents was not. More than defending their way of living, she was telling Alice Lee to mind her own business.

As Hannah spoke, the expression on Alice's face shifted, from mild dismay to a weary smile.

"Well, and then you wouldn't be here, would you?" Alice's tone had become maternal. "I suppose I can see why you wouldn't want to meet the people who tried to prevent your own existence! But . . . meeting you could very well be the thing to change their minds. It happens like that sometimes."

"They're both dead now," Hannah said. Hannah had no idea if her grandmother was also dead; but anyway, it *felt* true.

Alice sighed. She was looking at Hannah and thinking of something, though evidently not Hannah's supposedly dead grandparents. The light shifted and cast an Alice Lee-shaped shadow over the divan. "Well . . . I shouldn't speak disrespectfully of the dead, but . . ." She looked again toward the wall of photos. "Sometimes it's for the best. Moving on. The generations. Families can be the most difficult, the least accepting. Your parents . . . I don't know what their conflict was. For us, it was . . . obviously, it was being a mixed marriage. But we've managed to . . . Well in Korea it was even worse. There was no way we could stay there. I might have, on my own. But Charles . . ." Alice wasn't really talking to Hannah anymore; she'd gone somewhere in her mind, her memory. Then, abruptly, she was back, in the parlor, with Hannah and the photos. "It was complicated, but also not really. You see how all races are suspicious of other races . . ."

"What are you two *doing* in there?" Benny came stomping down the hall, halting at the threshold between entry and parlor. On this one thing, he'd been well trained.

Alice pepped up. Hannah felt the room tip, like a ship on a wave, toward Benny, and mild nausea threatened to rise to her throat. She squeezed her toes in her sandals, pressed her palms into the sides of her thighs.

"We're just talking, sweetie." Alice stepped toward Benny, across the threshold, and wrapped her arms around him from behind, cradling his chin in the crook of her elbow. She kissed his crown, her lips touching the valleys of scalp between braids, and then rested her cheek there.

Benny crossed his eyes and wriggled away. "Come *on*. We have to show her my *bath things*."

"Yes, darling. Let's take Hannah upstairs."

8.

At 4:30, Hannah fed Veda and Benny their snack. Benny pushed his apple slices to the side and scooped up peanut butter with his finger.

"You have to eat your apples, Benny," Veda said. She used the plastic knife Hannah had put out and spread her own mound of peanut butter over the green-skinned slices in frosting-like swirls. "You want me to spread it for you?"

"No." Benny opened his mouth wide, showing Veda his goo-smeared teeth and tongue.

Veda sighed, said nothing, and turned away. It was a very grown-up gesture. Hannah imagined she'd learned it from any number of adults, and yet it also seemed natural, very much her own.

"That's a pretty hairstyle on you," Hannah said. Veda's front hair was swept across her forehead, like the velvet drapery across a French window, and pinned to the side with a sparkly purple barrette.

"Amy did it. Amy wants to be a movie-star stylist when she grows up."

"Stylist?" Hannah didn't know what that was.

"That's only if she can't be an actress, which is her first choice."

"I wanna be a barber!" Benny said, kneeling up on his chair and hovering over them.

"Sit *down*, Benny." Hannah poked an apple slice into his open mouth. He'd eat anything if it was fed to him.

"Fat Mike! Fat Mike!"

"That's the barber," Veda said drily. "Benny had an *experience*."

Hannah had gathered that there had been some issue with Benny's braids, though she didn't know exactly what. No doubt Alice Lee did not approve: it was a gangster style. But what, Hannah wondered, did his father think? "What kind of 'experience'?"

Veda shrugged. It was her mother's word.

"What's your first choice, Veda? For what you want to be when you grow up?"

Veda sipped her milk, then dabbed at her white mustache with a napkin. "Supreme Court Justice," she said, reaching for her last apple slice. Then, before popping it into her mouth, "Or, maybe beauty queen."

Hannah cleared the children's dishes. It was 5:15. Suddenly, she felt rushed, and determined. To do something, change something. Her moods had been shifting and heaving like this lately. The bright reflected light from the parlor earlier had filled her head like a sharp pain. Now a different photo (one she'd come across in a shoebox in her mother's closet when she went looking for bobby pins) filled that white space in her mind: Soon-mi on a summer day many years ago, wearing a minidress, sleeveless with big brown sunflowers, and white go-go boots; her back straight, skin smooth and very pale, hair in a bouffant bob; the Washington Monument in the background and cherry blossoms cascading all around.

Hannah started to think that Alice Lee definitely did not know anything about being Korean. Somehow Hannah knew that it was simply impossible for Alice to know, and Hannah didn't like this nagging feeling of misunderstanding. The nagging spawned and then fed a blooming urgency that was now upon her.

"You guys okay for a few minutes? I need to use the bathroom upstairs."

"Why can't you use the downstairs one?" Benny asked.

"It's a girl thing. I'll just be a few minutes. Veda, you're in charge."

The small scissors had been in Hannah's mind ever since Alice had shown her the upstairs bathroom. Hannah didn't know what they used them for, or why they were in the toothbrush cup, but they looked just like the scissors Ms. Kwak at the Supercuts used. Ms. Kwak had been cutting Hannah's hair ever since she could remember, and it had been the same style—straight, shoulder-length—since forever. Except for last summer when she tried the perm: it had taken a full year, but finally it had grown out.

Hannah stood in front of the mirror, which covered half the wall over double sinks, and looked at herself. Her new glasses really were nice, she thought. She was wearing a plain white tank top and a faded denim skirt. Her posture was getting better (after years of her mother telling her to sit up straight), her skin was darkening to an olive-bronze from all that time at the pool. Her arms and shoulders were shapely. She had started wearing lip gloss (only away from home), which she'd bought at Strawberry's the last time she and Teresa went to the mall; a reddish color that looked purpler on her lips than on the label. Hannah grinned like a cat, then closed her mouth again: her front teeth were small and square and the one that was slightly turned made her top lip look fuller, and she didn't think that was a bad thing. She took her glasses off, pulled the rubber band out of her hair, and reached for the scissors.

She worked slowly at first, then hastily as she grew impatient. The scissors were very sharp and quick. Ten minutes later, she was almost done and anticipating a feeling of satisfaction, when a thundering against the door startled her. "What are you *doing* in there?" Hannah had been concentrating and hadn't heard Benny's footsteps on the stairs. The banging was like a punch to her elbow, and her hand slipped; the tip of the scissors nicked her above the eye, her new bangs now slanted upward, noticeably, right in the middle. There was blood on the scissors tip. Luckily the cut was tiny; it blended into a freckle just below Hannah's eyebrow.

"Just a *minute*, Benny. Go back downstairs. I'll be down."

"Hurry *up*! You're not even supposed to be up here without us."

Hannah closed her eyes, leaned on her hands and wrists on the countertop. She counted to three, slowly, the way her swim coach had taught her, to calm herself before a race.

"Benny?" She'd managed to tone her voice down, solicitous now.

"What."

"Get Veda for me. Now." Benny paused for a moment, then sprinted down the stairs, excited. Soon Hannah heard them both, a four-footed stampede, ascending.

"Are you okay?" Veda's voice sounded concerned; it filled Hannah with gratitude.

"I'm letting you guys in. Benny, you have to be quiet and calm." She had no choice; who knew what trouble Benny would get into otherwise.

She opened the door and stood there, let the children see. She held a wadded-up piece of toilet paper to her eyebrow.

"Oh," Veda said.

"What? What?" Benny said.

"Here," Hannah said. She handed Veda the scissors and sat down on the hard, lidded toilet seat.

Veda took the scissors and cocked her head, placid and thoughtful. Then she said: "It's going to be kind of . . . short."

"I wanna be the barber!" Benny shouted, seeing the passing of the scissors and gradually understanding.

"Be *quiet*, Benny. This is your *fault*." Hannah spoke through her teeth. Her father spoke like this when he was very angry, which was rare, and thus potent. Benny caught the sharpness of Hannah's tone, crossed his arms and pouted. Hannah ignored him. "It's okay, V. Just even it out. Small snips, little by little."

"I did this for Amy's salon Barbie head once. Your hair is kind of different, though."

"I know. So go slow. Small snips."

The operation went on for what felt like a long time, slow, and silent, and tense.

"What are these scissors usually used for?" Hannah asked in a near whisper. She needed to breathe, and to break the tension.

"My dad's beard. He's not supposed to leave them out, though. *He* might get hold of them." Veda pointed an elbow at Benny, who was sitting on the counter now, opening and smelling every jar and bottle within his reach.

Hannah had noticed that Charles had been growing a beard and mustache, seemingly migrating hair from head to face; she'd noticed, though she did not wonder why.

Veda worked slowly, carefully. She seemed to be cutting one strand of hair at a time. Every time Benny moved or made like he was going to say something, Hannah flashed him a look. She didn't know she had that look in her; it felt good to know that she did.

Veda stepped back and laid the scissors down on the Formica. She tilted her head, serious. Then she nodded. Hannah stood and turned to the mirror, put on her glasses. The bangs were very short—shorter than Jami Eisenberg's or Jessica Taft's, much shorter than Phoebe Cates's—but wispy at the ends, and even. It was a little girl's style, like a doll, or a cartoon; but it looked . . . stylish, too. "Pretty," Veda said.

"Ew, she is *not*," Benny said. He was playing with the open scissors, stroking the flat sides with his fingers like a pet hamster. Hannah let him. Then she had an idea.

"Here, Benny, you want to try at being barber? Here's a piece in back; you can try cutting it. Be careful, though. Just a little snip." She held out a lock of hair from underneath that wouldn't show. "If I let you, though, you have to be good and clean up here, okay? Just like the barber. And," she said, now leaning away from him, withholding the precious lock and dead serious, "let's not talk about this with your mom and dad." Benny nodded and held up the scissors, primed like a wind-up toy. Hannah looked to Veda, who shrugged her little shoulders. Maybe he would keep his promise, maybe not, they both knew. It was worth a try. Hannah leaned over and let Benny snip. His eyes were wide and a little crazy. "Okay, Benny, now you can sweep up." Benny hopped to. Hannah got the broom and dustpan from the hall closet and handed it to him. "Make sure to get all the little hairs, too," she said. Benny set to work; he seemed focused. Hannah let out a breath, then she and Veda went downstairs.

When Charles came home, he had a big bag of groceries, and another smaller shopping bag. He told them hot dogs for dinner, and

Benny cheered loudly. The boy was easily distracted from one thing to the next, and Hannah was grateful. From the smaller bag Charles pulled out three T-shirts, "from work." Hannah knew now that he worked for the Washington Redskins, in charge of security at the stadium. Or maybe he wasn't in charge, but he worked for the man in charge. One of the shirts was maroon, another mustard yellow, the third white. He gave the maroon one to Benny, the yellow one to Veda, and the white one he held out to Hannah. "Thanks for helping out in the evenings," Charles said. "And with everything."

Hannah took the T-shirt and said, not looking at him, "Thank you. I mean, you're welcome. And thank you." She pulled down on a strand of her bangs.

"That's number 28. Darrell Green, defensive back. Great athlete, first-round draft pick out of Texas A&M; all instincts and speed." He looked down, embarrassed suddenly by his enthusiasm.

The children put their T-shirts on over top their clothes. "Put yours on," Veda said. Hannah pulled the shirt over her head and struggled to pull it down over her tank top. It was a bit small, a child's size large.

"Your boobs are bursting," Benny said. Veda slapped his head, not too hard but not soft either.

"Knock it off, Benny," Charles said. Hannah's face flushed. Every day it seemed Benny acquired a new inappropriate expression. Yesterday it was *bitch on wheels*.

Hannah crossed her arms and pulled off the T-shirt. "Let's go," she said, grabbing Benny by the arm. "Bath time."

"Dinner in twenty minutes. Don't play around, or nothing for you."

Upstairs Hannah ran the water and waited for Benny to undress. She eyed herself in the mirror, sideways in profile. That good feeling, a powerful feeling, came back to her. "Get in," she said to Benny. "You heard your father. Don't play around."

9.

In August the family would go on vacation. They had been going for years to Rehoboth Beach, where Alice's maternal aunt owned a condo. Over breakfast, Alice suggested to Charles that they bring Hannah.

"Why would we do that?" There was something in Charles's voice. They both noticed, but neither knew what it was.

"The children like her. It could make things easier. You're always saying vacation is more work than work."

"I wouldn't say Benny 'likes' her."

Alice knew that Charles wasn't, in the end, going to refuse; but the discussion would continue. It was Charles's need to argue against any idea that was not his own. "Maybe not. But he listens to her. He's calmer. She has that . . . stoicism. For a girl her age, she's unflappable."

Charles wondered what this was about. With Alice, nothing was ever what it appeared. She wanted the girl to come along for her own private purposes. She always had private purposes. "Won't that be expensive? Full time for a week?"

"We won't pay her. We're taking her to the *beach*. Room and board. Clearly her own parents won't be taking her anywhere this summer; all she does is go to the pool and the mall, as far as I can tell. She seems very alone. Her mother is a good worker, they say, but not very . . . warm. I'm sure a week at the beach will be a treat for Hannah. Have you noticed how rarely she smiles?"

In fact he had. Charles hadn't thought of Hannah as lacking in cheer so much as filled with a gravity beyond her years. It seemed to Charles that Hannah now looked after his children not because they paid her to, but because they needed looking after; that Hannah had come to understand this. What he also felt, but could not have expressed in words, was that Hannah looked after all of them.

"I thought you were just saying you liked the fact that she's calm. Now you want her to smile more?"

Alice snorted a nervous laugh, then started to stack the breakfast dishes. The children had not cleared theirs, because Alice had told them to go outside and play so she and Dad could talk.

Charles watched Alice. She always busied herself when he'd hit upon something she didn't like to acknowledge, when she felt exposed. And now, he saw it. Or thought he did. What this was about. Alice's purposes.

When Veda was two, Alice had announced one day that she wanted to adopt—from an orphanage in Seoul where one of the DoD teachers she knew had volunteered. Charles thought she'd lost her mind. Alice had been home all day every day with Veda since she was born, sometimes alone all night when he worked the night shift. She was only twenty-four, Charles twenty-two, and they'd known each other six months when Alice got pregnant. When she told him, she was past three months along already. She'd known for longer and had been planning to have an abortion. Alice never said so, but still Charles knew. He didn't know what had changed Alice's mind, but regardless, he was determined to take responsibility—as his own father hadn't, as some of his fellow soldiers hadn't.

Adopting a Korean baby? Charles didn't even know Alice wanted another baby. She was on the pill, as far as he knew. Things were just starting to settle down, he was doing fine at work. Alice was coming unraveled, he thought. When she brought it up, she'd acted entitled and guilty at the same time. Like when she talked about her time in the Peace Corps. Charles wondered if this was about her family, defying them. Alice had told him all about their Florida plantation roots, her father's ambition, flying the coop to go north, to Dartmouth, where he was now professor emeritus. Dr. Nicholas Weaver Sr. was a supply-side economist, former advisor to the President's council, board chairman of a major energy company. His wife, Alice's stepmother, was a curriculum consultant to Christian grade schools.

When Alice started to show, they knew they had to leave Seoul; Charles would leave the Army, they would get married, and they would move back to Uncle Marvin's house in Pleasant Plains. It was all they had, Charles's inheritance (Alice did not want to ask for money from her father—who might or might not have given it— and on this, at least, Charles and Alice agreed). Essie and Marvin were both in the ground, along with Charles's brother Bobby. Derrick, the oldest, in jail, and Carl somewhere in Atlanta with a restraining order filed against him. Charles's sister, Rhea, a middle-school teacher who lived in Prince George's County with her much-younger husband, had written to Charles regularly and said she looked forward to meeting Alice and the arrival of the baby.

He had the job offer from the Redskins, which came through the staff sergeant who liked him—full time with benefits, junior assistant to the Manager of Gate Security. It was a good job, opportunities for advancement; Charles would take it, of course. It wasn't as if he and Alice could just pick a city or neighborhood anywhere on the map where this rainbow family would be accepted (if such a place existed) and then miraculously make a life there. Charles worried for his baby daughter. For *her*, little V, he would put his head down, do right, and make a family.

Adopting a Korean orphan, any orphan, was all wrong, for all of them. Was Alice serious?

Apparently, she was not. She dropped the notion nearly as quickly as she'd raised it. A year later Alice was pregnant with Benny, and the subject never came up again.

Alice stood and cleared the table. She wore denim cutoff shorts and a green tank top with no bra. Her breasts and buttocks had become flat and flaccid, her belly ample, but her legs were shapely and solid. Her strawberry hair had begun to gray when she turned thirty, and now, at thirty-three, it was brassy like wheat, but full and wavy, and she wore it a little unkempt. Her eyes were often open wide in a startled look.

Moments like these Charles pitied Alice. Her mother had died young and her father remarried a woman who wanted nothing to do with her. She left home for college and never turned back, chose her way farther and farther from her past. She was always somewhere into the future in her head, planning the next move. Scheming. Did she even know she did this? Did she ever consider what these schemes she thought up *meant*? Charles didn't think on it for too long. He'd stopped trying in earnest to figure Alice out a long time ago.

* * *

Alice felt her jaw harden, felt Charles watching her. She turned the faucet on and started to wash. He won't refuse, she thought. Just needs to make everything more difficult, needs always to be trying me for some crime or another. Alice focused on the dishes, scrubbed at dried egg yolk, which Charles never cleaned completely when he did the dishes. She scrubbed harder; she always felt better after completing a task thoroughly. When the dishes were done, Alice turned to Charles; he was reading the sports. He took his time more and more before leaving for work these days. She remembered when he left the house at 7:15, his collars ironed and eyes bright with purpose. She remembered feeling Charles's absence the moment he left, like a drop in temperature, and looking forward to seeing him at the end of the day, a little more rumpled and worn, but pleasingly spent from a day's work. Now, he lingered until 8:30, sometimes quarter to nine. She knew better than to ask.

"So," Alice said, smoothing down her hair with damp hands. "You'll ask her tonight?"

Charles raised his eyes, a stern look on his face.

That's just his face, Alice had told herself for years; and yet still sometimes it cut her.

Charles said, "Won't you be seeing her this afternoon?"

"I have to stop at the bank and the post office on my way out. I won't have time to talk."

What is this, Charles thought. She wants me to do it, to invite the girl. She wants to win. Well, fine then. He didn't mind. *He* liked the girl just fine, smile or no smile. She wasn't a lost orphan, she was a good-looking girl, provided for, a little odd maybe. Smart, observant girls usually were. Charles could see it a little already: playing with her looks and not quite easy in her body, which was clearly developing (he'd noticed her shoulders the other day, and how toned she was in the torso from all that swimming). Rhea had been like that—quiet and competent, awkward all the way through her teens, but she blossomed after that, found her own womanly style, unshowy.

This girl, Hannah Lee, she knew their family now. She was one of them. A family like theirs—maybe all families, Charles thought—resembled the Mob: loyal by virtue of silent collusion. Hannah understood the code, and embraced it naturally.

If Alice wanted to think of the babysitter as a needy child, let her. Let her think she's had a true triumph. "Sure," Charles said. "I'll talk to her."

10.

The car ride was long, and hot. They'd meant to leave at 8:30 on Saturday morning, before weekend traffic hit, but Benny had thrown a tantrum over wanting to bring all of his sandbox trucks instead of just one, and he'd locked himself in his room. They were delayed a crucial hour and a half.

Hannah had arrived, with her canvas duffel and school backpack, in the middle of the crisis. When they finally got Benny to open the door, half of his braids had been pulled out, the left side of his head now a willowy treetop of loose Afro. Hannah didn't ask what happened, if the tantrum precipitated the hair, or vice versa; or maybe they were two completely separate crises, which you couldn't put beyond Benny. And what did it matter, anyway: Benny loved those braids, and he'd done it to himself—undone himself—that was clear.

Hannah helped to hold Benny still while Alice and Veda finished pulling out the right-half braids. Then, while Veda gathered the brown bush into a low ponytail, Hannah tied it with an elastic. No one noticed the section on the left side that was just a little shorter than the right, nor the scissor tips peeking out from beneath Benny's pillow.

Hannah was excited. She was going to the ocean. At first she worried about missing swim practice, but when she told her coach, he said that swimming in the ocean, against the current, was the best training. *But be careful of the undertow,* he'd said. *It can be strong, and when it grabs you, it happens fast and all at once.*

Hannah didn't exactly know what undertow was. Her parents'

idea of a family vacation was a *kimbap*-and-watermelon picnic by the Washington Monument, or an outing to the shopping mall the day after Christmas, when all the sales were on—twenty-five dollars each for Hannah and James to spend. Last year she'd bought Ocean Pacific surf shorts and a big velvet bow-tie barrette with her money, both of which sat in the backs of drawers; they seemed childish to her now.

Hannah was also excited because he—Charles Lee—had been the one to ask. "Alice thought it would be good for the kids," he'd said. "Since they're used to you now." Charles had moved about the kitchen, opening and closing cabinet doors, looking for something he never did find. In his asking, he expressed somehow both reluctance and eagerness at once. Hannah did not know what this mixed expression meant, but she was always seeking out signs of their understanding—that private "it." She still believed in it, had no inclination to doubt: she was certain Charles sensed it too, but he was being more careful. It was the carefulness that Hannah took note of, and held, like a fragile robin's egg in her palms.

This wasn't a mere crush. A crush was how Teresa flushed purple and buried her face in Hannah's shoulder whenever Mr. Stevens walked by in the halls at school. This was different; Hannah's heart beat harder, but also slower, in her chest when Charles was in the room. She felt more alert, but also calmer, around him, as if a blurriness in her sight had cleared, a buzzing in her ear had silenced. Hannah had no name for her watchfulness toward Charles, and thus she treasured it all the more.

It was ninety degrees, and humid. Their late departure put them square into traffic at noon, the sun high and strong. The old Chevy wagon, no air conditioning, crawled across the Bay Bridge. Benny sat in the middle, asleep on Hannah's shoulder, his warm sticky cheek adhered to her skin. His head was a block of concrete, and he'd already drooled on her, but Hannah bore it: a sleeping Benny was better for everyone. Once, she caught sight of Charles's aviator glance toward them in the mirror. Charles was grateful, Hannah knew this; or thought she did.

Alice and Charles spoke to each other every so often, but Hannah couldn't make out what they were saying; their words were drowned out by the radio, tuned to an oldies station. When the Jackson 5 came on to sing "I'll Be There," she and Veda both quietly sang along.

On arrival they were rewarded with cool, clean, spacious lodgings at the Sea Colony. The condo had a living room, full kitchen and dining area, two bedrooms. Everything bone-colored or pastel, in wicker and faux bamboo. The children's room had two twin beds; they would call up a cot that Benny would sleep on. Hannah offered to sleep on the cot, but Alice said No, absolutely not.

"You're much too tall for it—or you will be by the end of the week at the rate you're growing." Alice winked at Hannah when she said this; her way of saying she'd noticed. It was true: in the last three months, Hannah had grown nearly two inches and had changed from a training bra to a regular one. It was Teresa who was first to say anything, and who went bra shopping with her.

Charles had stopped at a McDonald's drive-thru and now spread the wrapped packages of food across the round dining table. Hannah only went to McDonald's when James took her (otherwise, Soon-mi prepared every meal, every single day). She'd ordered a bacon double cheeseburger, large fries, and a chocolate shake, and Charles had turned to look at her before adding it to the order, a smile on his lips. As if to say, *Well all right, girl.* Alice, taking his look for a different kind of teasing, said, "Charles, for God's sake, don't make her self-conscious, the girl is *growing.*"

Benny marched from room to room, stuffing his mouth with fries from his Happy Meal box and inspecting everything.

"Sit *down*, Benny," Charles said. Benny obeyed, cheerfully. He was both tired (from the morning's battles), and refreshed (by the new surroundings and Happy Meal). The salty ocean air blew through the condo. Charles had opened the balcony door and all the windows when they first arrived. The smell of frying oil and meat mixed with the ocean air, and Hannah inhaled deeply. From her chair she could see the huge blue sky, the horizon stretching on forever. The sound of the waves crashing and lapping reached them on the seventh floor, and in the distance seagulls flapped and cried out. Hannah opened her mouth wide and bit into her burger; a burst of warmth and juiciness filled her mouth, and all at once she was overcome with two conflicting thoughts: what had she done to deserve such pleasure, and why so long in coming.

11.

At dusk, they went to the boardwalk. The air was hot and thick, but the ocean breeze cooled everything down, and everyone was out; you could hardly walk without bumping shoulders. Alice held both the children's hands, and Hannah and Charles walked behind them. "This reminds me of Seoul," Alice shouted, half-turning her head. She said it in a buoyant way, and Charles gave her a puzzled look that said, *This is nothing like Seoul.* Hannah wondered which one of them was more right and felt strange that she didn't know.

Suddenly, Benny pulled on Alice's arm. He turned around and pulled with both hands. They'd fallen into an especially noisy pocket, outside an arcade, so no one could make out what Benny was whining about; but up ahead the lights of the Ferris wheel glimmered, the tea cups darted and twirled. They continued walking, and Alice turned her head nearly full around on her neck to look at Charles, whose black eyes were filled with the gigantic wheel's circle of light. He shrugged and nodded at the same time.

"Okay," Alice said, "but just one ride. We need to have a proper dinner soon. We can come back another day to do the rest." The children's faces lit up. They dropped their mother's hands and ran.

"Slow down!" Charles shouted, and they did, but they turned and motioned for their parents to hurry up. It was Benny who led the way; Veda was giddy, deferential, full of trust in her brother's one-track exuberance, as if she'd been always waiting for this clearheaded Benny to relieve her of the burden of blithe maturity. She pattered behind him, carried along in his tailwind; like the little girl she was.

"You should join them," Charles said to Hannah. It was an invitation, an encouragement, not an employer's demand.

"Oh, Hannah's too old for the kiddie rides," Alice said.

Hannah said nothing, which did not seem rude or strange. The three of them were walking together, but looking ahead toward the children, speaking into the multitudes.

Benny chose the pirate ship. He ran up the ramp, elbows out, head down. He barreled through a young couple, breaking apart their entwined fingers.

"Benny," Hannah whisper-shouted, and she was off—up the ramp, apologizing to the couple—and on him. She put her hand on Benny's shoulder, and was surprised by how small he was—had she really grown so much? But then she realized he'd squirmed around her and was slightly down from her on the ramp.

Veda came to stand next to them, chin up and looking off somewhere. Charles came around the other side of the railing and handed Hannah three tickets. "Enjoy," he said, and Hannah took the tickets, smiling and dropping her eyes. Charles paused, a bare instant but long enough to see Hannah flush, before he walked back into the crowd of parents and grandparents at the base of the ship.

"Your face is so—" Veda started to say.

Hannah grabbed Benny's hand and rushed up the ramp to fill the gap in the line, waving her other hand in front of her face. "It's so hot," she said.

The great ship rocked back and forth, gently at first. Some teenagers in another row yelled "Whooooooaaaa!" in mock fear. Hannah sat between Benny and Veda, in the ship's very end row, which Benny had chosen. They'd watched as every row in front of them filled. The mechanical safety bar lowered and clicked into place, grazing Hannah's hipbones while hovering well above Veda's and Benny's legs, almost to their chests. Benny had barely made the height cutoff, and so he could stand—or at least raise up his bottom with his legs bent—which he did, hands raised, as the ship widened, and steepened, its arc.

"Sit *down*, Benny." Hannah tugged hard at his shirt.

The ship rocked wider and steeper. At the crest of the arc, the passengers hung suspended for what felt like many long seconds. Veda slipped her hand into Hannah's. Hannah looked over and saw that Veda was smiling with her eyes closed. Benny wriggled his hips, with his hands raised, and yelled, "Whoooooaaaa!" along with the teenagers.

Two more long, wide swings, then the ship tipped, inchingly, into full inversion. Coins spilled and clinked down onto the pavement far below. Hooting and hollering shot out all around. Benny's hands were still raised, but he'd been silent the last two swings. His face had turned a deep orange color, and his eyes were bulging. He wore a grimace, and Hannah couldn't tell if it was one of pain, or joy, or something else; but there was something unmistakably terrifying in that grimacing, bulging, orange silence. What was wrong with him? Something was wrong. Why wasn't he making any sound? Hannah could see the red veins of his eyeballs.

She looked away, then down into the crowd below. She looked, she looked . . . she found him. Charles. There were not many black people in the crowd. Charles's head tilted up, arms by his sides. Alice stood next to him, arms folded, one hip out. The ship tip-tip-tipped over and then swung full around again, whipping through the air. Hannah closed her eyes.

She opened them and looked again at Benny. He was the same. Something was wrong. He was ghoulish—metamorphosing, like the undead in those awful zombie movies James used to watch in the basement late at night. Hannah felt a sharp pressure in the space between her eyes, a dizziness spreading over her whole brain. Her mind was a psychedelic sheet of terror. She heard a piercing, high-pitched movie scream in her ears and suddenly realized it was her own throat making the sound.

The ship tip-tip-tipped again, and swung. Then again. And again.

"Owww!" Benny shouted. "You're hurting my ears!"

Hannah turned to see that Benny was no longer a terrifying zombie; he was the regular Benny again. She stopped screaming.

The ship swung several more times, no longer inverting, shallower and shallower in its arc, until it slowed to stillness. The safety bars dipped and hissed, pressing into Hannah's pelvis (someone else felt it too and made an *errgghh* sound) before lifting. The people poured out one side of the ship, as others poured in from the other. The children ran to find their parents and arrived at their sides, breathless.

"That was *awe*some!" Benny said.

"Hannah was scared," Veda said, giggling.

"Was that you?" Alice asked, with both disbelief and amusement. "We heard someone screaming bloody murder."

"That was *her*!" Benny shouted, shooting his whole arm at Hannah, his finger at her nose.

"Enough, Benny," Charles said sternly. "Why does everything have to be shouted? Stop pointing." He grabbed Benny's hand and yanked it away.

Hannah's heart pounded hard in her chest, but she tried to breathe as normally as possible. Alice was combing her fingers through Veda's hair, which had flown into a divine super-model mess.

"Worse than you thought?" Charles asked. It took a moment for Hannah to realize that Charles was speaking to her, but when she did, she also realized something else: it was him she'd been screaming for. Only he would understand what she'd seen.

Hannah blew her bangs, which were longer now, too long, out of her right eye. Her shoulders ached. "Yeah," she said, trying to say what she meant. "It wasn't what I expected."

"Well, you're all safe," Alice said. "I swear, I age an extra year every time the kids get on these things."

"We should ride with them," Charles said. "When did we stop doing that?" He asked the question pensively, hands clasped behind his back as he walked, like a much-older man. Alice had already headed for the park exit, her hand on Veda's back. Benny was walking a little apart from them, picking up red ticket stubs from the filthy-sticky ground. No one bothered to scold him.

Hannah was the only one to hear Charles's question. She was calmer now, her heartbeat back to normal, space opening up in her chest. She watched the wood slats go by beneath her feet; the occasional sparkle from a broken bottle or a penny below.

They walked, side by side. The space between them was that of a third party, a ghostly interloper linking their elbows. In his mind's eye, Charles turned slowly toward Hannah. The girl wore a turquoise jumper that tied around the neck and showed her collarbones and upper back. She was slightly pigeon-toed. He had asked his question—*When did we stop doing that?*—and there she was. Of course she doesn't know the answer, Charles thought. But then, Hannah looked up at him, and he saw in her face an eerie comprehension. She didn't know the answer, true; but she understood perfectly the meaning of the question.

12.

Hannah lay awake that night, fitful, and confused. Her mind and her body were both swarming—*swarming*—with she-didn't-know-what. She had a sense that there were different kinds of swarming, and they did not work together in harmony, but wrestled with each other, at cross purposes. She thought about that weather girl on Channel Four, the one with the perfect cleavage-to-waist ratio that Teresa and Raj both were always going on about—how she swirled her thin-fingered hands in front of the map to show high-pressure and low-pressure systems. If they collided, the weather girl warned, they would burst into a storm.

Their eighth-grade science class had actually visited the Channel Four station on a field trip (the station manager's daughter was in the class), which was how they had gotten extended close-ups of the weather girl's perfectly proportioned figure. The production staff showed the class how the girl was really gesturing toward a blank black screen. The images were on a monitor in front of her; she gauged her motions by looking into this mirror version of herself.

If Hannah's swarming was like high and low pressure, then she couldn't decide which was high and which was low, between her body and her mind. Didn't low pressure mean clouds and rain, and high pressure sun and clear skies? Everything felt stormy inside her, and hot. She kicked off her blankets. The air conditioning was on, and both Veda and Benny were nestled under the covers and sleeping soundly. Why was she so hot? At the same time, she could feel a shiver gathering up inside her, like a sneeze.

She rolled over on her side and stared at Veda, watching her little chest rise and fall, gently and evenly. Veda's lips were parted slightly, her long lashes curled out like tiny black butterflies at rest in the moonlight.

Some girls are happy, Hannah thought. She didn't know if this was a high-pressure thought, or a low-pressure one.

The room had a jalousie window facing the ocean. Alice had cracked the louvers open, even with the AC on, "to let the air circulate." Hannah hugged one knee into her chest; her stomach hurt. She closed her eyes, blaming the ocean, all this salt and moon and water that wouldn't stand still. She was swarming, and she just wanted to sleep. Tomorrow, she would swim. She would swim hard, and force out all the swarming.

A few minutes, or hours, later, a painful throb in her belly woke her. In her dream Hannah had been eating and eating at a table covered with her favorite foods—spicy tofu stew and cheeseburgers and dried wasabi beans—when suddenly, too late, she realized she was sick. Why hadn't anyone warned her? was the last thing she remembered feeling, or thinking, whichever one does in a dream. When she awoke, the aching pulse in her stomach, and that acute sense of injustice, slid together into one thing, as if the question had taken on the physical form of the throb. Her hands were tingling and stiff, and she was filled with rage, hungry to blame. She felt strange, not herself: her parents had taught Hannah never to complain, always to take responsibility.

She could not lie in bed any longer. She padded out into the main living area, then tiptoed to the bathroom, which was right next to Charles and Alice's room. The shower light was on, the door cracked. She tapped it open. No one was there. She thought they must have left the light on for the children's sake, although the apartment was bright with the glow of moonlight.

She bunched the hem of her nightgown into her armpit and pulled down her underwear; it was the sour smell that came strongest, then the darkness of the crusty stain, the color of BBQ sauce. Her stomach throbbed. Hannah sat down on the toilet seat and held her stomach with one hand, her nightgown in the other. She felt something plop out of her and looked down between her legs to see a thick red-brown glob floating and spreading. She peed, then looked again to see a bowl filled with pink, the red-brown glob smaller but still solid, like a yolk.

She stood, her panties at her ankles, nightgown still bunched in her hand. Now the pain had a color: Hannah imagined her stomach as a balloon filled with thick, stinky blood. How much would there be? How fast would it come out? She was so sleepy. She just wanted to lie down.

She'd paid attention in family health class. She knew words like "flow" and "uterine lining" and "ovulation." Teresa had started her period in the spring, and Hannah always knew when she was on it, because normally Teresa liked to wear miniskirts and dresses, but during her time of the month she wore dark-colored pants for days straight. How many days? Hannah tried to remember. Teresa would say she felt "like shit," or that she was PMS-ing; was this what she meant? She didn't talk about it much, not with Hannah anyway; Teresa had an older sister, and they were very close. This pain was worse than Hannah had imagined. Was this normal? How did Teresa stand it, for days at a time?

She sat back down on the toilet seat. She had to do something, but she was so tired.

The bathroom was large; it was at least three steps to the double basin and marble countertop, where Hannah eyed Alice's clear plastic cosmetics bag. She thought she saw something long and wrapped in pink-and-white shiny plastic. Ms. Bradford had said that young girls should use pads; tampons were for older girls and women. Hannah's stomach swelled and tightened. She thought what idiots most of her teachers were.

She breathed deeply, in, out. Closed her eyes. Counted to three. Opened her eyes, then rolled out a thick wad of toilet paper, placed it on her underpants, stood and pulled them up. Her steps toward the cosmetics bag, which were also steps toward the mirror that covered half the wall, were epic and absurd. Hannah wanted to cry, but she fought back her tears, thinking of Charles and Alice in the next room. She had to get out of this bathroom; she had to get back to bed.

The bag was unzipped. Hannah reached in and pulled out the tampon, which was one of three. Its familiarity reassured her; they'd passed them around in class. Despite her warnings, Ms. Bradford had shown them how to use it—which end was which, how to push the stringed end into the wider end like a plunger. Maybe Ms. Bradford wasn't such an idiot, Hannah thought. Maybe she understood after all that circumstances were not always ideal; that a young girl, like anyone, had to calculate, to prevail in matters of survival.

Hannah observed herself letting the wrapper fall to the floor. She would pick it up afterward, she would clean up everything. She just had to get through this. She inserted the tampon and pushed. She seemed to be out-of-body now. It was hard to get it all the way in, there was so much resistance. Was she doing it right? She kept pushing, and then, out of desperation, she pushed the plunger part too. Other than the sharp pain, like fingernails scraping inside of her, the pink-and-white paper on cream tile was the last thing Hannah remembered, before everything went black.

13.

Charles had been lying awake. Alice was deep asleep, having swallowed some pill or another before getting into bed. Maybe the pill had nothing to do with sleeping; Charles didn't know.

He heard Hannah in the bathroom. He knew it wasn't one of the children, they wouldn't have bothered with trying to be quiet. After a few minutes, he heard the crinkle of plastic, then a soft cry, a baby moan. Then, a strange sound he couldn't identify. He thought maybe one of the heavy condo bathrobes on the door hook had fallen.

Then there was nothing. Alice's loud breathing, one of the vertical blinds slapping in the living room, where the sliding door was cracked open. Nothing else. Not the toilet flushing or the faucet running. Charles waited a few minutes, then swung his feet to the carpet and stood in one motion.

At the bathroom door, he listened. A faint buzzing from the lights. The blinds slapping again in the living room. He put his hand on the knob, turned it, and waited. Still nothing. Slowly he pushed the door open until it wouldn't push anymore. It opened just wide enough for him to slip his upper body in and look around. Hannah was lying on the tile, blocking the door.

He did not think to wake Alice. He did not want Alice to wake. Perhaps he should have; anyone would have thought so. But Charles was a soldier. Had been. You had to think on your feet, rely on your wits. No one else was going to save you. *You* were the help, the savior, the one who had to act. And it was *her,* Hannah, lying there. He would know how to help her.

Charles sucked in his gut and squeezed into the bathroom through the narrow opening. Hannah's underpants were at her ankles, there was a smear of blood on the floor; blood in the toilet, blood on the girl's fingertips. He saw the Tampax wrapper, a thick wad of stained toilet paper. Charles crouched down and listened to Hannah's chest, put his fingertips on her wrist. With the thick elastic waistband between thumbs and forefingers, he pulled her lavender cotton underwear up, slowly, and he looked away just as he recognized the smell. Then he put his hand under her neck and head (they both nearly fit into the palm of his hand) and lifted them onto his lap as he eased himself down onto the tile.

Hannah's head, her whole body, was warm; her face was yellowish-pink. Had she been unusually pale, he may have done differently, might have woken Alice or called 911. But she was breathing normally, her color was full, almost cherubic. She wasn't clammy; there was no more blood as far as Charles could tell. She was all right. She'd had a scare maybe. She would be fine, she'd just had a scare.

He reached for a bath towel and bunched it into a pillow, slid it under Hannah's head. Then he stood and ran a stream of cold water on a washcloth, kneeled down and patted her forehead, cheeks, throat. He cleaned her fingertips, then wiped the blood off the floor tiles. He rinsed out the washcloth and hung it under a towel. He kneeled again, and waited, watching her. She slept very peacefully. She looked different without her glasses, both older and younger. He could see her dark nipples through her nightgown.

The mind is so banal, so simple sometimes. Charles let his eyes run over her body and did not feel ashamed. She reminded him of someone; of course she did. And of course he'd kept it from his mind until now. He sat there and let the thought take shape, though not the memory, exactly; and he was calm.

She seemed to be cooling down. Charles moved Hannah's hand, gently, and placed it flat on her sternum so her forearm covered her breast. He lowered the toilet lid, reached for the handle and flushed.

Hannah began to stir. Charles stood and turned off the shower light. Hannah rocked her head from side to side and pulled her knees into her middle. Charles squatted and scooped her up. The plastic applicator from the tampon fell out from under Hannah's nightgown when he lifted her, hitting the tile and clanking much more loudly than such a small object should. Charles told her to *shhhh* when she made a burbling sound like a small animal. He carried her into the children's room and shifted to hold her entirely in his right arm as he bent to straighten the blankets. Behind him, a squeaking of worn springs, and he looked over his shoulder to see Benny curled into a ball, facing the other wall, one foot hanging off the cot in a patch of moonlight.

Charles laid Hannah on the bed, then left the room, closing the door behind him.

In the bathroom he took one last look around. He picked up the plastic applicator and threw it in the trash. He went back to bed. Alice was still deep asleep.

In the morning Charles would wake Alice early and mention that he'd heard something in the bathroom during the night and had seen the Tampax wrapper on the floor this morning. "She might be unprepared," he would say, and Alice would immediately call Hannah into the bedroom for a private chat, to ask her, kindly, eagerly, if she needed to go to the drug store. Alice would take her, would help her, because she wanted to help her, after all. And that would take care of that.

14.

There was no denying it now: they shared a secret. If there was this one, then there were a thousand. Hannah felt strange, like a curtain was rising, the house lights falling, spotlight on. She'd had that dream before, about being the lead in a play and finding herself frozen before the audience, not knowing any of the lines. But in the dream there was no buildup, no anticipation. She was simply there, without warning, as if she'd just forgotten. Now, here, it was like an unveiling of something that had been pulsing, coming to life. There was a feeling of unbearable expectancy, as if she might die if she didn't arrive at her moment.

That morning, Alice had gone to the pharmacy and bought three sizes of pads. She'd stood in the bathroom with Hannah, facing the other way, while talking Hannah through how to pull the tampon out. Hannah was afraid: she'd never fainted before, was not eager to repeat the experience; and not with Alice. Charles had taken the children out for breakfast.

"You'll be fine, honey," Alice said. "Putting it in is the hard part, and you did fine with that." Hannah had figured out that Alice knew nothing about the fainting; about Charles putting her to bed and covering her tracks. About their secret. Hannah herself woke up having almost forgotten the whole thing, but then something came back to her; she remembered seeing Charles leave the bedroom, and close the door behind him. Imagining the rest filled her with an excited fear.

Hannah managed to pull the tampon out and put the pad in place, without incident. Then they sat down at the table, and Alice made tea. She asked Hannah if she wanted to call her mother. At first Hannah didn't understand the question. Call her mother? And say what? But then she understood, by Alice's earnest expression, that it was something she *should* want to do; something that Alice, for example, would want Veda to do. Hannah thought that if she were going to call someone, it would be James; but she definitely wasn't going to do that. So Hannah just said, No, but thanks, she was fine and didn't want to worry anyone; it could wait until she got home. Alice smiled at her, a sad smile that prompted Hannah to say, "Is there anything to eat?"

When Charles and the children returned, Hannah and Alice were eating granola bars and apples. Charles put two large Styrofoam containers on the table. "One is pancakes, one is waffles," he said. From his pocket he produced jam and syrup packets, and two each of plastic forks and knives, all of which he scattered on the table like nuggets of gold.

"Is she better yet?" Benny asked, tromping in figure eights around the glass coffee table and a chair.

"Why don't you ask Hannah that, Benny?" Alice said. "I'm sure she'd appreciate the concern."

"Are you better?" Benny's knees came closer and closer to the sharp table corners on every pass.

"Yes, I'm fine. Thank you, Benny."

"So let's go, let's go, let's go!"

"Put your trunks on, Benny," Veda called from the bedroom. She came out in her hot-pink plumeria blossom bikini.

"I'll take them," Charles said. "You two can relax here. It's in the mid-nineties today."

"Oh, no," Hannah said, quickly turning to Alice. "You should go. I'll stay. I'm fine. I'll just . . . I have a book." She'd brought *Claudine à l'école*, a new copy that Madame Glissant had sent via Raj (the note read: *Entre nous, ma chérie*). But even as she said it, Hannah knew that she would sit on the balcony, watching them.

"I thought you were *fine*," Benny said.

"Stop it, Benny," Charles said, and then he left the room to get dressed.

"What's she *doing* here if she's not even going to *come* with us."

"People can't help it when they get sick," Alice said. "Hannah gets sick sometimes, just like you do."

"I don't get sick," Benny said.

"He's got you there," Charles mumbled from the bedroom.

"God, I guess that's true," Alice said.

"Hurry *up*, Benny," Veda said. "Now *you're* the one making us wait." Keeping his rhythm, he tromped into the bedroom to change.

"Okay, then. Hannah, are you sure?"

Hannah nodded.

Alice stood, took a deep breath. "I guess I'll get dressed and then we'll head out in *five minutes*." She shouted the last part so everyone heard.

Veda went to the closet and came back with a stack of four yellow-and-orange-striped beach towels, which she placed on the table. She unfolded one and draped it around her neck and shoulders like a shawl. Then she sat at the table across from Hannah. "How come my dad had to carry you to bed last night?" She was now stacking the syrup and jam packets into a pyramid.

Hannah stared at her. "What do you mean?"

"It woke me up."

"You must have been dreaming."

Veda placed the last jam packet on top, then looked at Hannah. Hannah looked back. Neither said anything more.

After the family left, Hannah pulled out *Claudine* and went to sit on the terrace. It was hot, but the breeze was refreshing. She left the sliding door open, something she never would have done at home, not with the AC running. But the combination of warm ocean breeze and cold air hitting her from opposite directions was perfect; the pleasure on her skin shot a burst of happiness up to the very top of her head.

From her chair, Hannah leaned forward and watched the beachgoers through the iron bars of the railing. The spaces between the bars were just a little narrower than the top of her head. A cat could easily slide through, she thought. A shoe, a book, her glasses—

She saw Benny first, leading the way across the pool area, then down the wooden staircase to the beach. Benny ran, though slowed by the sand, which looked deep and silky. The other three stopped to take off their sandals. It was early still, so they had their choice of spots and found one, a few umbrellas to the right of the lifeguard stand. They were easy to spot, even from seven stories above. Charles was a lone dark figure among white and brown skin, and he wore a maroon baseball cap.

Still, Hannah had to squint to keep them in focus. She lowered and raised her glasses, trying to see them better. Benny threw off his T-shirt and ran for the water. Alice hurried after him with floaties. Charles went to the umbrella stand, then came back and stabbed the blue umbrella into the sand, driving it deeper until it was stable, and unfolded the chairs. He sat back in one of the chairs and stretched out his legs. Veda sat next to her father on one of the towels, knees up, burrowing her feet. After a few minutes, she stood and headed for the water.

Hannah turned the other chair on the balcony to face her and propped up her legs. The girl on the cover of her book had smoky eyes and wore a boyish sailor suit. Hannah opened the book and read the first page.

My name is Claudine, I live in Montigny . . . . this lovely region is atrociously poor and its few scattered farms provide just enough red roofs to set off the velvety green of the woods . . . . There are copses . . . full of sun and strawberries and lilies-of-the-valley; they are also full of snakes. Dozens of times near the rose mallow I've stopped still, panting, when I've found a well-behaved grass snake under my hand. It would be neatly coiled up, like a snail-shell, with its head raised and its little golden eyes staring at me; it was not dangerous, but how it frightened me! But never mind all that: I shall always end by going back there, alone or with my friends. Better alone, because those girls are so young lady-ish that they annoy me. They're frightened of being scratched by brambles;

they're frightened of little creatures such as hairy caterpillars
and those pretty heath-spiders that are as pink and round
as pearls . . . . Heavens, how I love the great woods! I feel
so much alone there, my eyes lost far away among the trees,
in the green, mysterious daylight that is at once deliciously
peaceful and a little unnerving because of the loneliness and
the vague darkness . . .

Hannah's eyelids grew heavy. Her body felt like molten lead—no longer swarming, but solidified into something thick and torpid. As her eyes were about to drop closed, she saw the maroon cap turn, and Charles's dark face raised up toward her. Hannah's eyes closed, then opened, then closed. She saw Charles's face behind her lids, the handsome face; she saw it as it was that first day—unbearded, off guard, slightly slack-jawed. Hannah did not open her eyes again but held this vision. She fell asleep with her right hand squeezed between her knees, ankles crossed, mouth open. The sun warmed her, and she felt neatly coiled up, deliciously peaceful. She dreamt of the velvety French countryside, and of venetian blinds flapping in mysterious daylight.

15.

On Tuesday, the third day of her bleeding, Hannah felt better. She wanted to go swimming in the ocean. She was tired of sitting, tired of lying down. The second day had been the worst, just as Alice had warned her. On the third day, Hannah told Alice in private that she wanted to try swimming. Alice nodded, and they went again together to the bathroom, where Alice handed Hannah a tampon, this one much smaller. "Just shout if you need me," Alice said, almost eagerly, pulling the door behind her but not shutting it.

This time Hannah had no problem. She changed into her racing suit and pulled her hair into a low ponytail. She felt good, and ready to swim hard against the current, like her coach had told her. She felt like one of those pretty pink-cheeked girls on the Tampax TV commercials, "fresh" and "ready for anything."

She came out in just her bathing suit, holding her clothes in a bundle.

"Finally," Benny said, mouth full of Cheerios.

"You look sporty," Alice said.

"I bet I'm faster than her," Benny said, then raised his hand to his mouth to catch the Cheerio dribble.

"You can only dog paddle," Veda said. "And besides, Hannah is, like, a *real* swimmer."

"It's just 'cause of the floaties," Benny said. "Mom said I could take off the floaties today."

"Only in the pool. Only in the shallow end," said Alice.

"If you want, I can take him to the deep end," Hannah said, cheerfully. "Look." She grabbed Benny under the armpits and lifted him to her chest. She used her legs to lift, and breathed out when she straightened. It was strange how strong and good she felt, as if the last two days had been a kind of metamorphosis. Benny kicked his legs and howled until Hannah let him down. "He's only a quarter this weight in the water."

"Let him swim," Charles said, rattling his newspaper. He'd gone early to the deli for cereal and milk and the paper, before anyone was awake. "We'll rent those boogie boards. The other children are fine on them."

"Boogie boards! Yessss!"

"I don't know . . . Hannah, have you ever . . ."

"Only at the water park, but it's probably the same. They're wide enough for two. I'll ride with Benny." Benny stopped jumping up and down and was about to pout at the idea of not having his own board; but then he thought better of it. It took Benny a moment longer than it might have an older child, or a smarter one, but he recognized that it was the best deal he was going to get.

Alice puckered her face, and they all knew she was going to say yes. "Veda, you stay close, too."

"I'll ride with Veda." Everyone looked at Charles, who continued to look at his paper. He'd spoken nonchalantly, but he knew, as they all did, that he'd made an exciting announcement. Charles had barely gone in the water, just waded in a few times to cool off, always wearing his cap. That's usually how it was—Charles supervising, surveying. On the rare occasion when he participated, the children knew it was something special. Hannah had watched him from the balcony, watched him watching; how when Charles was ready to turn from the shoreline and sit down again under the umbrella, he stretched out his arms and arched his back, like a surrender—to an enemy, or a god.

They were all giddy with shock, speechless.

"Well, hurry up," Charles said, looking up now. "Clear your bowls."

Hannah held her bundle tight against her chest. Dress rehearsal was over.

The sand was cool on their feet. The sun had been hidden behind fat white clouds all morning. They were cumulus clouds, and the patches of sky between them were blue. The day was bright, but cooler than the days before.

As Hannah barefooted through the sand, she smiled at her toes. The sand was gritty and ticklish, and she liked the funny feeling of sinking with every step, being swallowed by silky softness. The family made their way to the same spot, their spot now. It was quieter today, more older people and fewer teenagers. The tide came up a little higher on the beach, filling in holes where umbrellas had been planted and washing away a lumpy sand castle.

Once they'd set up camp, Charles reclined as usual in his chair. Benny and Veda, and Hannah too, sat on their towels and waited. Alice applied sunscreen, first to Veda's shoulders, then to Benny's nose and forehead; then to her own entire face and body. Hannah had shaken her head when Alice held the bottle out to her.

Charles sat back, and they all waited. They knew better than to rush it, to ruin a good thing. The muted sky was heavenly somehow, the air humid but not unpleasant; there was a stillness that seemed to warrant respect. They were all five of them in sync in their silence. They sniffed the salt breeze with their eyes closed, like newborn puppies. There were very few people in the water, no children. It was probably too cold yet. Benny began digging around Veda's legs and burying them, and she let him.

Hannah stood up. "I'll see how it is," she said. She wanted to swim on her own, even just for a minute, before having to bring the children in. It didn't matter if it was too cold, she'd warm up quickly if she swam hard.

"Okay, hon. Show us whatcha got." Alice grinned up at her, hand over her eyes like a visor. At a glance, Alice looked like she was saluting.

Hannah walked toward the water, then broke into a run. The ocean! It was indescribable. Sitting on the beach towel, beholding it from afar, Hannah had been eager but intimidated. It was so huge, and endless. It did not surprise Hannah that her parents had never brought her here; perhaps they'd never seen the ocean themselves. Now, her feet splashed in the shallow foam, she windmilled headlong into the emerald waves. When the water reached her thighs, Hannah sprang up from bent knees, hands clasped high and pointed like a gun, and dove. When she came up, she sputtered and shook her head. The water was cold, but not freezing, and saltier than she ever imagined: the sting at the corners of her eyes and the taste on her lips were strong but not unwelcome. Hannah leaned back, stretched her arms akimbo, and let her legs rise. The buoyancy of the salt water was a miracle, and she felt light as air. Her eyes were wide open, staring into the cloud-covered sun. She lay there a moment, felt for the pull of the current, carrying her out and away, then paddled and kicked her body so that her head pointed into the pull.

She began to backstroke. She stroked hard and fast for ten strokes, then slowed, stroking at an easy warm-up pace. She kept her eyes to the sky, kicking and stroking gently, in good form, knees rolling up and back, up and back, like perfectly calibrated gears. Hannah knew where she was: she'd stroked to exactly where she started. And she knew she was stroking in place, in proportional opposition to the current. It was like magic, this force of the sea, and Hannah was at home, its creature. She imagined them all on shore, imagined Charles especially, watching her. And they were.

Hannah stroked until her shoulders began to tingle, her breath grew shallow. She didn't know how long she'd been out—a few minutes, ten, twenty. She rolled over and swam breaststroke toward shore, then found herself caught at the crest of a massive wave and began freestyling hard. She rode the wave all the way in. Hannah knew instinctively how to ride it, how to let it carry her; how to join with it and borrow its velocity.

Years later, she would remember this first wave, this being carried aloft, like a feather, like an empty shell.

She would remember too how Charles had watched her, standing in front of his beach chair, hands on hips; how Charles and Alice both clapped their hands, laughing. Hannah would remember standing and walking up into the hot sand, winded and exhilarated, the sun now broken free from the clouds and illuminating everything with a blinding whiteness; and how, even in her blindness, she saw him there, Charles, on his feet, shoulders back, beholding, and pleased. She would remember that Charles was her destination, her sun-warmed celebration and homecoming.

And she would remember Benny, running toward her, catching her by the arm before she could reach them, reach him; pulling her away, off course, something about the boogie board man, *c'mon*, Alice's small woven money pouch in his hand. Why is he here, this boy, this mean stupid boy, Hannah would remember thinking; why is he pulling me, away, away from . . . Why does he ruin everything.

16.

Who's to say, in the end, who was at fault? Did the boy bring it upon himself? But he was a boy, just a child; can a child be responsible for his own fate? Charles was the only one who would wonder about this; and to himself, of course, never aloud.

Alice's eyes had just fallen shut underneath the shade of her peach sun hat. She lay on her stomach, cheek resting on hands stacked neatly one atop the other. Her elbows pointed outward and nestled in the warm sand. The seagulls squawked, and Alice heard them and didn't hear them. She was dreaming of Korea, of the little ranch house on the Army base: a warm bed, a warm breath in her ear, the bulk of a man settling on top of her, how good it was, so long ago and so good, the warmth and the weight.

Charles and Veda floated in a calm spot. They let themselves be carried downshore, toward another floating boarder who Veda was swearing was her dance teacher.

The lifeguard had climbed down from his tower to talk to his buddy, the bartender at the Crab Shack, who needed him to cover his shift later that night. The bartender had gotten a gig at a comedy club, and he was trying out some jokes on the lifeguard.

Hannah and Benny were just where they were supposed to be. Hannah kicked and paddled to keep within sight of their spot—of Alice's peach hat—on shore. But without her glasses, Hannah's distances were distorted; she relied more on instinct than on sight.

Benny was horsing around. He wanted to test how deep the water was. He lowered himself and threw back his head, with just his fingertips pressing the edge of the foam board. Hannah noticed how bitten-down his nails were, worse than usual. She hadn't noticed him biting them since they'd arrived; he must've done it only in private.

"Quit it, Benny," Hannah said. Benny wiggled his toes underwater, a good ten feet above the ocean floor. Hannah grabbed his arm to pull him back up.

"Are we going to catch a wave or what?"

"We should paddle that way, to your dad and Veda," she said. Hannah felt anxious, the farther away they drifted from Charles; the more distance between them.

"Daaad! Veeee-da!" Benny shouted right into Hannah's ear. She turned away, cringing. To make her point, she inched over to the other side of the board so that she was holding on to the corners of the short end. "Not in my *ear*, Benny." He was bobbing up and waving his hands in the air while still shouting. "Benny," Hannah said. Her back was to whatever Benny was shouting and waving at; she couldn't see them. Couldn't see Charles. She started to inch back to the other side of the board, when Benny pointed and said, "Look look!"

Hannah turned to look over her shoulder. It was Veda, standing on the surface of the water, and waving. Hannah blinked her eyes hard, then opened them again. Veda was still there, her legs long and straight, back slightly arched, waving like Miss America. It was some kind of mirage. Hannah couldn't understand what she was seeing.

"We have to get *out* there," Benny whined. Get out *where*? Hannah wondered. What *was* it? It was an invisible island in the middle of the ocean. Some kind of magic trick.

"Where's your dad? Can you see him?" Hannah squinted, scanned the horizon. Then she saw him, Charles, still in the water, leaning on the orange board. There was another figure next to him, on a blue board.

"Who's *that*?" Benny asked. They'd seen the blue boarder at the same time; it was too far to make out who it was.

They began paddling and kicking. Charles was just on the far side of Veda, Hannah didn't see him at first. They paddled and kicked, Hannah and Benny both determined to get there, toward a destination farther out than Hannah would have thought wise, since Benny had no floaties. But then Charles saw them, and he too waved his hand, and so Hannah kicked and paddled harder. She was pulling Benny and the board behind her, holding the board with her left hand, paddling with her right.

They were still some distance away when it happened. Benny was again shouting and waving. His puffy ponytail bobbed up and down. Hannah was doing all the paddling, and her arms grew tired, especially after stroking so hard earlier. She stopped paddling and instead held tightly to the board and kicked harder. It happened in an instant: one second, not even. The rip current shot through, carrying Benny with it.

There was silence, stillness. *Where, what?* Benny was gone, speeding away from her, from all of them, and the current was pulling on the far edge of the board. Hannah gripped it with both hands, she didn't know why; she didn't think. She kicked and kicked for what felt like a long time, until she ran into something solid. Her chest ached, her arms and her legs felt numb. The current was no longer pulling on her, and Hannah found herself collapsed on top of the board, lying on a soft wet beach in the middle of the ocean. She'd reached the magical island. Nothing at all made sense. The force of the current had come from nowhere, a beast had come to swallow them with its giant sucking mouth. She was exhausted. She opened her eyes. For a moment Hannah did not think of Benny, or Charles, or anyone. She thought: I escaped the giant sucking mouth that was trying to kill me. She thought: My bangs are in my eyes again, someone please push them away. She thought: My chest is going to explode.

Someone was screaming. It wasn't Hannah, or Benny. Neither of them had made a sound. The screaming came from somewhere on the other side of the island. It was an awful noise that filled Hannah's head as if it were coming from her own scrambled brain. Hannah would never forget that scream, Veda's primal scream that shot into the gray-blue sky that day, and voiced the horror that none of them—not Benny, not Charles, nor Alice—ever managed to voice.

The lifeguard was too late. Charles was too late. The blue boarder, who was, in fact, Veda's dance teacher, had been the first to see what was happening and pointed to where Veda and Charles saw the last of Benny alive, shooting away from them, weightless and tiny, like refuse down the gutter.

The boy never stood a chance. He did not have the strength to swim against the rip, nor the knowledge to ride it out then swim diagonally toward shore. The beast swallowed him, without mercy. Hannah understood later, when the rip current between the sand bars was explained to her, that had she let go of the board, had she let Benny have it, then kicked herself to safety, Benny may have survived. But no one said so. Not out loud. No one blamed her.

Holy Cross Hospital, Silver Spring, Maryland
1971

Many times she'd seen patients go under, as nurse assisting doctor; but this was her own first time. There was no question, at her age.

It's not the sleeping but the waking that stretches on, endless. It begins pleasantly, a floating, then dream and memory tumble in, flotsam and jetsam, shiny and broken...

Deep night, at the base of Jiri Mountain. She is holding her first child, baby boy, in her arms. Cold dirt floor, black silken sky through the window. Stars like diamonds. The child is tiny, and wet, and red. Come too early, far too early. Bleeding and pain, long pain, blinding blurring pain. This is not birth, she thought, this has to be death. The midwife is an angel of death; her husband the caretaker; this Quonset hut a gateway to the lower world. But then he wailed and wriggled, screamed at the stars; her heart wailed along, with joy, with relief. Her heart, her flesh. So tiny and red. He has his father's cheeks and brow. Their baby boy, alive not dead, tiny and alive, come into the world. Life, only life! The window offers the infinite sky. Enormous, kind mountain. Down below, tangled bedsheets. She is wet and throbbing. Warm and wet and throbbing...

In the hospital bed she floats, waking, slowly waking. Thrashing, murmuring. Endlessly waking, still.

Deep night. Running, running. Stars shimmer then disappear, shimmer then disappear. Thin clouds glide westward. She keeps pace, gliding. Light on her feet. The moon glows white noise. *In the pine grove, high on the ridge,* he'd whispered to her. They plotted all summer— not with words, but glances, the tension of their bodies. She runs the whole way, a lithe girl, only just started her flow last spring. She does not feel the autumn chill; breast thrumming with heat. She thinks of his small strong hands, intelligent eyes behind thick glasses. He is nineteen, a man; the landowner's first son. He sees her as a woman, sees *her*; not just the tenant farmer's little girl.

She arrives, giant pines rise up, reaching. Heaven above.

Breathing looking listening, in the dark, in the grove. Here he is; behind her now. She feels his bulge against the small of her back. Powerful sensation between her legs, a wetness, swirling, throbbing. The dark, sweet earth rising up beneath them, pulling them down, holding them up. Stars puncture the black sky above. Giant pines whisper, love whispers. Then his mouth, his hot breath, on her wetness, throbbing. This is death, she thinks, this is paradise, and she wants to die: surrenders, completely. Trembling, shuddering. His face now warm on her neck. He enters her, into the throbbing. Together now, they give up their breath, they die, they love, violently, perfectly, together. A war is on, but what does it matter, now, to them—North, South, Red, White—it is love that has invaded, conquered, taken possession.

She is waking, still waking, so long in waking. A tube twists, a needle digs into her vein. Fragments tumble then cease. Awoken.

A beige room. Blurry. A cold metal bar. A window. The buzz of yellow light. Eyes sticky, mouth dry. A face, lips moving. Arms holding it out to her, the swaddled bundle. The bundle is laid on her chest. Soon-mi shuts her eyes, wants to reach back to the grove, for the swirling and throbbing. But there is nothing. Where did it go. Her body is nothing, only a terrible ache and a tightness across her middle. This dry mouth, heavy head. The bundle moves, little elbows squirming. A girl, her daughter. Come too late, after everything; after too much. She is forty-three years old. Cut open in the middle. Where is her light-footed teeming body, her awakening soul. She looks down at the pink head and feels only loss, depletion; the end of love's invasion.

1973–1974

1.

Alice Weaver's eyes scan the words and images of the glossy trifold, unable to penetrate their meaning.

The DoD Education Administration of the Pacific provides a comprehensive and high-performing educational system dedicated to raising up the progeny of America's heroes.

Good order and discipline are the hallmarks of the military community we serve.

The plane flies west, chasing the sun—perpetual morning for almost twelve hours now. *Good order and discipline*, Alice reads. *America's heroes.* The words tilt and circle in the young woman's mind, searching for a landing strip, a clearing. The light streams in; Alice's eyes sting. She has been squinting for a long time. She'd tried to pull down the shutter, but it stuck halfway—the lid of a sleeping eye, still watchful.

The last two hours of a long flight are always the hardest. Alice knows this, having flown back and forth between Santiago and Logan Airport twice. The long leg of that trip—DC to Santiago—was ten hours; this time, DC to Seoul, is an endless fifteen.

Alice's friend Laila—who'd led their Peace Corps team in morning meditation and yoga—offered travel tips, to "keep her energy flowing." Alice had called Laila three weeks before, after sending in her DoD paperwork. "All transitions are traumatic," Laila had said on the staticky pay phone line. "You can minimize the trauma, with mindfulness." Panic had seized Alice: she had to get away, get out of her father's house and away from her stepmother; but a military base in Asia? Alice called Laila, because Laila had said, *Mi querida, mi hermana, we have to stay in touch*, and Alice believed she meant it.

Laila was the only one who'd chosen to stay in Chile after their two years were up. She would have left the Valdivia countryside by now, settled in Concepción to start on her new assignment. New roommates, new friends. Everyone loved Laila.

The first five hours had passed quickly. Alice re-read all the DoDEA materials—sent to the PO Box she'd set up at the Hanover post office after she saw her stepmother reading her postcards. The packet came from the high school on Yongsan base where Alice would be a teaching assistant (GS-4, biological sciences). Its contents were reassuringly thorough and clear—everything on crisp government stationery, a thickly embossed DoD medallion in the upper left corner. Arrival, transportation, housing, meals, post allowances, training and professional development, medical care; plus curriculum materials and an overview of the school's history and pedagogy—*Educate, Engage, Empower*—along with pay grade and benefits, which were comparatively generous and the main reason Alice chose Korea. There was a separate packet of recommendations for "Exploring Korea" on the weekends, listed by season. *The Wild Tea Festival in Hadong, Gyeongsang-buk Province, in May and June, is beloved and enjoyed by Koreans from all over the country.*

The impression of a cozy suburban community: there was a movie theater, library, bar and grill, two swimming pools, a park, a bowling alley. Alice found all this comforting. Everything, it seemed, would be taken care of, courtesy of the United States government.

In the phone interview, Vice Principal Mattison—wife of an Army captain—had told Alice that the school was both well-run and "progressive." The word was common currency, but Alice wondered what it meant to an educator of military children. The students, Mrs. Mattison said, were well-behaved, the teachers dedicated. When Alice said that she had little direct experience with the military (neglecting to mention protest activities in college) Dorothy Mattison said that was fine: the students needed a sense of normalcy, which was why they had begun to hire people from outside.

Alice reclined her seat halfway and sipped her ginger ale. She studied the photos of clean-cut, straight-backed children sitting at their desks; mist-crowned mountains in full autumn color; well-dressed officers' wives shopping for fruit in the busy streets of Itaewon. Soon she began noticing things, fixating: was that an insolent look on a student's face in the back row? Why was the sky overcast in all the outdoor shots? She put the folder away and flipped through her Korean phrase book. *Goh-MAP-sum-ni-DA. AHN-yung-ha-sae-YO.* Alice closed her eyes and mouthed out words, trying to hear them in her head. *MEE-gook-eh-suh-WAH-sum-ni-DA.*

She read a week's worth of the *Herald Tribune*, cover to cover, and realized just how out of touch she'd become. Two years in the Peace Corps, in rural Chile, and she—all of them—had gradually let go the daily connections to their old lives. Had they been back in the States, or even working in Santiago or Concepción instead of the tiny village of Colonia de Curfeo, they'd have kept up on the war, on Watergate, on US relations with China and Russia. During her junior year, Alice had gone to meetings, made posters, and marched almost every week. Meanwhile she'd studied organic chemistry early mornings and attended all of her classes, to prepare for med school applications. Needless to say, Nicholas Weaver Sr., whose professorship at Dartmouth had been newly endowed, and who'd be named, later that year, an advisor to the President, knew nothing of his daughter's political activities.

Midway through her senior year, Alice stopped going to meetings, stopped hanging out at The Rue where she and all her activist friends spent countless hours drinking and smoking and pairing off in dark corners late into the night. That winter, it was Gideon Roth, her lab partner—studious, on full scholarship, and seemingly unaware that a war was going on—who'd gone with her to the clinic when she was three weeks late. He never asked who or when (she had no definitive answer anyway, and maybe he understood this), or was she sure she wanted to go through with it. He went with her, waited while it got done, sat with her afterward on the dusty twin mattress on her dorm-room floor. He held her awkwardly while she cried. Gideon was in the closet, but they never talked about that either.

Alice moved out of the dorms, to an apartment five miles west of campus where no one she knew lived. She didn't apply to med school. She told her father, unconvincingly, that she would, eventually. Nick Weaver responded by instructing his accountant to cease payments to Alice's bank account, which didn't surprise her. That spring, Alice made her plans. Laila was a grad student in ecology; they'd met at a march. She was olive-skinned, with wavy chocolate hair down to her butt, wore cutoff jean shorts with construction boots and gauzy Indian-print tops; she could have been a model for a Peace Corps recruitment poster or the cover of *Vogue*, or both. Laila was signed up for the reforestation project outside Valdivia; there was still time for Alice to apply. *Come with me,* she said, and it seemed inconceivable to say no. Still, Alice hesitated: Chile? She literally had to look at a map. Then Laila said, *Do you like trees? We're going to help save them.* Trees, Alice thought. It sounded tranquil, focused, and important. In June of that year, 1971, they were off.

They'd meant to keep up with what was going on back home, and in Vietnam, and the rest of the world; but really, there was too much to do. They were on the move, constantly—by mule, scooter, sometimes a van with shoddy brakes when they were lucky—transforming tree farmers into entrepreneurs and the unemployed into their labor. It was so simple, and hopeful: plant trees, improve your lives, and your country. Laila was often pulled into meetings at the university, where they were developing new curricula; Alice happily stayed with the laborers, digging and planting, digging and planting. *Lengas, ñirres y coigües.* Trees whose names sounded to her like hope, like nourishment itself. Alice's arms grew strong, her skin golden; her hair glimmered platinum in the sun the way it had when she was a girl, before her father moved them from Jacksonville to New Hampshire, where not only did her hair darken, but also her mood.

Alice all but forgot everything that had seemed so dire just months before. She knew, somewhere in her mind, that the planet was going to shit; it was her country's fault, and she should care. But with so much actual difference-making work to do, here, now, she had the luxury—it was an odd word perhaps, but still the right one, for a life in which she cleaned latrines, bathed infrequently, and mended her one pair of sandals by hand—she had the luxury of thinking not at all about the future. She had the blessed good fortune of being absorbed in the necessities of the present. And in this essentially mindless, productive state, she passed her two years with the Peace Corps.

She could have stayed. She should have. But she didn't have what Laila had. Courage? Faith? The fact was no one had asked her to stay.

The on-flight meal was served—a rubbery oval of chicken, soggy cubed vegetables, disturbingly filling despite miniature portions— then Alice tried to sleep. Her head was crowded with headlines, like crows circling but never landing. *Brezhnev's First Visit to U.S. Pete Rose Hits His 2000th. Skylab 2 Lands. John Dean Testifies Before Senate Watergate Committee. Coup d'état in Uruguay.* None of it seemed real to Alice; she couldn't bring herself to care.

After returning from Chile, Alice lived for three months with Nick Sr. and his wife, Cheryl, in Hanover; and every day, Colonia de Curfeo, the happiness she'd found, grew more and more remote. She was desperate to leave, she had to find her way abroad again, anywhere, just far far away. Medical school applications piled up on the floor in her bedroom. She sat by the window in Nick Jr.'s room, at the opposite end of the house from her father's, and smoked the stale Marlboros he'd left behind (inadvertently, for sure) the year before when he went off to college.

Her father would have been able to arrange something; he was waiting for her to ask. It was a game of chicken between them, and Alice refused to surrender. She spent her days researching teaching programs at the public library, ate two-dollar meals at the diner on South Main. One day she came home to find ten women sitting in a circle in folding chairs in the living room. Cheryl was serving iced tea and lemon crisps. She introduced Alice as "home for just a little while." There was a stack of goldenrod mimeographed sheets on the coffee table: *National Right to Life New Hampshire Chapter, Founding Principles*. The women encouraged Alice to stay, but Cheryl said, "Oh no, Alice has other ideas." She looked at Alice and narrowed her eyes, almost imperceptibly. It was then that Alice knew—that Cheryl knew. She was an eerily shrewd woman. She would not have told Alice's father, would instead relish the private knowledge. Would use it to keep Alice away.

When Alice saw the DoDEA flyers in the window of the local recruiting office, she was ready to try anything; she made her plans—escape plans—hastily.

And now, here she was.

Alice leaned her head against the half-shuttered window. The couple sitting next to her whispered incessantly. The whispering seemed louder than if they'd spoken in normal voices. The man wore a starched button-down and pleated pants, the woman a collared denim dress and flat brown shoes. They reminded Alice of the Jehovah's Witnesses who used to knock on the door weekly in Jacksonville ("You have to be polite, but firm," Alice's mother would say, before opening the door and demonstrating impeccably). Each wore a wedding ring, but the way the woman put her hand on the man's bicep, along with her bright coral lipstick and nail polish (Alice's mother would have sniffed), made Alice think they were not married to each other. This suspicion, and their constant chatter, kept Alice awake for what felt like many hours.

Finally, she did sleep. Dreamt several dreams. First, her mother, in bed at home, the day ten-year-old Alice knew for certain that her mother was going to die: something in her face, a smile too forced, a grayness in her skin—all of which matched the facts of Alice's memory, but in sleep evoked the lonely terror of nightmare. Then, a scene from her college dorm, the halls long and labyrinthine, not being able to find her way back to her room; an elderly stranger, Walter Cronkite but not Walter Cronkite, guiding her by the elbow until they arrive at a door that isn't hers, although the stranger, now

000000

speaking a garbled, ghoulish Spanish, like a devil's tongue, insists it is. In Jacksonville now, at her grandmother Weaver's house, the ancient villa where Nick and Cheryl deposited her every summer during middle school: upstairs, in one of the bedrooms, there is a tumult, and Alice taps open the door to see a hospital room—doctor, nurse, a girl on a table, struggling. Alice doesn't know the girl, but still she wants to tell her to stop struggling, you stupid girl, don't you see you're making it worse? The doctor has his hand on the nurse's neck. Alice charges into the room, the nurse looks up, and Alice sees it is the whispering woman with the coral lips—

"Honey, wake up." A bony hand on Alice's shoulder. Alice opened her eyes, saw the woman's face straight on for the first time—no, the second time: the face was precisely what she saw in the dream. "You were having a nightmare."

The man was looking away, signaling the stewardess for coffee.

Alice sat up, smoothed down her hair, felt her warm cheeks with her palms. "Do you know what time it is?" Alice asked. The woman looked to the man, her hand again on his bicep.

"That would be . . . *EEL-gope-shi.*" He delivered his joke heartily, his accent proudly atrocious. "Seven o'clock," he then said, business-like. "A.M. Korea time."

"Thank you," Alice said, turning to the window and lifting the shutter. The sun flooded the row with bright white noise.

Two more hours; the last two hours. She'd slept a long time.

After breakfast, which she hardly touches, Alice begins to breathe deeply, in, out, through her nose, a small constriction in the throat, as Laila taught them. She closes her eyes, lifts her top chest; deep inhalations, long, slow exhalations. Inhale, soft belly, releasing tension in the abdomen. This was always hardest.

When she opens her eyes, Alice focuses on a green light at the front of the cabin. She wants to clear away distracting thoughts, the specter of waking nightmares, with a mantra. What will be her new mantra, now, on this new journey, this fresh start. On her way back from Chile, she'd chosen a Spanish word—*adelante, adelante,*

adelante. Breathing, releasing, Alice pages through the Korean phrase book in her mind. She finds *gwen-chahn-ta, gwen-chahn-ta; it's all right, it's all right.*

2.

With one hand, Soon-mi lays down the quilted changing mat on the countertop, between sink and wall. It will be tight, but Soon-mi thinks Hannah will fit. One third of the changing mat hangs over into the basin, but it will have to do; it's all there is. She is thankful for the mat—lent to her by a fellow night nurse at the hospital—which is coated in a plasticky layer, easy to wipe down. *It's a lifesaver*, the other nurse had said. There are so many new products and gadgets these days. Soon-mi hasn't kept up all these years; she never imagined she'd have to.

Hannah is heavy in her left arm. Soon-mi's hips are narrow; to rest the child there she has to jut out the right side of her pelvis, like a prostitute waving down a john. Perhaps she should have done as Chong-ho urged—just laid the child down across two seats in the baggage claim area while he and James retrieved the luggage. But Soon-mi did not see any other women changing diapers in public here; nor breast-feeding as she sometimes saw on the Metrobus. Here, in Gwangju, she cannot imagine such a thing, nor any of the immodesties she witnesses daily in America.

It's been ten years; so much has changed. Airport security is much more strict, for example; General Park's military personnel lurk and loom everywhere. As a woman with children, Soon-mi feels somehow less protected, not more. The new airport is really not so new, nine years old, but still, everything is too bright, too hard, too shiny.

Soon-mi has flown only once before—a decade ago, when they left Korea. She and Chong-ho and young James.

Hannah squirms, waking from heavy-headed sleep. Warm drool on Soon-mi's blouse. She straightens her hip, braces her legs, hoists the child up, then lowers her onto the mat. Hannah looks huge, squashed into this small space; she is in fact average for a two-year-old, but Soon-mi sees her always in comparison to James, who was a tiny, frail thing.

Hannah's eyes open wide, her face flushed and moist; her head tilts back against the wall, chin up, mouth open. The fluorescent lights buzz.

Exhaustion washes over Soon-mi like a mantle of lead. Fifteen hours. Direct flight is better, Chong-ho had said, and indeed he was always right about such things—thinking ahead, clear-minded, on their behalf. Hannah sat in Soon-mi's lap, not sleeping, but cheerful enough. Until the plane began to descend, and the child sobbed for thirty minutes straight, finally crying herself to sleep the moment the plane came to a stop.

Soon-mi wills away her fatigue—she is not a young woman anymore, but her will is strong as ever—and moves through the task at hand, swiftly, a little rough. Hannah marvels, eyes still wide, at the lights, the reflection in the mirror, the swirly stucco ceiling. The buzzing lulls her. Halfway through, a woman dressed in *hanbok* and heavily made up—a young woman—enters the bathroom and visibly recoils from the soiled-diaper smell; at which point Soon-mi notices the odor as well. Hannah twists her little shoulders and frowns. The woman stands at the far end of the counter and arranges her already perfect hair.

Soon-mi finishes the job and does not look up. She is aware that her own hair, wound tightly into a bun at the beginning of the journey, must now be a mess. She puts Hannah down onto sandaled feet, tugs at the skirt of the girl's wrinkled Winnie-the-Pooh dress; then straightens herself, ignoring the kink in her back, and wipes down the mat, folds it into her tote bag. On the way out, Soon-mi notices a small room off the square entry vestibule, where a tall American woman in a loose flower-print dress leans over a pull-down changing table. Hannah stares and sucks on two fingers. Soon-mi wonders how she missed it on the way in.

Across the baggage area, two carousels away, father and son stand together in silence, suitcases at their sides. They'd sat together on the flight, and just once during the fifteen hours, Chong-ho looked over at James's notebook, in which he was sketching an elaborate rocket ship. "It's for school," James lied.

James sees Soon-mi and Hannah first, and walks toward them. Only through thick, black-framed glasses does Chong-ho's vision come near James's twenty/twenty. At fourteen, James is taller than his father by a good inch (an inch and a half without the slouch), but lanky. He struggles with the smaller of the two suitcases, using both hands, while Chong-ho, compact and solid, carries the duffel bag and packed-full suitcase with relative ease. Hannah's feet bump her mother's every few steps, as Soon-mi beelines toward the boy and the man. Soon-mi has always had sharp eyesight as well.

Chong-ho leads them out to the taxi line. The humid air hits them like a sodden blanket.

"Won't it be very expensive?" Soon-mi asks. From the airport to Chong-ho's father's village, in the Hadong countryside, is some fifty miles. The skin of Soon-mi's cheeks and armpits is suddenly red and bumpy with heat rash, but she resists the urge to scratch and awaits Chong-ho's answer.

But Chong-ho does not answer. It is his way of saying, *Do not question me.* It is his way of rejecting the question and assuring his wife that he knows better: there are stronger imperatives than money.

Chong-ho and James load the suitcases into the taxi's trunk while the driver stands by. He is white-haired and stooped, holds a cigarette that's burned down to the filter. He takes one last toke, then tosses it into the roadway. Chong-ho sits front, even though, with Hannah on Soon-mi's lap, there is room in back.

"Umulkol Village," Chong-ho says.

"Eh?" The old man inclines his ear cartoonishly.

"Just go toward Hadong. I will tell you the way." The driver puts the car in gear with enthusiasm, nearly peels out into the lane. This fare will cover two, maybe three days' worth of his normal fares.

"Of course there is an extra zone charge, for out of town." Chong-ho does not answer. It is James, staring out the window and seeing everything, sharply and at once, who understands best that this time his father's silence means, *Your cheating lies mean nothing to me, old man.*

Once they are on the highway, the driver attempts to make conversation. "You from Seoul?" Chong-ho shakes his head no. In fact, neither he nor Soon-mi has ever been to Seoul. "You're visiting at an odd time. It's quiet in these parts in August and September. It's the springtime, May and June, when it's busy, when everyone comes for the tea festival." Soon-mi's ears perk up, and a distraught look passes over her face. She always loved the tea-harvest season. "It was a big one this year, one of the biggest harvests they've had; because of *Saemaul.*"

"My father is ill," Chong-ho says tersely. "I am the eldest son."

The driver nods and grimaces, grinding his teeth on a ginseng candy. There is nothing more to say in response to Chong-ho's statement. It is a heavy burden, and unavoidable. What every first-born male must bear. The old man steps heavier on the accelerator, and James's stomach, always sensitive, lurches.

Saemaul? Soon-mi wonders. A strange word, it must be something new.

From Hadong, the journey is south and east, along winding roads. The air cools, even as they move southward, as they ascend into the mountains. Twice, unsure of the turns, Chong-ho asks the driver to pull over so he can step out onto the shoulder—in one case, to the middle of the road—and take in the panorama of the valley to get his bearings. The roads they are traveling are new; they have route numbers and yellow painted lines. Chong-ho is not sure if these are the same dirt roads he remembers, now paved over and numbered, or completely new ones that follow alternate paths. They are surrounded by mile after mile of golden rice paddies, as if every paddy from years before had spawned a family. Packs of workers crouch and climb with their harvest buckets on new peach and melon farms; on vast pear orchards, fruit blossoms en masse like so many well-ordered platoons. Gone are the familiar thatched roofs, and, in their place, brightly colored tiles and armies of concrete buildings flash by in clusters.

"What are they?" Chong-ho asks.

"It's incredible," Soon-mi whispers.

Hannah's mouth hangs open at the brilliance of colors—the gold and green of the rice paddies and orchards, the bright blue of the roof tiles.

"The government," the driver says, vaguely. "General Park gives them concrete to build meeting houses for local officials and village leaders. Who knows what happens inside, but the more they build, the more they get from the government."

"The government owns everything now?"

"Well, it's hard to say," the driver says. "Officially the land belongs to the people. But the people . . . who do they belong to?" A bitter laugh loosens the old man's tongue. "My cousins in these parts say the village leaders compete, for everything—first it was concrete, then steel. Then better rice seed and equipment. Sometimes the farmers are forced to donate land for 'village improvement.' That just means the government cronies are stuffing their pockets. If you are a friend of the Saemaul leader, then you are doing well; but if you are not . . . My cousins wanted to grow traditional rice instead of the new high-yielding variety, but the Saemaul leader cracked down and now has it in for my cousin's family."

"But the fields . . . everything looks so rich," Soon-mi says.

"Yes," the driver says. "My cousin is doing much better, they have food enough and his children are going to school. He invited me to bring my family to live with them, but . . ." He makes a pained sound, sucking spit through the gaps in his teeth. "I prefer the city. I am more independent. We get by, anyway."

Saemaul, Chong-ho thinks. *Saemaul Undong*: The New Community. What, he wonders, has become of the old one.

They have been driving for almost an hour and a half when Chong-ho sees it: the Chinese parasol tree, in late bloom, deep-green leaves and creamy yellow flowers. It rises up from the melon field. It has grown taller and fuller, but it is unmistakable. Behind it he can just make out the gingkos that hover over the lookout shed.

"There are no melons," Soon-mi says softly.

"They have let it go fallow," Chong-ho says. His tone is disapproving. It is true that the soil must renew itself, but really Chong-ho is not concerned with farming techniques. In Chong-ho's mind and heart, the melons from that patch will always be the fruit of Soon-mi's family's labor—not this new tenant's, whomever he may be. Perhaps there is no tenant; perhaps it is Chong-ho's younger brother who is now making decisions about the land.

The taxi rumbles down the dirt road along the field, then climbs through the trees, circling the base of a blunt-topped mountain, two, three times around, ascending steeply. They come to a clearing—a cluster of low, flat houses and a dusty road that continues on toward more houses, a general store, a school, and, beyond that, farther up the mountain, a burial ground.

"Here," Soon-mi says suddenly, her forehead against the cold glass. Chong-ho, James, even little Hannah, look to her, surprised. The taxi stops short of the first house; forests of oaks surround on either side of the road. Other than that, nothing. "Look," Soon-mi says, pointing. Chong-ho and James look out the window in the direction of Soon-mi's finger, while Hannah sucks her thumb.

"It's just trees," James says. With great effort, he holds back a complaining whine. His parents, this whole trip . . . he resents being dragged along. He is old enough and could have stayed home alone. But he knows better. His father made his decree. There was something of significance awaiting them, a *family matter*, whatever that meant. They would all go, no discussion.

Hannah kicks her legs, bouncing on her mother's lap. Her eyes move around like a searchlight.

Only Chong-ho understands Soon-mi's sudden command. It is always like this, between them; always has been. He sees the ancient stump at the head of the path. At the end of that path, a long way through the oaks, is a ridge, high above the village. There, thirty years ago, the two of them arrived one night, hand in hand— the master's son, the tenant farmer's daughter—breathless under the moonlight. They continued along the ridge until they found a grove of black pines, heavily canopied, a refuge for their illicit love. Hidden from even the moon and the stars.

3.

Sunday morning, Alice wakes to a pounding between her eyes and hot, sticky breath on the back of her neck. Her brassiere's underwire digs into the ribs on her right side. On the floor beside the bed her dress is crumpled into a puddle of polka dots. The sun streams in through jalousie slats, and the room is sweltering; no one had thought to turn the fan on last night.

This morning, rather. Alice can't recall what time she came home; can't remember coming home at all. She assumes they weren't all together—she, Pauline, and Suzanne. Or were they? If not, who came home first, who last? Abruptly she sits up, her head spinning. Once she can see straight, she scans the room: who was to say they all came home at all?

A warm, tiny hand flops into Alice's lap. It was Suzanne breathing on her neck just before, curled up close, nearly spooning. Now Suzanne has rolled onto her back, mouth open, her other hand draped across her eyes. She is fully dressed, in collared gingham, buttons done all the way up except for the very top. Alice pulls lightly at Suzanne's skirt and sees that she's still got her hose on. Well that's a relief, Alice thinks: what hysterics they'd be in for if Suzanne had lost more than just a little self-control with the soju.

As far as Alice can tell, the only signs that anything unusual occurred last night are the bobby pins sticking up every which way on Suzanne's head, her brunette tresses frizzed and flyaway like the "before" on a Breck commercial. That, and the fact that it's Sunday, and Suzanne is not up and gone to church.

Alice's senses come to her one at a time. She smells Suzanne's sour breath, then tastes her own. Sound arrives more slowly, like a dial turned up: soft snoring, Pauline sprawled out on her bed, head turned toward the far wall, one foot and one hand hanging over the edge, like the chalk outline of a murder victim.

It had been Pauline's idea to go to Itaewon—"We should celebrate," she'd said. It was the end of summer term, and they had only one week off, after all, before classes started up again. They'd been working hard—five classes a day, and Korean immersion classes on Saturdays—since June. On Sundays they did laundry and grocery shopping, the occasional trip to Dongdaemun Market to shop for trinkets, then dinner with the Mattisons. Suzanne went to the Presbyterian church in the morning (there were no Lutherans, it was the closest she could find) and sometimes spent the afternoon with her church friends.

Alice lifts Suzanne's arm with two fingers, turns her wrist to see that it's almost noon. Suzanne mumbles, rolls over; Pauline is stone still, the snoring periodically noisier and throaty. No church, no market-browsing today. If Alice can stand steadily on two feet, dress, and make it down the hall to the kitchen for a glass of water, it will be the day's great accomplishment.

Why Suzanne volunteered to call her fiancé's cousin—a private on a hardship tour at Yongsan—Alice still can't fathom. Suzanne said she'd met him once before, back home in Duluth at the engagement party, just before he shipped out. "A nice quiet type," she'd said, and Pauline's eyebrows went up and down. Dorothy Mattison had warned them about the soldiers, and everyone warned them about Itaewon; but Pauline was on a mission, to "blow off steam." "Aren't you guys curious? We stay inside these gates like it's a convent or something. I need to get *out*." She managed to recruit Suzanne to her cause.

In fact, Alice had been feeling it, too: while they had everything they needed—a comfortable house, a kind (if overly maternal) supervisor, friendly and helpful colleagues, diligent students—the schedule had been rigid. They hardly ever went out at night. And here was prim Suzanne, eager to see this "other side" of Seoul. Suzanne's fiancé was in Bangladesh doing missions work, and she suggested that this foray into the den of licentiousness was her Christian duty. "Christ would never just stay in the nice part of town," she said, as she ironed her gingham. This comment had unsettled Alice: she thought of Laila, who had left her post as researcher and administrator in Concepción—too much paperwork, too much time in the office, she'd written—and gone back south, to a poor village outside Valdivia, to start an artisan cooperative with Mapuche women.

Alice scoops her dress off the floor. She fishes through a laundry pile and puts on a pair of clean drawstring pants and a T-shirt. On her way out, she flips the ceiling fan switch. The blades begin to move the air in a hushed whir.

Alice is rarely in the kitchen at this time of day. As she pours herself a tall glass of iced bori-cha from the refrigerator, she scrunches her face at the greasy countertops and cabinet doors. The house is modern, everything in the kitchen in white veneer with walnut handles, and it was spotless when they arrived. But the two girls in the west bedroom—younger girls, straight from college—had never lived on their own before, and they were sloppy. Alice runs a *haeng-ju* under the faucet and starts wiping down everything in sight—cabinets, countertops, stove, sink, fixtures. A mysterious urgency takes over as she scrubs harder and harder. Soon she finds herself on hands and knees with three sponges and a bucket of soapy water. The floors are in fact the cleanest of all the surfaces, but still, she will scrub until it is all done. A memory of her mother comes to her: as a little girl, Alice would sometimes help Mary, the housekeeper, with chores, out of boredom, and her mother would scold her for it. Cleaning was for common women, she'd say, and Alice was not from common people. But after her mother got sick, when Alice spent more and more time with Mary, her mother put her pale hand on Alice's cheek and said, "It's good that you can take care of yourself. Eventually, we're all on our own."

Alice scrubs and scrubs. The circular motions begin to work their way into the throbbing in her head, clearing out space, quieting the hammers.

* * *

What happened last night?

They'd met Andrew—the cousin—at The Angel Club, a bar in the heart of Itaewon. The English-speaking taxi driver knew exactly where it was. They couldn't decide if this was reassuring or not.

Andrew was there with a group of fellow privates, huddled together at a table near the bar, drinking and laughing. The table was covered with Bud Light bottles and steaming bowls of *boodae jigae*. The boys were young—nineteen, twenty—and harmless. The restaurant itself was crowded, and noisy, and dark, and there were no other foreign women. Alice wished they'd come earlier—it was after ten—surely there would have been a few other DoD people, maybe some young Army wives. At The Angel, Alice was even more conspicuous than usual: both Pauline and Suzanne were shorter than she, and brunettes. The place was filled with Korean women, two to one over the soldiers. Some of the women were ordinary-looking, they could have been housewives; others were heavily made up, in short skirts and platform heels, their hair slicked and tightly curled. But all of them were obviously poor. Suzanne's "mission," Alice noted, might just be accomplished.

"What were you guys talking about?" Suzanne asked Andrew, after they'd made room and pulled up extra chairs. Pauline ordered a beer, and Suzanne asked if they had wine, to which the waitress did not respond, but scribbled something down and then looked to Alice. "Soju," Alice said, which elicited boyish hoots and murmurs from Andrew's friends. "When in Seoul," Alice said. She wanted to establish that she knew how to handle herself in the face of the staring eyes all around.

Three Dog Night was playing too loudly, and across the room some kind of rowdy drinking game involved two women as the main players and a group of older-looking soldiers as spectators. The scene was not so unlike that of the bars in Gainesville, except that Alice was never conspicuous at The Rue or bars on the Ave. And there was something else, something that made her additionally uneasy—unspoken rules, both strict and unknowable.

Alice wore a dress she'd bought at the Sunday market—modest polka dot boatneck, gathered at the waist, blousy—and she was glad. It dawned on her suddenly that it was the women in the room who made her nervous, who carried danger—not the men.

"We were talking about the abduction," one of the young privates shouted over the music. He had dark eyebrows and a Roman nose, New York or New Jersey in his accent. "It's crazy. Nobody here knows anything. The news is wrapped up like a fuckin tourniquet. We get everything from the Army reporters, and they have a hard time getting it, too. It took almost a week for the local papers here to get hold of it."

"Get hold of what?" Suzanne asked. She sipped her sweet plum wine and waved away cigarette smoke with a pink little hand. She blinked her eyes wide.

"Not you, too?" the soldier said, laughing.

"Ah, lay off, Cassaro," Andrew said. "They're teachers. They spend all day behind walls, with Mattison's wife as den mother."

Alice flushed but said nothing. She became aware of her frumpy dress.

Andrew was on his fourth beer and starting to show it. He leaned forward, and the girls leaned in as well. "Kim Dae-jung? The opposition leader, President Park's nemesis? He was abducted. Three weeks ago, in Japan. But we didn't hear about it until a week later. Then, a week ago, he was released. They just dropped him off on the street somewhere. He made a statement, but *that* wasn't released until just yesterday. Everyone knows Park and his cronies did it, but no one says so publicly. It's amazing how an entire country can just agree to pretend like that."

"Are you bull*shit*ting us?" Pauline had spent her childhood in England; remnants of her inflections surfaced most with expletives. The boys assured them they weren't, taking turns telling what they each knew, excited to be in the know.

Alice ordered another soju. The conversation receded from her, and her from it. She'd been here before: things were happening in the world, important things, terrible things. And she was not a part of it. She was in the dark, on the side, and doing what exactly? Why had she come to Korea? To hide, and avoid. She *had* been, once, a part of things; but no longer. In Curfeo, they may not have been protesting the war, or American imperialism, but still they were working for the greater good; solving real problems for real people. Sitting now with these American boys, she felt ashamed; but more than that, she felt a yearning—for a lost time and a lost self.

The group continued to talk and laugh; they'd moved on to other subjects. Pauline and Suzanne scooted their chairs in closer and asked about other camptowns, where some of the boys had gone for training. Itaewon was "the best," whatever that meant. Alice watched the other two girls relax and enjoy themselves. As it got closer to midnight, the number of women wearing makeup and high heels increased, and the soldiers got drunker. The boy called Ocampo stretched his arm out behind Pauline. Alice downed the half-bottle of beer in front of her—who knew whose it was—and then tugged at the neckline of her dress.

"Alice? Alice? Are you okay?" Suzanne was shouting into her ear. Alice leaned away. Why was she shouting?

Alice stood. Her chair wobbled over and one of the soldiers caught it before it fell. She mumbled that she needed to pee. On her way to what she thought was the bathroom, she dropped her purse, and when she bent down to pick it up, someone shoved her from behind; she fell over into a soldier sitting at the bar. He was an older man wearing a different uniform from the others, and he was alone. Alice noticed his eyes, which were giant dragon eyes, blood red around the edges. The man helped her to her feet, and Alice smelled his breath; she thought, *dragon breath*, and pulled away. She looked now again at the spot where she'd dropped her purse, and it was gone. Alice's instinct drove her now, back toward the poolroom through the crowd, and she barreled through, not even noticing the stares. Then she saw her—a young woman in a fake-leather bodice and miniskirt, hair kinked and lips red—standing by a pay phone outside the men's room with Alice's green-leather purse clutched in her hand behind her back. Two soldiers, one black and one white, both tall and broad, stood with her.

Now Alice really did have to pee. That discomfort, the bodily urge, put her over. She made for the woman, arms outstretched. The distance to the pay phone at first seemed short, but then it became infinite. There was the sound of bar stools scraping the floor, and a woman's roar (hers?). Something happened then, everything happened. A sharp pain at the crown of her head. The last thing Alice remembers is a flash of her own reflection, distorted, monstrous. Was it a mirror behind the bar? A darkened window? She could see fat pink splotches on her neck—the sure sign she'd drunk one too many.

The floor is shiny in the spot where Alice is scrubbing. She is dripping sweat and rubbing it into the linoleum. Her left shoulder aches. The floor is sharp under her knees.

"Oh, Jesus!" Pauline jumps when she sees Alice there, kneeling. She'd come down the hall in a rush. "What are you doing?"

"Sunday cleaning," Alice says. Her voice is froggy; these are her first words this morning. She raises her hand and Pauline takes it, helps Alice to her feet.

"There's . . . someone here to see you." Pauline's expression is half-teasing, half-concerned. Her arms are crossed, and she flicks a tentative finger toward the window. Alice inches over and peeks out from a side angle, but she can't see the front door. She steps closer and leans, chin first, to see him standing there, cap in one hand, green purse in the other. He stands very straight, almost at attention; his khakis are perfectly creased. It comes back to Alice then, from last night, that reflection she saw: sunglasses, aviators, on a dark face.

"Oh, my God," she says.

4.

They walk through the village. Soon-mi stays close to Chong-ho, just behind his right shoulder. It was her impulsiveness that put them in this position, walking a mile up the mountain road with their luggage. Chong-ho does not speak of it, though; it is a forgiving silence, not a hard one. After the taxi drove off, they'd stood together at the entry path to the forest, all four of them, still and watchful for a few minutes. The children did not understand, but they stayed quiet.

With her left hand, Soon-mi holds the front end of a large duffel bag while James holds the back. Hannah's bottom rests in the crook of Soon-mi's elbow; the child wraps her limbs around her mother's waist and neck, like a baby chimp. Chong-ho looks straight ahead, suitcase in each hand. They walk with heads down, along the hot, dusty road, a private procession. Every so often an old woman or a child peeks through curtains. A shirtless boy sits on a wooden folding chair in front of a small, neat house, pulling at the legs of a grasshopper. When he looks up to watch them pass, Hannah waves.

The switchback takes them into a canopy of ancient pine trees, then Chong-ho leads them down a narrower road that opens into a clearing. A tall, wall-like gate rises up before them. The gate door is ajar. Chong-ho hesitates about whether to ring, call out, or simply walk in. Soon-mi squeezes his arm, a fortifying gesture, and he reaches then to push open the heavy oak door.

In the courtyard, a woman is stooped over a ceramic jar. A yellow dog stands beside her wagging its entire body, trying to alert her to the presence of strangers, though it does not bark. She swats the dog's nose away, then raises her head and looks toward Chong-ho, who has stepped forward. The woman stands up, though still hunched, and squints. A deep frown pulls down her whole face, from forehead to cheeks to chin. In her eyes, though, are recognition, a hint of joy. Both Chong-ho and Soon-mi immediately apprehend what the conflicting expressions add up to; but to a child—to James, to Hannah—the woman appears tormented, and frightening. James lets go of the bag, takes a half-step back; Hannah begins to whimper and fuss, and the dog breaks into hysterical barking.

"*Aigoo! Owhat-goon-yo!*" Chong-ho's eldest sister, Yoko, claps her hands together, and the two walk briskly toward each other. A sliding door from the right-side wing of the U-shaped compound opens, and more relatives begin to spill out. At the sight of his mother standing by the door, choosing not to descend into the courtyard—shrunken, eyes arid and void—Chong-ho knows for certain now what's happened: he is too late. His father has passed from this world.

"It's a long time, Taru," his sister says. "Almost twenty-five years, neh?" Chong-ho flinches at the sound of his boyhood name, as his sister pulls him into an embrace. That his family continues to address each other by their Japanese names should surprise him, but it doesn't. The children puzzle.

Yoko settles Chong-ho and his family in one of the spare rooms. She is the family's messenger, matter-of-fact. "Mother has left you behind in her heart. The rest of us resolved long ago that we have no eldest brother." As the sun sets behind the mountain, the large room—once his father's study before the third building in the compound was built—takes on a hazy yellow glow that makes the children look sickly.

"Father, too? He did not mention me in these last days?"

"No, Taru. Not for a long time. And no one expected him to. Nichi is prepared to perform the rites. He has taken his place as eldest son."

"So everything is set for Saturday?"

Yoko nods. James, who is sitting on top of the duffel bag now, picking at frayed threads around the zipper, bristles; his father flashes him a look. Today is Wednesday: for James, Saturday is an eternity away. Soon-mi, sitting quietly with Hannah on her lap, meets eyes with James as well, but with sympathy. She lets out a heavy sigh, in solidarity.

"Very well, then," Chong-ho says. "We will not interfere. But *nuna*, he was my father, and these are his grandchildren, and Soon-mi is my wife. We will participate as family. If my brother objects, then I will discuss it with him." Chong-ho speaks in a tone both firm and respectful, almost magisterial.

Yoko's eyelids are swollen with fatigue. She shakes her head. "It is not Nichi you must worry about. It is Big Uncle. Who will stand up. He will insist that you are beyond forgiveness."

Suddenly a boyish guffaw punctures the tension. "What the h—?" James's outburst is involuntary and gets caught in his throat. He finds himself standing and has succeeded in startling everyone in the room, including himself.

"James!" Soon-mi hisses.

Chong-ho is speechless, and his face expresses something inscrutable: it is not anger. It is closer to curiosity.

James doesn't have time to decipher, but he recognizes that his window to speak will close in an instant. He is tired, and cranky, his inhibitions have evidently worn away. Enough already. Beyond forgiveness? What does that even mean?

The boy finds his voice. "We're *right here*, I can understand everything she's saying. How much you wanna bet *she* can understand, too?" James nods his chin toward Hannah, who has stuffed four fingers of her right hand into her mouth. "They're saying *Appah* has to be forgiven for having us as a family, right? That we're all mistakes, or sins, or something?"

Soon-mi looks into her lap, clenching her jaw, while Chong-ho stares straight ahead, past his sister, past the walls of the room, into some void. A beat passes, and Soon-mi looks up to see Chong-ho, still staring ahead: it is shocking, but not unwelcome, that her husband has not leapt up to silence James, one way or another.

"It all sounds like bullcrap to me." James mumbles the final words of his monologue, receding instead of punctuating. His face begins to crumple and redden, but he holds back tears. His stomach churns; he puts his hand to it. He thinks of his mother's anxiety and seriousness while preparing for the trip—*You must behave like a grown boy. This is a time to stand behind your father.* Well okay then, he thinks now. I tried.

Yoko, who speaks no English, does and does not understand her nephew's eruption. She thinks, What kind of son is my brother and his peasant wife raising? She thinks, Taru has always had a good

and solid heart, but he believes too much in freedom. Beholding
James now, Yoko remembers a different boy, a toddler, shy and
intent on his pile of twigs, or blocks, or chopsticks—figuring out
how things went together or came apart. Chong-ho had brought the
boy secretly, to meet his grandmother. It had been ten years since
he'd run off with Soon-mi, since the war. Their father would have
beat them all if he found out, so Yoko arranged it with greatest care,
did not even tell her mother the real reason for their trip to Hwagae
Village, inventing something about a new market stall with the best
hanyak in the valley. Their mother had held the child, did not reject
James outright; but later she told Yoko never to do that again. She
had no son, no grandson, as far as she was concerned.

James clearly wants to flee the awkward silence, but there is
nowhere to go, nowhere to hide. They are like animals at the zoo
here, everyone ogling them from a distance, both afraid and superior.
He sits down again on the luggage.

Finally, Chong-ho says, "Nuna, please leave us."

Yoko sits up, her shoulders back, in disbelief. The implications of
Chong-ho's words are unmistakable: he is dismissing his elder and
allowing the boy to stay, unpunished. Propriety and respect have
been flouted.

Soon-mi has to control herself from interjecting—*No, no, Sister, I
will take the children away so you two can talk*. She knows she cannot
do this. Chong-ho is resolved.

"And nuna, my name is not Taru. Not Kitaru. I am Chong-ho."

Yoko raises herself from kneeling to standing without assistance,
but not without pain. She takes one last look at them, this doomed
family—her rogue brother and his melon-patch wife, their insolent
son. Maybe there is hope for the little girl, she thinks, to fall far
enough from the tree, but doubtful. "By the way," she says, just as
she steps out the door, and looking now at Soon-mi. "Your aunt is
dead. The last of your lowly people are finally gone."

The ejected family continues its procession, up the mountain
road, then down again toward the lake. To passersby, they look

like vagabonds. It is almost nine o'clock; they have not eaten since breakfast on the airplane.

Kim Young-shik's wife, Yoo-na, answers the door. The village has been her home now for over twenty years (she is from Taegu, she and Young-shik met at university) but she has never met her husband's closest childhood friend. "Yeh?" she says. Her expression is both confused and concerned as she beholds this ragged crew on her doorstep.

"I am Lee Chong-ho," Chong-ho says, bowing. "Is Young-shik at home?"

"Yes, but . . ." She hesitates. The sullen boy and the moon-faced woman with sweaty hair, dusty city shoes, and a sleeping child in her arms evoke pity. "Your name you say is—"

"Lee Chong-ho."

Soon-mi's eyes fix on her husband. Even now she marvels at the steadiness of Chong-ho's voice, his alarming stamina. He speaks with dignity, as if it were perfectly normal to knock on someone's door unannounced at nine in the evening, suitcases and children in tow, in need of a meal and a bed. Soon-mi beholds Chong-ho's straight back and his rough hands, which he holds in loose fists at his sides. It is as if no time has passed since their years of wandering, after the war, when they *were* vagabonds. He took care of them, every day—one day at a time, when each day felt like it could be their last—believing utterly in their survival.

The woman at the door seems now to recognize the name. "Just a minute," she says, and disappears into the house. The screen door shuts, but she leaves the inside door wide open. There is a mild ruckus inside, a chair scraping the floor. Heavy footsteps barrel forth.

"*Aigoo, aigoo!*" A fat man with a crew cut, in undershirt and boxer shorts, throws open the screen door, arms outstretched. "My old friend! You've come! Prodigal son! It's a miracle! Come in, come in!"

The children eat everything on their plates, and though Soon-mi has lost her appetite, she eats to keep her strength up. The men eat separately in the living room.

"You did not even sit at their meal table," Young-shik says.

"It was not offered," Chong-ho says.

"But you will still go to the ceremony?"

"Yes. This is between me and my father. And the ancestors."

"And what about your uncle?"

Chong-ho scoffs, shakes his head. When he was a boy, he feared his father's eldest brother—a wiry man with a mean, hawkish face, who lost his wife and daughter during the war; later, his son ran off to Seoul. When Chong-ho was still in touch with Yoko, she told him that their cousin was consorting with American soldiers, black men who frequented prostitutes and did drugs. All this made Big Uncle even meaner.

"My uncle likes order, and authority; as my father did. They chose the Japanese, and General Park, because they believed that hierarchies and power would bring greater stability for country people. Perhaps they were right, strictly speaking." Swaths of rice fields and the armies of orchard workers with their buckets flash across his mind. "At any rate, my uncle also hates the rebellious son who leaves his home village for a different life."

"He is a tough sonofabitch, your uncle. Your father was tough, too, but your uncle, he has that nasty streak. He takes money from the officials, you know. Ever since *Yushin*. It's more than just support for Saemaul now. He's become a part of the machinery. We call him deputy around here."

Chong-ho nods. None of this surprises him. It was his grandfather's trait—the conviction that some ruinous wrong had been committed against him, and the resulting hunger for power— that his uncle inherited. Chong-ho's grandfather came to the country from Seoul, dispossessed of prestige; the details were never spoken of. "My father and uncle lived with their father's discontent and sense of inferiority. They came to understand that, for a man, being able to choose his work, his life, is everything. But then, when it came to love, my father, he just never imagined . . . he was too proud." Chong-ho does not look in Soon-mi's direction; there is no need, their story is all too known. "Perhaps someone more gifted in argument and proofs could have changed his feelings. I did not have that gift or temperament."

"You know you never did make it easy on them, my friend." Young-shik lights a cigarette and leans back, laughing. "Everything was a battle for you back then."

Chong-ho laughs, too. "We were all in it together, weren't we? You were our instigator. Those pranks against the Japanese administrators at the school? And remember *Oo-ri Hangul*? That was *your* doing."

Young-shik holds up a finger and stands to leave the room. When he returns, he has a slim book in his hands. The back cover is plain black linen, the front embroidered with a green-and-blue geometric pattern. He hands the book to Chong-ho, whose mouth hangs open.

"You've kept it all these years."

Young-shik nods. "I look through it every so often. To remind me. It was all so urgent back then. We knew what we were fighting for, and against."

Chong-ho remembers clearly that day, their last year in high school, 1942, when ten of them together planned the moment they would drop their Japanese readers onto the hard dirt floor of the classroom. Then they would stand, each reading a short passage from *Oo-ri Hangul*, the chapbook of stories and poems they had written themselves. They were works about liberation, about the Korean spirit of resistance, of *han*. They were love poems to their homeland, to independence and human dignity. Five of the poems were Chong-ho's—more than any of the others. All of it was written in *hangul*, their native alphabet.

Chong-ho runs his thumb over the book's spine. "Does it still feel present to you? Do you remember?"

"How can I forget?" Young-shik lifts his undershirt and twists to show his bare back: two purplish stripes, slightly raised, diagonal from shoulder blade to shoulder blade, like fat earthworms burrowing under the skin. Lower down on the right, a smaller scar where he'd been kidney-punched several times: they'd rushed him to the hospital, the kidney was removed.

"They picked you because you were the easiest target. We all got beaten, but you . . . they were like savages."

"Well, like you say, I was the instigator."

"We all did it."

"I was the fat boy."

"Despicable cowards."

"You were the real leader. I felt I was playing my part by taking that beating. You may not have survived it. I could take it."

Chong-ho too lights a cigarette, and they smoke in silence for a few moments.

"They are good poems," Young-shik says.

Chong-ho smiles a sad smile. "I've written better ones since. About Soon-mi, about our journeys. Refugee life makes for good art."

"You have many tales you have never told. I can see that. Tales of hardship."

"We all have them. Ours are no different."

"But they are. Yours are tales of exile. Here, when the Reds were finally gone—most of them, anyway—we still had whatever family we had left. We helped each other. But you two . . . we all wondered about you. Were you alive? Were you dead? If you were alive, what kind of life could you be living?"

Yoo-na brings a tray of soju and persimmons. Chong-ho looks up but doesn't see her; he is too deep in thought, in memory. What kind of life? He puts back the shot of soju, absorbs its warmth and sting. Not *life*, he thinks. *Lives*. He and Soon-mi—before the war, during, after; all those years they lived like nomads. Then, their sojourn to America. He is forty-nine years old and has lived a dozen lives; has died as many.

Soon-mi and Yoo-na chat quietly in the kitchen. Soon-mi tells of their journey from Maryland, about the plane ride and how her heart skipped when she saw Jiri Mountain in the distance. She is careful not to say too much. James snacks on persimmons while drawing in his sketchbook and seems calm now, oddly at home. Soon-mi stands and cradles Hannah in both arms, the child's head hanging over Soon-mi's arm, neck exposed, like a rescued drowner.

Hannah is getting too big for this, but Soon-mi is slow, will always be slow, to see her daughter as she is. She swings the girl's legs up in the air, almost to vertical, her head dangling inches above the floor. *"Uy-shah!"* Yoo-na claps her hands, playing along, and Hannah, red-faced, opens her eyes wide to the upside-down world while her mother readies to swing her once more.

5.

Both Suzanne and Pauline could be trusted not to tell Dorothy Mattison, but Pauline was the one to voice her "concern." She warned Alice to be careful. She did not say about what, exactly. Maybe the dangers could not be parsed out, maybe it was the whole-thing of it: a soldier, overnight in their house, in Alice's bed. Three times this month. Strictly against the rules, playing with fire. Alice might lose her job; worse, she might be discharged dishonorably, if that was even possible for a DoDEA employee. Certainly it was for a private in the Eighth Army. The stakes were higher with the government, a red mark following you around. Maybe that was what made Alice shrug it off; by now she'd had quite enough of good order and discipline.

That Charles was black was the unspoken part. Alice wasn't sure if it was because of Mrs. Mattison, or Pauline's own prejudice. Suzanne played it nice, wouldn't dare come forth with anything overtly racist. Pauline had less self-control; Pauline was more honest. Alice in fact appreciated this. That part of "be careful" was Pauline's way of saying, *Don't be naïve.* She said once, half mumbling, "Opposites attract, but you can take that too far."

Alice awakes in Charles's arms. The sky is still dark, a faint glow rising. She sits up and pulls the covers over her bare shoulders, squints to see movement—frenetic white dots—through the window. Snow. Tiny flakes, spilling rapidly, like a waterfall. Charles lies next to her, filling all but a narrow sliver of her twin bed, lightly snoring.

The toilet flushes across the hall; the patter of slippered feet—Suzanne, whose bladder rarely made it through the night. Charles stirs, opens one eye. Alice leans over him, letting the blanket slip off. Charles opens both eyes now, then closes them. He reaches around and gathers Alice in. She listens to his chest: Charles breathes deeply and slowly, infusing pulsing veins with air, and life, and calm. This arouses Alice—the way Charles contains his own arousal until just the right moment. He is good at waiting, and stillness. No one ever told her that this was what to look for in a lover.

Yes, lover. For longer than a month now. It had started before the overnights. Today is two weeks to Christmas. They crossed the threshold on a rainy night just after the leaves had peaked, and fallen: It was a heated, clunky, and thoroughly ecstatic affair one evening, after hours, in the Quonset hut that was Alice's classroom. He wanted to see the school, Charles said, what the semi-civilian parts of the base were like. Even on post, each had his place, and everybody stuck to their assigned areas. Alice still has no idea where the barracks are.

Twice after that, they rented a cheap room at a *yeogwan*—a 10x10 windowless box with a thin foam mattress on a hard, heated floor— just outside the base. Finally, Alice insisted he come to the house on South Post, to "meet the girls." If he came for dinner, then stayed over, he wouldn't be wandering South Post after dark.

It seemed fitting, anyway—that they would continue to meet in forbidden territory. It was how they first came together. The Angel Club, Alice learned later, was whites-only. Charles, too, had been unaware of the owner's reputation for bouncing black soldiers. Whites-only meant that neither black GIs nor Korean men were allowed; as white women, Alice and her roommates were an odd sight but were left alone. After midnight, though, the hostesses would have started eyeing them down; they'd want unencumbered access to Andrew and his friends, and the owner would back them up. The sexual ecology of the place was crucial for business.

Charles was there on a fluke: he and Dennis had been walking down the street with Kang, a KATUSA in their company, when Kang stopped suddenly, frozen in front of the window of the club.

Smoke just about came out of his ears and nostrils, as Charles told it. He was mumbling and hissing in Korean.

Kang had seen his sister through the window; she'd run away from home, a small town outside Incheon, six months before. He'd feared this very thing, that she'd taken up work as a hostess in a club. Their father was a respected teacher of mathematics in their hometown; the girl had rebelled because she wanted to be an actress, which their father deemed disgraceful and forbade. "Charles, you have to go in. You have to go in and bring her out. My sister. I cannot go; the owner, he knows me. His wife is from Incheon. He knows my family. I cannot." Charles had looked to Dennis, who held up his hands and backed off like a man pleading innocent to a crime not yet committed; then he looked at Kang, who was desperate, near tears. Charles scanned the streets to see if there was anyone he recognized, a white private from their company. There was no one. Then he stepped up to the window and looked inside: he saw someone he knew, Sanders, a Private First Class who lived down the hall in the barracks. He was a quiet guy from Oregon, not exactly friendly, but not unfriendly either. He was the guy who told the other guys to clean the fuck up after themselves in the bathroom.

Alice understands better now, the risk Charles had taken—what it was like, for the black enlisted men, even among the higher ranks. She'd heard about the riots at Camp Humphreys; and there were smaller incidents on and around base that she now paid attention to. At the school, there were only a few black students, and it was understood that their being at the school at all meant their fathers outranked the other students' fathers. They were never harassed or mistreated; the children perceived rank better than anyone. Alice understands too that Charles's friendship with Kang is an oddity: the KATUSAs were ignored by the other soldiers at best, taunted at worst, though they came from families of stature and education. But Charles was drawn to Kang's interest in history and books and what was going on in the larger world. He and Charles talked about things; Charles was learning the language from Kang, phrases other than "big dick" and "how much for a blowjob." Alice found that admirable.

They'd met for dinner a few times before Charles told her the real reason he'd decided to go into the club that night. When Kang pointed out his sister through the window, he could see that she was probably no older than fifteen, sixteen at most. Alice brought that night back into her mind and realized that he was right, and she was mortified: she'd nearly assaulted that teenage girl for taking her purse. Charles saw her embarrassment and smiled. He said, "Good thing you were smashed; your aim was pretty far off."

It wasn't until they'd spent the night together on South Post for the first time that he told her the rest. "Dennis and I had been going to this place, The Lotus, pretty regularly. We went mostly just to hang out, you know; it was what there was, it was one of the mellower places where we were allowed. Sometimes, though, things would get outta hand, and at that point we would leave. Anyway, one night, I don't know, it had been a bad week: one of our buddies had gotten into a fight with a KATUSA out on the street, and the MPs got into it, and everyone was a mess afterward; Dennis had just gotten word that his father had passed. I guess we were coming up on a full year, and it was like, what the hell were we doing here. The madam at The Lotus knew me by then, she called me *chakhan gagman*—basically sweet nigger—because I left the girls alone. But she saw that I was looking pretty low, so she said Here, go upstairs to room four, a special treat for you, and handed me a key, all smiles. So I went. I opened the door, and there was this girl, lying on a dingy mattress, on her stomach, naked. When she heard me come in, she didn't look up, or turn around to see who it was, she just got up on her hands and knees and stuck out her ass. That's what she was told to do, I assumed, by the madam." Charles paused then. They were lying in Alice's bed, it was the middle of the night. He'd said too much. He was talking like someone who just needed to talk; like a ghost caught between this world and the next.

But Alice whispered, "And what happened?"

Charles took a deep breath. He'd stopped wanting to tell this story, but Alice wanted the rest. "We'd smoked some weed. I was pretty out of it. I unbuckled my pants and went for her. It wasn't like

. . . it wasn't really human or anything. It was just. It wasn't real. It was a nightmare. When I got up on top of her it scared her, and she turned her head, made this noise like a small wild animal. I looked at her face. She had all this makeup on, and she smelled like cheap perfume, but Christ . . . she was maybe thirteen or fourteen."

They were both quiet then. Alice was sleepy, and the story made her feel hard and cold inside. There was a feeling of having been passed an anvil to carry. There was a feeling of curling up with it and wanting just to sleep. Three AM was the hour of absolute quiet on the base; in an hour the officers would rise, the recruits shortly after, and at five the day's activity would begin; the sins of the night before would be buried and all but forgotten. Charles slipped out at five after five, and Alice slept another hour. After school the next day, Alice found a note in her staff mailbox: *Not all my stories are that sad. —Charles*

He hadn't told her the ending. She wasn't sure she wanted to know. But she did wonder what had happened to Kang's sister.

A few days later, he told her. "After your friends picked you up and got you outta there, the owner threw us out—me, the girl, Sanders. Kang laid into the girl, right there on the street, slapped her a couple of times, put her on a bus back home." It was Saturday, Alice played hooky from Korean class, and she and Charles were off post—their first time, together—hiking in the mountains north of Seoul. Alice hiked in front, he let her set the pace, which was brisk, and they were both winded. They paused at a lookout point—the leaves were aflame in gold and red and orange. Alice and Charles beheld the sight as if they weren't also in it, as if there wasn't another pair, on the other mountain, beholding them. Alice did not pause for long; she led them on, up and up, more steeply as they trekked higher and higher.

Charles still had not finished his story. The last thing he said about Kang's sister was, "She went missing again, last week. This time she packed everything, didn't leave a trace. Probably someone helped her, with her getaway. Maybe there was a john, or a GI. Who knows? But it was predictable, I'd say. A girl like that, if you lock her up like a prisoner, all she's thinking about is how to escape. A girl like that wants to be free; free and hungry and hooking is better than locked up and well-fed." Alice kept going, up and up. Her heart was big and pounding in her chest, the cool air sharp in her lungs.

Neither of them liked the story. Charles reported what had happened. There were no heroes, but no real villains either. It was a sad story with a bad ending. Alice wanted to argue—on behalf of the girl, on behalf of all women and girls. But she felt cornered somehow and didn't know what to say, how to win. Alice also felt ashamed. About the purse. She wanted to find Kang's sister, give her the damn purse.

Neither of them goes home for Christmas that year; what was there to go home to. Agnew had resigned, Nixon was dirty; it was just a matter of time before a man with a funny voice, whom no one elected, became President. Dennis's cousin, who went to Vietnam, wrote in letters about coming home, about people holding "Saigon Puppet" signs and shouting at them when they got off the plane.

Alice and Charles have the house to themselves. They stay in, mostly, go out a couple of times for groceries. When they aren't making love or cooking or eating, Charles reads the paper, listens to sports on the Army broadcast station, reads his *The American Story* textbook to get a jumpstart on the US history course he is taking next term. Alice helps him prepare for his math placement test— quadratic equations, geometry. Charles wants to finish his degree sooner rather than later. He wants to go home with it. Alice likes helping Charles, and Charles welcomes it.

Charles shows Alice the essays he wrote for his writing class: a profile of J. Edgar Hoover, a memoir about being a pallbearer at his mother's funeral, an analysis of George Orwell's "Shooting an Elephant." Alice tells him he is a good writer, and that he has a lot to say. She means it, but somehow it sounds false when she says it out loud, like she is trying to buck him up.

Alice asks Charles what he wants to do with the rest of his life. Charles says he thinks he can make NCO by the time he is thirty-five. Alice asks, Is that what you really want? Charles says he doesn't know. Then he says, "Don't laugh, but . . . when I was a kid my mother made me help out at the church on Saturdays. Someone donated a box full of spy novels. I stashed them and read all the Bond books, then I got really into Matt Helm, and then Ludlum. I always thought . . . I'd make a good spy."

Alice does laugh; they both do.

Charles says, "What about you?"

"I was supposed to be a doctor."

"Supposed to be."

"Yes. Lots of supposed-tos. My father. My mother, too. I mean, she would have wanted me to be independent. Professional."

"What do you want?"

She pauses. "Don't laugh."

"You bet I will; it's my turn."

"Fair enough." She wraps cut-up potatoes in a dish towel and squeezes; they are making fries. "I want to make the world better." She lays the towel down on the counter. When she looks up, Charles is not laughing, not even in his expression. He looks genuinely confused. "What? Don't you think America, the world, it's all going to hell? Don't you think we should try to . . ." She doesn't have the words; aren't they self-evident?

"Try to . . ."

"Try to . . ." Alice waves her hands, grasping.

"Save it?"

"Well . . . and why not?" She girds herself. Mentally, she has her fists up. So far, Charles has dominated whenever they talk about serious things. He always has the last word.

"Depends on your definition of 'better'."

"What does that mean?" Alice dumps the potatoes into the hot oil, too quickly, and it splashes her cheek. "Ow!" She jumps back from the stove. Charles calmly runs a towel under cold water and dabs her face. Alice holds still, trying to catch Charles's eye, but he is focused, tending exclusively to the burn.

Charles tosses the towel into the sink. "Think about Kang's sister.

He was 'saving' her, right? Her life was supposed to be 'better' if she was back home."

"Maybe it would have been."

"But maybe isn't enough, is it? If you're going to go to all that trouble. Of 'saving' someone. Are we making Korea 'better' by being here? Well, maybe *you* are. Me, the guys in my company. It's a toss-up at best. And Vietnam, I mean c'mon. You gotta ask yourself; see the big picture. You gotta be smart about the savior business."

"And you want to be an officer in the United States military?"

"I didn't say that."

"Right." Alice sighs and laughs. *Defeated again.* She could tell Charles about Curfeo, about Laila, and the tree farms and the Mapuche cooperatives; but she hesitates. She told him that she was in the Peace Corps, but didn't go into details when she saw the way he smiled and nodded, as if she had told him she liked puppies. She waits to see if he'll ask about it now. He doesn't. Alice ladles the fries out of the oil, lays them on a paper-toweled dish; lets them cool before the second fry. Charles makes perfect plump patties out of the ground chuck he picked up from the PX, along with beer and wine, a head of lettuce, a tub of mayonnaise, Tabasco, and sesame seed buns. Oreos for dessert.

Charles is a fast eater, no nonsense. They don't talk anymore about saving the world, or about the Army, or about Kang's sister. They quiz each other on American presidents and laugh when they get to the thirteenth and Charles has to look it up in his textbook (Millard Fillmore). It is strange how comfortable it is, like they are an old married couple. In the evening, Charles reads on the sofa wearing just his boxers, shouts at the radio when his team is flagging. Neither of them thinks about the fact that there is no one else around, that it is just the two of them, inside the walls of this neat little ranch house (nor does Alice think how differently Charles acts, and talks, for instance, when Dennis is around).

At the end of the week Alice begins to think about the future. How long will she stay in Korea. What will things be like between her and Charles after this week is over. After the school year is over. After Charles's tour is over.

The future comes fast. In February, Alice is four days late. One night, over *kalbi-tang* in their favorite hole-in-the-wall *kalbi-jib*, Alice says she can't eat, tells Charles she doesn't feel well, and prepares to tell him why. But then, she doesn't. She can't. Alice does not want to have this conversation with Charles, with anyone. She does not want to hear about "options." She does not even want to be told it's "her choice." Because it's not for anyone to tell her that. Saying it implies there is some question. There was no question the first time. She told no one but Gideon Roth. It was private; *is* private. Charles still drives their discussions, he thinks faster on his feet. He controls the silences. Not even knowing what Charles will say, Alice decides she won't have it, his reasoned viewpoints, his calm authority. Not this time. She has a nightmare one night, Charles and Pauline wearing black capes, both shouting at her about being naïve, about considering the realities. Alice does not tell either Pauline or Suzanne. She wants to tell Laila, but it's too much for a letter.

What does she really want to do with her life? It's clearer than it's ever been. This. This child. Mother. Don't laugh, Alice tells herself. Vaguely she is aware of the notion of karma, and she wants some part of it, another chance, the universe offering up redemption. It is not rational, but it is also unquestionable. This is what she will do with her life. With or without Charles.

Charles is called down to Pusan for a month of training in March. In April for the spring holiday, Alice and Pauline and Suzanne decide to go to Kyoto. When they return, Alice decides it is time, she will tell him. They see each other for the first time in over a month, and both of them recognize that something is different. Charles is at once solicitous and distracted. Alice thinks, He's been with a whore. Or two, or three. She thinks, I will do this alone. That's how it will be. Charles says, What's wrong? Are you all right? Alice is pale and fidgety and fierce, like she wants to start a fight.

When she interrogates him about not calling from Pusan, Charles doesn't play her game. "What is it? If you have something to say . . ."

He drags it out of her. Alice breaks down, weeps in Charles's arms. "It's all right," Charles says. "It's going to be all right."

Six months later, when Alice goes into labor, Charles is on night duty at the stadium. Alice calls the security office, calls a taxi, and off she goes to Providence Hospital. When the pain comes, she cannot believe it; but her scream is silent, the taxi driver undisturbed. Alice is sure she will die before this child comes into the world. If she lives, how in God's name will she be able to love something that has caused her this indescribable pain.

6.

Saturday is long in coming. Chong-ho smokes, pages through Young-shik's old newspapers piled by the TV. On Friday morning Chong-ho goes for a long walk alone. Soon-mi rises early to help her host with kitchen chores and laundry; the rest of the day she stares out the bedroom window and naps at odd hours, alongside Hannah. James keeps his nose in a sketchbook, looks up to ask whomever will listen for something to drink, do they have any colored pencils. He finds bori-cha in the refrigerator, and Soon-mi makes a weak effort to find pencils but tells him he'll have to wait for Yoo-na to come in from the yard.

Young-shik is gone to town where he works at the post office; Yoo-na tends to the chickens and pigs. When Soon-mi wakes from one of her fitful naps and looks out the window to see Yoo-na wading in pig slop, she thinks: I should go out and help. But weariness and revulsion overcome her, and she lays her head back down, pushing her cheek into the dense mat that separates her from the hard floor. She drifts off again, and in the moist warmth of half-sleep thinks, That woman will be rewarded in this life and the next, for her goodness; I, on the other hand . . .

Hannah wakes at two in the afternoon, toddles into the main room, where James is reading a comic book, the one he's read three times already.

"Are you hungry?" James asks. Hannah nods. She has dragged along the bedsheet, which trails behind her like a veil. "Gimme that," James says, and takes the sheet from her sticky hands, rolls it into a ball and looks around for where to put it. The clean laundry is hanging on the line outside. James tucks the sheet into a corner of the sofa. "Here," he says, ladling out some green liquid from a pot on the stove into a silver bowl. "It's still warm." James sits Hannah on his lap at the table and hands her a spoon. "Don't make a mess." Hannah reaches with a wobbly hand, dribbles seaweed pieces and broth into her lap and James's, but manages to get most of it into her mouth. The garlic taste is strong, and she likes it.

"Hurry up, my leg's falling asleep," James says. He reaches around her and lifts the bowl with both hands, tips it into her mouth. Hannah slurps. "You can do it. Here. Both hands." He puts her hands on the sides of the bowl one at a time, and just as he pulls away, a deep, muffled voice sounds from outside the kitchen window. Hannah drops the bowl, which crashes onto the hard wood. "Jesus!" James hisses, shoving Hannah off his lap and jumping up out of the chair. Hannah looks down at the slimy green-black seaweed bits clinging to the tops of her feet and spreads her toes wide.

"What's happening?" Soon-mi bounds into the main room, face flushed, hair flattened on one side. James doesn't answer. He bends down to pick up the bowl and spoon and seaweed and beef bits. Then, the deep voice again. All three turn toward the window. There are two voices now, similar in timbre; it is unclear whether they sound angry.

Chong-ho's brother Nichi is one year and one week younger. They were never close, but still they looked out for each other, out of respect for their father. Chong-ho was always the better student, Nichi the more popular and genial.

"We have both aged," Nichi says, "but you have become much older than me than you ever were." The comment is meant as a jest, but Chong-ho knows its truth, evident in his graying head and cracked hands. The two have not seen each other in over twenty years.

"There is the body's age and there is the soul's," Chong-ho says. "I used to think they evolved independently, but now—"

The front door opens, and Soon-mi steps out, with Hannah in her arms. Nichi turns, his face tightening, then going flat. He nods, and she nods back, smoothing down her hair as she drops her eyes to the ground.

"Let's walk," Chong-ho says to his brother. James comes out just after they have turned to leave, and he watches the backs of the two men recede into the woods.

They walk down a path they have traversed many times before. The trees have grown tall, and yet the forest still seems smaller to Chong-ho; he wonders that he ever lost his way here.

"I am sorry I was not at home when you arrived. Big Uncle and I had to bring the news to the relatives in Taegu." Nichi's formality and statement of the obvious bode ominously.

Nichi has come, Chong-ho assumes, representing the family. Perhaps Big Uncle is trying to keep him from attending the burial. No matter: Chong-ho is resolved. He will not be moved. Not by his brother, not by anyone. "Of course," Chong-ho says.

"Big Uncle can be harsh, and unforgiving," Nichi says.

Chong-ho wonders warily at his meaning; for what is his brother softening the ground?

Nichi stops at a clearing and runs his hand over the bark of a great oak, then circles the enormous trunk. "Remember this?"

Chong-ho does remember. One of the boys had gotten hold of his father's bow and arrow; they made a target—a face—and took turns. Young-shik and Chong-ho would say, "These are the Jap commander's eyes: aim for dead center." Nichi came along at first, but then fell in with his own crowd, the sons of other landowners. Chong-ho's friends had started going by their given Korean names; Nichi and his friends never did, nor did the family.

It is hard to make out, but there it is—the target, the face they'd carved.

"Young-shik was the best marksman," Chong-ho says. Then, turning away and walking on, "My eyesight was never as good."

They come to another clearing, near a stream with a swimming cove where families would sometimes pitch tents in good weather. The men and boys would fish, girls and women scrub each other's skin with stones. Embers from a recent fire flick orange in the pit. The two brothers sit on a fallen log that was years ago hacked into a bench.

"*Hyung*, you can't come to the ceremony," Nichi says matter-of-factly, almost casually. There is something in his voice, an authority that, even now, after all that's happened, Chong-ho feels is out of line. But there is also a wincing note of regret that is even more unsettling.

"And why is that?" Chong-ho responds in a low, even tone, like an innocent worn down by a long trial. "Is it because Big Uncle is a bitter, petty man?"

Both brothers look straight ahead, into the dappled light that reflects off the water in bright bursts.

"Hyung." Nichi crosses into a paternal tone that Chong-ho does not like at all. "Father did not forgive you. He would not want you . . . you cannot come."

"Again, brother, I ask you: Who is to say? This is between our father and me." Chong-ho stands, walks a few steps away, then turns back to see Nichi looking down, shaking his head. "What is it? What is it you have come to tell me?"

"Kimiko came back." Nichi's eyes are arrows, and Chong-ho the reviled target. The impossible statement, the invocation of that name, stuns Chong-ho. "She came to see Father. A year after you disappeared."

"But Yoko never mentioned . . ." Chong-ho's words erupt before thoughts can form.

"She didn't know. She does not know. No one does. Not Big Uncle. Not even Ummah."

Chong-ho sits down again, a few inches farther from Nichi than before. What does it mean? How could it be? He'd put his first wife, the woman his father had forced him to marry, out of his mind. He'd embraced relief—because what else could he do?—when he learned she'd died early on in the war. Neither he nor Soon-mi ever spoke of it.

"And how is it that *you* know?"

"It just happened that way. She wandered up to the house out of nowhere. Ummah and Yoko were in town, picking up the week's rations."

Chong-ho looks sideways at Nichi, who has lit a cigarette and now offers it to Chong-ho. Chong-ho takes it, and Nichi lights another for himself. "Yoko told me she died during those first terrible months."

"Her whole family died. She was alone. Destitute. Neighbors took pity on her even though they had nothing, because of . . ." Nichi pauses, takes a long, squint-eyed drag on his cigarette. "Because she was pregnant."

Chong-ho closes his eyes. He was already braced, because he knew. Not precisely what his brother was about to say, but that whatever it was, it would fell him; like one of these trees in a lightning storm. Somewhere, somehow, hasn't he always known? Wasn't Kimiko's quick and early death just a bit too convenient?

They had married in the late winter of 1950. Chong-ho was twenty-five years old; Chong-ho's father had learned of his affection for Soon-mi years before and conveyed his disapproval by ignoring it, while at the same time reducing Soon-mi's father's melon plot by half. The engagement to Kimiko was a foregone conclusion, and Chong-ho's protests fell on deaf ears. Even Yoko, who in those days passed along to Soon-mi clothing she'd outgrown and sometimes invited her along to the river to bathe with her and her friends, offered no support. At the engagement party, Chong-ho drank too much and whispered to his future mother-in-law that her daughter had been sold into a doomed marriage.

A married man, Chong-ho still went to Soon-mi, and she soothed him. But Soon-mi had resigned herself; life's realities did not surprise her. What was unfulfilled love next to poverty, a mean alcoholic grandfather, her beloved sister's death from tuberculosis? She would love Chong-ho, even when he married; even when she, eventually, was married, to some ugly old tenant farmer with a tiny rice paddy. She had no expectations for happiness. Their secret nights, in the pine grove on the ridge, seemed to her the full blessing of her life.

But Chong-ho was a poet, and a romantic. Soon-mi was his truth, and his beauty. Three months after the wedding, his sham marriage became intolerable. Chong-ho took Kimiko home, to her parents' village. He held Kimiko's bags, stood on the doorstep in front of her. When her father came to the door, Chong-ho put down the bags and said, "I am returning your daughter to you. It is better that we part now than continue on like this. She is unhappy, because I am unhappy. If you force her to come home with me, you can be assured that I will not be faithful to her, that I will grow to hate her, that she and I will behave horribly toward each other." He took Kimiko by the shoulders and pushed her into her father's arms, then left.

A month later, North Korean soldiers invaded Seoul and began the march southward. City people came pouring into the southern towns and villages. Villagers fled further south to Cheju and Koje-do. Chong-ho's family would make their way to Sorok-do, to his mother's people. Soon-mi's family had nowhere to go. Chong-ho refused to join his family unless Soon-mi and hers came with them.

"It is not the tenant family you should be concerned about," his father raged, "but your wife's!" Chong-ho's father had every intention of forcing Chong-ho back to his marriage, but the soldiers' approach upended everything. And so, in the chaos, in panic and desperation, Chong-ho parted from his family and found Soon-mi. He convinced her to go with him. At first she was hesitant— leaving her mother was the hardest—but she said yes, she would go, wherever he took her. They had nothing; and nothing but war and hardship awaited them. They knew they would never return home—never again be someone's son, or daughter. They would have no name, no people.

Years upon years they wandered, from town to fishing village to island. They would stay months at a time, find labor for a season, then move on. Once, they stayed in a village on the far side of Jiri Mountain for almost two years, built themselves a thatched hut where they kept warm and fed until the growing population of wolves and coyotes threatened their safety. They had a child now, Jae-yoon, later James; they had lived through much worse, but now, they could not risk it. James had been born seven weeks premature, a sickly baby who would've died, but for the village midwife who'd tended to him with herbs. He'd survived; the war was over; they had now to ensure the child's health. They settled in Sacheon, where Chong-ho was able to find work as a research assistant for a botanist, and Soon-mi enrolled in nurses' training. After a year, they gave her a certificate and she applied to a proper nursing school.

Chong-ho's eyes have been closed for just a minute now, but it seems like he and Nichi have been sitting on the log for an eternity.

"You were gone," Nichi says. "You were dead. Even if you were alive, you were dead to the family. To father's honor. Kimiko arrived half out of her mind." She was starving, and had been raped by the soldiers—who knew how many times? The neighbors could not care for her anymore. There was no room, no food, no doctors or medicines; there was cholera in the household, and she had the baby. Who knew how long she'd wandered alone, or how she survived. Who knew how or when the baby was born. But it was. Born alive. "Shortly before she came to father, she'd drowned the baby in the river. She came to father and begged him to help her die. She'd tried, but couldn't do it. Would he please help her, she pleaded. Did he have a weapon, or poison." She had such wildness in her eyes, Nichi tells him, that their father was not sure she even knew who he was; she may have just wandered to the first place where someone was home. They'd been among the first to return.

"What did he do? What happened to her?" Chong-ho speaks through his teeth.

"He found a place for her. In a hospital in Gwangju. We took her there. Then someone sent word a few months later that she'd died, from cholera."

Soon-mi had once described to Chong-ho watching a man die from cholera, at her first clinic placement. A victim of cholera dies of dehydration, the organs shriveling and shutting down one by one.

Chong-ho is still sitting on the log but nothing beneath him or around him is solid. He has a terrifying urge to tear at his brother's smooth, undisturbed face. Who is he to deliver this news? Who is he to speak for the dead? "How do you know, about the child . . . if it's true?"

Nichi exhales a long cloud of smoke through his nostrils. He smiles an ugly smile. "If you had been there—if you had seen her, heard her—you would not wonder that. And you would have seen, you would have known, as *true*, that your abandonment destroyed her; she suffered a fate worse than death. If there was a child—and I believe there was—it was destroyed by you as well."

Chong-ho returns to the house alone, breathing hard, a single vein bulging across his forehead. Young-shik is sitting on the porch steps, barefoot and smoking. Chong-ho stomps past his friend and throws open the screen door.

"Ho ho, my friend, sit and relax a while. We'll eat in ten minutes' time."

"*Yo-bo!*" Chong-ho shouts into the house for Soon-mi. "James, get your things and your sister. We are leaving now." Everything halts; the chatter and bustle of meal-making turn to stone silence.

Soon-mi puts down whatever she was chopping and comes gingerly to the door. "What is it?"

"We must go. It is time to go."

There are no more words, except for the mortified apologies Soon-mi offers twenty minutes later, as she and Chong-ho and James and Hannah hurry into the taxi that Young-shik has called at Chong-ho's irrefutable request. Chong-ho shakes his friend's hand, nods to Yoo-na with lowered eyes. He cannot explain. He only knows—and his friend vaguely understands this as well—that they will never see each other again.

In the taxi, there is too much time, too much silence. James chews on the skin around his thumbnail. Soon-mi's knees tremble beneath Hannah, who pinches at the flesh of her mother's thighs and sucks on a piece of thick, garlicky seaweed. Chong-ho stares dead ahead at the road, jaw clenched, as Soon-mi tries, unsuccessfully, to catch his eye in the mirror. Stop it, he thinks sharply. Stop trying to know. You cannot know this. You'll wish you didn't.

But the wall he is erecting is weak; it will crumble. Soon-mi is complicit, he has made her so. They are one in every way, and there is no line in the sand, no caste division, no worlds apart—not even now, when Chong-ho wishes for privacy to mourn, to despise himself. Soon enough, he will tell her everything. The two will live together in this knowledge, in these deaths; and the wordless weight of them will always feel like too much to carry. Like sinking into a bottomless pit of cold clay.

They will forge on and survive; they always have. But henceforth with a persistent, disquieting sense that with one more burden, all will give way. One more blow—to themselves, a loved one—and they will be swallowed whole.

Providence Hospital, Washington, DC
1978

They arrived just past 3 AM—calmly, quietly. Too calm, too quiet. Given the wife's condition. Her water broken, contractions coming hard, but slow. The doctor took one look and pronounced it would be a while. The woman said, *No epidural; no matter what,* and the night nurse almost laughed out loud. The doctor kept his poker face. *This could be long,* he said, *and not easy.* The husband bent over, a stiff, dark hand on his wife's back. *Don't decide yet. Leave the option open.* The woman clutched her hot water bottle and clenched her teeth. Red-faced, brassy hair flying wild on one side, flattened and moist on the other; sweat beading at her temples.

No. If you let them, I'll never forgive you.

The pretty little girl, long-haired and chocolate-skinned, sat in a chair swinging her legs while the other nurse asked how old she was. Three fingers, and a grin. Dark-purple gums, and dimples.

The nurse watched the little girl, then looked over at the woman and the man. She remembered: three years before, this couple—white woman, black man. The delivery had gone fine, the man went to get food. But when she brought the baby to the woman, the woman became hysterical: *No, where's my baby, my baby boy, where is he, that's not my baby.* Slurring words, making no sense. The nurse had taken the pink bundle away, come back and put a cold towel on the woman's head. She'd quieted down but kept saying, *my baby boy.* Wild eyed, she whispered: *He came to me, in dreams. He told me he was a boy, and he was coming, he's been waiting all these years, to come back to me. He said it's all right, he's all right, he's coming back. My baby boy.* The nurse remembered these haunting, baffling words. She'd dabbed the woman's forehead, soothed and shushed her; some women reacted strongly to the drugs, just needed to sleep it off.

She remembered the craziness in the woman's eyes. She remembered thinking, Thank goodness more doctors are encouraging parents to learn the sex of the baby beforehand.

This time the labor is long, and not easy. The woman does not take the epidural, and she tears badly. Five stitches.

In the waiting area, the nurse tells the husband she remembers them, when the little girl was born. He nods, but she can tell he doesn't remember; or doesn't want to. His face had been unreadable, back then, when she'd told him, about his wife carrying on like that. She remembers trying to read his face, but it was like she'd spoken in a language he couldn't comprehend.

Now, tonight, when the nurse brings the child—the boy, Bennett—the woman takes him in her arms, looks into his face, weeps, laughs. *You're here*, she says. *You're finally here.* The woman and the baby fall asleep, soundly; on her face, a faint smile. A long-awaited rest.

LATE SUMMER–WINTER 1984

1.

There would be no open casket. Charles's sister, Rhea, raised the question on behalf of the family, but Charles knew she would not insist. They all moved through the arrangements in controlled motions, like factory workers on the line. No rebellions, no complaints. There would be no open casket because there would be no demonstrations, no feeling at all. Alice had made clear, in not so many words, that she wanted none of it.

It was just Rhea and her husband, Marcus, from Charles's side; on Alice's, her father and brother, Nicholas Sr. and Jr. (*You'd best not bring Cheryl, Nick,* Charles had advised his father-in-law, in a voice that warned him of a scene between Alice and her stepmother best avoided.) Dennis Rhodes came alone (his wife had recently left him), and when Veda asked if Amy could come, Alice gave a weak smile and said, *Sure, sweetie.* Then Karen Mitchell called, *a bit concerned,* and they agreed that Karen would accompany her.

It was Sunday. Five days had passed since the drowning, though no one could have said so. Time no longer meant what it used to, and any reality seemed possible.

Alice had traveled back from Rehoboth General Hospital in the medical van with her son's body. Charles had packed everything up and loaded the car, while Veda and Hannah sat in back. Hannah sat behind the driver's seat and hugged her duffel bag in her lap; Veda sat in the middle. The two girls did not speak, or touch, but there was between them a palpable need to be proximal, together, in some way.

Charles could smell the salt on their skin and in their damp hair. They were still wearing their suits, wrapped in sun-striped towels at the waist. He kept to the speed limit the whole way, and as they drove, Charles wondered if they were cold, did they need to put on sweatshirts. But then he realized that he was drenched at the armpits, his neck sticky. It was in the nineties, sunny and humid; it was a day identical to the day they'd arrived.

The morgue, then the arrangements. In the midst of it all, Charles wondered about Hannah. When he'd dropped her off, no one was home. He got out of the car and asked her if she'd be all right. Hannah nodded. Charles put a hand on her shoulder, and Hannah fixed her eyes on his other hand, which hung by his side.

"Good-bye, Mr. Lee," Hannah had said, then turned and walked toward the house.

Today, the day of the wake, Charles woke early. Alice had taken a sleeping pill the night before, then another in the middle of the night, after getting up to make a call (to her friend Laila, in Chile). She would likely sleep another two hours, at least. Nick Sr. and Nick Jr. were at the Marriott. Rhea and Marcus were in the downstairs guest room and would be up soon. Charles stepped down the hall to Veda's room. Alice had asked if she wanted to sleep with them, and Veda had said no. Charles didn't blame her; their bed did not offer the warmth of comfort. Veda would have sensed this. Or, maybe she was simply old enough to feel her own sadness without any help.

What does a young girl think or feel about anything? Charles realized more than ever that he had no earthly idea.

He tapped Veda's door open to see that she was not there. The covers were thrown off, as if she'd slept soundly then awakened with a start. Charles stepped back and walked down the hall: Benny's door was open, and there Veda stood, next to Benny's bed, in her nightgown and bare feet.

She was surveying the room, which had been a mess the day they left for the shore. She'd made the bed and put away the trucks and trains in the big plastic bin they'd bought so optimistically. A pile of his dirty clothes lay neatly just next to the door. The carpet was filthy; a vacuuming would be the next logical task. But beholding the silence was the thing now. Silence and order.

Charles stood still, but the floor creaked anyway—as if his insides had settled down into his feet. Veda looked over her shoulder. The expression on her face was enigmatic. Sad, yes, but maybe more confused. She whispered, "Can you show me how to do the laundry?" Charles felt something sink hard in his chest, sucking air down his throat. He'd felt this when Rhea called to tell him Essie had died. And again when they lost Bobby. He couldn't associate the feeling with sadness, or anger, or fear exactly. Because he'd also felt it when Alice told him she was pregnant, with Veda. And what Charles had felt then was something he still couldn't describe in words.

Maybe that wasn't true. Maybe he'd been plain irritated. Now, though—since that news had become flesh-and-blood Veda—now Charles looked back and couldn't feel it, whatever it was, so simply. It wasn't possible to feel anything simply anymore.

Charles nodded. "Let's get the sheets then, too," he said.

"No," Veda said, now turning her body as if to guard the bed. "We have to leave it for now. We have to let something smell like him for a while."

Charles was speechless. His daughter was not often insistent. Veda had spoken in a tone mostly confident, but also with a hint of uncertainty. She needed her father's confirmation. "Yes," he said, finally. "Yes, we do."

The Weaver men arrived at 9:30, crisply suited and having breakfasted at the hotel; Reverend Haywood shortly thereafter, in black robes and red tie, unshy about asking Rhea to fix him a cup of strong coffee and toast with margarine. He'd been widowed the year before, and while the church ladies were busily identifying among the widows and spinsters the best next match for him, he lived alone. Alice liked Rev. Haywood well enough. He was even-tempered, and honest. And from listening in on Rhea's and Charles's talk of the comings and goings of ministers, he was no dime a dozen. There was no question, at any rate, that Rev. Haywood would officiate. The Weavers' Episcopalianism had lapsed instantaneously after Alice's mother died; there was no one but Rev. Haywood for a time such as this. Even Nick Sr. conceded.

Joe Haywood was tall, light-skinned and thin-lipped, and both Alice and Charles knew, though did not say, that this was better than if he weren't. Who ever knew what would set Nick Weaver off; he was a man accustomed to ruling every room he entered—to thinking and saying whatever he damn well pleased.

Alice busied herself in the living room, rearranging and straightening pillows and chairs that were already arranged and straight. She spoke softly to herself—*Now let's see, that's better*— as if readying to host a holiday party. It was obvious that she was avoiding her father and brother, who sat in the parlor, feeling no need to either socialize or make themselves useful.

Charles and Veda stood in the foyer, staring out through the screen door. Charles wore his only suit, Veda a navy sundress with an organdy collar that Rhea had bought for her last Easter. Charles had his arm around her, and Veda held the hand of that arm with both of hers. Neither wanted to be in the parlor with the casket. They stood without speaking, waiting for their friends to arrive.

Dennis and Amy and Karen walked up to the door at the same time, like an accidental family. They didn't bother making introductions but went straight to the parlor, and shortly after, the service started. Rev. Haywood led them in "Precious Lord" and "I Won't Complain," and his voice was so much stronger than the rest that it sounded more like a solo. Then they all sat down in folding chairs. Rev. Haywood spoke of death and resurrection, darkness and light. When he called Benny "Bennett," Alice let a single tear fall; her great-grandfather was the only person in all the family whom her mother had loved. The reverend then spoke of God's nearness, His presence incarnate, His greatness transformed into earthly form. "In times of grief there is nothing but the Lord's comfort. We must unclench our fists and our hearts, we must let Him come in." Charles saw Alice look down at her hands; she'd laid them flat in her lap, like a little girl practicing her manners.

The cemetery was a five-minute drive. Karen and Amy said they would walk. Veda wanted to walk too, but when she looked to Charles he shook his head. The men loaded the casket into the hearse, then Charles, Alice, and Veda drove directly behind. On Kenyon Street, people sitting on their porches stood up; some clasped their hands together in prayer. The few neighbors from the old days, who knew Uncle Marvin, nodded their heads. Alice stared straight ahead. When Charles reached over, he felt her hand balled into a fist, and after a few moments, when she didn't unclench it, he drew his hand back.

The sun shone brightly, though a pleasant breeze cooled things down. Alice wore large sunglasses that covered nearly half her face. During Reverend Haywood's prayer, Alice crossed her arms and turned her head away. No one saw her biting the inside of her lip so hard she could feel the pain shoot to the top of her head. The burial was brief and no-nonsense. As they began to disperse, Veda bent down and scooped up a mound of dirt with both hands, then fanned out her fingers to let the loose brown earth spill into the hole.

Afterward, in the parlor, Nick Sr. broke the ice. "Thank you, Reverend," he said, shaking Joe Haywood's hand heartily. "God's mercy." Charles watched his father-in-law proceed to work the room, shaking hands and delivering lines about "What a tragedy" and "God's comfort." His fleshy pink face and silver hair made Charles think of an elderly relation of Lee Atwater, and he noted with some relief that this burst of sociability meant that his father-in-law was soon to make his exit. No doubt his flight was scheduled for early afternoon.

When he left, Nick Jr. shut the door behind him, then made himself a plate of deviled eggs and carrot sticks. He came to stand with Charles and Dennis, a good half foot shorter than Dennis, who towered. Nick shook his head, crunching a carrot. "Christ, what a sonofabitch," he said. Dennis busted out laughing, then covered his mouth. Charles, too, chuckled. When Alice shot a silencing look their way, Charles thought, what a shame. She might have laughed, too.

"So how's your team looking this year?" Nick asked. "Got any intel on draft picks?"

"No way y'all can top last year," Dennis said. Dennis's people were originally from Dallas, die-hard Cowboys fans.

"What goes up must come down," Nick agreed.

The security manager's office was completely separate from the training and coaching department. Only the Director of Security,

Charles's boss's boss's boss, would catch wind of preseason rumors.

"Y'all just smartin from old wounds," Charles said. The Dolphins-Redskins match the year before had been some kind of breakthrough for him and Nick, who lived in southern Florida. When Nick called for Alice the week before the Super Bowl, and Charles had answered, each argued his team's obvious advantages. After the Redskins won, Charles called Nick down in Boca and left a boisterous, taunting message on his machine (Nick was at a sports bar, drunk and getting drunker); he'd even gotten Benny to whoop like an Indian into the phone. "Enough, for God's sake," Alice had said, but Charles knew it pleased her.

The three stood together a few minutes longer, shifting weight, holding plastic cups emptied down to ice cubes, before Charles excused himself to the bathroom. He walked by Rhea and Marcus, sitting together on the stairs, whispering while Marcus massaged Rhea's neck. Charles kept walking, past the bathroom, and headed through the kitchen to the back door, with the idea of taking a solitary moment in the yard. He found Alice there, putting out a cigarette. Neither of them had smoked in years. Where had she gotten it? Maybe Dennis, Charles thought. Or Karen Mitchell.

"Got another?"

Alice didn't seem startled, or surprised. She held a pack of Camels in her left hand, held it up for him to take it—the whole thing—so he did.

"It wasn't how I remembered it," Alice said.

Charles didn't know what she meant, what exactly she was remembering. She'd smoked in high school and college but had quit by the time they met. "They took all the nicotine out," Charles said. "Most of it, anyway."

"What's the point then? If it's going to be bad, it should be good." Alice's voice was floaty, a little spooky. She'd put on a very dark lipstick today. Those big sunglasses. Charles didn't know her at all.

They stood together in silence while Charles smoked. They went back in together, and for another hour told their friends and family that they were doing fine, just fine. Thank you so much for coming.

2.

Charles took a week of bereavement leave. Only three days of it was paid time, and those two extra days worried him. The burial had cost. And he wanted to go back to work, wanted to be busy, to get away from the silence, from Alice, who wasn't speaking at all.

Alice's own leave of absence was "indefinite." They needed the money now, but Charles didn't say anything. If she took too long, the home might replace her, they both knew that. Charles thought, well, no need to put money in Benny's college fund anymore; and though it wasn't much, they could transfer the balance into Veda's. No need for a babysitter, either. The thoughts ambled in, like deadbeat old friends who took liberties, and Charles shook them away. He knew he had to be careful about such thoughts, had to keep them to himself.

On Monday and Tuesday, Veda stayed mostly in her room. School would start in a week, and she needed some things: a list had come in the mail from school. Charles would be the one to take her. Alice spent all day in the kitchen, putting loose photos into a gigantic leather album she'd dug out of a drawer. When she wasn't doing that, she was upstairs sleeping. In the middle of the night, Alice whispered and cried on the phone downstairs, to Laila, and to another friend—Pauline, Charles guessed, who lived in England.

Charles took Veda to the Kmart. She didn't complain, like she usually did, about how *ghet-to* it was, about wanting to go instead to Peoples, and then to Sizzler afterward. Benny had always liked the Kmart. Charles thought about this, for the first time—that Benny had had a personality, and preferences. Benny had liked Kmart because it was usually disorderly, a little grimy. What did this mean, Charles wondered. Who would Benny have grown into.

Protractor and compass. Glue stick. Yellow highlighter pen. Posterboard, two different sizes. Erasable pens, blue or black ink (*Please, no red!* the teacher had written in bold letters). Erasable pens, Charles thought. What a contradiction. What was wrong with good old pencils? He always carried a mechanical pencil in his shirt pocket, along with a Bic ballpoint to fill out carbon-backed forms.

The school-supplies aisle was a mess: items pulled off their chrome posts and tossed here, there, everywhere. Certain areas were piled high, others bare. The impression of dregs. But they'd come at the dinner hour, six o'clock, so it was quiet, the wreckage after the storm. Veda stood there, arms out to her sides and palms out, a stance of both irritation and despair.

"It's okay, V," Charles said. "There's still a lot of stuff here, we just need to sort through it." He remembered clothes shopping with Rhea and Nona at the Salvation Army when he was young. He'd hated that vision of dregs, too—everything pawed over, the smell of vinegar. Why couldn't he have new things, like Dennis, whose father was still around, a pharmacist with a degree. Charles had drawn the line at secondhand stores when it came to his own kids. Alice shopped at thrift stores for herself, and one day brought home almost-matching rugby shirts for him and Benny. "Aren't these great?" she said. "Like new."

"No," Charles had said. He took the shirts and marched outside, stuffed them in the garbage can.

"Here," Charles said, handing Veda the shopping basket and the list. "Think treasure hunt. I need to go look for a thermos for you, okay? Your mother says you need a new one." It was the only thing Alice had said as they were leaving the house. "Don't leave this aisle. I'll be right back." Veda nodded, sighing. She'll be okay, Charles thought. She was going to roll up her sleeves like the good kid she was.

Charles squinted up at the signs above the aisles. Was it sporting goods? Or maybe the soup and coffee aisle. He began to move briskly, up and down the aisles. The fluorescent lights suddenly seemed too bright; they were sapping Charles of energy and clear thinking. Since the funeral he'd not slept well, or much. And he'd not gone for a run or to the gym since before they'd left for Rehoboth. When the painkiller/sleep aids aisle presented itself, Charles found himself drawn, and drifting.

It was a long aisle, and at the far end, he saw her. The lone girl, bespectacled, black-haired, long-limbed. She was reaching for small boxes, taking them down, reading the labels, replacing them on the shelf. Charles took a tentative step, then another, toward her, to make sure it was Hannah. It was. She wore her brown purse slung across her front, as always.

There'd been no question of inviting Hannah to the funeral, no discussion; Charles thought to bring it up but knew Alice wouldn't have it. Hannah's absence was conspicuous, though. She'd been with Benny nearly every day for four months; what else could it mean but that she was being held responsible? That Benny's loved ones saw Hannah as the black hand of his death.

Charles stepped backward up the aisle, slowly, like a bystander backing away from a crime scene. He'd seen her but did not want to be seen.

Good-bye, Mr. Lee, she'd said. Seeing her now, he heard her words in a new way. *We can't know each other anymore*, was what she'd meant. *We have to erase everything.* Charles took another step backward, then another. His body and his mind crossed each other, moving in opposite directions. He wanted to know . . . how she was. Had something changed, broken. Was she all right.

Why did he want to know?

It didn't matter why. Different things mattered now. There were things Charles wanted to know because he just *did*.

But he did not walk forward. He turned and headed back to aisle nine, back to Veda. She was practicing the ballerina foot positions Amy Mitchell had taught her. Her basket was nearly full. Charles grabbed her hand.

"Wait, what about—"

"Leave it." He walked and talked, trying to sound casual. "You know, let's drive over to Peoples. Then we can head to Sizzler for dinner. I'll call your mom."

Charles led Veda out the automatic doors into the parking lot. He did not look around. They got into the car and drove away. He had kept Veda from seeing Hannah, kept Hannah from seeing them. Even so, Charles knew, as he drove, that he was not running from her, but was rather compelled by a different idea altogether.

3.

The last days of August were unusually cool and cloudy. The oldest among the porch sitters stayed inside; there were grumblings about whether they'd be able to hold their Labor Day barbecues.

Charles went out to Wheaton for the third morning in a row. He took the Metrobus early Friday and didn't say where he was going. No one asked. He came home to make lunch for Veda, and then went out again, to Barkley's, which was Dennis's daily watering hole now that his wife, Sherisse, had gone. The two men would drink in broad daylight and stare at ESPN on the TV and say little. Once, Charles was tempted to talk to Dennis, to tell what he'd been doing in the mornings; what he'd seen, what he'd learned. But he took one look at his unshaven, red-eyed friend and knew that Dennis was in no shape to listen, really listen, to what Charles had to say. He would take it the wrong way. Then again, just what would be the right way.

Hannah was home alone in the mornings. Charles had counted on that. The first morning he went, he just stood on the street, watching the house, until he felt conspicuous. Then he walked across the road to the bus shelter and sat on the bench. After about an hour, and five buses, he saw movement in one of the downstairs windows. He couldn't see very well, but he knew it was Hannah. When she disappeared from the window, he imagined her going upstairs to her room, or maybe downstairs to the basement. Maybe the TV was down there.

Benny had always nagged about finishing the basement of their house. He'd enlisted Alice as his ally. "They do need a playroom," Alice said. "We can put the TV down there, and a foosball table." The foosball was her sweetener: Dennis and Charles had grown up on foosball, they'd play at Dennis's all the time. The other thing they used to do in Dennis's basement was smoke cigarettes and, eventually, weed. Did they want to create these hiding places for the children so soon? Charles liked watching TV upstairs with Veda, and Benny was just getting interested in football.

Was Hannah hiding in the basement? If so, what did she do down there?

On the second morning, Charles brought his Perrini Greens, with the high-powered zoom. Suddenly he was brought back to boot camp. Eighteen years old, in the middle of the forest, charged with locating the most inconspicuous lookout spot with a direct sightline. He'd been singled out for these assignments by the training officer, and it was never quite clear if this was reward or punishment. Maybe there was no difference.

Today's objective was easier. The yard behind the house was small and descended into a wooded area. A tall hedge had been planted alongside, and the neighbor to the east had built a six-foot wooden fence. Charles walked between the hedge and the fence invisibly. His perch behind a thick-trunked maple was further obscured by spent corn stalks at the yard's perimeter. He could see directly into every window at the back of the house, including the sliding doors that led from patio to kitchen.

Hannah's bedroom faced the back. She spent most of the morning there. Once, she left her room and walked into the hallway. Charles watched her stand in front of the hallway phone and stare at it for some time before picking it up. She held the phone between her shoulder and her neck, then twisted herself into the cord like a mummy; she was talking to someone she knew. She hung up and went downstairs, pulled out the Yellow Pages from a cabinet. Charles watched her page through then scan a page with a Band-Aid-tipped finger. He wondered how she'd injured herself. A blade or knife slicing the fingertip open? Or just a hangnail, chewed off by teeth sharp enough to burst a vessel.

Hannah picked up the kitchen phone and dialed, held the phone with both hands and stood rigid. She said something into the mouthpiece, robotically, as if she'd been told to say it. Then she hung up.

Charles watched from behind the maple tree. Nothing else happened, and then suddenly it was noon. He was good at this—standing still, on alert—and his boss liked him and trusted him for it. The others too often wandered off their posts out of boredom. Now that Charles was Senior Assistant Manager of Gate Security, he spent most of his time in the office. Every so often, though, he missed those watch assignments; he missed the solitude of vigilance.

At 12:10, a white Chevy Nova pulled into the driveway. When Charles caught sight of Soon-mi stepping out of the driver's side, his heart sped up, and his hands grew sweaty. He dropped his binoculars, wiped his hands, then raised them again. He saw a small woman wearing pink scrubs, gray-haired. Charles had expected Hannah's parents to be closer to his own age, and Alice's, but this woman was easily in her fifties. He considered the fact that Alice had never mentioned it. No surprise, he supposed; they had different ideas about what was notable.

Essie Lee had also been in her fifties when Charles was a teenager. She died when he was sixteen—an unnecessary death. The main reason for such late detection of the cancer was Essie's stubborn mistrust of doctors. Charles remembered little about that time: one day, Nona and Rhea took Essie to the emergency room; a month later she was gone. No one told him so, but Charles understood that she'd decided against treatment. *For what?* he could hear her saying. *Six months of sick and bald?* She was weary by then, and lonely. A parade of boyfriends had come and gone, and Charles had been staying away, over at Dennis's most of the time.

Rhea tried to explain to Charles once that his father, Frank, had been Essie's one true love; none of the others after him ever measured up. *Whatever*, Charles had said. The man left her with his kid, and she's mooning over him? *Whatever*.

Charles watched Soon-mi carry groceries into the kitchen. She carried also a flat paper bag, folded over at the top. Charles made out a Sports Authority logo. Hannah came bouncing into the kitchen, and her mother handed her the bag. Hannah unfolded the top and peered inside. A smile spread across her face. It was a strange smile, light and intentionally childlike. Too light. And the bouncing . . .

Soon-mi continued to put away groceries, and she waved her hand at Hannah. Charles watched and deciphered. *Go, take that, and off with you*, her hand said.

Hannah turned on her heel and again bounced out of the kitchen. When she got to her room, Hannah dropped the package on her bed, stared at it. Her face had changed. Charles remembered something now—that strain he'd seen the first day she arrived at their house last May. The effort of politeness, of pleasantry. Hannah had made that effort for her mother just now. Why had she done that?

Charles focused the binoculars on the paper bag. It was a few moments before Hannah reached in and pulled out a swimsuit—Champion tags, navy blue with red and white racing stripes. She stepped over to the mirror and held it up to herself. Her face was blank, and strange. Slowly, she pulled her T-shirt over her head then pulled off her jeans, stripped down to naked but did not look in the mirror.

Charles let down his binoculars, then let a beat pass; when he raised them again, Hannah was pulling on the swimsuit. She stood in front of the mirror, and Charles could see from the back that it fit Hannah perfectly. He could see the long arch of her spine, her shoulder blades framed prettily by the crisscrossing straps. In the mirror he could see the ripple of her ribs; small breasts like mounds of soft, sweet dough, nipples like chocolate chips perched on top.

Hannah turned and moved toward the bed, lay down on it and curled onto her side, hugging a yellow-butterfly pillow. Charles watched her. Hannah lay there, still.

Downstairs, Soon-mi had finished putting away the groceries. She sat in a lumpy recliner, snacking on whole peanuts, breaking them out of their shells with her teeth. She opened up a garden catalog and pushed back on the recliner, which seemed to resist her, until the footrest popped up. She closed her eyes. Charles saw bits of Hannah in her face—the rectangular forehead and dark mouth. Her skin was smooth and freckled with age spots, and it was her hands, knuckled and pruned, that most betrayed her age. Her hair was not gray, actually, but black and streaked with white. Charles felt her fatigue, sensed she had things on her mind, things distracting her from her catalog. Or, the catalog's purpose was to distract her from what was on her mind.

What was most strange was that Hannah's mother's mind was somewhere, but not on the girl curled up alone on her bed upstairs. But then, why would she be concerned—that girl was bouncy, and pleasant, and obedient.

Suddenly, it was clear. Charles understood what he was seeing: Hannah had not told her parents—had not told anyone—about Benny.

4.

On Tuesday, when Charles went back to work, he left home earlier than usual. He drove a local route, past the high school in Wheaton. He'd not gone to watch Hannah on Sunday, or on Labor Day, and he needed to see her. Needed to. Needed to check on her. Needed to know more. It didn't matter why.

The school parking lot was packed. The freshmen were arriving on buses, the upperclassmen in groups of four and five in junky, noisy cars. Charles pulled over across the street, cut the engine, sat and watched. Hannah's first day of high school. He wondered how she was feeling—did she spend all morning getting ready, what would she wear. Which Hannah would show up—the polite, strained, bouncy Hannah? Or the one he knew, the one he'd known.

Did he know her? He did. He knew her. Somehow, he did. Blood on her fingertips; the weight of her head on his shoulder when he'd carried her to the bed. How he'd felt her like a shadow, dense and yet weightless, sitting behind him on the car ride back. Veda eventually fell asleep, but Hannah had stayed awake. Charles and Hannah were together, awake; silently impolite in their thoughts. They both thought: This isn't really such a tragedy as everyone will make it out to be. They thought: The world won't miss him, not really.

And: Not everything that seems so important actually is.

And: How did I get mixed up in all this, how can I get away.

Good-bye, Mr. Lee, Hannah had said. Maybe she'd been right; but Charles didn't like it. They knew each other, but that had to be finished now. Written in solid ink, then erased.

Hundreds of kids. Mostly black and Asian. Some Arab kids. The white kids wore caps turned backward, baggy jeans, fat sneakers. If he stayed and watched long enough he would see her, he knew he'd be able to pick her out. But he had to get to work. It was his first day back, and he was late already.

The employee lot at the stadium was also packed. The season opener was three weeks away. Charles shared an office with two other assistant managers. Bart Sheridan, former All-American, Notre Dame '50, was a recovering alcoholic: sober six years, 93 days, according to the AA flipchart on his desk. He'd lost his wife and kids in the wreckage. Bart put his head down, did his job, didn't say much. Smoked cigars and looked about a hundred years older than his fifty-something. Charles and Mike Brown, the other assistant, joked along these lines. Mike was a few years younger than Charles, son of a Morehouse professor. Mike had his sights on moving into the management side of things. Charles liked Mike all right, they were friendly if not friends.

"Hey, man." Mike extended a solid hand, they each gripped with two and held it. "Good to have you back." Bart looked up from his desk and nodded.

"He been around yet?" Charles looked at the wall clock. He was twenty minutes late.

"Nah, not yet. Don't worry. He'll go easy on you for at least—"

"Twenty minutes?"

Mike laughed. "Yeah. I was gonna say a coupla days, but you've probably got it right."

The morning went by quickly. Charles caught up on paperwork, looked over shift schedules. The boss, Terrence, called him in to his office at 11:30, sat him down, offered condolences. Told him about some recent incidents—tagging on the southeast wall, two cars jacked from the employee lot—and said that sold-out crowds were expected from day one: his staff needed to have their heads in the game. Was Charles really ready to be back? Yes, he was, Charles answered. How was the wife doing? Fine, Charles said. As fine as could be expected, he added.

Terrence nodded. "You know, we've all been praying for you.

Coach Gibbs got word of what happened, he said a prayer, too." Charles blinked his eyes. Coach Gibbs? He'd never even been in the same room as the man. Anyway, Charles nodded and thanked him. He opened and closed his fists, digging his nails into the fleshy part of his hands. Terrence looked him over one last time, then said, Okay, get back to work.

It was good to be busy. At lunch, Charles and Mike went to the Roy Rogers at the mall. Mike asked, his mouth full of roast beef and sesame bun, "So how you holding up?"

Charles chewed his cheeseburger and nodded. "Takes time, I guess." He didn't know what he meant, but he was feeling his way around, trying out lines.

"The Lord giveth," Mike said, shaking his head. Charles cringed, but hid it behind his burger. It irritated him when people mindlessly trotted out *The Lord*. "Every day's a gift, I guess. Just do our best, the rest is in Someone Else's hands." The words floated up and away. Mike was soft, everything pretty much came to him easy.

"It's harder on Alice," Charles said. A tiny weight lifted. He had said something true.

Mike nodded. "Makes sense. A mother's heart. But, man. Your *son*. Your *boy*." Charles turned to look at the fountain just outside Roy's. A fat man sat on the ledge, licking the drippy pink streams of strawberry ice cream off the sides of his cone. Charles narrowed his eyes, gritted his back teeth. When he picked up his soda, his hand felt unsteady, teeming. He didn't like what Mike had just said. For the first time, the thought came: what if it had been Veda?

The afternoon flew by. Charles did his work, and he didn't think anymore about what Mike had said—or about what *The Lord* does after he *giveth*. He glanced at the clock at three and suddenly knew he had to leave. He made up an errand. "Gotta drive over to the suppliers in Beltsville to make sure the new monitors'll be ready in time." Charles said this in one breath, to the middle of the room, while packing up his bag.

"Sure, man," Mike said, putting his hand over the phone. Bart furrowed then raised his bushy eyebrows.

School let out at 2:45. Charles knew he'd have missed her, but he drove to the school anyway. He found himself panicking. He realized this might not even be her school. He'd parked and was halfway to the main entrance, walking briskly, before he knew what he was doing, what he planned to say. In the office, a hook-nosed woman with a Russian accent asked if she could help him.

"I'm looking for . . . my goddaughter," Charles said. Words spilled out, knowing words that surprised him. "I'm supposed to pick her up from swim practice today. Her parents had an unexpected . . . they forgot to tell me where." The woman paused, looked Charles over, shamelessly. He straightened his shoulders, buttoned his cardigan vest.

"There's no practice yet," she said, "but tryouts are at the recreation center."

"Thank you, ma'am," Charles said.

He felt bold now, mission-driven. Reckless was not a word he was willing to apply. He had to look out for her. Someone had to. At the rec center, Charles walked right past reception, flashed a stadium badge. From the viewing window, high above the pool, among some thirty or forty girls clustered on one end, he spotted her. Navy blue, red and white racing stripes. Hannah's figure appeared even longer and suppler with her hair up in the bathing cap. She walked toward the starting block from the other end of the pool, dropped her goggles, which had been dangling off a finger. A boy—goggled, six-packed, and broad-shouldered—bent to pick them up and handed them to her. An exchange of half-smiles, then off in opposite directions. Charles's jaw clenched; he imagined how warm and moist it must be down there, amidst all the bodies.

He watched from his perch, still and focused. The coach shouted orders and blew into a whistle; the swimmers obeyed, and swam. Hannah swam long distances—several laps of freestyle, then a period of rest, then backstroke. She swam smoothly and prettily. Charles could see that now. Hannah was a formal swimmer, disciplined, her arms and legs cutting the water's surface like blades. He'd watched her from shore at the beach, but he'd recognized only her endurance then, not her form.

The swimmers did not race each other, but rather a stopwatch that the coach's assistant held and clicked. Charles remembered that stopwatch, and the whistle, too, from high school track (he ran his sophomore year, until he was kicked off for smoking weed underneath the bleachers with Dennis and two freshman girls). He remembered it from boot camp, too. He was fast, and he also had good form. This was what made Charles a good soldier: he could be fast, or still, whatever was needed.

Hannah's last trial was a medley—two laps each of the four strokes. Her butterfly was her weakest, her breaststroke good enough. When she was done, she sat on the lower bleachers, catching her breath. The boy from before, the goggles-retriever, sat down next to her. They talked to each other sideways, without looking. They watched the other swimmers.

Charles saw that the boy was harmless. He wore Coke-bottle goggles and sat with his knees together, hunched over.

The whistle blew, and the boy got up. Hannah did not follow him with her eyes as he walked away. Instead, she stared into the water. Then slowly, she raised her head. She looked up. Hannah looked at the dark face in the window high above. She lifted her goggles to her eyes, then lowered them, her head still raised.

Charles remained still, at his perch.

Neither of them flinched. It was a long time—it seemed so to both of them—before the whistle blew and Hannah stood to join the huddle of swimmers.

5.

In late September, Charles asked Alice through the bathroom door if she planned to go back to work. She didn't answer. She flushed the toilet.

Alice had been filling her days; with what, Charles didn't know. She'd joined a bereavement group, which she went to on Thursday nights, maybe other times too during the day, Charles suspected. Veda went home with Amy Mitchell after school twice a week, to ballet class once a week. Alice was there with her, in body if not in mind, on Tuesday and Thursday. Nights, she stayed up reading downstairs and came to bed late, sometimes staying up to call Laila. Charles was gone before Alice awoke in the mornings, just barely in time to get Veda off to school. There had been two incidents of Veda going to school lunchless, so Charles started making her lunch.

He left early because of his stop at the high school. Every morning. After that day at the pool, Hannah had looked for him, in the parking lot, as she got off the bus. She looked for him. Charles saw that. When she saw him, parked across the street, she smiled, just barely, then turned to go inside. He stopped too at the rec center on his way home. He'd bought a membership so he could go in every day. He would watch from above at the window until Hannah was out of the pool, in between heats, and looked up. They would both smile. Charles was proud of her. Hannah had made the varsity team, as a freshman. When the whistle blew, Hannah would go back to the starting block, and Charles would leave.

One morning, Hannah did not get off the school bus. Nor the next day. On the third day, Charles drove to her house; parked on the opposite side of the street. The white Nova was in the driveway. Hannah's mother should have been at work for the early shift. Charles grew worried. Maybe Hannah was sick. He wanted to wait, and watch. But Terrence had been stopping in more often, checking up on him. Charles wondered if Bart had said something, about his sometimes leaving fifteen minutes early to get to the rec center.

Charles cut the engine. He would call Mike from a pay phone, he decided. Tell him he'd had car trouble.

At 9:30 the front door opened. Soon-mi came out first, Hannah following with her head down. Hannah's hair was tangled, her face puffy. She wore a purple warm-up suit and flip-flops with no socks. No coat. It was cool, in the fifties. Hannah held her hands clasped in front, like a perp in handcuffs.

Charles followed the Nova to an office park in Upper Marlboro. It was one of the new townhouse developments, where black doctors and accountants were setting up offices. What could they be doing here? Charles wondered. No way this is their doctor. They probably didn't even have a family doctor. Alice had told him that most Koreans didn't have insurance; they paid other Koreans under the table for all their services, medical and otherwise.

Charles drove past, then made a U-turn and parked at the gas station across the street. He got out of his car, walked to the edge of the road, and read the sign posted for drive-by traffic. One of the names on the sign read Suk-joon Rhee, Certified Public Accountant.

He did not understand. Hannah had stayed home from school two days. She looked sick, unhappy. She was being forced to make this visitation. To an accountant? It angered him—this incomprehension, this wall between him and . . . between him and the solace. Of their understanding. He was not going to be able to figure this out, without her help. She wanted him to know, Charles was sure; Hannah would want him to know.

At home that night his problem was solved. Half of it, anyway. It was Alice who bridged the gap. "I gave notice," she said. "I'm sorry. We'll just spend less." That was all. But she said it in a way that made Charles suspect she'd done this some time ago, and was just now telling him. He knew then what had happened.

Alice's resignation, and the reason for it, would have reached Hannah's mother by now. She would have learned about Benny, about Hannah's lies, whatever she may have told them about why she was no longer working for Alice Lee's family. Maybe now, too, the mother knew about Charles, that Hannah went to the house of a black man every day for four months, had gone on a beach trip with him. Hannah's parents would be shocked, they would be angry, surely. But what would they do? Which part would be most punishable in their eyes? And who was Suk-joon Rhee, CPA?

Good-bye, Mr. Lee.

Charles did not want her to be right about that; about them not knowing each other anymore. But she was no longer free, no longer his to watch. Someone else was watching Hannah now. They were watching her in the wrong way, though; not looking out for her, but accusing her. Why were they doing that? Couldn't they see that she was just a young girl? Hadn't they seen her swim, her body so free and strong?

On the fourth day, Hannah was back to school. She came off the bus but didn't look Charles's way. When Charles went to the rec center, Hannah didn't look up from the bleachers. Charles was there, at the school, and at the pool, alone. She'd left him. He was angry, but not at Hannah. It wasn't her fault. They'd gotten to her somehow, he could see that. He could see that she was completely alone, too.

He stopped going to the school and to the rec center. He stayed longer at work, threw himself into reports, jump-started a new protocol for night-watch accountability that Terrence had been keen on. He started running again—mornings, along the canal, in the cold weather. He met Dennis at the gym, and they both got into better shape, while they talked even less. Charles put his head down. He cooked three-course dinners, read spy novels late into the night. He knew how to do this; it was remarkable, really, how he could soldier on, as they say. Unthinking.

Alice did not remark on these shifts; she barely noticed. In addition to the support group, Alice now went to the Episcopal church on Wednesday evenings for prayer service. She seemed to Charles either more peaceful or more numb, he couldn't tell which, but there was color back in her face, and he was glad to see it. He smelled cigarette smoke on her clothes, though he never saw cigarettes in the house. Charles considered buying a pack and a lighter and leaving them out for Alice on the table, though he never did.

A week before Christmas, Alice and Charles were sitting at the dinner table. Veda sat up on her knees and reached over to stab a piece of chicken off the platter. She focused on her fork as she brought it back to her plate, watching the precariously hanging chicken with cross-eyes. She was clowning, and Charles smiled;

Veda seemed to be doing all right. Alice spooned steamed carrots onto everyone's plates, serving herself last. Veda sat back down, her mission accomplished. Then she said, "Guess who walked me home today."

"Didn't you come home with Karen and Amy, hon?" Alice unfolded her napkin into her lap.

"I would have, but when I came out from school, Hannah was there."

Alice paused before putting carrots in her mouth, then chewed slowly. A piece of chicken threatened to lodge in Charles's throat.

"What was she doing there?" Alice's eyebrows moved independently of each other. She reached for her wine glass but didn't lift it.

Veda shrugged. "She just came to see me. She said she missed us."

"And what did you guys talk about?" Charles asked. Alice flashed Charles a look. They were both attempting to extract information, but Alice's glare conveyed skepticism of an alliance.

Veda shrugged again. "I just told her about my new teacher, and ballet class, and other stuff. She didn't want to come in, she just left when we got to the gate." Charles paid very close attention as Veda spoke. She didn't seem anxious or careful. She was simply reporting. "It was nice to see her again," Veda said. "But, it's okay with me that we don't see her all the time. I like that it's just us now."

Charles began to breathe more evenly, and Alice exhaled slowly, as if through a narrow tube. There was a pregnant, fraught feeling that either of them might burst into tears, or a violent rage. Veda cut into her chicken thigh, concentrating her eyes on her plate.

Alice breathed in, tucked her hair behind her ear. "V, honey, what have we always said about going with strangers?" A spooky sweetness in her voice.

Veda made a face, somewhere between confused and annoyed. "But she's not a stranger."

"Well, that's true. But she doesn't work for us anymore. So no matter what, come home with who you're supposed to come with, okay? Unless me or Dad tells you different. No matter what."

"Okay." Veda continued to eat, calmly. Too calmly, Charles thought. She was aware of her movements in a way that made Charles sad.

"Good girl," Alice said. She sat back and dropped her shoulders. Her relief had nothing to do with Veda, and it pricked Charles.

"You know, this can't have been easy for her," Charles ventured. Alice knew exactly whom Charles meant by "her." "Don't you think maybe we should . . ." Charles did not finish his sentence; he did not know how to finish it.

"I don't want to talk about it," Alice said. "Let's please close the subject." She stood and cleared the plates Charles and Veda were still eating from.

At the sink, Alice froze, looking out the window. She made a strange sound—an airy gasp, thwarted in a cavernous throat.

Veda and Charles both looked up and saw what Alice saw, what had delighted her instinctively but fell short of expression. Veda was up out of her chair, standing at the back door. "Look how big they are!" Snow was falling, lots of it, and in giant flakes. The white puffs seemed to Charles to both float weightlessly and rain down with force. How did they do that, he wondered. How could the snowflakes be so gentle and so hard.

Veda cracked open the screen door, put her hand out. "It's so warm!" she said, looking first to her mother, who was putting on yellow rubber gloves, then to her father, with a look of desperate eagerness.

"All right," Charles said. "Put on your coat and boots. Why don't we *all* go." He said this for Veda's sake.

"You two go ahead," Alice said, turning the faucet. "I'll clean up here."

Charles was disappointed, if not surprised. He didn't really expect Alice to come out with them, but the snow had sparked something, that gasp—an instant of delight she couldn't contain. He was about to coax her; but he'd missed her: she was gone, fully committed to her task, as if scrubbing away the residue of the preceding moment. He watched her briefly. What might happen if he went and stood behind her? She might stop her scrubbing; they might watch the snowflakes together.

Alice finished the dishes and began scouring the inside of the basin. Charles stood and left the kitchen.

He would recognize later how easily he'd let it happen. Maybe he could have stopped it, could have encouraged Veda to fight for her mother's presence. Instead, they silently allied; they allowed Alice to pull away, to drift. They would learn what to expect, how it would be from now on.

And when Veda came flying down the stairs in her snowsuit, Charles knew he did not really want Alice to come along. Veda had been with her—with Hannah. They'd walked together, and spoken. Maybe Veda had hugged her.

Outside, in the front yard, Veda stuck out her tongue and held out her mittened hands. Then she lay down. She spread her arms and legs and moved them up and down, jumping-jack-style. Instead of opening her arms and legs and closing them in sync, she opened her arms over her head while closing her legs together, then vice versa. Charles had never noticed that before. He tried to remember last winter, when Veda and Benny made angels in that same spot in the yard. They'd made them side by side, but had they moved their arms and legs in the same way? Charles lay down next to Veda and began working on his own angel; but he was too conscious of the motions, too noticing. He couldn't figure out which motion was instinctual, which came more naturally.

He stopped thinking about the motions and just swung his limbs, up and down, up and down. He thought about making an angel. And he thought about Hannah—that she had come back to them, to him. She wanted Charles to know that she was okay. They had not gotten to her. She had not been erased.

6.

The snow did not let up for four days straight. It piled to nearly three feet. Cars were buried, the Metro and buses shut down. School was cancelled across the district and counties. Charles called in and told Terrence he was coming, he could dig out his car, but Terrence told him *Stay put, it's a mess out there.* Charles knew he would say this, but he had cabin fever.

He shoveled every day during the storm, and every day the snow piled up again. He shoveled in front of Mrs. Lang's house, two doors down; she was elderly, her grandsons were unreliable.

The plows roared down the street, twice a day, but everyone else was on foot. Karen and Amy Mitchell came by, flying saucer in tow; they were heading to Rock Creek Park.

"C'mon, Alice," Karen said, gently. "It'll be fun." Both Karen and Amy waited patiently, eagerly but not too eagerly, for Alice's answer. Alice was in a sweatshirt and scrubs, her hair, now down to her shoulders, was tied back in a ponytail. Veda had already darted upstairs to put on her snowsuit.

Charles pretended to read a magazine. He knew better than to encourage Alice to go. He heard the silence, then soft voices, then suddenly, "Yay!" from Amy.

Alice came into the kitchen. "They want us all to go. Rick, too. His office is closed. If you come, he'll come."

"Make him an offer he can't refuse?"

Alice laughed. The laugh escaped her; she would have held it back if she'd felt it coming. She loved *The Godfather*, they both did; they'd seen it together for the first time in Korea, dubbed, which was awful, but still they loved it. "Something like that. We'll swing by their place on the way."

It was the first time she'd needed Charles for something in months. Charles didn't particularly like Rick Mitchell—he was loud and laughed at his own jokes. He'd participated in sit-ins back in college and mentioned it too often. Charles laid down his magazine. He needed to get out of the house, one way or another. "Let's go," he said.

It was a long walk, but they didn't mind. Families were out everywhere. The snow fell in flurries now. Veda and Amy hopped like jackrabbits into powdery snowdrifts, buried almost to their waists. The snow was too soft, too fresh, to pack into snowballs. Instead, they squealed and splashed fluffy powder at each other like kids at the lake in summer.

"Easy does it, Ames," Rick said.

"Darn, I forgot the camera," Karen said.

Alice said nothing, she looked away. She did that—looked away—whenever Veda laughed.

Alice and Karen walked ahead together, and Rick and Charles followed, dragging sled and saucer. Rick tried to talk football, but in fact he didn't follow the sport too closely. The two men had nothing in common, except for their daughters, and that they were both fatherless at a young age. Karen had confided to Alice that Rick's father had drunk himself to death.

A plow drove by, spraying snow up onto the sidewalk. The girls screamed with delight. Charles admired their joy, while blocking out Rick Mitchell's too-loud laugh.

At the entrance to the park, Karen asked, "Which way?" To the east was an open field. To the west were woods and hills. The most popular area for sledding was farther north. But the girls were getting impatient, and they'd walked a long way already.

"If we go to the fields, it'll be you and me pulling like mules, buddy," Rick said. Charles didn't mind the idea of getting his blood pumping. "You girls want to fly like those Olympic tobog-ganers, right?"

"Yeah!" both girls shouted, though Veda had never watched tobogganing. Charles flashed her a look of mock irritation, and Veda pushed out her lips.

They turned up the west path and climbed the uphill road. Ahead, Charles saw two figures huddled together on a bench beneath a canopy of snow-laden oaks. The figures were familiar. One man wore a black knit hat and puffy jacket, the other a baker boy cap and gray overcoat. The man in the baker boy had his hand on the other man's shoulder. Their heads were bowed; they were praying.

It was Reverend Haywood and Dennis. As they drew closer, Alice saw them, too. She looked over her shoulder at Charles. Alice and Charles read each other's faces. Hers said, *Let's not do this now. Let's just keep walking.* Alice had never liked Dennis. Charles's face replied, *All right. Fine.*

They passed the bench and ascended the hill. When they reached the near top, Charles said suddenly, "I think I dropped something. Go on ahead. I'll meet you all there." He turned and jogged back down the hill before anyone could question or protest. Before he could catch Alice's glare.

The path had been plowed but was covered in two inches of snow, and beneath that was a sheet of ice. Charles jogged and skated, jogged and skated. He held his arms out, like the wings of an airplane. He'd done this as a boy—he and Dennis, on this very same path. When Dennis and Joe Haywood came into sight, Charles stopped. The two dark heads were still bowed. Charles had warmed up from both the climb and the jog; those two must be freezing, he thought. The reverend was not a young man anymore, and though he was "strong as an ox," by his own estimation, Charles didn't like seeing his dark cap turned to white under an inch of snow. What could be so important that they didn't go inside and sit somewhere warm? It was foolish, and it wasn't like Dennis; he hated the cold.

Charles assumed Dennis had come to the reverend about Sherisse. She'd taken up with a man five years younger, who made better money as a mechanic than Dennis did as manager of a Houlihan's. Their son, Lawrence, was staying with Dennis's mother. Dennis had been sinking to rock bottom, shakier and lower every day.

Finally they raised their heads. Rev. Haywood squeezed Dennis's shoulder with a large gloved hand. Charles continued down the hill toward them.

Dennis saw Charles first. He waved enthusiastically. It struck Charles as an odd gesture; Charles had gotten used to the bar-sitting, morose Dennis. In truth, his friend had always been a jokester type. But the gesture now was different; it was discomfitingly earnest.

"Yo, fancy meeting you here." They grabbed fists in their customary way. Charles eyed Dennis, who looked away.

"Reverend," Charles said, reaching out with both hands. Their greeting formed a brawny mass of leather and fleece.

Rev. Haywood stood and tipped his cap. Snow spilled to the ground like confetti. "Well," he said, spreading his arms, "it's just like the old days." He meant those Saturday afternoons when Dennis's and Charles's mothers had sent them to church to help clean out storage closets and pick up crumpled offering envelopes from the pews. In the springtime, Rev. Haywood had had them pull weeds around the hydrangeas and weeping cherry. This was when they were ten, or eleven, when they still listened to their mothers. "You were good boys then," he said. "And I believe you are good men now." It was the sort of sly admonishment—a subtle tough love—that church elders perfected. "How are you, son? And how is your wife?"

"We're just fine," Charles said.

"Well I suppose there's more to it—if I know anything about this life—but I'm glad to see you out here enjoying God's good earth."

Charles blew into his hands and shifted his weight from right leg to left. It was too cold to stand still, yet he was the only one fidgeting. "Alice and Veda are up the hill with some friends. They're sledding."

"That's wonderful to hear. The small joys. That's the road to healing."

Charles smiled weakly. He was waiting for Haywood to leave them, so he could ask Dennis what this was all about.

"The small joys," Rev. Haywood said again.

"Ain't y'all freezing?" Charles asked. It was always natural for him to talk like a thug when he was around Dennis; even more so with Dennis and the reverend.

"Warm-blooded," the reverend said. "Always have been. But I do need to get on back to the church. We've got coats to distribute. God bless you boys." He gave Charles an arm pat and Dennis a nod, then turned and walked briskly toward the park exit. Dennis and Charles both watched him until he was out of sight.

Charles rubbed his hands together and waited for Dennis to explain himself. It had been years since either of them had been to church—since before they enlisted. They'd never talked about it; Charles assumed they'd both outgrown it. Church was for the weak, for people so lost that all they needed in life was kindness and nothing else. Religion was for the older generation, like spats, and castor oil.

Dennis said nothing. He was still looking off in the distance.

Charles realized he had something to say, it was on the tip of his tongue. Something along the lines of, *Aw, D—not you, too?* First Alice, now Dennis. They were all surrendering their right minds.

But Charles didn't say it. He too said nothing, and this conveyed something unnatural between them. Dennis cleared his throat and looked over Charles's shoulder, up the hill. "You goin' back up?"

"Yeah, man. C'mon. We can run the girls back up when they come down. I ain't been to the gym since the snow started." Dennis nodded, and they jogged up halfway, then crossed through the trees and followed the high-pitched sounds of little girls in flight.

Afterward they all came to the house. Alice served Swiss Miss with mini marshmallows on top, and the men stood by the back door in a row, holding their mugs. Everyone's cheeks were glowing, they'd all gotten a good workout; even Rick had taken a couple of turns dragging the girls uphill. Karen took a turn sledding, and Rick tried to drag her up, too, but she jumped off and said, "Don't even try it." Alice watched mostly, though she clapped her hands when the girls went speeding down the hill. She played along with the girls now as they dipped their upper lips into their mugs and came back up with foamy mustaches.

Dennis had been quiet, and Charles had an urgent feeling—like he was losing his friend. Like everyone around him was being lost. There was something sinister out there, *getting* to everyone, and they were all giving in—acting helpless, like children. Mindlessly offering themselves up to be swallowed whole.

Dennis elbowed Charles. He said, "Hey man, I should get going. Need to shovel the driveway, straighten up the house. My moms is bringing Lawrence by tonight."

"I'll walk you out," Charles said.

On the porch, before Dennis reached the steps, Charles grabbed his shoulder from behind and pulled him around, a little too hard. "Yo, man, what's going on with you?"

Dennis put his hands up, showing his palms. "Yo, what's up? What I do?"

"*What I do?*" Charles mocked. "You ain't done nuthin, man. You ain't done shit. What's that old man feeding you? That bitch ran out on you, and for what? A fancy car and a Jacuzzi bath? You ain't done *shit*, you hear me? Don't let that old man tell you different."

"Whoa whoa, take it easy. It ain't like that. Reverend Haywood, he just . . . I got myself into this."

"*Sherisse* got you into this."

"No man, listen. Just listen. I lost it last night. I met up with Teddy over on Fourth. I bought some skag offa him, and then, I dunno. Then I ended up over at Brother's."

"Brother's?" Charles shut up and listened now. This was going somewhere. Brother Dee's was a dive bar across the street from the church, and Dee's back room was where serious junkies went to shoot up. For decades, the reverend and the deacons had been going over there to witness—Fridays, every week. Every so often they fished someone out and cleaned him up for Sunday service; but soon enough, whoever it was would be right back on the other side of the street.

"Yeah, man. I was thinkin bout Sherisse and that motherfucker and their Lincoln fuckin Navigator; and about gettin *fucked up*. And when I got there, I thought, yeah, I'm as hopeless as these shitsacks. But it was Friday, you know, the day Haywood and the deacons come by. And they found me. The reverend grabbed me up by my armpits and took me back to the church. I slept there, and when I woke up, he gave me coffee and food. And then we got to talkin, and I was a mess, you know. Blubbering like a pussy. And he says to me: 'You knew where you were going. You knew where the Lord would find you. It was your cry for salvation.'"

Dennis pointed his finger in Charles's face, the way Rev. Haywood had pointed it in his. Charles put his hand up and leaned away from Dennis, as if he'd caught a whiff of something rancid.

But Dennis kept talking. "I'm sayin, there are other forces, you know. Bigger than us. Maybe it's the Holy Ghost; maybe it's somethin else. At some point, it just don't matter. When you're between living and dying, when you're drowning and someone pulls you out, are you really gonna ask for ID?"

It was unclear who realized first what Dennis had said—*drowning*—but both of them turned away. "Yo, man—I didn't mean . . ."

But Charles had already moved on to other things in his mind. It wasn't any use, thinking about the unidentified bigger force that did or did not pull someone out.

Charles was thinking instead of Hannah. Her *cry for salvation*.

She'd shown up at Veda's school. Maybe, like Dennis, just finding herself there. This part was true—that sometimes you found yourself acting without thinking. If you thought too much, you were bound to ask Why. Why do it, Why *not* do it? And when you couldn't satisfy yourself with reasonable logic, you didn't do it, whatever it was you had the instinct to do. *Why* mattered less and less. *Why* didn't mean the everything most people thought it did. So what if you knew why. So what if you didn't. Why was the boy dead; why were the rest of them alive.

Why did Hannah come to Veda.

Why think of Hannah now. Why not.

Dennis said, "I'll see ya later, man," and then he left the house. Charles went inside and closed the door behind him, already forgetting Dennis's story, but hearing in his head, like a mantra, *cry for salvation*.

7.

They would be home for Christmas Day, as usual. Alice went alone to a Christmas Eve service at All Saints; she did not ask if either Charles or Veda wanted to join her. She'd put on a skirt and stockings and her favorite heeled boots. She was eager and upbeat when she left, but returned spent, flattened. Sitting in his recliner, Charles watched from the corner of his eye as Alice pulled off each boot, dropping them on their sides by the stairs. She was asleep when Charles came to bed. Charles lay awake for a long time, first with the light on, then off. Alice didn't stir. She was really sleeping. Charles hoped that somehow this was a good thing: Alice hadn't slept soundly, not at night, for months.

Rhea and Marcus would be by for supper at five, after they'd had Christmas lunch with Marcus's mother. They'd all agreed on Chinese takeout from Peking Palace, which had been Benny's favorite. It was Veda who'd suggested it, two days before. Alice and Veda were making Christmas sugar cookies, and Veda was standing on a footstool stirring the batter. She spoke thoughtlessly, licked her finger after she said it. Alice was measuring out vanilla and said, "That sounds good," and Charles was confused for a moment. He'd been prepared for the air in the room to go tight and brittle. "Yay!" Veda said. Charles had stood outside the kitchen and listened. A woman and her daughter were making cookies. The mother was praising the daughter for using a rolling pin for the first time. Everything seemed very normal, and a wave of aloneness washed over him. He really didn't know who that woman was.

Early Christmas morning, Charles set to making breakfast. Pancakes and bacon. Later on he'd do eggs made-to-order. He'd hardly slept. It was still dark, but he was wide awake.

While the bacon sizzled on low, he walked into the parlor with his coffee. He'd gotten the tree and done his shopping before the storm. Alice and Veda had not done theirs. Veda was disappointed, said she'd been saving up her allowance; but Charles told her he didn't need anything, and she should save her money for other things, though he was hard-pressed to think of what. He and Alice had agreed to keep gifts to a minimum, which they both understood meant only gifts for Veda. But Charles didn't like the idea of the two of them watching Veda open presents by herself. So he bought Alice a few small things—a pair of bedroom slippers, some bath bubbles—and even bought himself a new shaver, from "Santa" (whom Veda had outgrown years ago, and Benny had never believed in).

Charles put Nat King Cole on Uncle Marvin's old turntable, switched the volume down to low. He never liked "The Christmas

Song," so he put the needle ahead to "God Rest Ye Merry Gentlemen." When it got to verse two, he could smell that the bacon was almost ready. *O tidings of comfort and joy, comfort and joy*, he sang along in his head. He turned to leave the parlor but paused as the King started on verse three: there was a dramatic modulation, an upswinging change of key. He wondered that he'd never noticed it before; playing the record low seemed to bring it out.

The bacon was crispier than he liked, but then Alice preferred it that way. Charles mixed the pancake batter and put it in the refrigerator. It was 7:15, the sun just coming up. It was going to be a clear but cold day. Once Veda came down, they'd get right to opening presents. Then breakfast. Then the whole day to pass before Rhea and Marcus arrived.

7:25. Charles pulled on a sweatshirt and laced up his boots. Grabbed his parka and hat. Wrote a note and tucked it under the plate of bacon on the kitchen counter: *Gone to Dennis's to check on him.* Dennis would be heading to his mother's today, to spend Christmas with her and Lawrence. Alice might or might not find the note strange. It was hard to predict these days.

The buses were running, and Charles caught one before long. There was no traffic, and just one other person on the bus, an old woman with big white eyebrows, head wrapped in a scarf. Once Charles transferred, it was only five minutes to the stop opposite Hannah's house.

The white Nova was parked in front. The porch light was on, and Charles guessed they were the sort to leave the light on all night. Nona used to scold the neighbors for doing that: *That porch light says, I'm afraid o' you, I know you out there. It says, I got somethin worth stealin.* Nona had a brother and a cousin who were both thieves and always liked to think she understood the mind of a hoodlum.

Charles sat in the bus shelter. He blew into his gloves. His sweatpants were thick but not windproof. He stood and jogged in place. No one was around. He sang under his breath while jogging. *Tidings of co-omfort and joy, comfort and joy, O-oh ti-idings of co-omfort and joy.* Charles had a nice singing voice, everyone always said so, though he hardly used it. He stopped jogging, stood flat-footed, at attention. He sang two more verses and then thought, Okay. Arms hanging at his sides. I brought my tidings. He slumped a little and sighed out white breath.

Then the porch light went off. Charles froze, as if a light had gone *on*, shone on him like a searchlight. The garage door opened. Soon-mi came out. She was wearing a brown coat and a knit hat. Behind her, Chong-ho followed. He wore a tweed baker boy cap, like Rev. Haywood's, gray parka, large owlish eyeglasses. Charles saw the two of them for only a moment before they got into the car. Soon-mi drove. Hannah was not with them.

Charles looked at his watch. Veda would be up by now, or any minute.

There was no question what he would do next.

The garage was open, but Charles went to the back patio, to the sliding door. He wanted Hannah to see him, fully, through the glass. He did not want her to wonder or be afraid of who was behind the knock.

At first he knocked softly. He knocked with his glove on, one knuckle. When no one came, he knocked again, glove off, two knuckles. He waited. There was a poinsettia on the table, a stockpot and a glass kettle on the stove; a large chef's knife and cutting board on the counter. The lights on both the oven and range were lit red, and a light cloud of steam rose from beneath the lid of the pot, which was covered but not fully. Charles raised his hand to knock again, but then there she was. *There she was.* Hannah seemed to appear from nowhere. It was like she had been there all the time, watching him. But Charles knew that was impossible.

Hannah wore those same purple warm-up pants, and a faded long-sleeved T-shirt. Her hair was tied up in a knot, the ends sticking out and radiating like sun rays. The frayed sleeves of her shirt hung over her hands, and she looked at him, straight on, no eyeglasses. Hannah's expression was inscrutable, but Charles decided she seemed sad. He felt that he was smiling at her but somehow wasn't sure if he was.

They stood there, both of them unmoving, for what felt like a long time. Charles pointed to the door handle. He could see that it was unlocked, the latch was down, but he waited anyway. Hannah nodded, and Charles slid the door open, stepped inside. Frigid air blew in behind him, and Hannah wrapped her arms around herself.

There she was.

There they were.

Something was happening. Charles saw Hannah, felt her, anew. She was no longer in his employ. But it was more than that.

She's very becoming, Alice had once said about one of her brother's girlfriends. She'd meant it sarcastically; the girl was an airhead, and a debutante. But Charles understood the word's meaning now. *Becoming.* Yes, Hannah was *becoming.*

The room had warmed again, it smelled of simmering meat and something else. A wonderful earthy smell; to Charles, a familiar smell.

Christmas morning, Charles thought. Comfort and joy. He did not think, My wife and daughter are at home, waiting.

Hannah spoke first. "They've gone to the airport," she said. Her voice was low, it did not startle the silence, but gathered it in. "To pick up James." Charles nodded. He knew that James was Hannah's brother, even as he wondered if she'd ever told him.

The airport. An hour and a half, two hours they'd be gone, at least. There was time.

Time for what?

Neither of them moved, though Hannah relaxed her stance. She fidgeted with her sleeves.

"Are you all right?" Charles asked.

Hannah didn't look up. "I thought you might come," she said.

Charles smiled at the indifference she was affecting now. Like they were young sweethearts; like she was playing hard to get. Probably she didn't mean to be that way, but that's how it came off.

"Is that why you went to Veda's school?" He played along, a light mock-scolding.

Hannah nodded, then straightened her back. It was a conscious movement, a self-correction. Her strong, narrow shoulders were now pushed back. She didn't want to play. She wanted to be serious.

Okay, then, Charles thought. He was willing to follow her lead.

"I missed her," Hannah said. "I missed . . ." Neither of them could fill in the blank.

But this wasn't a moment for uncertainty.

Charles's soldier's training had taught him—to know when, in the face of doubt, to be cautious; and when to push forward. "What have they . . ." *They.* He meant her parents, but it was unseemly to invoke them. He started again. "What's . . . happening?"

Hannah's shoulders relaxed again. She knew what he was asking. There was relief in just hearing the question. She said, "Do you like barley tea?"

That was the familiar smell. There was the meat, boiling, but there was also the tea. Every hole-in-the-wall, every side street in Itaewon, had smelled of it during the daytime. At first, the smell was awful, like medicine. But then Charles grew to like it. The smell of an open field, harvest-ready, in high summer. "Sure," he said.

They sat at the kitchen table with their hands cupped around their tea, like old friends recalling old times. Except they weren't—either of those things. The poinsettia was large and garish, the pot wrapped in shiny green tin foil. Charles nudged it aside. Then he said, "You're in some trouble."

Hannah nodded. "At first they were going to go talk to you—to Mrs. Lee. They were going to . . . I don't know . . . I guess in Korea when your family is shamed, when someone in the family disgraces, there is some kind of, like, a formal . . . a confession."

Charles listened. Part of him wanted to stop listening. It was unnerving, the hard silence of the Koreans. He felt he knew well their anger. Maybe guilt and shame were the flipside, the fuel. He drank his tea and stared at the lip of the cup, where his mouth had been. The poinsettia was a red flame blazing in the corner of his eye.

Hannah told Charles that her parents had decided not to go to Alice. Hannah knew, she said, that it was partly because they did not want to meet him, Charles. She said this, and then said that her parents were not racists, that wasn't it. It was "something else."

Charles laughed a short, sardonic laugh. Hannah continued. "They just . . . they're protective. They keep to themselves." Hannah's face was grave, her eyes flat. Charles didn't laugh this time. Hannah believed what she was saying. She believed there was *something else. Something hard to describe.* Charles did not say, *When you get older, you'll see it's all a lot simpler than you thought.*

"They're sending me away," Hannah said.

It was strange, how she said it. As if she was breaking the news to him. As if it was Charles who would suffer, who needed to be gently informed. It was strange, because it was uncanny—how right she was. She knew this news would break Charles's heart.

Good-bye, Mr. Lee.

Something gripped and yanked at Charles's gut; something was sucking the air out through a narrow passage, a life-sustaining opening that was beginning to close.

Hannah went on. "There's this man they know. His nephew goes to a boarding school. They know someone who helps people get their kids in. The money part, too. My swimming helped, I guess. What's the word, when they put you out of sight, because of shame? It's like in those scary fairy tales, like in old England."

Charles didn't know what word she meant, but he saw it like a cartoon now in his mind. He saw *Suk-joon Rhee, CPA,* in a wig and puffy pants; he saw a stockade. He saw, too, solitary confinement.

"Banish," Hannah said, with relief and an incongruous smile. "That's the word. They're banishing me."

Christ, Charles thought. That's exactly what they're doing. And she knew it better than they did. That in 1984, banishing was like something out of an outdated history book, or those Grimm Brothers books that Alice stowed in the basement.

That feeling was back, what Charles felt when he saw Dennis with Rev. Haywood in the park. The feeling of everyone near him being lost, of losing them—to something he couldn't name, or clutch, or kill.

"To where? For how long?"

"It's in Virginia somewhere." She didn't answer the second question. "They have summer school, too. The brochure looks nice."

Charles winced. He imagined the smiling faces, black white brown yellow. Everyone healthy and well-dressed in bright colors. The Army brochure had been like that, too. There was a Yongsan brochure that he and Dennis had looked at together after they'd gotten their assignment. They'd laughed at it, how corny and obviously staged it was. And yet hadn't they secretly wished and imagined it would be like that? Bright city lights and blue mountains and petite satin-robed women with long, silky hair?

"It's not so bad. I might as well go. They have a good swim team. Staying here is probably worse. If I stay, then . . ." Hannah shrugged.

If you stay, then I can look after you, Charles thought. I'll be there, in the parking lot at your school, at the rec center, every day.

But Charles said nothing. He stood up. The chair scraped rudely on the linoleum. He stood still for a moment while Hannah sat, looking into her lap. Then Charles started pacing behind her. He wandered into the next room—a carpeted room with wood paneling on the walls; the room where he'd seen the weary woman, perplexingly unaware, leaning back in the recliner. The couch was old, the upholstery worn. The coffee table was black lacquer with silver etching, an Oriental pattern. Everything was mismatched—color, style, American, Oriental. It was an ugly room and seemed intentionally so, and Charles hated it and walked back into the kitchen.

"Can I see your room?" he asked.

Hannah looked at him. He'd surprised her. He'd never seen that look before. Something changed then, Charles was taking the lead. It felt right to him. Something was happening. Hannah was becoming. Her feet were resting on the bar of the chair, her knees fell apart.

Charles moved toward Hannah and crouched next to her. Their faces were close, and Charles could see a small, pretty bump on Hannah's nose bridge he'd never noticed before. Her ears were pierced but she wore no earrings; there was a greenish smear around the hole on the right lobe. She had a brown mole on her left eyelid. She smelled of fruity shampoo and her breath was a little sour. Her bangs fell long and tickled her eyelashes.

Hannah blinked, three, four times in succession. Then she turned to face Charles—eyes wide open.

Charles was confused by how familiar and how strange Hannah looked to him; how, from the moment she appeared on their doorstep, months ago, he seemed to know her by her solemnity. *Haa-nah*, she'd said. That aspiration: wide, flat *a* like *apple*, like *hat*. That expansiveness, which Charles felt now in his chest. Hannah knew *him*, too. And she knew Alice, and Veda, and Benny. She knew them and knew what the tragedy meant, and did not mean.

Charles pushed away Hannah's bangs. Her mouth fell open slightly, and he saw the pale pink of her tongue.

Gently Charles took Hannah's wrists, and Hannah wrapped her arms around Charles's neck. He scooped her up from the chair, straightened from his knees and thighs to standing. She was light in his arms, but she was also solid—lean, thick muscle of her hamstrings and across her upper back. Hannah buried the cool skin of her forehead in Charles's neck. Again, as during the drive home from the shore, Hannah and Charles shared unspoken thoughts. They thought, No one understands, No one knows. They thought, Not everything that seems so important actually is.

They thought, We are alive, even though others are dead.

They thought, This is how it is.

And, There isn't much time.

They ascended the stairs. Charles did not think of what would come next. He did not see anything at all of the future. He only felt her, Hannah, her *becoming*. And she was. Neither of them wondered Why, about anything. Neither was confused, and everything seemed very simple. They knew each other. Hannah was solid in Charles's arms; she breathed on his neck, her elbows were snug around his shoulders. Was she afraid? Was he? No. They were not afraid.

This was how it was, and there wasn't much time.

What came next was as important as it seemed.

It was Christmas morning. Charles hadn't turned off the record player. By now it would be spinning the sound of silence.

BOOK TWO:
Les Bien-Aimés

Kenyon Street, NW Washington, DC
May 1988

He caught it on the second ring, but still it woke her up. She came downstairs, stuffy-headed from a cold she'd caught at school. She stood in the hallway, frowning. Rubbed her eyes. Barefooted, too-big purple pajama pants brushing the floor. Sniffle. *Where are you going?*

He hung up the phone—*Goddammit, D*—pulled on his sneakers. Laced them too tight. Go back to bed, he said. Emergency at work, I'll be right back. He tried to sound casual. He hated to leave her alone. She was thirteen, old enough, but still. It was 2 AM.

Alone. Her mother gone, to who knew where. Veda understood it was for real.

The emergency room on a Thursday night. Two shots to the chest. They said he drew first. *They*: Sherisse and her ex-con boyfriend. They said he was high. None of this unlikely. But his gun wasn't loaded. Hers was. Police said the boyfriend pulled the trigger. Doubtful; she'd have done it.

The boy, Lawrence, upstairs sleeping. (Probably why he took out the bullets, he had that much sense at least.) Dennis had come for the boy. What the hell did he think he would do? Run off with the kid, live on the lam? The bitch had won custody two weeks before. No visiting until he was clean and sober. They'd talked about it over the fourth beer at Barkley's. Charles knew his friend was in bad shape. But *this*.

He waits for Dennis to get out of surgery. His moms waiting too, stone-faced. The doctor comes out, says he's stable but not conscious. Edna Rhodes asks, He's all right, then? When will he wake up? Doctor says, Ma'am, there's been significant blood loss. The old woman is confused. Spell it out, Charles interjects. Doctor glares at him, knows he's not kin. Says, I'm afraid it's wait and see.

The born-again phase had lasted a year. Maybe it would have been better if it stuck. He didn't know. He never liked it and said so.

But *this*.

Laid up, all tubes and machines. Wait and see. God fucking dammit, D.

On the way home, he thinks, They were always heading here, weren't they. Only one of them would make it; wasn't that the statistic? One in two. Young men in their 'hood. Now Charles knew; he was the one. Alive. Free. Time to go. Not everyone gets the chance. Live the life you want. Erasure, all of it that came before. Survival. Opportunity. Restart.

1985–1988

1.

The old woman's prickly matter-of-factness did not put Alice off. She preferred it to the childlike compliance of patients at the home. Mrs. Oh was an elegant, haughty woman, more bark than bite. At eighty-seven, her hair was still thick, mouse-gray with wiry strands of silver, blown regularly at the hairdresser's. She wore long skirts, flowy cashmere tunics, silk-linen in summer. Monthly manicures and pedicures, skin porcelain under expensive creams. Wine-red lipstick, every day. It was not hard to imagine the smart, finely made contents of her shoe closet, though Alice came to Mrs. Oh's only in the mornings, when she wore satin house slippers.

It was a good job, as easy as they came, and well paid. Alice was thankful to Mr. Hong, the director at the nursing home, for recommending her to Mrs. Oh. Alice did not mind her former employer's pity.

The old woman did have her moods. "Useless," she liked to say, waving an age-spotted hand back and forth and referring to any number of things: arthritic fingers, her memory, her two sons and their expensive wives. She was a no-nonsense woman who evidently had stories to tell—something in the downturn of her eyes, the lines around her mouth. That she never told them seemed a source of strength; Alice took her cues. Though one day, when Alice said she had to leave early for her daughter's teacher conference, Mrs. Oh said, "You have a daughter?" Then she laughed, incredulously. "No, no. But you are alone, all alone, I can see. Like me."

Another woman brought food at midday. Occasionally Alice stayed for lunch; more typically, Mrs. Oh would lie down for a nap at eleven and Alice would slip out.

Alice's days churned, one into another. It was fall again. She had money in the bank, her own account now, and Veda was back to school. The apartment near Dupont Circle was above a pool hall and overlooked a string of gay bars and tattoo parlors. It was a strange neighborhood, people who didn't belong together. It would be fine for now. Alice had put down the deposit and didn't tell Charles for two weeks. Then, just before leaving, "It's month to month," she said. "Just for a little while. I'll be home in the afternoons and for dinner. Veda will hardly know the difference." This last part was true. Alice was gone to Mrs. Oh's before Charles and Veda woke up.

She'd packed a suitcase and one box. Some clothes, toilet items. A box of old photo albums. A folder full of letters (she'd been writing to Laila, and Laila wrote back—about artisan cooperatives and irrigation and trees). Alice did not in her mind connect the apartment with Rick Mitchell, but of course it was easier than him coming to the house on his lunch hour.

They were nothing to speak of, Rick's weekly visits. One restless summer evening Alice had gone to see Karen. She found Rick at home alone—drinking, unshaven. Karen and Amy had gone to Karen's parents in Connecticut after they'd argued. Rick told Alice this, told her too much, and then it happened. Clunky and sweaty on the family room rug, an itchy old thing.

He was older than Charles by a few years and wore a sweet aftershave Alice didn't like. But his body was soft and warm, and he took direction hungrily. He had a fat tongue and thick, slow fingers that he sometimes pressed into the outer edges of Alice's spine. Afterward he always showered, rinsed his mouth with Listerine, and Alice didn't mind. Sometimes, before getting up, Rick would want to talk—about Karen, or his dead father. Once, he said, "You and I, we have both lost someone important," and Alice asked him right then to leave. But the next time he came, Alice was apologetic. She wanted his warmth, needed his hunger. She demonstrated her remorse sexually, as she'd learned to do with Charles. Or maybe she'd learned it long before, she really couldn't remember. That time, Alice let Rick talk. It was fine as long as she didn't have to respond, as long as he kept her out of it. "Karen keeps telling me to go to a shrink, to work on my 'issues.' She wants me cured. She's a wonderful woman. It makes me hate her. Only people who've never been broken think that others can be easily fixed."

Mornings with Mrs. Oh. Coffee shops and mall food courts in the afternoons, where Alice wrote to Laila. She'd exchanged a few letters with Pauline, who'd married a Brit and lived in the English countryside. Three children, two dogs, chickens, horses, and pigs. They homeschooled and brewed beer. Neither had kept in touch with Suzanne.

Evenings on Kenyon Street, where Alice cooked from recipes on pasta boxes and soup cans, smiled and half-listened to Charles and Veda talk about their days. She washed the dishes and avoided going upstairs. Rick Mitchell once a week in her echoey apartment that always smelled of fried foods from downstairs. It was in her clothes, her hair; she grew used to it.

Alice's days churned, sometimes, it seemed, without her. Time passed. A year, two years. Charles worked long hours, got promoted. Veda's feet grew long and she shot up, taller than Alice.

Twice a week there was group. Here, Alice "worked out her grief." By the third year she'd become the longest standing member. It was a dubious honor; others had moved on, graduated. Callie, the leader, believed in capital-T Truths. *Death is a part of life* was one, and *The reality of death is what gives life meaning* its corollary. The others repeated these out loud, but Alice never did. It sounded to her too much like *You can't have your cake and eat it, too*, something her mother had started to say toward the end of her life. Also, *You make your bed, sweetie, and then you have to lie in it, so choose a firm mattress and the prettiest linens you can afford.*

The dreams started again. The old dreams, from when she was pregnant with Veda. Rick Mitchell shook her by the shoulder and said, "You were moaning and mumbling. *Don't go, don't go.*" Alice never told Rick about the dreams. She never told Callie, or Charles. The dreams were hers. They were what she had left. Alice dreamt of a boy who tried to come close, because he loved her and wanted to be with her. He tried, and tried again, but he was always just out of her reach. Always departing, disappearing, swirling away like refuse down a drain.

Every time she dreamt it, some piece of her went spiraling down into the same futile darkness. Alice wanted to chase the darkness. It was hers. All hers. The darkness and everything it consumed.

"What is it, Alice?" Callie asked when she came to group drawn and dark under the eyes. "Tell us how you're doing." Shut *up*, Alice wanted to say to Callie. Callie with her strapping sixteen-year-old son who stopped by to pick up car keys and waved hello to the group. Truths with a capital T. Here are some: *Nothing is really yours. Your best is nowhere near good enough. Bad things happen, things fall apart, good intentions turn to shit. You are not loving, or good. You are a pile of tired bones, heart like a toy chest—filled with moods and feelings that come and go, make loud noises and flash bright colors; then break.*

Sometimes Alice went for long drives. Once, on her way back into town, she found herself pulling off the beltway and driving to the V.A. Charles had gone there for minor things, but Alice had never been. She saw the sign and something made her turn off. She sat in her car with the engine running. After a few minutes, she parked and walked in. In the lobby she stood frozen. A petite woman wearing scrubs asked did she need help. Her eyes were unbearably kind. "I'm fine, no," Alice managed to say. Alice walked through the lobby to an atrium, where she could see into a courtyard. There were paved paths and a very green lawn and low purplish plantings. Orderlies wheeled patients around; a few men moved slowly on crutches or with walkers. Those in wheelchairs had all their limbs; those trying to get around did not. Alice sat on a bench and watched them through the glass for some time. She wondered: who was worse off, those trying to walk, or those being wheeled? She thought: I could watch them forever. But the sun began to go down, and the nights were cool now; everyone came inside, one by one. They re-entered the building on the other side of the courtyard, and Alice felt them moving away from her, leaving her. She hugged her handbag in her arms. She saw the frayed, hanging pant leg of an amputee sway back and forth as he made his way down the path. It swayed, loose and empty, and Alice began to weep. She wept as she drove home and never returned there.

Later, Alice wondered if that day at the V.A. had actually occurred. If the courtyard wasn't a mirage, or a nightmare. If she'd actually wept those tears. The days churned one into the next. Alice felt like an alien creature, living outside time, apart and alone; even when, especially when, she was among other people.

Another year went by. It was 1988: Sonny Bono was elected mayor in California, Cher won an Oscar, and scientists had genetically engineered a mouse. Alice wasn't sure anymore who was the alien, her or everyone else. One day in spring, Charles told her to pack and move all of her things. He didn't say why, or why now, just, *You've been gone a long time; so you should leave.*

2.

Soon-mi and Chong-ho saw Hannah off at the Greyhound station on a snowy January afternoon. Their car would not do well on wet country roads, they reasoned, and thirteen was old enough to travel alone. Hannah had one large suitcase and a duffel bag.

Soon-mi had knocked on Hannah's closed door, asked if she was almost ready; she said *Yes.* Then, *Will it be as cold there?*

Soon-mi said to the door, *I think so. Pack your naningoo. Always good to have it.*

They watched Hannah hand the ticket to the driver and board the bus. Soon-mi saw how Hannah looked the driver straight in the eye and said, *Thank you.* Then Hannah disappeared down the aisle behind tinted glass and Soon-mi left the boarding area. She wandered the parking lot looking for the white Nova—a red Bronco blocked it from view—and once she found it pulled around to the front of the station. Chong-ho was waiting, hat covered in large fluffy snowflakes. They drove away and turned left at the first intersection, while the bus came up just behind and turned right.

It was dusk. The days were getting longer, but it didn't seem so. They stopped at a diner. The previous summer, when Hannah had started coming home later from Alice Lee's house, they went out like this a few times, the two of them. Once in a while, not often, Chong-ho craved a hamburger and French fries. Soon-mi usually ordered spaghetti or baked chicken. Tonight she ordered from the breakfast menu, steak and eggs, and Chong-ho had fish and chips. Soon-mi ate Chong-ho's pickles, and they shared a hot-fudge sundae for dessert.

Hannah called later that evening. There was a shuttle that picked students up and brought them to campus. She had no particular impressions to share. Before they hung up, Soon-mi said, *Make sure stay in touch with your brother.* James had a job lined up in Seattle and would be moving in June.

They did not hear from her. In the spring James told his parents that he'd tried to get Hannah a summer internship at his company. But Hannah said she preferred to stay at the school, where she would work part time for room and board. Something about an independent project in French, and swim training, James said. Chong-ho and Soon-mi didn't ask questions.

The lilac bushes finally bloomed after fours years; the *Baptisia* grew vigorous and full in back, an indigo oasis around the patio. Soon-mi and Chong-ho worked in the garden every day, and Soon-mi brought cut flowers for the residents at the nursing home, zucchini and eggplants for the staff. The long winter was finally over.

Within weeks of Alice Lee's resignation back in November, they all knew what had happened: the drowned boy, on Hannah's watch. It was enough, these two facts together, to generate a radius of silent pity around Soon-mi. But then, the boss's wife, while searching the drawers of Alice's old desk for paperwork, found a family photo. Charles Lee, everyone soon learned, was a black man.

The radius grew wider; there were whispers now. How could Soon-mi not have known, all those months? Or did she? Which was worse? Soon-mi kept her head down and continued to care for her patients.

Neither she nor Chong-ho had given thought to how others would perceive Hannah's departure, but Soon-mi understood soon enough that the act of sending their daughter away (word spread via the accountant, Mr. Rhee) had gained them exoneration. The boss and his wife, the other nurses, they were easy and friendly with

Soon-mi now. *You did the right thing*, is what the friendliness meant. *A bad seed is not your fault, it is your misfortune; you have managed your shame appropriately.*

Time passed. Chong-ho turned sixty-three and took early partial retirement, a phase-out plan they called it. Two afternoons a week now they strolled three miles, to the park and back, arms locked. Like a couple much younger, or much older, than they were. Days upon days—months, then years—passed in relative placidity. They were together, as always, together, alone. They'd managed their shame appropriately.

James was doing well in Seattle. The pictures he sent of his new condo showed emerald-green lawns, beige carpeting, a ceiling fan, and a terrace where he kept his bicycle. They had not visited, but next year they would; he was engaged, the wedding would be the following summer. James's fiancée was from L.A., her name was Grace. Her father owned two designer handbag stores, and her uncle was a minister. Hannah had been gone two years, and James had not seen her. She wrote him occasional postcards. Hopefully she would come to the wedding, too, he said, though he did not actually sound hopeful.

One cool morning in the spring of 1988, on the way back from the park, Soon-mi mentioned to Chong-ho in passing an errand to the post office. She wondered aloud what sort of delivery system they had at Hannah's school; it had been three years, and she had never before sent a package there. Hannah would be graduating in June. James's wedding was coming up now, in July, but Hannah had not said whether she would be there.

The line gets long after noon, Soon-mi said. Chong-ho said nothing. He looked up at the bright white sky and watched gray clouds gather, thickening.

Soon-mi had begun knitting a poncho in the fall. Two shades of red with gray and purple flecks, a soft angora wool blend. She knitted in fits and starts. Finally she finished, but here it was late spring, too warm to wear. Well, she would send it. Autumn would arrive soon enough. Also in the box were wasabi beans, seaweed chips, dried spicy squid, powdered ginseng for tea. At the last minute, she'd scooped Chong-ho's special growing mix into a Ziploc bag, tucked in a few seed packets. Only later did Soon-mi realize she'd sent last year's leftover packets instead of the new ones. Probably the seeds would germinate, but still, she felt an old frustration. An off-pitch twang inside of her.

Standing in line at the post office that afternoon, Soon-mi thought, Does she still like spicy foods? What has she been eating? And what is she going to do with plant seeds anyway? Hannah had never shown interest in gardening.

"Excuse me," a terse, impatient voice behind Soon-mi said. A moment later, a poke on her shoulder. She turned to see a chin raised, pointing toward the gap between her and the next person. Beyond that were at least ten more people.

Only one clerk was on duty. No one knew why. There'd been much grumbling and sighing, which Soon-mi did not, like some, find comforting or cathartic. "Sorry," she said softly, and shuffled forward with her box.

Finally it was her turn. "Any perishables or combustibles?" the clerk asked. He was a small Indian man, with tinted glasses. He had a high forehead and sunken cheeks. He appeared to Soon-mi disturbingly skull-like. She shook her head no. Perhaps the growing mix was perishable, but she didn't mention it. "Any stamps for you today, madam?" He must be new, she thought. So polite. This was why it was taking so long.

"No, thank you," Soon-mi said.

The clerk nodded. "Parcel post, $8.50. Priority, $18.25. Overnight, Monday arrival, $43." He said the last figure like a grand finale: FOR-ty three DOL-lars. He raised his black-caterpillar eyebrows. She couldn't see his eyes through the tinted lenses. A drop of sweat trickled down his skeletal forehead, and Soon-mi felt suddenly warm herself. The box packed with winter clothing and desiccating dirt (why hadn't she double-bagged it?) and foreign foods was ridiculous. A wave of futility washed over her.

"Just . . . the regular mail," she said.

He nodded. "Cash or credit?" Soon-mi handed the clerk her card. The clerk printed and stuck the postage label on the box.

On her way out, eyes lowered, Soon-mi did not see the brassy-haired woman standing in line. "Madam, Mrs. Lee," a sing-song voice called from behind the counter. "Your credit card, Mrs. Lee." The woman in line looked up from her tattered paperback and turned her head. But Soon-mi didn't see, or hear. She kept her eyes on her feet and walked out the door, into the gray afternoon. The clerk had to follow her, waving the card. The other woman's gray eyes opened wide, then wider, as they tracked the other Mrs. Lee out the door.

On the way home, Soon-mi turned in to the parking lot at White Flint Mall. She did not like to come home in an unsettled state and wanted to clear the embarrassing episode from her mind.

It was the expensive mall, where she and Chong-ho sometimes wandered on rainy or cold days, or during heat waves in summer. Soon-mi went occasionally by herself, when Chong-ho thought she was grocery shopping or working overtime. She parked in the covered lot and did not notice the black clouds gathering. If she had, she might have hurried home to help Chong-ho put away his shovels and tools. Instead, Soon-mi entered the mall at the ground level of Neiman Marcus. She liked to wander this store in particular, because it was never crowded, not even on weekends. There were not many places where Soon-mi felt she could truly escape, but this was one of them. It was for her like entering a dream, where she forgot herself completely; where the gleam and sparkle were more real than her gloom—than echoes and twangs haunting her. The salespeople and perfume girls knew she would never buy anything, and yet they did not let on: the place was too high-class for that. The perfumes here were light and fresh, the scent of perpetual spring, exotic flowers like plumeria and freesia. Soon-mi liked to finger the cool silk of richly colored blouses, the velvety cashmere of gloves and sweaters. In home furnishings on the top floor, she sometimes sat down in a plush armchair or recliner for fifteen minutes, half an hour—just reposing, beholding the vision of tranquility. She could not have named the music playing quietly overhead, but if she were to hear one of those songs elsewhere she would surely recognize it. It might summon her back into the dream, like a hypnotist's trigger.

No, on second thought: if she heard the music anywhere else, in the real world, it would only ring an atonal key. This world was apart from the other, a delicate mirage.

After wandering clothing and shoes, Soon-mi returned to the ground floor. She was thinking of James now. There was a brief time, during high school, when he'd had some trouble, fell in with the wrong friends; but he'd outgrown it, gotten back on track, and now he lived in a nice community called Mercer Island. It was, in fact, an island, right there next to the city. There were such islands off the coast of South Korea, but they were primitive places mostly, hillbilly backward places. Or else exotic and tropical, mainly for tourists. Where James lived was simple and serene.

Soon-mi approached one of the jewelry counters. She squatted to peer inside the display case. Suddenly a woman's midsection came into view, a gold-link belt hanging low on bony hips, around a stretchy black dress. "May I help you with something, ma'am?" Soon-mi stood to see a petite woman with a pixie hairstyle; her little-girl's voice matched her perfectly.

Soon-mi froze but did not break eye contact with the salesgirl. She stared into the girl's green eyes, not seeing the girl but something else; then Soon-mi pointed, her eyes following her finger. "That one," she said. It was a men's Rolex, silver and gold. The salesgirl slid open the display case and reached in to take out the watch. She held it out to Soon-mi, loosely draped over her wrist; and Soon-mi felt her eyes grow wide like a child's. It was exquisite. It was perfect. The girl was saying things about the watch, its features and what sort of gold and what sort of silver, but Soon-mi was not listening. Neither did she heed the $9,000 price tag, which she saw and did not see. She just knew the watch was something good, something solid, it would last and last; and James would know that she wanted this lasting goodness for him. He would know without doubt or confusion: the watch would always be proof. Soon-mi nodded every time the salesgirl asked her a question, until the girl was putting the watch in a box and wrapping it in tissue paper. Meanwhile, Soon-mi floated to the other side of the counter, where she saw a sapphire pendant, an oval, like an elegant lady's manicured fingernail, surrounded by tiny diamonds. It was a deep indigo blue, like the endless sky on those cold winter nights at the base of Jiri Mountain after the war; when they lived off the land in the Quonset hut they'd built with their own hands. The diamonds were just like the stars on those cold, clear nights. James had been born during that time. They'd laid him down under the window that looked up at those stars.

Grace. Her daughter-in-law-to-be was named Grace, and Soon-mi could see in her mind a pretty girl named Grace with this midnight sky hanging from her pretty neck. They would be so happy, James and Grace, and these gifts would be the grand finishing touch to that happiness. Soon-mi pointed to the pendant, and soon the salesgirl was bending down behind the counter to find a velveteen box; then lining with red tissue paper a small shopping bag of gold and pearl. The corners of the paper fluttered over the bag's edges like flames. Soon-mi watched the girl, whose back was to her, as she placed each of the two jewelry boxes into the bag.

And then, all at once, knowing what came next—what the girl would say when she turned around, the amount she would utter, the pale, terrifying palm she would hold out—Soon-mi woke from her dream. Faster than the girl could turn and look up, faster than she could catch Soon-mi's panicked, mortified eyes, or her hunched figure shuffling away, Soon-mi was gone.

3.

February 6, 1985

Dear James,
I picked this one from all the postcards at the campus store because from above you can see the huge forest, and the campus looks small. It doesn't always feel like that, but when I

remember, I feel better. It's not so different from before, really.
You don't have to worry.

—Hannah

Hannah knew she was serving out a sentence. What it meant was that there was an end date. In the meantime nothing was unbearable. She had no idea where she was, what sort of place she'd arrived to. It was thus easy, finding her way: French class and swimming, the familiar things. She formed a simple schedule around these.

There were acres of woods a half-mile from the school, and she went for walks. She discovered a wetland area where a colony of white-petaled flowers with blood-red centers bloomed, and she wondered if they were related to Claudine's rose mallow. She never found snakes, well-behaved or otherwise, though she kept looking. Hannah loved, like Claudine, her aloneness in those woods.

In general, she kept to herself. She read and re-read *Claudine à l'école* and looked for signs of intrigue among the girls and her teachers; alas, *rien*. There was a quiet girl from mainland China who tried to befriend her, but with her slouchy shoulders and dry, blinky eyes, she was no Luce—and anyway, by the second year, the girl was teasing up her bangs and saying *ya know* and *nuh-uh* like everyone else. Hannah became friendly with the staff of the sports center and the language lab; she sometimes stopped in for tea with her dorm counselor, Ms. Marcioni, who taught physics and coached cross country and introduced Hannah to old movies like *The Apartment* and *Sullivan's Travels*. Sometimes they baked cookies together, with Bob Dylan or Joni Mitchell playing in the background.

Hannah's swim coach, Mr. Modeste, was an ex-Marine and doubled as the coach for the nearby military academy. He was tough, and Hannah liked that. In the middle of February, though, Coach Modeste came down with pneumonia, and his son, Omar, took over practices for two weeks. At the end of the first week, they had an away meet two towns over. On the bus, Hannah sat alone in the second row, behind Omar. His head was shaved bald underneath his thick wool hat, and his skin was very light—lighter than Hannah's—but with lots of tiny chocolate freckles across his cheeks and wide nose. Omar sat sideways in his seat, looking out the window across the aisle, and Hannah crossed her arms over the seat back and leaned her head on her stacked forearms. It was an icy, slushy day. Omar said, "Nervous?"

Hannah raised her head and shook it no. "I heard they're no competition."

"That's probably true," he said. "But what does that matter?"

Hannah smiled. She liked Omar's answer. He said it like a dare. He was sucking on a green lollipop. Hannah guessed probably he and his father didn't get along. He seemed about twenty-five, definitely not as old as thirty.

Hannah said, "I don't get nervous. I mean, this is one thing I don't get nervous about. I just get ready." She stretched out her hands by her knees then made fists, twice, three times.

Omar smiled. He liked her answer, too. He leaned in and was about to say something conspiratorial when the bus swerved and fishtailed. The driver held on tight at 3 and 9 and pumped the brake while the bus skidded back and forth, back and forth. The girls screamed at multiple pitches. Omar grabbed both Hannah's shoulders and pressed his forehead, hard, into hers. In a few moments, the driver regained control. Luckily there'd been no other cars within slamming distance.

"Are you okay?" Omar's eyeballs were an inch from Hannah's. His breath was ragged and smelled of cigarettes and sour apple.

Hannah nodded.

Omar stood up. "Everyone okay?" His voice boomed and shook at the same time.

Hannah didn't turn around. She heard mumbles and swearing, and she studied Omar's face as he scanned the rows: his mouth twitched at one corner, and the whites of his eyes made a moat around dark irises.

They arrived safely, and they won the meet, a clean sweep. It was decided that the roads were too dangerous for night driving, so the girls were given sleeping bags and would spend the night in a common room of one of the dorms. They had dinner at Friendly's, and Hannah sat with Omar in a two-seater booth. The girls were used to Hannah gravitating toward adults; the waitress was on her third shift and barely looked up as she took down orders.

Hannah ordered a tuna melt, and Omar ordered a Reuben. When the food came, Hannah leaned forward with her chin out and said she'd never had one of those. Omar picked up half and held it out to her; she wasn't sure if she should bite right out of his hand or take it with her own. It was a big sandwich. He pulled it back and cut off a quarter, then slid it to her on a napkin. When Hannah bit into it, she thought it might be the strangest, and most delicious, thing she'd ever eaten.

"You have good form," Omar said, leaning back with his arm across the red pleather. "Very smooth and patient. And still with speed. Not something you could have learned, just natural."

Hannah nodded and chewed her second bite of Reuben. She was easily the best swimmer on the team, and she knew it. After finally swallowing, Hannah said, "So, what do you do normally?"

Omar laughed. "You're funny. For a quiet girl, you get right to the point." He waved down the waitress and ordered a coffee. He pointed at Hannah to see if she wanted one. She considered, then nodded. "At the moment, I do nothing, really. I do this. I tried the school thing. A few times. Didn't work out."

Hannah lowered her chin solemnly. Then, "Where does your accent come from? Coach doesn't have it." It was the word "this," which he pronounced *thees*.

"Ah, good ear. Hardly anyone notices anymore. Can you guess? Same place as my name."

Hannah thought hard. She wanted to get it right. She had a feeling the answer would be satisfying. "It's not French. But it sort of is. Is it like . . . the Middle East?"

"Close. Morocco. My mother was Moroccan. I lived with her most of my life."

"In Africa?"

"For a few years. Mostly in Brooklyn."

"Where is she now?"

"She? Died. A year ago. That's when I came to live with my father. It's only temporary, though."

"How did she die?" The waitress brought the coffee and looked back and forth between the two, then turned and walked away. Hannah wrapped both hands around her mug. The coffee smelled bitter and a little chocolaty.

"It was a car accident. Actually. Her boyfriend was driving. I was in the backseat." He stretched his neck to one side and pointed. A thin raised scar the color of ash ran along his hairline from temple to jaw.

Hannah could still feel the sharpness of bone on bone in the middle of her forehead; she was sure there was a red mark there. Neither of them spoke for a moment. Hannah almost said, "I was with someone when he died, too." But she didn't. She knew that to say it would do no good and would not be satisfying. She thought probably he already knew; she understood that people could recognize each other without words.

The bus dropped them off at the dorm. Omar and the driver would stay at the Motel 6 and be back for them in the morning. Hannah was the last one off, and she felt wrong, leaving. Omar stood and nodded at her; he stuffed his hands into his pockets and smiled. She walked by him, then slowly down the steps, like a prisoner, back to serving out her sentence. She did not say *Goodnight*, because that felt wrong, too. It would have been nice to stay up late with Omar, on the bus. She had the sleeping bag. They could share. Hannah wanted to hear about Morocco; maybe Omar could tell his stories in French. That wouldn't happen, though; and if it didn't happen tonight, it would never happen. Coach would come back to practice; Omar would leave town. That's how it was. How things were. It didn't matter that Omar had seen her body and known her—her natural form and strength. Or that his great fear was imprinted on her skull, right between the eyes.

Hannah pinched her face as she left the bus. For the first time she felt how gravely the wrongnesses were muddled. She'd do her time, but she should keep her head straight about it. Hannah kept on and descended the steps—one, two, then down onto the icy black pavement that looked swampy under the street lamp. She stood there a moment before following the girls to the common room. She breathed white winter breath into the yellow light. Hannah felt Omar watching her, but she did not look back.

In the late spring of that first semester, there was an especially lonely time when Hannah called Monique Glissant. She had a small card on which her teacher had written her phone number. On Hannah's last day, Madame had handed Hannah the card, saying, *Tu peux m'appeller, quand tu veux—when you are in need.* She'd looked at Hannah inquiringly. Her look said, *What has happened to you, what is happening?* Hannah took the little card and said, *Merci, Madame. Je vous remercie.* She was not avoiding the inquiry. She simply did not know what to answer.

When she finally called, Hannah did not know if, or of what, exactly, she was in need, but Madame seemed to understand. They spoke regularly from then on, always in French, and thus in the way of communication that lacks adequate vocabulary, both vague and intimate. *Oui, je suis contente, mais je pense beaucoup. Rien ne me manque mais il manque quelque chose.* The school's advanced classes were too easy, so Hannah made up an independent study, reading through Colette's works and translating short chapters and stories. On her dorm-room wall, by her bed, where other girls had pictures of Patrick Swayze and Rob Lowe, she had a 5x7 postcard that Madame Glissant had sent her—the actress Polaire as Claudine, sailor-suited with cropped hair and smoky eyes.

There was summer school, but it cost an additional tuition. Instead Hannah worked in the language library and saved up. They let her stay in the dorm with paying students in exchange for collecting the garbage and cleaning the bathrooms, and she could use the pool in the early mornings. After work hours and on weekends, Hannah sometimes took the bus into town, especially when she craved a juicy cheeseburger or a Reuben sandwich. At the diner, she sat at the counter, sometimes with a book, sometimes with a few postcards and a pen. She wrote to James, and twice each to Teresa and Raj. It was interesting to try to say something in the small space of a postcard.

By summer's end, the waitress at the diner knew to bring Hannah coffee with lots of milk and two sugars, and she came around to warm her mug, pursing a smile and eyeing her. The girl sat there, drinking her coffee and staring into space, just like some of the old geezers she'd served for decades. One day she saw Hannah opening an envelope and unfolding a letter. Hannah sipped her coffee with extra care, as if tasting for either flaws or flavors, and she ordered a slice of cherry pie instead of her usual chocolate milkshake. The waitress left Hannah alone until the third refill, then asked, "You got a sweetheart in the service or something?" Hannah looked up, as if considering the question seriously—as if it were not a yes-or-no question. Hannah then folded her letter and asked for the check, very politely, and the waitress raised an eyebrow before turning away.

Hannah went home only during the Christmas break after the fall semester, for two weeks. In her parents' house, there was a feeling that nothing at all, and everything, had changed. During the days, Hannah went out by bus and Metro, to see foreign movies at The West End or to the botanical gardens looking for rose mallow. By silent agreement, the three of them ate dinner together every night. Soon-mi cooked multi-course Korean meals, and Hannah ate gratefully, like a guest. The familiar smell of barley tea filled the kitchen, and there was a poinsettia on the counter as always; still, there was something mysterious in their midst upon which Hannah felt she was intruding. Chong-ho and Soon-mi were to Hannah more contained than ever—like bottles of black ink, opaque and impenetrable.

Just before New Year's, Hannah went to Madame Glissant's in Friendship Heights. It was her first time visiting, but she felt at home. They looked at photo albums of a Parisian childhood, and more recent pictures of summers in Paris. They cooked buckwheat crêpes, and Monique made Hannah a Kir, which she sipped slowly and savored. Monique herself drank nearly an entire bottle of red wine. The alcohol made Hannah sleepy, her head pleasantly blurred. There was something she wanted to tell Madame. Or, was it something she needed to ask? The warm buzz from the Kir insisted both that the difference mattered and made it difficult to distinguish. Was it something about Claudine, maybe? *If my face looks younger than my age, my figure looks eighteen at least.* Or about Renée the dance hall performer, *La vagabonde? From the open lawns rises a quivering silvery incense. On such a winter morning as this, surely even in the full flower of adolescence I was neither more firm nor more supple nor more sensually happy* . . . It was on the tip of Hannah's tongue, whatever it was.

She'd felt this same thing that previous spring, the lonely time, when she first called Madame. Hannah had received a letter. At first she'd thought she wanted to tell about it, but then immediately she knew she didn't. In the end, she thought maybe what she'd wanted to express was simply her desire to keep talking to Madame, no matter where she was.

There had been more letters, over the summer and fall—the one she'd read at the diner was number three—and there would be many more to come. Neither their arrival nor their contents surprised Hannah. They were familiar somehow, and steady; reading them was like swim practice, the smooth middle laps before she had to push through fatigue. Hannah heard their warm woodwind tones in her ear more than she analyzed the words in her mind.

And yet, something was stirring in Hannah. She thought of bread-baking in home ec class—the dough rising, soft and yeasty and slow. Maybe she was being impatient, punching down the dough during the first rise with her urge to quiet the stirring. Hannah recalled the tangy aroma of the ballooning, fermenting bread; she inhaled deeply as if it were now filling Monique's living room.

Monique's eyes were drooping. She had a contented smile on her face, a flush in her cheeks; her feet were curled up under her, feathery black tresses brushed her shoulders. Hannah finished the last of her Kir in a gulp. White heat ballooned in her chest and warmed her cheeks. She did not want to lose Monique to sleep, because she was not ready for the evening to end. She blurted, "Are all French girls like Claudine?" She could see the words in the air, like a spy code on a ribbon.

Monique became thoughtful. She sighed, hugged an embroidered pillow, a gift from her Lebanese grandmother, and laid her head in the crook of the sofa's arm. "Well," she said dreamily, "you wouldn't ever call Claudine typical; or Colette for that matter. But the French recognize themselves in both of them. Colette is the kind of romantic we understand. For us, love is more . . . aesthetic, you could say, than moral. There is this great difference we feel with the Americans: you have so many wrong kinds of love." Monique closed her eyes. She searched for the simplest words, for the girl's sake. "I think Colette would put it this way: if love is truthful, it is beautiful. If it is beautiful, it is right. That is all there is to it." The wine had loosened Monique's tongue, and her heart was warm and full. Without the wine, she might not have continued: *"Et bien, le vrai amour peut sembler tout tort."* True love can appear all wrong.

These last words were half-slurred; Monique drifted into sleep. Hannah was wide awake, her thoughts glowing and buzzing like June bugs. There was some wine left in the bottle, two swigs worth, and Hannah took them. The fruity acid taste made her think of wetlands and garden snakes. In her mind Hannah began mapping the Metro route to Kenyon Street. It was not at all a direct route. It was almost midnight. The letters came again into her mind. Not the words, but the bright white paper—always just one sheet, folded into perfect thirds, written on one side. The handwriting was small and neat with wide spaces between the lines. Warm and steady in her ears—a gentle harmonic line threading through her own internal music.

Monique snored softly; her eyes opened then drooped. Hannah spoke again, in a forthright voice, as if performing a monologue. "My teacher at school didn't like me reading *La Vagabonde,*" she said. "She said it was not appropriate for a freshman independent project. So I read it during the summer. It's funny to wonder what she meant." Was it that Renée, once a promising authoress, was now, after her divorce, *une dame seule qui a mal tourné*? Or was it something about being "sensually happy"? *Shy senses, normal senses . . . slow to rouse but slow to quench—in short, healthy senses.* Hannah wondered if the teacher meant they were the same thing—a lone woman who made a "bad turn" and one who had healthy senses.

The following spring, when she had to write an essay to go along with her translations, Hannah wrote: "Sidonie Gabrielle Colette was a woman who loved everybody she was meant to love—men, women, boys, girls, dogs and cats. She had many, many loved ones." Hannah did not write *des proches*—meaning kin, the people who are close by—but instead *des bien-aimés*: literally, the loved ones, the ones she well-loved. Hannah wrote: "Colette died alone, an old woman with her butterflies and baubles. She lived truthfully and beautifully." It sounded right to Hannah. The loved ones. *Les bien-aimés.*

4.

She had been gone three months when Charles began to dream of Frank. By then he felt how Hannah was disappearing from him. The loss was severe; it was too much to sort out with thinking alone. He bore it like a maiming, an amputation—the twitching of something you feel is there that isn't.

Charles believed that if Hannah came back, if he could just see her, watch over her, he could preserve it. Dig into it. Make it real. Whatever it was. All Charles knew was that it was something, and now it was gone. Going. Gone.

He heard nothing from Hannah, or about her. How could he, why would he? Once, he thought about how Veda might again surprise him and say that Hannah had come to see her. But that didn't happen.

In his dream, Charles saw Frank's face: thick eyebrows, bottom teeth that showed big and crooked when he smiled; nose wide and flat with a point at the end like . . . just like the boy's. Benny's. The face came with a voice, deep and smooth like molasses, but in that dreaming state Charles was never able to make out words. Frank did not exist in Charles's memory, he'd disappeared from their lives right after Charles was born. Charles had never even seen pictures—Nona did not allow it, destroyed every one—and yet he knew, without a doubt, that the dream image was true. The face, the voice. When he woke, Charles knew he'd dreamt of his father.

The knowing was always followed by thoughts of Hannah. It was an eerie layering of unrelated pictures and sensations. What did it all mean? It was too much to sort out with thinking alone.

Charles and Alice went on—days piling on top of days, then weeks, months. He thought of Benny sometimes, but there was no sadness. His thoughts were infrequent and uncomplicated—shrugging sentiments, echoes of his grandmother and the church folk, who'd drop their chins and say, *Weeehhhl* in the face of all things unspeakable. Nona would never shrug, though. She'd shake her head and squint her eyes at the needle she was threading or the newspaper she was reading. What was she really thinking—when they lost Uncle Ernie. When the Lang girl next door was found dead—violated, her face kicked in—in back of the Greyhound station. Nona never wept. Not that Charles ever saw, anyway. Was she sad? No, not sad. Something, but not sad.

Weeehhhl, Charles thought. The boy came, and then he went. No guarantees on him. If Alice could hear the thoughts underneath these . . . *Wasn't heading no place good, anyways.* Thankfully, she could not.

What Charles hated to think of—he did once, and then never again—was the drowning itself. It took three minutes, they said. Three minutes. Your mind crazy with panic, water devouring your air. Three minutes was too long. Thirty seconds was too long. It was no way for anyone's child to die.

Charles didn't know exactly what Alice felt when she thought of Benny. He had an idea that when you thought and felt something all the time, you really didn't think or feel it at all.

One day Alice said she would begin caring regularly for an elderly woman with diabetes near Great Falls. Soon after that, she took an apartment; said she wanted to "try it out." She would come home for Veda in the afternoons and evenings. They would barely know the difference. Charles couldn't argue that.

The dreams came on, and Charles began thinking of Hannah Lee every day. The twitching, her absent presence. Then one day he decided *Enough with the thinking*; he wrote a letter. As soon as he finished writing it, he didn't think of her for a week. Then Charles wrote another letter, and it went on like that. He found that he could put Hannah out of his mind by writing to her. The letters were short, and there wasn't much to them: he wrote about the day-to-day, his passing thoughts. Somehow the agitation quieted. He sat at his desk when he wrote, always around 2:45, when she'd be coming out of school. The writing absorbed Charles—the short, simple letters still took concentration—so much that he didn't notice Bart Sheridan watching him.

Charles didn't dare send the letters. He'd file them away, and then a few days later tear them up. The ritual just evolved: write, wait, trash.

Spring came, and with it something lazy and sour in the air. Charles realized that he was forgetting Hannah. Forgetting the *it*. The writing hastened the forgetting, as if each word turned substance into fog. He'd long forgotten how she felt in his arms, her slender, solid body opening up to his. When he tried to remember, Charles couldn't keep the images and sensations from melding with the magazines that lay around in the men's room stalls at work (sometimes hidden beneath a newspaper, just as often out in the open); and this sickened him profoundly.

The days grew longer and hotter. Charles brooded. Then he became frightened. Bart Sheridan watched Charles flick his pen at his desk, clench his jaw. One day, at 2:45, Charles went to the high school. He hadn't thought too hard about what lie he'd tell, but it came easy: she was their babysitter, he owed her last wages, he said.

He really shouldn't have let it go this long. The secretary was young, and new, that was lucky; maybe she'd been a babysitter herself not so long ago. She smiled, looked in her file and gave him the name and address of the other school, where they had sent Hannah's transcripts. Charles went straight to the post office, addressed and stamped his most recent letter, and mailed it.

May 1985

I've only ever written letters to my sister, back when I was stationed in Korea. She wrote long letters with news of the family and the neighborhood. I wrote back short bits, usually half-truths, to spare her what it was really like. I remember sitting down to write as if it were a class assignment. "Write 250 words in which you put the recipient's mind at ease." I was pretty good at it.

Time passes slowly these days. It's always the same amount of time—a day is twenty-four hours, a week is seven days. It's one of those mysteries. There's time, which never changes; and there's the experience of time, which is always changing. But without both, what would be the point. We're serving some purpose, by making something out of those ticks on the clock. When you're waiting, you can think about the fast-moving experiences and try to savor the slow ones.

At work time passes a little more quickly. The key is to give yourself just a little more to do than can easily be done. Or make it harder, create a problem to solve. That race against the ticking is what makes the time go faster; you've made the ticks scarce, more valuable. Maybe, if you're trying to make time pass a little more quickly where you are, you can give it a try.

When I have trouble sleeping, time goes more slowly. The nights are hard lately. It's these dreams I'm having. I see and hear my father as a man about my age. My father had a deep voice and thick eyebrows and a wide, pointed nose. I didn't know him, but that's what I feel sure I know about him.

And writing to you, I should say, is about trying to say things that are true. The assignment is, "Write a page in which you do your very best to tell the truth."

He drove away from the post office and felt instantly better. Then worse. He shouldn't have sent it. But why not? What had he written? Charles tried to remember his words. *Time passes slowly these days* and *At work time passes a little more quickly* and *My father had a deep voice and thick eyebrows and a wide, pointed nose.* The words were true. They expressed something simple and definite.

Expressed. Not *communicated.* It troubled Charles that he had no way of knowing whether his expression would be received, or how. The next few weeks Charles waited. For what? A response?

Then he began imagining Hannah reading the letter—just opening the envelope, unfolding the single page, and reading—and he felt better again. He held to that image and no longer waited for anything. He sent two letters during the summer, another in the fall. He sent one just before Christmas, too.

Frank disappeared from Charles's dreams. As mysteriously as he had appeared.

Time passed. Charles applied himself at work. It was true that by setting challenges, solving problems, day after day, you could pass the time quickly—months, a year, then another. He remembered what a good soldier he could be. The boss was pleased that he was improving things, tightening up. He got two title bumps in two years; Bart Sheridan chuckled when he heard. "I've had my share of those," Bart said. "You can be sure the paychecks haven't changed as many times." Charles couldn't help wondering how Bart managed the brand-new Coupe de Ville he'd driven up in a few months before, but he didn't care near enough to ask.

Alice lived in her own world now, and Charles asked himself if it had ever really been otherwise. By the time they'd lived apart nearly three years, certain things started to come clear—that he'd married Alice because of what it would have meant not to marry her, for one. Back then, he'd wanted *out* of the way of things—the way of the triflers he came up with, who ended up in the back room at Brother Dee's, or in the pews, or prison, or dead. The way of so many GIs who took up with local women then left them to take care of "accidents." The way of his father. Charles had married Alice and thought, This is a way out. A better way.

But it wasn't. He was young, and his ideas were too simple. There were other ways, could have been. It was Veda who Charles meant to do right by, and he still could have—done right, and done elsewise—if he'd just had more wits about him. He'd begun to see this when the boy came: Alice had stopped using birth control without telling Charles. He'd missed it, wasn't paying attention. When he realized, it was too late; they never spoke of it.

Veda was growing up now, literally—long-limbed and straight-backed. A dancer's body. Graceful, light. The other womanly developments were slower, and Rhea (who knew, without a word spoken, that Alice had left) said, *Count it a blessing.* There were long phone calls and boy-girl parties at the roller rink and tube tops that didn't look to Charles as innocent as they used to. But Veda was doing fine. She started junior high and made a new set of friends—black girls whose fathers were doctors and lawyers and listened to jazz. She took an interest in Uncle Marvin's old LPs, and for her twelfth birthday Charles bought her a hi-fi with turntable. She kept on with ballet, and jazz dance, and made the drill team. That year they also took in a yellow kitten that had mewed in the backyard for days, and Veda named her Josephine Baker.

One of the new friends had a single mother, Angela. Her daughter, Nicole, was head of the drill team, and Veda spent a lot of time at their place in Shaw. Angela was an executive assistant, taking night classes toward a business degree, and Nicole was in the ninth grade, two years older than Veda; there was an older brother who'd been in some trouble. Rhea suggested it would be a good idea to meet Angela. One Friday evening, instead of letting Veda take the

Metro, Charles drove to pick her up. Angela came to the door in a turquoise sleeveless sheath, sheer black stockings and no shoes, and a stopwatch in her hand. Her eyeglasses were perched on top of her head, and she was cheerfully out of breath. The girls had been practicing; she'd jumped in to help with timing as soon as she came home from work.

Charles and Veda stayed for dinner—they ordered pizza, and Charles paid—and when Nicole's brother, Malcolm, came home, he grabbed a slice, headphones on, nodded at Charles, then went to his room. "Grounded," Angela said to Charles, raising her smooth brown eyebrows. "At least he acknowledged you. That's an improvement."

"He took a plate *and* a napkin," Charles said. "I'd say you've got him on the right road." Angela smiled and held up her wine glass. Nicole rolled her eyes at Veda, who fought back a giggle.

The year Veda turned thirteen, Alice started coming only on the weekends. Charles preferred not to be there. Sometimes he went early to the batting cage or the gym, and then to the movies. Sometimes, when Angela wasn't studying, she joined for the movie. But Charles mostly preferred his solitude (and Angela preferred light comedies). There were places popping up in the neighborhood where you could sit all day and read a book and drink a strong coffee for three dollars, and no one thought any of that strange. Charles read Gerald Seymour and Chester Himes and Nelson DeMille and Ludlum, devoured them like he used to as a boy. It felt like the recovery of something, a revival. He looked around and saw that he was among complete strangers, hidden in plain sight, and he drew a kind of fortitude from the anonymous human energy around him. Charles felt clearheaded, and he remembered things.

He remembered the toy miner's lamp Rhea had gotten him so he could stay up reading until dawn. He remembered sitting in church, still high from smoking weed the night before, smiling stupidly and thinking he wasn't really there, a body in the pew; he was invisible, and invincible. He remembered taking first in night infiltration at boot camp; arguing geopolitics with his friend Kang over a stinky bowl of *boodae jigae*. He remembered who he was, before. It felt exhilarating, like a hundred tiny resurrections from the dead.

And throughout this time, Charles wrote to Hannah. He wrote about it all. In his way.

One day in the spring of '88, Bart Sheridan asked Charles to go for a drink after work. Say what? he almost replied. Eight years they'd worked together and never gone for a drink; what was this about. It was mid-season, the team was away that week, so what the hell, they took off early, went to a Holiday Inn in Largo. Leave your car, Bart said, and he drove them in the Coupe de Ville, maroon with cream leather interior. At the bar Charles ordered a beer, Bart had club soda. Bart asked Charles did he ever drink anything stronger, and Charles said not usually. What Bart told him next—what he asked Charles—made Charles laugh out loud, from his belly, as he hadn't in a long time. You *ain't* serious, Charles said. Bart said he was, dead serious, and Charles saw there was no doubting it.

Two months later Dennis's ex-wife shot him twice in the chest. Dennis survived but didn't wake up for weeks. By that time, Charles had said to Bart Sheridan, *All right, then. Tell me more. Tell me what's next.*

5.

Mrs. Oh was in one of her moods. Eyelids puffy like mushroom caps, the skin of her face sagging like wet leaves. Hair mussed on one side, lips pale and chapped. She wore her old reading glasses, squashed and crooked. The drapes were drawn; the old woman had forgotten to open them, which she always did, just before sunrise.

Alice said, "You were up late again." She laid out four pills and prepared the insulin. "Were you reading those awful books?" Mrs. Oh had lately taken up blockbuster thrillers.

Eyes flashed. "Why it's your business what I am reading?"

Three years now as her health aide, and Alice understood Mrs. Oh's sharp tongue as a kind of trust, and affection. Alice took a breath. "You need your rest." She'd arrived agitated herself. Yesterday she'd gone to the shipping store in Silver Spring to pick up boxes. *You should pack up your things*, Charles had said. He seemed resolved about something. Eager. She wasn't going to ask. Anyway it wasn't unreasonable, Alice knew. Boxes stacked in the trunk, she'd gone to the post office for airmail envelopes. The line was long. Someone called her name, *Mrs. Lee, Mrs. Lee*. Then she saw her. *Mrs. Lee*. The girl's mother. That girl.

Mrs. Oh rolled up her turtleneck from the waist. Alice saw parchment-like skin, a grotesquely jutting hipbone. Spindly blue veins like a wilderness of waterways. Alice held up the syringe, flicked at the liquid; then fumbled and dropped it.

"What's the matter? Maybe I am not the one who needs rest."

Alice bristled. In fact, she did often stay up reading. It helped her to sleep. She'd gone back to classics, pocket paperbacks from the Goodwill. Currently, a tattered *As I Lay Dying*.

Alice bent down, picked up the syringe. Re-sterilized it. Steadied her hand.

Mrs. Oh said, "How is your daughter these days?" The shots evidently hurt more and more as the old woman's veins became thinner; she made small talk, for distraction. Or so Alice thought. Why was she always asking about Veda? It irked her.

"She's fine," Alice said.

"I was the only daughter," the old woman said through a grimace. "My mother always loved me best. Secretly, of course. Daughters were worth nothing."

When Mrs. Oh lay down for her nap, Alice left. She left like someone in a hurry. Really she had time to kill. One o'clock, Charles had said. After the housekeeper leaves.

Alice sped along Canal Road. Fleeing. Repulsed. She saw Mrs. Oh's yellow, desiccated skin. Frail skeleton beneath. Wrong glasses, mussed hair, no lipstick. Tiny turns toward the end. At eighty-nine, it happened quickly, there were no margins. She would be the one to get the call, Primary Emergency Contact (Mrs. Oh had made the switch on her forms last year). Alice pressed the accelerator with a heavy foot.

A family of deer grazed along a thin strip of grass between the guardrail and the pavement. There were three. They were awfully close to the road. The little one looked up and made eye contact. Then dropped its head—

A hard thump beneath the car. Left side. Alice felt it in her seat, a punch from below. *Shit*. Her heart punching too. She did not slow down. In the rearview mirror there were no other cars. Alice saw clearly the mess of fur and guts, black and white and red; a fat, fluffy tail, comically intact. The odor overwhelming. She drove on, faster. A mile, two. Then pulled over into an unpaved parking area by the canal. Heart slowing, now a hard ache. Drizzling now, but she needed air. She'd never hit anything before. The impact was harder, bonier, than she'd imagined. Alice cut the engine and got out to walk along the horse path.

The path went on for miles, all the way to Ohio. Alice walked, then found herself jogging, chin up. Her feet began to hurt, leather clogs without socks. She'd gone more than a mile from the car. The drizzle turned to warm rain. She turned and jogged back.

Alice drove down K Street, then up New Hampshire Avenue. The agitation had moved to her stomach, which grumbled. She was hungry. She made her turns without signaling, pulled into the short driveway alongside the house on Kenyon. There would be food, she knew; the housekeeper, a Jamaican woman, stocked the refrigerator with stews and skewers and patties. Alice had peeked once, while waiting for Veda to pack her overnight bag. She'd sighed—bitter, relieved—seeing all that food. She herself now survived on yogurt and baked potatoes. Veda was better off with Charles.

She had three hours before Veda came home from ballet. On the porch she put in her key, but it stuck. Swollen metal, needed to be jiggered. Alice wondered if Charles would ask for it back now.

The key turned, Alice stepped inside. The dampness brought out smells—curry, cat litter, sweet strawberry shampoo. A new hall clock ticked loudly. She slipped off her clogs, padded barefoot down the wool runner. At the bottom of the stairs, Alice looked up. A climber gauging elevation. She hadn't been up in a long time. At the top she paused. Breathed. Remembered how hungry she was. Remembered the boxes in the trunk. She turned and pattered back down. In the kitchen Alice made herself at home: opened the refrigerator and pulled out a Tupperware. Chicken and rice. Took down a plate from the cupboard—the one bearing Veda's grass-and-flower drawing from kindergarten—and forked out half.

She sat at the table and ate. The hallway ticked. Alice did not hurry. She ate, and enjoyed, the food. She did not think, I am eating Charles's food. She did not think, In the middle of the night, the phone call will come. She did not think, That woman at the post office, that girl's mother. Alice ate. She looked into the backyard and saw something, but then it was gone. She blinked hard to see if it would come back. It was yellow. A yellow dump truck, the size of a large cat. No. It was the cat.

Alice finished her food standing up, left her plate and fork in the sink. The rain came down more steadily, pitter-patter drops. She thought of Laila, who'd written about capturing rainwater. Alice had started taking shorter showers.

Her feet were dry now, but she could smell them. She again mounted the stairs; walked quickly past the bedrooms to the bathroom. She sat on the edge of the tub. A washcloth hung on the bar, still damp. Alice drenched the washcloth then rubbed her feet with the cold, wet cloth. Winced as the blistered skin rubbed off. She dropped the soiled cloth into the tub and stepped out onto the mat. Burrowed her toes into the soft fibers until they were dry.

She had not turned on the lights, but now she did. Alice looked at the face in the mirror.

There was a thirty-nine-year-old woman with frizzy hair, thin lips, clear gray eyes. She did not look terrible, this woman. She looked like the woman who attended bereavement meetings every Tuesday, the woman to whom a sad man made love every week. She looked like the woman who wrote letters, read novels, appeared at teacher conferences.

She did not particularly look like a world-changer, or a peace activist. She did not look like a patriotic educator of impressionable minds, or a pioneer of interracial marriage. She did not look like a compassionate caretaker of the elderly. The lights over the mirror were bright, the reflection loud. The rude image wanted to keep telling Alice what she did and did not look like. Alice wanted to walk away, but the woman wouldn't let her.

You do not look like the mother of a ghost child and a drowned boy. You do not look like a mother at all.

She walked abruptly out of the lighted bathroom. Paused to notice her own breath, still breathing. Jaw clenched, Alice did not go down to the basement where her abandoned things awaited her. Instead she went straight to the second door and opened it.

The room was now sage green where once it was dark blue with a stenciled train along the top trim. White sheets and a crocheted afghan covered the bed. The boy's desk was there, now piled with *Sports Illustrated* magazines, Uncle Marvin's encyclopedia set, other tattered books, three generations old.

There was nothing else to see. No other traces. Alice exhaled and almost turned to leave; but then she didn't. She lingered, just a moment. Her feet moved forward then, stepped to the closet. She slid the door open. There were spare pillows, Charles's two suits and Army uniforms, the Jamaican woman's cardigan sweater and loafers. Alice looked up. On the top shelf, just one item—a Happy Days lunchbox, metal; Fonzie straddling his motorcycle, thumbs up, Richie and company flanking. He'd wanted a leather jacket, Benny had. Alice had told him, *Next year*. She'd thought, Maybe when he's ten, if he still wants it.

She took down the lunchbox, sat on the bed. Her feet were clean and cool, her stomach full. Alice opened the box. Why would she hesitate? Charles had probably saved the box because he thought he should save something. Maybe there were Matchbox cars inside, fortunes from fortune cookies. It would be all right, seeing these things. *Take small steps*, Callie would say. *You can do it.* They were just a child's things, any child.

When she opened it, Alice was calm; then she wasn't. Her eyes became blurred and hot; her stomach turned.

She saw first the matching thermos: Howard's double chin, Joanie's scarf, Marion's sly smile. The images had faded to disembodied fragments.

Nestled beside the thermos were two little bundles, each the size of a thumb, tied around the middle with black string. They were the same but different: locks of hair, one light brown, the other black. One was fluffy and light; the other shiny like lacquer, pin-straight. The bundles lay side by side, like an arranged couple on their wedding night—decidedly, astonishingly, together.

Alice's trembling hand reached in, took the fluffy brown bundle in her palm. It looked like steel wool but felt soft like a rabbit's foot. The black string was a piece of thin shoelace, from a pair of dress shoes Benny had abhorred. The string was tied in a square knot: he'd been learning Boy Scout knots at school.

Alice dropped the bundle back into the box. It was as if it had ignited and singed her. Benny's hair landed on, then rolled off the girl's. There was a glimmer, like a winking, the light reflecting off glossy black; mocking her.

Alice shut the box, flipped the latch. Fought the urge to retch. With great concentration and without breathing, Alice placed it back onto the high shelf. Slid the closet door closed. Left the room, pulled the door shut, descended the stairs. At the bottom, Alice's feet found her clogs, and she exited the house. Locked the door behind her.

And then she sped off—for the second time that day.

Alice knew and did not know what she had seen. It had to do with them—the three of them—Benny, Charles, and that girl. (That girl, who was still alive, while her son was dead.)

Alice knew and did not know. And she understood somehow that an opening, an escape, was presenting itself. She understood that knowing or not knowing was something she could decide.

She drove away. Fumbled with the keys hanging from the ignition, removed the metal ring that held the house key; rolled down the window and tossed it.

In the morning Alice sent a telegram to Laila. *I'm coming.* She called a home healthcare agency and told the person on the phone to send someone to 44 MacArthur Boulevard, 7 AM sharp, experience with the elderly and type 1 diabetes. *Tell Mrs. Oh that Alice Lee had a family emergency. Send someone experienced, but let them know it won't be . . . it won't be a long assignment*, she said.

Adelante, adelante. Two days later Alice was going, going. She had a new mantra now. *L'oscuridad, l'oscuridad.* It was hers, all hers. The darkness. Alice reclined her aisle seat, closed her eyes, nestled into her precious darkness.

6.

Soon-mi returned home agitated; Chong-ho could see that. First, he heard it: the tires squeaking as she nearly knocked over the wheelbarrow. En route to the front door, she stepped in a mud puddle. Chong-ho watched her pay no mind. Why was she using the front door anyway. The garage door was wide open.

He'd finished turning over the beds just before the downpour. While the rain pounded he looked out from the greenhouse and envisioned planting schemes. He'd rotate the tomatoes and beans; plant more lettuces around the squashes; try a new eggplant variety. You always wanted to make more with less.

Chong-ho had been retrieving a trowel from one of the beds when Soon-mi drove up. After he watched her go inside, he turned back toward the greenhouse. Something made him stop: a tickle on his skin. A slug on the backside of the trowel tip raised its antennaed head, stretched toward Chong-ho's index finger. Chong-ho flipped the trowel over and shook the slug onto his palm. It fell on its side then righted itself. Fat and slick, it stretched nearly all the way across. The sky brightened as a heavy gray cloud passed and a wispy white one replaced it. The complex colors of the slug's shiny skin came into relief. Chong-ho watched the slug. The slug did nothing. Then, he felt an emission of moist warmth between the slug and his skin. With the trowel point, he lifted the slug off his palm by its middle. A trail of goo smeared across his lifeline.

Chong-ho walked toward the patio, palm upturned, slug and trowel pointing forward. The rain had filled Soon-mi's rain boots, set out to dry and forgotten after the last storm. Chong-ho bent over and tipped the trowel into the boot; gave it one hard shake. The slug fell into the boot. The surface of the water parted like a mouth. The slug sank a little then slowly floated back up. He left it there, then— to float, sink, breathe its last breaths. He set the boot aside so he would remember to empty it later.

In the kitchen Chong-ho listened for Soon-mi but heard only his own blood beating. He studied the ooze on his palm. With his finger Chong-ho spread the ooze so it covered other lines, not just the one. The liquid was thicker than he expected. Gummy and now cool. He held it up to his nose, and winced. Slugs produced various kinds of fluid—one for mating, for example, with alluring qualities; another for defense. Surely this was the latter. It made Chong-ho's eyes sting and smelled intensely of something rotten he couldn't name.

At the sink, he squeezed soap onto his palm; spread it around carefully, then more vigorously. After he rinsed and dried, Chong-ho went upstairs to find Soon-mi. She'd been gone so long. Why had it taken so long to mail a package.

In their bedroom he found her lying on her side—hands stacked palms together under her head like a pantomime of sleep, her eyes open. The tips of her sneakers hung over the edge, one sneaker mud-splattered all the way to her ankle. Two buttons of Soon-mi's shirt, one at the top and one at her belly, had come undone; she wore one of Chong-ho's ribbed undershirts instead of a bra. He'd noticed the other day a new package of undershirts in his drawer. Now he understood where the others had gone. Chong-ho rarely watched Soon-mi undress anymore.

He sat on the edge of the bed, in the crook of Soon-mi's curled-up middle. He wanted to stroke her cheek. Her neck. Kiss her eyelids so they would soften and close. Often he wanted to do this; he'd never stopped wanting to.

It had been years since the two came to their understanding: the ardor they'd once embraced defiantly, like a holy calling, evoked too many shadows, the suffering of others; a trace of obscenity even. Celibacy—more than that, sensual austerity—was their penitence. They never spoke of it. They circled each other's suffering and contained their desire with priestly stoicism; though not before any god. No one was watching. Only themselves, watching each other.

They watched, and they abstained—a taut and cloistered accord.

How long had it been? Chong-ho did not believe in keeping time on atonement. It surprised him that he even wondered. But there was something in Soon-mi's present dishevelment that moved him: she lay there, loose and disarranged. Chong-ho saw now that Soon-mi's cheeks were blotchy, her breathing irregular. He listened to the tremors. Something like panic was either rising or falling, he couldn't tell which.

Her glassy eyes settled on him, and at once Chong-ho was startled: he saw, unmistakably, the perfect fright—all passion and fragile trust—of the young girl whose love he had claimed more than forty years ago. It was as if Soon-mi had seen a ghost; the ghost had seized her ascetic spirit and left behind only flesh and ragged want.

Chong-ho held up his palm. He rubbed at his lifeline with his thumb, three long strokes. Then he pressed his hand into the small of Soon-mi's back. Immediately, he felt it—tiny flutter of a muscle. The live wire of their touch as charged as ever. He was surprised, but then not at all.

How long? Here she was. It had been no time at all.

Soon-mi rolled onto her back. She took Chong-ho's hand, held it to her dry lips. Her eyes stared. Some days there was a faint light in those eyes. The light said, *I am still with you.* Today, the light flickered like an SOS.

Chong-ho unlaced Soon-mi's sneakers. The sneakers fell to the carpet with a soft thud. Soon-mi closed her eyes and pulled Chong-ho's hands to her breasts. Then she let go, let her hands fall. When she opened her eyes again, Soon-mi looked at Chong-ho directly, and seriously.

Take me back, she was saying. *Take me back to the grove. High above on the ridge.*

Chong-ho did not have to recall. It was there, right there, always. Chong-ho began to move his callused hands over Soon-mi's body, gently, slowly, underneath her clothes. Soon-mi closed her eyes, but Chong-ho watched her. She was the most familiar sight to him, more familiar than his own face, yet today he felt her flesh anew. Her bones and lumps and rough patches were a map of years and denials and disuse. They both closed their eyes now. That rotten smell came back to Chong-ho: he knew now that it wasn't something, it was everything—like a feast abandoned to the flies. He didn't wince; he took it in.

Take me back. It was neither far away nor long ago. Chong-ho laid his forehead on Soon-mi's broad sternum. He breathed warm breath into the valley between her breasts. The undershirt was thin and loose. He lifted the shirt and slipped his fingers beneath the waistband of Soon-mi's pants.

He took her back, back to the grove. Soon-mi whimpered, and moaned softly. He moved, and she moved, and they both breathed, smooth and calm like dancers on a stage, building toward a grand lift. Then Soon-mi cried out—a girl's cry, brittle and virginal. She was both reaching and letting something go. She arched her back, and her body shuddered. Finally she let out one last low whimper: all her flesh gave way, sinking into the bed. Chong-ho watched Soon-mi as her breath deepened, then quieted. The furrow between Soon-mi's eyes relaxed, and her mouth fell open.

He sat with her, letting out his own held breath, then laid his hand on her forehead like a doctor feeling for a fever. Chong-ho still did not know what was behind her flickering eyes. What particular fear or sorrow had met Soon-mi on the road between home and the world and back again. He knew well how flashes of mortality could singe the soul without warning these days; but Soon-mi had never been one for morbidity. She was the fatalist (he the romantic) and took each day for what it was. Was it something from the long-ago past haunting her freshly? Or was it something to do with Hannah? Perhaps these were not so easily distinguished.

Soon-mi curled onto her side and began to snore softly. Chong-ho stroked her hair and put his lips to her forehead. Then he left, clicking the door closed behind him.

In James's room, now Chong-ho's study, Chong-ho sat at his desk and reached for the last notebook in the series he kept on a shelf he'd installed just above. They were tape-bound books he'd made himself, filled with poems—complete poems, line fragments, phrases arranged and rearranged. The first three notebooks had come with him from Korea. In recent years, he did not write often, and when he did, he wrote plainly. If Chong-ho were to title the volumes, which he did not, they would be, just, *Sarang gwa chun haeng*: Love and War.

He sat with pen in hand, notebook open. His mind was moving, his senses high and full. He wrote:

Hana-ae sarang, oori neun soopuro do ra ga

Loved one, we go back to the grove
we breathe pungent earth and sweet flora
into each other's valleys
we show each other the way
with hands
hearts
thick skin on thin
together we climb and heave and sing out;
but we are not young again
our meal is meager
it is enough.
We bring our bones and lumps
and rough patches.
Our denials and disuse.
Your flesh is as always my flesh.

Your face more me than mine.
Loved one, we succeed only, ever, at sorrow and love.

Chong-ho closed the notebook, returned it to the shelf. He exhaled once, fully, then pushed out more air, and still more; until he was empty and hunched over the desk. He listened to the silence all around. A bus hissed to a stop across the street. People boarded. The bus lurched, and pulled away.

Then Chong-ho's lungs sucked in a sharp breath. He sat up. He began to heave and tremble; his hands made fists. A sob—a low rumble at first, then a coarse wail—poured out. He heard it in his ear as if it had come from another creature. Chong-ho fell forward, arms spread like a prisoner giving himself up; forehead pressed into the hard wood of the desk. Chong-ho's shoulders shook, and he wept, but without tears—open-mouthed and now silent.

In truth, it had been a long, long time.

It had been as long as Chong-ho had been fatherless. As long as he'd stood accused and shamed and disowned.

He lay sprawled over the desk for some time. His breathing calmed and slowed. When finally he lifted his head, the room had dimmed: a dusky glow illuminated the translucent shades. Chong-ho found himself standing but did not remember having done so. He walked out of the room like a sleepwalker.

Before descending the stairs, he paused outside Hannah's room. The door was closed, as usual. He did not open it but stood square before it. The door was like a blank, hard face. Soon-mi was dead asleep in the other room. Chong-ho stood square, and alone.

Hannah. How long had it been? It had been nearly Hannah's lifetime. This—these long years of parsimony, of their love cloaked in mourning garb—it was all Hannah knew. And of course she had been watching. There may not have been a god standing in judgment, but Hannah was watching.

And wasn't it for this that they'd sent her away?

For her own good.

Chong-ho had not asked questions about the family whose boy had drowned; but he knew that Hannah was not innocent. She had kept it a secret. This dark thing, like it was nothing. And the man, the father, he was black. She hadn't said. Probably there were other secrets.

From where else had she learned to lock everything away, batten down tragedy? It was *for her own good* that she go away from them. They told it to themselves; they had to believe it.

Chong-ho knew now that he'd been right about Soon-mi—something from the long-ago past, something to do with Hannah. The years had passed quietly, too quietly. Hannah was graduating now, going forth. They would let her go completely. But if Chong-ho had resolved, Soon-mi had only deferred. Not because she disagreed, but because she took the failure upon herself.

She had never been easy with Hannah, Chong-ho knew; never opened her heart. Never knew Hannah as her own, not like James. James was their child of hope and resolve; their love was full then, determined. Hannah came too late: whatever the girl needed from them had been spent. For Soon-mi, their plan had signified defeat, not resolve.

Would Hannah too be known and loved? Chong-ho had no idea. He hoped she would. He hoped that her heart would not go rancid, abandoned on a banquet table. Such a fate would be the real obscenity. Chong-ho was content with his own lot: he had chosen love and admitted its sorrows. But what good is such love, the heart's pure fervor, if only the lovers can live in its depths?

Chong-ho turned away from the door and continued on—down the stairs, through the kitchen to the patio. The rain had ceased; the clouds were parting. He surveyed the yard and assessed the tasks remaining. Calculated what he could accomplish before dark. Behind him, the *Baptisia* pushed out tiny blue buds on bushes that had grown wild over the years. The drowned slug floated in the boot.

7.

June 17, 1988

Dear James,
Congratulations. Yours is the first wedding invitation I've ever received. It's funny to see your name in fancy script, but it's exciting too. You and Grace look handsome in the picture you sent. How'd you get her to say yes? (ha ha) I'll send back the RSVP soon. (You shouldn't say, "Ummah and Appah really want to see you"—as if.) Graduation is coming up fast, finally. Thanks for the advice about college; you're right that it's good to think about why you're there and what you want out of it.
—Hannah
ps: On the front is Colette's gravestone in Paris. It's shaped like a bed.

Once she started, Hannah realized that packing wouldn't take long. Books, clothes, few personal items. She'd never made herself at home, like the other girls. She filled a large trash can with notebooks, term papers, old granola bars and instant cocoa, socks with holes in the heels . . .

In the bottom desk drawer was a stack of letters. White #9s, a single trifolded sheet inside. Bound by a wide rubber band. She'd seen similar stacks in other girls' rooms, but tied in satin bows or tossed into pretty boxes. A girl named Judy, who lived across the hall, received a letter every week, sometimes with an enclosed Polaroid. Hannah couldn't understand why the boy sent pictures of himself with his handsomer friends. There was one with a bulldog puppy that was nice. Hannah couldn't imagine holding the letters to her chest the way Judy did, but she did read them slowly. Certain lines stayed in her ear like a melancholy tune that's also soothing. The letters reminded her of something she knew she didn't want to forget: sadness can comfort; plainness can make you feel things. She read in one of her English textbooks that newscasters report on outer weather; poets report on inner weather. That was what the letters were like—*reporting; inner*. Hannah liked the way the sheets were creased and folded crisply, and so she always refolded them and put them back into the envelopes she'd sliced straight across with a letter opener. It was almost as if the letters had not been touched.

Hannah opened the drawer and considered briefly tossing the stack into the bin. She felt that the letters, their music, would stay with her, whether or not she packed them. But then she thought of the time Judy saw her with a letter and asked who it was from. When Hannah answered, "A man I once knew, I looked after his kids," Judy made a face. A stupid face.

Hannah tucked the stack into her suitcase between sweaters.

There was a knock at the door. "Yes?"

"Someone downstairs for you."

"Coming."

Parietal hours were over, but it was senior week, the night before commencement; the rules went lax. Even so, Hannah fished around the entry table for the pen that had gone missing and, when she found it on the floor, signed in the boy she knew would be there (no sense risking it, so close now to the end). The boys' academy down the road had graduated two days earlier. He was officially free and hadn't yet left for home.

Upstairs in Hannah's room, he said, "You really have hardly any stuff." He turned over a book in her pile of to-pack. "DurrAH," he said, hamming up the accent. He'd gotten through intermediate French last term only with Hannah's help.

"DurrAHSS," she said.

"That makes no sense."

Hannah shrugged. "Are you all packed?"

He laughed. The boy had a nice laugh. "No way. I have so much shit. They let us stay another week. My parents don't come until Tuesday."

Hannah stood with hands on hips, surveying. *What's next.* She would be ready—more than ready—to leave tomorrow. The boxes would go by airmail, straight to Rue Pascal; she would have to call a taxi. She could have asked the boy, he had a Wagoneer, but Hannah didn't want him to see the address. Everything else she planned to take on the bus.

"Why don't you come stay with me, after tomorrow? My roommate's gone, the house counselors are barely around. You can meet my parents. My little brother, too. He's a trip."

Hannah was still thinking about whether everything left would fit in her second suitcase. She looked up, realizing what he'd asked, and smiled. "That's nice. But, no thanks. I have to get going."

The boy pouted. "The invitation to Nantucket still stands." He came up behind her and rubbed his hardness against Hannah's lower back. Hands squeezing her shoulders. "My parents are cool; they'll let us have our own room."

Hannah let him kiss her neck; she closed her eyes. He was warm, and nice, and not as stupid as some others. She was his first. He'd said so anyway, and he was so nervous their first time, and fast, that Hannah believed him. He didn't ask if he was hers. Maybe he didn't care, maybe he assumed; maybe he was afraid of the answer. Hannah realized quickly how easy it was with a boy who had never done it before: relax, let him do the moving, move just a little. Let him lay his head on your chest afterward. Say yes when he asks if you liked it. She knew that he was working his way toward doing more, making her feel more. But he wouldn't get there. Hannah could not imagine surrendering to this boy in that way. For what he wanted, it should be fearless. With no question of wrong or right. But he was afraid of too many things—of doing something wrong, of not doing it right, diminishing himself in her eyes. It was fine the way it was. It was nice. It was how it should be, between him and her.

The boy would be going to UVA in the fall (over Duke), and Hannah chose to believe it had nothing to do with her. They'd only met last winter, at one of the coed mixers. They had talked about where they'd applied. Hannah had applied to just the one school, and she'd been accepted.

"And there's a private beach. In July, at high tide, you can actually ride waves." His hands ran down her hips.

Hannah had been thinking only of buses and boxes. An airplane. It would be her first time (second, actually, but she'd been too young to remember). When he said *ride waves,* Hannah stepped out of his reach and turned to look at him.

"What?" The boy's eyes shifted sideways—blue and swirly like marbles.

What. Hannah wasn't sure. It was a long beat. She'd been moving fast, moving toward the light at the end of . . . this. The boy came back into focus, and she almost told him what she had already decided not to tell him. Not to tell anyone—her parents, James; Coach Modeste, who had put in a good word for her with the assistant swim coach. That she wouldn't be going to UVA in the fall. Wouldn't be going to college at all.

"Nothing," Hannah said.

The boy looked at her. Smiled. *Always fucking inscrutable.* For now, he enjoyed the challenge.

"Help me pack," Hannah said.

In the morning, Hannah turned toward the wall and shoved him out of the bed, sent him on his way. Before he left she handed him *The Lover* and said, *DurrAHSS,* and he took the book and laughed. He kissed Hannah's cheek and said, "See you later." He planned to come to her graduation, didn't know that when her name was called, Hannah would be on a bus to DC. It would matter little in the long run; he would of course grow tired of challenges.

From the bus stop, before boarding, Hannah called Madame Glissant to confirm arrival time. Hannah would spend two nights in Friendship Heights. She and Monique would fly to Paris together. *My family owns a building in the 14th,* she had said on the phone. *There's a small flat on the top floor, very sweet.* That first mention months ago had been only half-serious, but Hannah could not let go the idea. France. Paris. Where Colette lived and wrote. Where Claudine had her adventures. She wanted to pay her respects at Père Lachaise; to Duras too at Cimetière Montparnasse.

In her translations there were words Hannah encountered and clung to: *essence* was among her favorites. It meant spirit, the heart of the thing; also gasoline, fuel for the journey. Hannah would go, to the place of *essence*. And to the place of *bien-aimés*.

She would go; her sentence was over, she'd done her time. Madame understood this. *Pourquoi pas?* Madame would finally write her historical novel, Hannah would help with research.

The bus pulled into the loading bay, ready for boarding. Just before hanging up, Monique said, "You are sure, Ah-nah? Your parents, your teachers, they all want you to go to college, *bien sûr*."

Hannah considered, for an instant, what her parents would say. It was easy enough to imagine: nothing. They would say nothing. What could they say. At some point an alternate plan had crossed her mind: go home for the summer, live the next three months in their house, lifeguard and wait tables. Pretend she was going to college. Hannah thought how easy it would be, this deception. How deep and wide the gap between her and them, how little possibility for friction or discovery. A part of Hannah had relished this plan—feeling the gap fully, inhabiting it. She had submitted to their banishment; she could play it out to the very end. It would be a kind of preparation, fueling up. She would be *pleine d'essence* before leaving and never turning back.

No. She would go now. Her boxes were getting on a plane. Hannah had said a final good-bye to the boy, without him knowing.

"*A toute à l'heure*, Monique," she said, then hung up. It was the first time Hannah had called Madame Glissant by her given name.

The bus was only half-full. Hannah relaxed into her seat and leaned on her duffel bag. Three hours to DC. She slept lightly and dreamt fitfully of the ocean—the salty air, sun high and strong, her body aloft and riding the massive wave's velocity all the way to shore. *What did I do to deserve this, and why so long in coming.*

8.

There was the question of Veda, which kept Charles awake nights but did not keep him from going forward. One step at a time, no commitments just yet. There would be training trips over the summer—Vegas in June, North Carolina in July; Vancouver in the fall to seal the deal. Rhea and Marcus would stay at the house. Charles had told them the training was for the stadium—a new government requirement for venues that drew high-volume crowds. Bart had told him what to say.

Veda had her own busy life now—friends, school clubs, dance classes and recitals. It was the year of clothes and makeup and *hanging out*, which Rhea would manage better anyway. Veda would be okay, Charles told himself. *Will you be okay?* he asked her. *Dad*, Veda said, rolling her eyes then rolling over on her bed to dial someone's number. Charles had let her have a phone in her room. She was getting so tall, her toes nearly reaching the edge of the mattress. She'd be okay, he told himself.

Alice was gone. Charles had been thinking things over, planning on Vegas, but he wanted everything else to be cleaner, clearer, before proceeding. Wanted Alice out, and told her so. (A legal divorce would be next, he thought, but one thing at a time.) But who knew she would disappear? She hadn't taken her things, though evidently she'd come by the house to get them. Charles went to Dupont Circle but didn't know the apartment number. He stood in the lobby and asked a few people; no one knew Alice, no one knew anything. Charles couldn't remember the name of the old woman she worked for. Chung, or maybe Park? Maybe he never knew. He wondered if he should call Nick Jr. The whole thing was bizarre, an ominous shadow.

Even so, Charles felt relieved. Alice had been leaving them for a long time; now, finally, she was gone. She didn't want to be found. When Charles told Veda, she asked was there a note or anything. There wasn't. Charles saw that for Veda there was a difference— between Alice's half-presence and her complete absence. He didn't know was it a big difference or not. He was sorry for it.

It hadn't taken long for Bart Sheridan's proposition—after its first ridiculous clang—to resonate. Dennis was the clincher. Dennis laid up like that, tubes and machines, it spooked Charles. Like he'd been waiting for it and it made no fucking sense at the same time. But Bart was making sense. The whole thing was wacko, so Charles trusted it. Over steak and lobster on the terrace at Phillips, Bart told Charles about his illustrious career, pre-alcoholic meltdown, in paramilitary; his migration to private security once he'd sobered up; his eye on Charles over time as a potential recruit. You heard about it at Yongsan, side comments from higher-ups, about hired guns and soldiers for rent, the black market of national security. But as Bart explained it, it was less cloak-and-dagger and more money-and-lifestyle. "It's a no-brainer for guys like me. Like you. Salary, benefits." Bart paused when the waiter came, as if on cue, to replace the plates piled with lobster carcasses with sparkling new ones. "Even flexibility. You can say No. I couldn't fucking believe it at first. 'No, I'd rather not go to Tora Bora next week; but Tangier next month sounds good.' It's a life, and not a bad one." Bart sat back, looked up to admire the big blue sky over the Potomac. Ordered another club soda.

Glasses clinked around them. Sweat beaded on Bart's forehead. A patch of summer had come early, it was May and ninety degrees. Charles squinted at Bart through his aviators. Bart could apparently see, or detect it. "You're wondering why the stadium job." Bart had been at it now ten years, and Charles was in fact wondering. "At first I needed it. My sponsor said a regular schedule was important. Then it was a good cover. I was leading trainings mostly anyway. Then my kid had a kid. My kid hates my guts, but he said, 'You can be grandpa if you're actually going to be around. Reliable.' So now I recruit on the side. I'm a contractor for the contractor."

Charles asked what had to be asked: how dangerous was it; why him. Surely there were more seasoned MP types, or Navy SEALs. "At Tier 2, you're more the shepherd than the hunter. It's a lot of sitting and watching. Sometimes it's hand-holding assets, getting them from A to B. Or straight body-guarding for guys with significant enemies.

The point is you're invisible, they barely know you're there. Safety means not having to think about danger; you're the one paid to think about it. Keep everything steady and easy. I've seen you. I think if you had to you could balance a china teacup on each shoulder while the circus stampeded through here." The MPs, the SEALs, former Special Ops guys, they were geared toward Tier 1—black ops, hard core. Bart's firm was building up Tier 2, for overseas work. "You got a lady friend or anything? Someone who'll ask questions about where you're going or where you've been?" Evidently Bart knew he and Alice had split. Bart knew a lot of things he hadn't let on. "Swear to Jesus, it's not the Russians or the Iranians who give us the hardest time, it's the wives and girlfriends."

Charles hadn't seen Angela in a while. She'd finished her MBA and taken a job with ruthless hours. Veda was probably more disappointed than he was; Nicole was in high school now, she didn't see much of either of them.

"A sister," Charles said. "And my daughter. But they're . . . they'll be all right."

Rhea had said: *Three trips in six months? Hasn't V had enough upset? She needs you home.* Charles couldn't say, *No, she really doesn't.* Rhea would balk, might refuse to step up while he was gone if he said that. What V needed Charles couldn't precisely say, but it wasn't him waiting with dinner salads and checking her algebra. Rhea and Marcus would be just enough of what she needed. For now.

The money would help. Charles was doing fine enough, but a college fund would be nice. It wasn't the money, though. He would do it because he wanted to. Dip his toe in, anyway. Bart said, Start with the training: no obligation, no guarantees. Both sides are trying each other out. If the training clicks, everyone knows it's a go; *then* you quit the day job. "I've seen guys rush in, all Rambo and adrenaline, pumped up to fight the bad guys. They don't last long. It's not what they expected." Bart grinned a yellow-toothed grin. "But you might like to know I'm a top recruiter these days. It seems I have the eye."

Sure, he would try it, see if it clicked. One thing at a time. But Bart was making sense, and Charles knew it in his gut. Three weeks later, he was off to Vegas. The day before leaving, Charles sat at his desk at 2:45 and wrote another letter.

June 1988

By my count, you'll be graduating. I'm glad for that, though I can't presume whether or not you are. So I won't say, "Congratulations." What I mean to say is that you're finishing something you didn't choose to start. It doesn't mean you didn't make good on it. But it's over now, so that's something.

One way or another, you're starting new. At your stage of life, that can be exciting. I wish I had had more wits about me when those moments came. Those moments of change and decision.

Often you don't feel like you're making a decision at all, but when you look back you see that you did. It was yours to make. With a little different thinking or influence, you could easily have decided different. No, not easily. If it were easily, then life would be much simpler.

I'm about to start new, too. I'm going away soon. A new job. It's going to be a different kind of life. The one I think I was supposed to live. I'm ready for it. It took a long time and some half-aware decisions along the way. But anyway it feels like finally I am both making a decision and aware of making it.

I have felt that way about decisions I've made in relation to you. Somehow that's true. Every time I write I seem to know better, somewhere inside but apart from the words, why that is. Maybe someday I'll find the actual words.

You haven't written to tell me not to write. I believe the letters are reaching you, so you are either reading them when they arrive or not reading them. Both possibilities seem reasonable to me. When I think about it, I can't predict which it is. Where I'm going I'll always be able to find you, so I'll keep writing. It means something to me. That you know I'm writing. Every letter a decision.

In the Nevada desert, there were a dozen of them, a few around Charles's age, but most on the far side of forty; one woman. They'd all served overseas, except for one, who made clear his past was off-limits. The training was relentless, dawn to dusk, later for night tactics. There was little small talk, meals were quick and silent; everyone seemed to prefer this. A short bony-faced guy called Mitt, the woman, and Charles were the top performers in almost all the exercises. On the last night, the three found themselves congregated in front of the dorms. They were up on a hill; the lights of the strip flashed in the distance. The woman said, *That was nice work.* She meant the motion-sensor exercise. Charles had completed the course without tripping a single light, and had detected an IED that no one was expecting. *You, too*, Charles said. Her defensive tactics—her ability to get out of any hold by any aggressor—had prompted applause. Mitt said, *So what mess are you guys trying to get away from?* The woman harrumphed. Mitt grinned and moved his eyebrows up and down. *Seems to me this is a lot like witness protection, but the pay is a whole lot better.* Neither Charles nor the woman confirmed or denied this. Mitt put out his cigarette and said, *Well, I hope never to run into either of you out there*, and went to bed.

In between trainings Charles had to maintain, and up, the fitness. It wasn't easy. But it felt good. Charles felt how, at thirty-six, there were only two options: soup yourself up, stronger than the nineteen-year-old you were, or go soft in the middle, an old man in a wifebeater. School was out, but Veda got up early with him to go to the track, clicked the stopwatch. They took turns, for fun. Veda was a natural, fast and graceful.

A week before Charles had to leave again, Dennis woke up. Charles went to see him every day. Dennis was groggy from the painkillers but he wanted to talk. He spoke slowly, and said uncanny things.

I gotta get outta all this. Get away.

Where's the fuckin window that's supposed to open when the door slams.

Sometimes it's like I just wanna disappear, off the grid; some desert island. He joked, *Like witness protection, man. Find me someone else's crime to witness.*

I worry about Lawrence. What's gonna happen to him. All this mess. Where's his fuckin window.

One day, after he'd talked and talked, Dennis seemed to remember Charles; everything that had happened.

You had it all, man. You were on track, it was gonna work out for you. Stupid bad luck. Or else holy wrath. Seems like what's the difference anyway. Reverend Haywood was dead a year now, went peacefully in his sleep.

Charles wondered if he could tell Dennis the truth. A part of him wanted to. Felt like he owed it to him. One in two. He was the one. Not Dennis. Dennis laid up. Dennis paralyzed on his left side. Charles had a window, and he was jumping out. Jumping in. Whichever.

The truth was: it wasn't bad luck. It was good luck.

Charles woke before dawn the morning he left for North Carolina. He tapped Veda's door open and watched her sleep for a few seconds, noted the neatly folded pink T-shirt and baseball cap she'd laid out on the chair: today she was starting her first job, scooping ice cream at Mazza. She and her friends were too young for the jewelry or clothing jobs, but they liked the upscale mall, and the pink uniforms. He closed the door and silently headed out. Rhea was up. She handed him a thermos of coffee and crossed her arms over her bathrobe.

The drive would be long, but Charles didn't mind. About halfway, he stopped for breakfast at a diner in a small town outside Roanoke. Main Street was flanked with American flags. Charles knew the town, had written its name on at least a dozen envelopes by now.

The last one had come back: RETURN TO SENDER, ADDRESSEE NO LONGER AT THIS ADDRESS. He guessed the private schools finished earlier than the public ones; or maybe Hannah hadn't checked her mail at the end.

Charles ordered oatmeal, ate quickly while it was still warm, and when he paid the check he asked the waitress where the school was. She pointed at the window that faced up the hill. "You're a little late," she said. "Or early. It's pretty deserted up there. The summer school doesn't start up until after the holiday."

All the flags: probably a parade this weekend for the Fourth. He nodded. "Just wanted to take a look around."

The day was humid and overcast. Charles parked near a building that looked like an athletic complex—sprawling and metal-roofed. He made his way to the main quad. The buildings there were red brick, one with white columns and a portico, which he assumed was the main hall. He walked toward it and stood in front, then turned a slow 360.

Charles saw pale green lawn with tufts of straw-yellow, muddy-brown brick under the muted sky. No trees or plantings. White shades were drawn in all the windows, like eyes with no pupils. A bronze statue of a man with chin up and hand tucked into breast pocket stood atop a dry fountain and seemed intended as the tableau's centerpiece; but it was too small.

Charles clenched his jaw and inhaled. The humidity should have brought out smells, but there weren't any—nothing teeming, beneath or beyond. He swallowed a gulp of tasteless air.

A fly buzzed overhead, too close. A small gray bird with a blue chest flitted over the quad, looking for a tree branch; finding none, it settled on the statue's upturned chin. The fly buzzed in Charles's ear and he let it.

Hannah was nowhere here, and Charles wanted to know, somehow, that she'd survived this. That they hadn't gotten to her. Erased her. That somewhere she'd found an open window, maybe even broke one to pieces. This place was like an insensible ghost, uninformed of its own death.

With a pang Charles suddenly envisioned Hannah standing outside on Kenyon Street the day they buried the boy—at the bottom of the steps, head lowered, hair tied back too neatly and dressed in a borrowed black dress. The house would have looked just like this place from where she stood—like nothing. Dumb and proud and bloodless. Pretending to do honor; upholding something or other.

If she'd actually come, Charles would have gone out to stand on the sidewalk with her. Would have lifted her chin and said, *You're all right* and *You're supposed to be alive.*

A cement path wove toward the far corner of the quad and threaded between buildings. Charles made his way briskly across and out. He emerged into another, smaller quad, much the same, and beyond that was a path that led downhill. He wanted to wander a little longer, keep looking for her, some sign or sense, but he was running short on time, had to make Asheville in under four hours if he was going to arrive at the training site by 5 PM sharp (no excuses). He looped back to his car and drove the ring road in the opposite direction. Past some other buildings, beyond a large parking lot and a maintenance building, the campus seemed to open up onto something green—deep, rich green, with textures. Tiny flashes of gold. Charles rolled down the window and craned his neck to see as far as he could. He stuck his nose out and sniffed like a dog. Charles thought he detected a sweet scent, pine or cedar. The hint of something floral.

He hoped he wasn't inventing it.

Charles gunned the accelerator and drove on.

He decided to believe in the scent and hold to its consolation—the proximity of the forest and its enchantments—like a kid staring at his night-light to quiet the monsters under the bed. He clung too to the fact that, once he started the new work, it would be easy enough to find her. And he would. He would always find her. He'd said so, in the letter that was in his briefcase, that would soon be in her hands. And Charles meant, always, to tell Hannah the truth.

BOOK THREE:
L'Essence

Sarang Pyong-hwa Nursing Home,
Silver Spring, Maryland
Spring 1992

The arrangements have all been made; everything in writing.

Last time, four years ago, her useless sons rushed to the bedside—vultures more than babes. The end was near, the health agency people said. She knew this was not true, but the stroke had taken her speech. She would have said, *Not yet, not yet.* And, *Where is that damned woman.* If Alice Lee had come, her sons would never have known; that was her wish. Useless, everyone useless.

When the dust settled—the sons gone back to their wives, back to their lives—she thought: *Not yet, not yet. I can still do something.* She called her lawyer.

She herself does not know how much time has passed since then. Months? Years? It seems not at all long ago. She remembers: *That woman. Where has she gone to.* Her mind had fixated. She was not dead yet. *I can still do something. The damned woman's daughter; poor daughter! The daughter always suffers. Like I suffered.*

How long has she been here? Mrs. Oh wonders. They treat her like an old-timer. The man in charge is familiar, acts as if they are old friends. If they are friends, why can't he get her more closet space for her things.

Her sons moved her to this placid, pastel place with its hideous ferns and too much sunlight. She remembers her home, her lovely things. When you reach the end, it's the colors that matter. Deep purple, wine red, luscious creamy white. The drapes wide open only at dawn and dusk. Too much sunlight bleaches everything. Here, everything watery and thin.

She regained some words; more than she lets on. She makes weak gestures; let them figure it out. She is tired. A woman spends her lifetime trying to be understood.

Now. Now it is time. Her body tells her this. She has been lying in bed. Day after day. The lawyer has come. The lawyer says she has been here almost four years. A week ago she had another stroke.

The lawyer is a man. A Korean man. He does not understand. Like last time, he tries to talk her out of the wishes she put in writing. It's my job to advise you toward sound decisions, he says. To foresee the long-term repercussions of these documents, their stipulations. To ensure that your loved ones are cared for.

No, she thinks. *Your job is to do what I say. I stayed married fifty years, and now I have money. With money, I employ you. My mind is quite sound. Time is scrambled, but the order of things is not so important anyway.* The lawyer should know better than to tell an old woman who her loved ones are, how to care for them. No one knows. No one can tell you. *It's all scrambled in the end, can't you see?*

With the documents, she can do something. Just a little unscrambling, for a girl who got the short end, like her. *The documents stand. You may call my children now.* She waves a crooked finger in the air. For the last time she makes herself understood.

When her sons arrive, she is already gone. At the inquest, one is enraged, one is in shock. *Crazy bitch*, says one. *This is wrong*, says the other.

AUTUMN 1992

1.

Her first passport stamp. Her first passport. It would be a year of firsts. Veda turned eighteen in September and actually felt different. She'd often been told how mature and grown up she was. She never liked those comments. Now she'd be free of them. Never again would she "seem" adult. She simply was one.

The customs officer opened Veda's blue booklet and held it up. His eyes shifted back and forth—her photo, her face. Veda's skin and eyes changed tint in varying light. People always told her that, too. "Have a good trip," he said. A faintly lurid smile. She took her passport back and walked on; it was never her goal to be noticed, but she was used to it. Once, on the Metro platform, a man carrying a leather purse grinned his gold front tooth and handed her a card and said, *You should model, call me.*

She would fly first to London. Over the summer she'd run into Nicole, who went to Wesleyan and was wearing her hair natural and carried a Prada bag. She kissed Veda's cheek and said *I miss you, you should visit;* she'd be on study abroad. She said, *Come to London, then we'll take the weekend in the country.* Nicole had been to London the summer before, with Angela, on one of her business trips.

Veda felt how big the world was; she'd hardly seen any of it. The idea of travel had made her anxious, in both senses of the word. It still did. But she'd made a plan: a week in England, then on to Paris. She knew no one in Paris. Well, possibly someone.

On the plane Veda paged through *Vogue*, then *National Geographic*. She thought of her interview at Howard. She'd said she wanted to double major in theater arts and biopsychology. It was her best guess. She'd applied to schools in other cities but wanted to stay near home; if she went somewhere else, she might never see her father at all. Howard sent the acceptance letter, then a month later the letter saying they'd over-enrolled. She had the option of starting in January. Veda had jumped at it. She wanted that pause. For what, she wasn't yet sure.

She clicked off the overhead light, put away the magazines. Closed her eyes and thought of the money sitting in the bank. How could she not think of it. Mysterious money, come from nowhere. Then Veda tried hard not to think about it. It was tiring her out. As an abstract idea, it unsettled her. Like a brown paper package with no addressee. Like a face with no features.

She wouldn't have thought to go to Europe. It was a fluke, running into Nicole, who'd been in town visiting Malcolm. He still lived in Shaw, paid rent to Angela, had been in and out of juvy, and was now holding down a UPS delivery job. Angela lived in New York, worked in finance; it was her boss's sister who would host Nicole, and Veda, in Dorset. Veda got the sense that the boss was more than just a boss.

Rhea thought travel was a *wonderful idea*: she was the one to bring up Paris. *Autumn in Paris*, she'd said dreamily. *You can see where Josephine Baker got her first standing ovation.* Veda had sat at the kitchen table and stroked the cat, who was fat as ever. Paris, she thought. She bent her mind four years back and saw words on an envelope—her father's handwriting, and the name that was both surprising and familiar. She strained her memory a little harder and saw *Rue Pascal, PARIS FRANCE*. Rhea said, *Happy Graduation, honey*, and bought Veda a plane ticket.

The money in the bank stayed untouched. Charles was looking into the source—the certified documents that came in July. The documents looked real, did not appear to be a prank. There was a serious intention to remain anonymous. What had turned up so far was the name of the lawyer. It was a Korean name. An extremely common name. The PO Box address in Bowie didn't help. Maybe, probably it had to do with Alice.

Alice was long gone. She lived in Chile, almost four years now. It was Veda's grandpa Nick who'd hired a private investigator back then. He found Alice, "living like a goddamn lesbian bohemian." Veda didn't want to think of her mother right now. It was possible she was dead, the money an inheritance. Doubtful, though. Why the anonymity. There would have been a death notice. (And lesbian Peace Corps bohemians did not accumulate wealth.)

"You can check," Veda told her father. "I don't want to." She had a different idea.

She'd begun to understand why she wanted a pause. She was eighteen. When she was nine, her little brother died. After that, everything started to spin; everyone flung outward and away. *Centrifugal force* (the only useful idea Veda had retained from junior-year physics). Veda wasn't spinning, it was everything else. Veda still lived on Kenyon Street. She went to school. Did her chores. She was a good girl; that was what Rhea always told Charles. Veda had watched and seen things, and sometimes grew dizzy. Dance and drill team helped her settle the dizziness. *Biopsychology*, Veda had told the interviewer.

Four years ago she'd seen an envelope in the mailbox. She came home from school, and she and the mailman had arrived at the same time. He handed her the mail, and as she was walking up the steps, she noticed it—the white corner of an envelope peeking out from the letterbox by the front door. Wait, she'd called. She ran up and reached into the box, pulled out the envelope. She scurried back down the steps and handed the letter to the mailman. As he took it from her, she saw to whom it was addressed.

It had surprised her—like the sharpening of a sound she hadn't realized was staticky.

The envelope, the sharpness, went away from them; it went at first to Virginia. But then it came back. NO FORWARDING ADDRESS. Charles had put the envelope in his briefcase. In those days, Veda snooped in her father's briefcase.

She didn't open it. At the time, it made her queasy to think of reading it. Then Charles spun away again, to another training, somewhere in Canada. When he came home, Veda watched him, watched the mail. Soon after she saw another letter. It was an airmail envelope, going to Paris. Rue Pascal.

Then there was the lunchbox.

It was August, the following year, and Veda had awakened one morning with a lonely thought in her mind: five years. Five years since she watched her brother drown. She wanted to go to the grave.

She would ask Aunt Rhea to take her. They rarely went into his room, but Veda did that day, to see if there was something she could bring. That's when she found it, in the closet. It was the only thing on the shelf.

Time to pause now. Veda had questions. She was eighteen and tired of the spinning and flinging. Suddenly, this money. A Korean lawyer. Maybe it had to do with her mother. But Veda had a different idea. Maybe it was something, someone else.

2.

September 1992

> *Sometimes I've wondered what you might say or think about this, or that. Sometimes I think I know—what you think, who you're becoming, year after year. You have a birthday coming up soon. I don't think of you as becoming older; just becoming.*
>
> *I used to worry that it was selfish—to keep writing. To express one-way thoughts without two-way conversation. But I also figured it was right that you didn't respond. Right meaning it made sense. I was writing, and you were reading, and somehow it mattered.*
>
> *And right because there was nothing false in it. That was the important thing. It's too easy to get stuck on selfish, or wrong, and not care enough about false.*
>
> *I had a thought the other day, though—sudden, like a bell in my ear. It surprised me, but then not really.*
>
> *This thing happened, and I want to tell you about it. But not just tell you: ask you. I was wondering your opinion on something important. For the first time, a voice inside me said:*
> Well, why not ask . . .

For her twentieth birthday, Hannah had gone traveling in the south. The year before seemed like so long ago. The year she turned eighteen was the year Hannah arrived in Paris, but she herself forgot her birthday until the day after. There was one year when James sent a card. Hannah couldn't recall which year. Probably the second. It was odd, piecing together time in this way. Connecting the years with the day of your birth.

She couldn't remember how Monique knew it was her birthday. Probably when she helped with the visa renewal, she saw the DOB on the form. (Hannah did remember how her friend Raj used to tease her on her birthday: *10/4, good buddy*, he'd say.) Anyway, it was a surprise. A beautiful *gâteau*, her favorite cream filling.

"Twenty-one. I know it's an important one in America," Monique said, smiling with her sad eyes. She'd become more sad and more content at the same time since returning to Paris.

Their neighbors on the third floor had come by, with their twin daughters whom Hannah tutored; Monique's editor, Chantal; Antoine, the bartender-tattoo artist from downstairs; Monique's mother, who lived on the second floor and had made the *gâteau*. By the time everyone left it was after eleven.

"Thank you," Hannah said to Monique. "You didn't have to."

"Well, obviously I just wanted to have a party." Monique winked. When she was not writing, she hosted and gathered. A mother hen. Hannah the first chick.

Antoine told them to come down and have drinks. Monique said, "You go ahead. I want to get these pages to Chantal tomorrow." It was a précis and first chapter for her second novel. The first had been published, to good reviews.

Before Hannah left, Monique handed her a rectangular package wrapped in brown paper. A book, obviously. "Open it later," she said.

"You are 'legal'," Antoine said in English, chuckling and pouring champagne from behind the bar. Hannah sipped and ate olives with her right hand, and with her left she fingered the letter she'd folded into a small square and tucked into her coat pocket. It was the only time she'd folded or carried one of them with her: the rest remained in their original crisp trifolds, stacked together and held by a thick rubber band in her drawer.

Hannah did not respond to Antoine; she was staring at something over his shoulder: a group of students sat at a long table, drinking and laughing. Attention suddenly turned on one boy, at the far end. The other boys clapped and hooted; the girls giggled and leaned into one another. All eyes followed as the boy, lanky with dirty blond locks tickling his eyes, loped to the other end of the table. He grabbed the hand of one of the girls, pulled her to her feet. She was short and shapely with black pixie hair; pale cleavage burst from her scoopneck top. The boy leaned down and planted a long kiss on her lips. She resisted, only a little; her face and entire chest now cherry red. Hooting, louder hooting. Hanging jaws, giggling. Everyone else in the bar glanced over, then ignored them. Americans.

The girl pushed the boy in the chest, both of them now looking away, laughing nervously. The girl stumbled, evidently drunk. Hannah noticed the boy had closed his eyes when he kissed her; the girl's eyes were wide open. The kiss was electric; perhaps long in coming. It was meant to happen, for sure, though it may not have, if not for the public element and the wine.

"You should join them," Antoine said. He chortled, yet seemed earnest. Hannah watched as the drama dissipated.

"What did you do on your twenty-first birthday?" she asked.

He poured her another glass, smiled knowingly. "Ha, well, you really want to know?" Did she? Antoine came from the *banlieus*, had wild stories to tell. But Hannah's mind was wandering. The party, the champagne. The kiss. It was after midnight. Her mind loosened and roved. Twenty-one. She knew it didn't mean anything, but it reminded her that there was a way of thinking about things. Adulthood, childhood. Time. Thresholds and labels.

A waiter brought more bottles of wine to the students.

She could join them. Part of Hannah wanted to. But she wouldn't have giggled. It was meant to happen. A warm voice told her, *There was nothing false in it.*

Antoine wiped down the bar while Hannah watched the students. She said, finally, "I guess not really."

Antoine looked at Hannah curiously. He was not offended but amused. "You are a funny one, Ah-nah." He poured her another glass. "*Bon anniversaire, ma chérie.* All grown up. *Une vraie femme.*"

Hannah awoke late the next morning, head throbbing. No, not her head: fat pellets of rain against the window. The phone had rung earlier. James's muffled voice on the machine. Belated birthday call probably. He still made an effort, even when she didn't.

By the time she dressed, the clouds had parted; the sky was peach and bright. From her *petit balcon* Hannah watched the dome of Val-de-Grâce rise and darken against the midday light. The market would be open another hour. She went out.

Hannah took her time. Browsed produce and fish. Bought bread and eggs and pears. Stopped at the *pharmacie.* Decided to walk around Parc Montsouris, since it was almost three in the afternoon, her favorite time of day in autumn. Hannah ordered a coffee and sat at an orange metal table and now wished she had let Antoine tell his story. It would have been a good one, an adventure, and mostly true. Maybe he didn't get to tell it that often, from his side of the bar. But did French bartenders spend as much time listening to patrons' stories, their histories and woes, as American ones did? Hannah guessed not. No one in Paris ever asked, So what's your story? She came to Paris and immediately she was *Ah-nah.* Silent H. Monique's *Ah-nah.* No one ever questioned who she was before. It didn't matter. Anyway, if someone had asked, what would she have answered? Maybe she would have said, *It's Haa-nah.*

She walked home under a rust sky, fast-sinking sun. Autumn chill nipping at her ears and fingertips. Hannah stood outside and looked up at her little window. She waited. Sometimes she did this—fixed her eyes at her own life, from the outside. Tried to see it—or hear, taste, feel it—anew. Sometimes she waited for loneliness to come—not just *seule*, but *solitaire*—and it did. But tonight, Hannah felt grateful and alert. *Shy senses, normal senses . . . slow to rouse but slow to quench—in short, healthy senses.* The warm voice came into her ear again, its vibrations, then settled behind her heart.

I was wondering your opinion on something important.

Hannah looked up to see a pale dusk moon. It was the sort of moon that appeared in silent movies she'd seen at Le Champo, and under it, a reel of memories flashed through her mind. She remembered marching up to Madame Glissant at the mall. She remembered seeing the ocean for the first time and riding the waves that summer. She remembered handing a ticket to a bus driver, and cleaning toilets, and searching for Claudine's velvety green in the woods. She remembered packing her boxes for Paris.

Her window was darkened now, but the moonlight glowed and Hannah could see the silhouette of the lamp she would switch on when she came in from outside. It was an antique oil lamp that had belonged to Monique's grandmother. Hannah fixed her sight and saw herself turning the switch. The flare of light. The light was small but bright, and in the vision Hannah perceived something definite: the oil and the radiance were one thing, coupled and continuous. *L'essence c'est l'essence.* The two meanings, fuel and spirit, were distinct but inextricable.

She had come this far. From the street, under nightfall in Paris, Hannah sharpened her gaze—all her senses—and fathomed her own life. She was twenty-one—*une vraie femme*, or *une femme qui a mal tourné*, all grown up or badly turned out, and it didn't matter.

It was he, Charles Lee, who had always known. That it didn't matter. That what mattered was *l'essence*. He was the one. In knowing, he had both fueled and lit her spirit.

Now he was asking her for something. *Your opinion. Something important.* She was alert and grateful. She was glad he asked.

3.

Charles had been home for a week over the summer—back from a three-month assignment before heading out again—and badly needed a haircut. He hadn't been to Vernon's in years. There was a new sign—Fat Mike's BARBER SHOP—and Charles didn't know when it had changed. He decided to go in. It was late afternoon on a Friday; the place was buzzing. Charles almost didn't recognize Mike, who said, "Well look who it is." Mike wore a big graying Afro and had lost weight. "The great disappearing act, Charles Lee. Now ya see him, now ya don't. Couple presidents now?"

"Just about," Charles said. "How ya been, Mike?"

"Can't complain." He told Charles about his boys, now in middle school and managing to stay off the corners.

"Vernon?" Charles knew the answer.

Mike nodded. "Almost two years ago. He went easy. We were glad for that."

An old man lowered his newspaper and cleared his throat. "You're Essie Lee's boy," the man said.

Charles and the old man eyed each other. "Yessir," Charles said.

The man went back to his paper. It seemed that was all he'd be saying about that.

Charles looked to Mike, who shrugged.

Mike patted his chair, and Charles sat down. Mike worked quickly, all business. There was a line now. Fat Mike's was a place where the job got done, and the wait wouldn't be long. Charles was in and out while the old man leaned back for his shave.

He walked home the long way around the block, taking in all the changes in the neighborhood—For Sale signs on nearly every block, a Vietnamese nail salon, a coffee house on the corner. As Charles turned onto Kenyon Street, an old Lincoln pulled up slow beside him. The driver rolled down the window. "I knew Frank," the old man said. He was wearing a porkpie hat now, but Charles recognized the voice from before. "We ran together in those days."

This thing happened, and I want to tell you about it.

At the house the Lincoln pulled over, and the man, his face now shiny and smooth-shaven, climbed out with his cane. They stood at the bottom of the stoop. Charles invited him in, but the man begged off. His name was Clarence Crawley. He lived in St. Louis now but was in town burying his aunt.

The old man told me that Frank was alive, living in Senegal last he heard. Followed a woman there. Before that, San Antonio, for a while Chicago. He didn't know much else. He said, "We ran together. Frank, he was no prince. But he weren't empty-headed either. Frank wasn't a punk. He had ideas. It was a long time ago. But I thought you might want to know."

I could go and find him. It wouldn't be hard. But why should I? I've been thinking about this. Frank and I, we're not so different. Neither of us wanted what we got stuck with. That's the truth, and it never changed.

But you knew that. You knew from the beginning.

I've been writing to you a long time. I wonder who you've become, what you think is important now. If you think any of this is.

The letter went on, it was longer than usual, spilling onto the other side of the page. Charles made sure to write a return address—a PO Box he kept in McLean—on both the outer envelope and on the letter itself.

He left for his next assignment, would be gone through December. He was glad for the distraction, moving the time along. He was still doing Tier 2 work, wherever they needed him, and he was as good as Bart had predicted. His assignments almost always became bigger and more interesting than they were at the start— risk factors and responsibilities inching upward—because of how good he was. He'd be body-guarding an asset's mistress, mostly to appease paranoia; then they'd move him to the asset himself. Or he'd observe and report on a contact, then they'd put him on the higher-up—there was always someone up the chain, often a government official—that Charles had identified.

If he stopped to think about the danger, he might flinch or falter, but Charles never did. He kept his eye on the ball. He watched and waited and knew that to move too soon or too suddenly was always a mistake. The best guys waited longer, then moved on a dime. Sometimes it was a matter of seconds; sometimes days or weeks.

Neither did Charles ask why, or which one was the good guy, which one the bad. He understood that the answers would not be satisfying, and knowing that, the work made sense to him.

"Now that's a frightening statement." The woman from the first training in Vegas sat next to him at an airport bar. They both had layovers and time to kill. He'd recognized her first. Her hair was different, long and flowing and a different color, and she was wearing heels—probably she'd need to use feminine charms to get what she needed, wherever she was going—but he'd known her right away. She went by Anita.

"What's really frightening," Charles said, "is when anyone tells you, 'We're the good guys.'" He was glad to see her. She was easy to talk to, and it was like no time had passed.

"Yeah, but c'mon. There are some really bad guys out there. Like a hundred and ten percent bad. And anyway, none of it makes *sense*."

Charles raised his glass. "Agree to disagree," he said, smiling.

Anita paid the tab and led him to a staff restroom at the end of a hallway near the lost luggage office. She clicked the lock and began unbuckling his belt.

Charles let her kiss his neck, but then grabbed her hands, and lifted her chin. Her lipstick had smudged to one side of her mouth, and he saw how dark the circles under her eyes were. He whispered, "How about—" and reached into his bag, pulled out a small film canister—"this, instead." He popped off the top and, from a cluster of Q-tips, pulled out a joint.

She laughed and seemed relieved. He handed her a paper towel for her face and buckled his belt. She said, "You know, this leather skirt is a bitch to get out of anyway."

They slipped out of the bathroom, the joint tucked into Anita's bra, and she asked did he have another. He did. "I know a guy in air traffic, with a windowed office."

"Seriously?"

"Don't worry; he's just a charts-and-graphs guy."

They stood by the open window and watched the planes take off. Dave the data analyst went out for his break, grinning and greedy. Charles let Anita have the joint. "I think you need it more than I do," he said. He didn't smoke much anymore. Once in a while for the jet lag.

"Jeez, a Boy Scout type. I could sort of tell, back in Vegas." Charles didn't say anything to that. "You religious or something?"

He laughed.

"Or—and I got nothing against it or anything, but back there in the bathroom—you . . . queer?"

He laughed again, a little louder. He wasn't offended. But it was a nervous, off-guard laugh. Truth was, he didn't have a better explanation—for why he'd refuse a good, no-strings fuck with a woman he liked.

Off he went. He worked through the fall. In January Veda would be back from her trip. They would have a few days together. In the new year, he'd have time off coming to him: he'd worked too many days, too many assignments, one after another—according to Bart, who was on him about it. "Take the time," Bart said. "I've seen this before. You get sucked in. Mistakes get made." Maybe he would take the time; spring in west Africa, why not. He would wait and see. Wait before deciding. Maybe there would be something in the PO Box when he returned.

4.

Veda spent a month in England. She got comfortable and put off her trip to Paris. Toward the end, Nicole took up with a medical student from Wales whom Veda found irritating, so she bought a train pass and set out on her own. In Berlin, she caught the end of Oktoberfest and learned how to roll a cigarette. Amsterdam was cold and rainy, and the best museums were closed for renovation. One night a pimp approached Veda with a wad of cash and a proposition; she got on the morning train and headed south. She took her time making her way to Paris—Bruges, Lille, Amiens. For two more weeks, she sat in

cathedral pews, stood on bridges, ate bread and cheese. It was easier
than she'd thought, getting around, traveling alone. To keep men from
harassing her, she took to wearing baggy jeans and her father's old
Army sweatshirt, her hair up in a Redskins cap.

Veda was three days in Paris before venturing to find Rue Pascal.
She checked in to a hostel in the Latin Quarter and kept busy doing
laundry and browsing tourist sites the first two days; on the third
day she sat on a bench by the Seine, pensive. What was she doing
here. What was this all for. When finally she found her way to the
14th arrondissement, she walked up and down the street for an hour,
then sat in a café. She didn't know which building. It was a small
street, but still there were at least twenty buildings. She thought
there was a 5 in the address, but she couldn't recall for sure. She
came the following day at sundown and waited for the lights to go
on in the windows. One of the buildings had a blue front door—a
vibrant blue that was somehow also serene. She'd been drawn to it
right away (plus the number was 51), so she focused on the windows
there. A woman with twin girls approached, and Veda made like she
was walking in the opposite direction; she looked over her shoulder
and focused on the fingers punching in the code.

Veda knocked on the door of the ground-floor apartment. A
woman answered in bare feet and wrapped in an enormous shawl.
Her black hair was tied up in a messy chignon. When she saw Veda,
Monique's expression changed from mildly annoyed to solicitous.
"Are you all right, my dear?" Monique said in English. Veda was no
longer wearing her protective disguise—she'd put on a purple dress
and tall Doc Marten boots—but something still gave her away as
an American. She had the look of someone in search of something
definite and specific. "Can I help you?"

Veda said who she was looking for, and Monique became
animated. Yes, yes, Hannah Lee lived here, upstairs. Was she
expecting her? Obviously she knew Hannah well; was more than
just a neighbor.

"No," Veda said. "Not at all. It will be . . . a surprise." She tried to
sound casual—an old friend passing through. In fact, Veda was not

shocked to have found Hannah; somehow she knew that finding her
would not be the hard part.

Monique made tea. They sat at one end of the large oval dining
table. Hannah would be back soon, she'd gone to the museum library
to do research. "We have begun a new project," Monique said. "A
novel, based on the life of Balthus." Monique went on to describe
who Balthus was and why he interested her. Soon, Veda knew more
about the painter than she did about the woman speaking. She
hadn't even said her name.

"A man like Balthus, there has to be more than meets the eye, you
see," Monique was saying, when they heard the squeal of the heavy
blue door, footsteps in the building foyer. Monique had left her front
door cracked open.

The footsteps ascended the stairs, then stopped. Slowly they
retreated. It was unusual for Monique's door to be open. Monique
put down her cup, pushed back from the table, and stood. "Ah-nah?"
she called. She walked to the front door and opened it wide. "*Viens.*
You have a visitor."

Veda Lee and Hannah Lee stood at opposite ends of Monique
Glissant's table, staring at each other.

Their postures became taut—as if a force pulled forward from
their chests, locking them together.

Monique cleared her throat. "We have been having such a nice
chat. You are surprised, Ah-nah? She said you would be."

Hannah pressed her shoulders back. "I . . . yes. What a surprise."
Hannah's voice was flat, and controlled.

Veda remembered that evenness; her babysitter's persistent
calm. She tucked her hair behind her ear and focused on the scuffs
on her boots. Then she lifted her eyes and said, "I thought . . . it
wouldn't be so hard to find you. I guess it wasn't." Veda wanted to
get this part out of the way—that she'd come looking for Hannah.

Hannah re-gripped the handles of her tote bag. Her face
flushed, but her expression was inscrutable, and Veda remembered
this, too.

"I've been telling your friend about Balthus," Monique said brightly. "Just when you came."

A beat of stillness. Darkness clicking down outside.

"You have not seen each other in some time?" Monique looked back and forth between them. Then she leaned over the chair and began gathering the pot and teacups, a few scattered papers. Creating motion, moving the air.

"A pretty long time," Veda said.

"You've . . . you're so tall," Hannah said.

Veda laughed at that. "You look the same," she said. "But different."

Hannah continued to hold her tote bag off the ground, her shoulders square despite the weight of thick art books pulling on one side.

"Sit, sit," Monique said, waving her hands. She left the room. There was rummaging in the kitchen.

Veda slid back into the chair and stacked her hands in her lap. She tucked her chin and lengthened her neck; it was something her dance instructors had drilled into her. *Soft and hard, like steel lace.* Hannah put her bag by the door. She came forward and pulled out a chair, but did not sit. It was not unlike the first time the two met— Veda sitting, statuesque, and Hannah standing by, stunned by the sight of her. Back then Veda had taken Hannah's hand, full of trust and confidence. Now, eight years later, neither recalled the memory.

Their eyes pulled toward each other and locked as their beating hearts had moments before. Hannah sat down.

"Your friend is nice," Veda said. She knew she should say more. She did not want to beat around the bush. Almost two months she'd been working her way to this moment. Longer, really.

Hannah said, "So—how did you . . ." She did not finish her question. Maybe she would have, if Veda had not started in, all at once.

She told Hannah about the letters—the one in the mailbox that came back; the one in Charles's briefcase. She took them back four years in an instant. "He didn't know," Veda said, "my dad. That I was looking. That I saw." She twisted a pink stone ring around her index finger. She'd bought it on the street in London and was proud to have bargained with the vendor. "He doesn't know I'm here."

Monique returned with a plate of bread and butter and olives, and a bottle of Viognier. Hannah and Veda sat silent with hands in their laps, like children receiving their punishment. "So," Monique said, "tell me. You were schoolmates?" Hannah explained how they knew each other. Monique was surprised to learn that Veda was so young. "Come all this way *toute seule*? *Quel courage.*"

Veda told them about her travels. She didn't yet mention the money. "I'm starting at Howard in January," she said.

"Your parents must be proud," Hannah said.

Veda just nodded. She wondered what Hannah knew. About Alice and her father. She wanted to find out. "So, you live here? Upstairs?"

They stood in Hannah's tiny kitchen. Veda was armed with her questions, her need to know. She told Hannah about the mysterious money. "It's sitting in the bank," Veda said. "I'm supposed to claim it, I guess." She mentioned the lawyer. It was an even more bizarre story when she said it out loud.

Hannah listened. Then she said, "I don't know anything. I'm sorry."

Veda had not anticipated how she would feel, either way. She found herself neither surprised nor disappointed. And she found herself believing that Hannah knew nothing—about the money, about her mother. It seemed ridiculous now that she imagined Hannah would have the missing piece. *Her* missing piece. "It's probably Alice," Veda said. "Though I have no idea where she'd get money." She said it in a defeated way that did not invite a response. And she said *Alice*. In her mind, Veda had been calling her mother by name for years; saying it out loud felt both strange and liberating.

Suddenly there seemed to be nothing else to say. Nothing at all. Veda's hunch had not panned out. All the buildup of the last two months. Now what? Did she have another hunch? Another *different idea*? What was her next question? What did she really want to know? It was getting late.

The force that had pulled on their hearts waned. Veda could almost hear the click, the unlocking. Her dance instructors would cringe to see her sagging shoulders, dropped chin. Veda realized she did not want to ask, or know, anything more. About the letters. Her father. He had always had his own mysteries. Still, he was known to her; a certainty. Nothing was as sure, and she wasn't going to start doubting. Veda felt at once that she knew everything; that there wasn't anything to know; and that, if there was, it had nothing to do with her.

The spinning again. An image of bright lights by the ocean at night, teacups twirling. Weariness came over Veda all at once: she missed Kenyon Street and Aunt Rhea and her cat.

She said: "Do you know where Josephine Baker performed?"

The grand foyer of the Folies Bergère was all greens and golds, like an underwater palace. Enormous candelabras, red spires illuminated, flanked the staircase.

"Wow. This is . . . something." Veda stepped up behind Hannah's shoulder. It was the following night, and they'd agreed to meet by the stairs. Hannah had picked up the tickets at Will Call, from Monique's friend. Veda scanned the upper floor. "What's with all the horses?"

"And this paint job."

"I guess it's supposed to be 'gilded'."

"Not quite worthy of Josephine?"

"Not really." But Veda wasn't actually disappointed. It was exciting, and she felt somehow at home. She wore an ivory sweater, her hair pulled tight in a long ponytail. Both she and Hannah noticed people around them noticing her. Veda stepped to the side, underneath the staircase, as if accustomed to the strategy. She would perfect her strategies in years to come—refusing to be taken for something she was not.

Hannah said, "Do you remember saying once that you wanted to be a beauty queen?"

"I said that? Really?" Veda considered this. "I guess that idea seemed simple enough at the time."

Hannah took a moment to reply. She said, thoughtfully, "Yeah. I think it was your backup."

They milled around the lobby. Hannah told Veda that she'd never been inside, only walked by. "Have you been to Josephine's house, the Chateau?" Veda asked. Hannah had not. "I've seen pictures. My aunt told me about it. It's . . . I mean, you can't believe it. Like a fairytale. Did you know she was a spy for the Resistance and adopted twelve children from twelve different countries?"

Hannah nodded. "Monique considered her for the next novel. She housed refugees in the attic, right?"

"I think so. She had this huge idea of family. Everyone was family. But then she died pretty much alone and broke." Veda sighed. When Rhea told this story, she swooned. Veda didn't want to burst her aunt's romantic bubble, but she figured the takeaway was that love and idealism could go completely wrong.

"You should go," Hannah said. "If you have time."

"Maybe." In fact, Veda had nothing but time for the next few weeks. It made her nervous to think of it.

The lights flickered. An announcer urged them to take their seats. Veda and Hannah found their way to the lower mezzanine and sat between a man and a woman, who motioned over their heads.

"They want to sit together," Veda whispered. Hannah spoke to the woman, who thanked her profusely, *Merci, merci, c'est gentil*, as they shuffled around each other.

"These are good seats," Veda said, once they'd resettled. They were front and center.

The musicians were warming up. Hannah took off her coat and folded it into her lap. The program was a modern dance medley, called *EsSense*. "I think this is going to be good," Hannah said.

Veda flipped through her program. She hoped so.

There was an awkward delay while the musicians retuned. Hannah asked Veda about college. Veda said, "They're starting a new dance major this year. I'm excited about that." She meant it. The thought of starting college was newly comforting. "They recommend double-majoring. I'm interested in science; but the history department is the strongest. They're big on the whole sankofa thing." The lights flickered one last time, and a hush came over the hall, now full.

Hannah leaned over to whisper a question (*sankofa?*), but, too quickly, the darkness swallowed the light.

The curtain rose. A drum went boom, the brass section blared. The woman who'd switched seats hooked her arm into the man's and nestled her head into his neck. Veda looked over at them, then leaned back in her seat.

Veda and Hannah both sat very still, transfixed. Hannah hugged her coat. The dancers strode across the stage, their bodies fluid and sensual.

As they watched, Veda and Hannah did not speak, or touch. In the darkness, they lost themselves in the beauty of the movements. Questions went unasked, and unanswered, and yet both felt proximal, together, in some way.

.

Wheaton, Maryland
December 1992

She has been thorough, methodical, attentive. Still, she pauses for a moment, sits on the edge of the bed by his side. Watches his chest rise and fall—slow, rattling. Chong-ho spoke his last words two days ago. Yesterday, darkness swallowed his vision. The end came quickly, the illness did not prolong; as he would have wanted it.

She holds his hands, clammy and very cold now, searching his face one last time. His eyes are open, pupils large and cloudy. She waits, and watches. Perceives no struggle, no eleventh-hour doubt—*Call the doctor. Take me to hospital. Save yourself.* Their resolve came simultaneously; plans made with a word and a nod. In the week past, all has held.

In the bath, he was docile, calm, while she scrubbed his skin. He offered up his limbs as she dried and dressed him.

The bed is made. Soon-mi pulls the spread just over his knees. Now straightens the tie of his *hanbok*, straightens the bow of her own. Licks her thumb, presses down a rogue strand of hair along his temple.

Outside the sky is indigo, the night cold and clear.

Two vials, two needles. Two rubber ties. Two pills. Easily acquired by her from the nursing home. One pill between his lips, back of the tongue. A sip of water, tip his head back slightly. Swallow. One minute, two for good measure. Her hand on his chest, the other clenched to brace her nerve. The second pill in her own mouth now. Swallow. The bitterness.

Ties his arm above the elbow. The vein presents itself, plump and royal blue. Needle in; plunge. Her lip quivering. Steadies her hand, finger pressing, needle out. Gently.

Careful to lay out everything on the nightstand: needle, vial, pill bottle, rubber tie. No doubts, no mysteries or complications. Their final word: their love everlasting.

To the other side of the bed. Much easier to administer her own, no trembling or hesitation.

In the lamplight she leans over, kisses his mouth, a long kiss. Switches off his light, then hers. Lies back, hands stacked on her breast. She should lie still, lie flat, most dignified this way. He would have wanted that. But she can't. She reaches under the blanket, finds his hand. Together, again, they die, together, again. This time without violence. Outside the moon shines bright, silent.

WINTER 1992-1993

1.

In November, the heat in the building was out more than it wasn't. Hannah worked downstairs at Monique's, portable heaters blowing at their ankles. Monique worked on early chapters about the painter's youth—Rilke, cats—while Hannah focused research on Thérèse Blanchard, Balthus's infamous child model. Thérèse was the neighbor's daughter, age eleven when she first posed. There was little information. She died of "unknown causes," age twenty-five. Hannah studied the paintings in books—angular Thérèse in provocative poses. It was hard to say if she was warm or cold, vital or ruined. *It's none of your business*, the girl seemed to say. Don't try to appraise. Perhaps her refusal to be gauged was her *essence*. Or was it the artist's.

Once or twice, Monique inquired about Veda. *Quelle jolie fille*, she sighed, already nostalgic somehow. Hannah had nothing to report. She did not expect to hear from Veda again. But after Veda left—probably for the south, she hadn't quite decided—an old memory rose to the surface of Hannah's mind: she'd been in town, on her way back to campus from the diner; a city bus turned a corner too fast. There was a rollerblader in the crosswalk. A young girl stood on the curb alone, waiting for her mother, and screamed. An awful scream. A familiar scream. Hannah had walked quickly in the other direction.

There was a series of calls from James, the messages progressively urgent: *It's Appah. He isn't doing well. A new prognosis. Getting worse. I'm flying home. Call me. Call me, Hannah.* Hannah didn't call. She would. Soon. More likely after. It had started six months before, the illness. It had been wait and see back then, neither hopeful nor dire. She knew what it was, and understood what was now happening. She didn't share James's need to participate. Just let it happen. What else is there to do.

The mother of the twins knocked on the door one evening in December. "Your phone is ringing, all day long. Every thirty minutes." She wore an apron, and there was flour in her hair; she'd been baking her bûche de Noël.

Hannah went upstairs and dialed, but she got James's machine. Her phone rang early the next morning.

"Both of them," James said. His voice was eerily subdued.

It was 4 AM: heavy charcoal sky and stone quiet. Still, Hannah sat down at the kitchen table, put a finger to one ear and pressed the receiver into the other. She wasn't sure she'd heard him right.

"They did it . . . she . . . together." A pause and an audible swallow. He was laboring toward normal volume. "I found them. In their bed."

Hannah released her finger. She'd heard him. She stood up. Her front teeth began to chatter. A biting draft was coming through cracks in the rickety window. Why hadn't she asked the porter to seal it before the winter chill arrived. Paris autumn was so mild, it was easy to believe it would last forever.

James continued. He uttered the words "homicide" and "suicide" and "lawyer." He said, *Your plane ticket is waiting.* Hannah hung up and started moving. She took a very hot shower. Got dressed, packed a bag. Made coffee then sat and watched the sun come up. Her mind was a blank white sheet.

She waited until just before leaving to knock on Monique's door. With her coat on and bags at her sides, Hannah explained that she was leaving. She said "accident," and she was sure Monique heard something hollow in her voice.

Hannah's plane landed late afternoon. It was the first day of winter—a watery daytime moon was out by the time Hannah stood on the curb. The airport shuttle took her straight to the house. James had been there all morning. The EMTs, police, a trial lawyer, all come and gone. James was sitting at the kitchen table with another lawyer—the estate lawyer—when Hannah walked in.

James halted in mid-sentence and stood. Squawking chair on linoleum. Bed hair, unshaven. The two stepped to each other. James hugged Hannah tight. Hannah smelled fast food grease and something antiseptic. The large prim woman in tweed smiled thinly.

"My sister," James said. The woman closed her eyes; offered dramatic sympathy. Hannah made no response. "Excuse us a minute." James led Hannah to the living room. He held her by the shoulders. "You're all right?"

Hannah squinted slightly. James looked wiry, like he'd been digging ditches instead of selling software for the last six years. His hair was thinning. Bloodshot eyes. "Are you alone?" she asked.

"Grace and the kids are at The Sheraton." There was a new baby; Hannah had yet to meet either.

They sat down on the lumpy sofa. James said: "He wouldn't go to the hospital. They could buy time, the doctor said. I really thought Ummah would help me convince him. We came to talk sense into him. But when I got here . . ."

Hannah tasted something acrid in the back of her throat.

"It was all quiet. Everything was normal. They looked like they were just resting." James's lower lip trembled. His first show of emotion, Hannah guessed. "She'd bathed him, combed his hair. The blanket was pulled up." James took in a breath and blew out hard, brow furrowed, like an athlete readying to launch.

"Did you . . . what did you . . ." Words came up; Hannah didn't know where from.

"I didn't touch anything. Suddenly I realized." James was working hard at telling her. At not skipping anything. "I realized. What she'd done. How she'd done it. I went downstairs. Called the ambulance. I didn't touch anything. I waited. Then they all came. They took over."

Hannah said nothing. Her mind still a sheet. Blinding, blank. After a few moments, she looked around the room. "Is there . . . anything else?"

James shook his head then leaned over his knees, fingers laced behind his neck. The woman in the kitchen coughed. James lifted his heavy head and said, "Ummah went to see her—" he gestured with his eyes "—a month ago. There is one thing, though." He sighed. "The ashes."

James finished with the lawyer, and Hannah sat on the sofa

and waited. She barely moved. The lumps were worse than she remembered, and this made her sit even more still. The hushed voices in the next room sounded like the tapping of muted keys. Hannah listened as if from underwater.

They went for dinner nearby. James told Hannah what the police had told him. Mostly, he made sure she knew that it had been deliberate, consensual. They'd been careful to leave no doubt. Then he said, "We'll go for Christmas. Grace and the kids can visit family in Seoul. You and I can go south to their village and . . . do this thing."

Hannah said all right. She picked at her noodles. Then she said, "I want to go back to the house for the night."

James tried to talk her out of it. "When we get back we'll pack everything up, throw stuff away." Really, he was too tired to argue.

"I know," Hannah said. She felt herself darkening into an ink blot, opaque and impenetrable. "Just one night."

Hannah moved methodically through the house, turning lights on in every room. Everything was the same. She knew it would be. The kitchen was spotless. An orchid bloomed on the counter, the spider plant hung near the sliding doors. Hannah tapped the moss in the orchid pot: still damp. On the stove was the large pot—the one with the red electrical tape holding the handle in one piece— where her mother kept clean frying oil. She lifted off the top. Empty. Scrubbed clean.

The wall clock ticked, its gears whirred. All the sounds still muted and watery in her ears.

Upstairs, the bedroom doors were closed. By the police? By James? The synthetic carpet felt scratchy, even through her socks, and everything felt small, like a child's playhouse. Hannah went to their bedroom at the end of the hall. Opened the door slowly. The bedspread hung off the side of the bed; the pillows were smushed to one side. On the velveteen bench beneath the window, someone had left a blue rubber glove, an empty Newport soft pack, a plastic grocery bag. The disorder annoyed Hannah, then angered her. She rushed in, picked up the glove at its wrist edge with thumb and forefinger, tossed it into the plastic bag. Tossed the cigarette pack in after it. Tied up the bag tightly. She proceeded to make the bed, smoothing and tightening the tuck of the sheets, then she stopped: *No.* She yanked the sheet hard, gathered and stuffed it under her arm, pulled off the fitted sheet and pillowcases. Made one big ball and rolled it toward the door.

In the bathroom, a night-light glowed. All was immaculate but for the smudge of a large shoe print on the tile. They could have taken off their shoes, Hannah thought. They should have. They come with badges and gloves and "sir" and "ma'am" but don't bother to honor the household's ways. Her instinct to defend these ways surprised her. Remove your shoes. Bow your head. Never speak aloud of tragedy or shame. She could hear the technicians' and policemen's too-loud, flat voices, describing each part of the scene to one another—like a sports match, or a soap opera.

There was a shower chair in the tub, and a bedpan. Who are— were—these aged people, these frail bodies? She didn't know them. Neither did she know them when they were young, alive to the world, if ever they were. Sadness filled Hannah like sleeping gas, smothered her sense of purpose. She would try at least to finish what she started. Plastic bag in one hand, bedsheets hugged to her chest, Hannah went to the basement.

A dusty smell. The hum of a dehumidifier set low and still going. Hannah loaded the bedding, set the cycle. The plastic bag hung from her wrist. She went back upstairs, slid her feet into the slippers by the door, walked out to the street. The neighbors had rolled their bins to the curb. Hannah opened one and dropped the bag inside.

From the street the house looked neat, and peaceful. By the neighbor's floodlight she made her way through the side yard to the back. There it was completely dark, save the illuminated picture of the kitchen framed by the glass doors. Hannah shivered. She stood at the edge of the patio, looking in. She knew that from inside, at night, you could see only yourself, reflected. Hannah crossed her arms tight and turned to survey the yard, covered now in a thin layer of icy white. Her eyes adjusted: at the far end, near the property line, stood her father's greenhouse; halfway to the patio, six rectangular wooden boxes, covered in frozen leaves and snow.

Neat and peaceful. Outside, a world of ordered growth; inside, only night blindness.

She heard a rustling in the trees. A raccoon, maybe, plotting with masked eyes. Or a lost fawn, foraging alone.

Back in the basement, Hannah sat on the washer and waited. Eight more minutes. Her father had erected a metal standing shelf— paint cans, rollers, and Mason jars on top; gardening tools, plant food, cracked clay pots in the middle.

On the bottom shelf, a cardboard box. It was covered in shipping stickers—like a cartoon trunk heading for an around-the-world tour. Hannah came off the washer and stepped closer. She saw her name, followed by the school address, in her mother's childlike mix of print and script: in the zip code, a 2 looked like a 7, the 3 like an 8. She had not written the name of the school, or Hannah's box number. NO FORWARDING ADDRESS, PAYMENT UPON DELIVERY, ADDRESSEE UNKNOWN were scrawled all over the box, each with a black line slashed through. Hannah squatted and spun the box around, saw that it had been re-taped a few times and shipped to four different addresses: Virginia, Arkansas, North Carolina, Louisiana. Several postmark stamps, the dates faded. Hannah lifted the box off the shelf—its corners were crushed and soft, but intact—and placed it on top of the dryer. Under the single overhead bulb, Hannah found the most recent label: RETURN TO SENDER. It was addressed to "Ummah," what was written on the original return address. April 18, 1991. Almost two years ago.

The washer began to whir, airy and rhythmic.

Spinning, whirring, faster, faster, frantic. Then quiet. Still. Hannah leaned over the box and sniffed. She couldn't identify the smell, only that it was unbearably familiar.

Hannah noticed that the top of the box bulged slightly. The tape had been sliced. She pulled the flaps open and removed several softcover notebooks that appeared to have been stuffed into the box later. She stacked the notebooks carefully, then removed the rest of the box's nested contents, one item at a time. Not the mice, nor the moths, nor the US postal system, nor any act of nature, had damaged or destroyed a single thing.

In the morning, before James came to pick her up, Hannah sat at the kitchen table and paged through the notebooks. They were filled with the familiar Korean characters she'd seen on the spines of her father's books but couldn't decipher. She would show them to James later; he'd be able to read at least some of it.

The notebook on top was only half-filled. Hannah turned to the first blank page and stared at it for some time. She reached for a pen from the jam jar by the phone. She wrote, *Dear—*

Then there was a honk outside, James's rental car. Hannah tore out the page, carefully, and tucked it in her purse with the pen.

2.

Charles was now used to spending the holidays in transit. Buses, trains, taxis. One year in Tunisia, on a camel under a gigantic orange sun. That was something Charles would never forget. Rhea always made her honey ham, and Charles called from wherever he was, but this year, since Veda was also traveling, he wouldn't bother. He did send his annual gift to Dennis—a check. First for medical bills and physical therapy. Then, after he got back on his feet, Charles had said to Dennis: Fuck drug rehab. Go back to school. Get a lawyer, get your son back. Dennis did. He was finishing his bachelor's. Thinking about a master's in education and teaching high school. He saw his son every other weekend now. Sherisse had kicked out the man who'd supposedly shot him; who knew why. Charles never told Dennis, in so many words, that he felt lucky. The checks were his way of telling him.

Veda had said on a staticky phone line, with the minutes on her phone card ticking away, that she'd spend New Year's in Barcelona, or maybe Rome. They'd see each other a few days after, then, at home. She seemed to be making the most of her time, and Charles was glad. He didn't know that in the south of France, at Château des Milandes, she'd met a boy—he was from Miami, and his grandmother had been at Josephine Baker's infamous desegregated performance there in '51. Of course Rhea would gasp, wide-eyed, when she heard this. Charles would chuckle and think it was a pretty good story, too.

On Christmas Eve, Charles found himself alone in a motel room in Zurich. It was a training site for European assignments, and he'd been asked last minute—volunteered—by Bart to fill in for a colleague who'd gone MIA. It happened sometimes—not because of the work necessarily, but because of who got into it in the first place. Charles didn't mind; he'd never been to Switzerland. Bart told him he should pick up some training work anyhow—good pay, easier pace. They got Christmas Eve and Christmas Day off, for example.

The two other trainers invited Charles out for a drink and a big meaty meal, but Charles declined. He had a Chester Himes autobiography with him, and that would suit him fine. For the holiday especially, Charles preferred solitude over keeping company with whomever was around. He was tired, too. That was the thing about "easier pace"—once you slowed down, the exhaustion set in. He felt noodle-limbed, and dull around the edges of his mind.

Charles lay back on the squeaky mattress and clicked on the lamp. He studied the book jacket, and the photo of Himes on the back cover. Himes wore sunglasses and a well-cut trenchcoat; he stood outside a French food market with one foot up on the doorjamb of a classic car—an old Ford, maybe a Model C, or maybe a Peugeot. The caption read, *Himes in Paris, at the height of his popularity in Europe.*

Charles put the book down, clasped his hands behind his neck. The young recruits were drinking and roughhousing next door. Charles stood and looked out the window. The place was up high, in the mountains; probably a school, or maybe a sanatorium, a long time ago. The surrounding peaks were craggy and snowcapped. It looked to Charles like a painting in a doctor's office. None of it felt quite real, himself included.

He should get out of the motel. The place was barely a notch above an army barracks. There was a moldy smell that stung his eyes and was probably poisoning his brain. He hadn't seen much of Zurich after the airport. Truth was he didn't much care for an easy pace; had come to mistrust it.

His colleagues had taken one of the company cars. Charles had the keys to the other. The fuel gauge showed full. He had all the maps he needed, along with the latest navigational gadget. He flicked the lights to make sure the high beams were working; they'd wound up a narrow back road to get here.

Charles started driving. He made it to the bottom of the winding road just as the sun smudged and faded over the peaks. He found the highway, then took the turnoff for Basel/Belfort. He just took the turn, didn't think about it. He guessed he wasn't actually interested in exploring Zurich; probably he knew it when he set out.

He pressed on the accelerator. All at once Charles couldn't bear the thought of the next twenty-four hours up there, at the training center. He'd spent many holidays working; why was this one different. He was not sentimental about Christmas, nor New Year's resolutions or fresh starts. But this year there were some things to think about: Veda would start college. Tier 1 was calling, if he wanted it, probably now or never; he wasn't getting any younger. Maybe sell the house—wasn't it about time. There was still that mysterious money to deal with; Charles was glad Veda was as suspicious of it as he was—her father's daughter.

Where was he heading, Charles wondered, where was all this going. His life. This car. This too was what happened when you slowed down: questions came gnawing.

Charles looked over at the passenger's seat and saw a glove he hadn't noticed before, stuffed in the crack. He pulled it out: black leather, women's. The female trainer had small, strong hands. She took care of her hands and nails, he'd noticed that, but only now realized he'd noticed. Had there been teasing disappointment in her eyes when he'd declined dinner? Maybe.

Charles drove, and wondered, and drove faster. Time off in the spring: it sounded like more work than work. He sighed. A pilgrimage to Senegal? Maybe Frank was still there, alive, maybe he wasn't. Pilgrimage was a melodramatic word. Charles thought about it on and off, but not too hard. He was waiting. He thought more often about his PO Box in McLean. Charles began to wonder if that last letter wasn't a mistake. Everything had become a little less real since then, hadn't it? He'd been working and living, going along, a solid restart; but now he saw painted replicas instead of mountains and sky. He was slow to notice what he noticed. What if a pilgrimage was a real thing, an important thing; not melo-anything.

Charles felt blurry in the head, at the same time he knew exactly where he was heading. He was halfway to Paris.

Outside Langres Charles pulled over. The gas tank was just about half-full. Or half-empty. He'd pulled off onto a wide turnout, but it was pitch black and hardly anyone was on the road. He needed to think. Charles's hands began to shake. He should've stopped to eat something.

What had made him think Hannah would write back? He thought she would. Charles held out his hands and breathed out, a loud white breath. He was forty-one years old. He had gotten his wits about him, or at least more of them. He wasn't good or great, but he thought that if he took care, he could be true. Steer clear of false. That was the heart of it, of everything, and he should keep his eye on the ball. He thought, I do believe she'll answer, and, It is important. He thought, Let it be. No sudden moves, none too soon.

The night was black and cold. A pair of headlights came full on from behind and sped past, leaving a blacker darkness in their wake. Charles saw Hannah in his mind now, swimming—that smooth, strong backstroke—in the middle of a vast ocean. She was going somewhere, getting there by strength and intuition. She didn't look over her shoulder, just kept stroking.

He needed to let it be. Let her get where she was going.

His job was to watch and wait. A while longer.

Charles held his hands out until they steadied. Then he turned the car around.

He drove back up to the motel on the mountain. He relaxed as he drove, kept to the speed limit. He thought maybe when he got there he could find his colleagues at the bar they'd mentioned. There was a small, cold hand in need of a glove. All the petrol stations were now closed, but he'd have just enough to get there.

It didn't matter, Charles thought. What did or did not arrive in his PO Box. "It doesn't matter," he said out loud. He had written to her, written everything he knew to be true, for a long time. It really wasn't much. That was the thing: it usually wasn't—the part that matters.

In his mind, Charles read to himself words he'd written, which he'd read over several times and, he realized now, had committed to memory.

> *Frank and I, we're not so different. Neither of us wanted what we got stuck with. That's the truth, and it never changed.*
>
> *But you knew that. You knew from the beginning.*
>
> *I've been writing to you a long time. I wonder who you've become. What you think is important. If you think any of this is.*
>
> *I could find him. Frank, my father. Then I'd look him in the eye. I'd say*
>
> *You and I are not so different.*
>
> *I had good luck, not bad luck. I had a window, and I jumped.*
>
> *It wasn't ever the boy's fault. It never is.*
>
> *Three minutes is too long.*
>
> *He was your grandson, and he favored you, and Benny was his name.*

3.

"Where'd you get these?" James took a piece of dried squid from the open bag on the seat between them. "Ick, they're stale." He spit it out into a cocktail napkin.

Hannah looked out the window onto the blinking night lights of Gwangju. Duras's *The Square*—Monique's birthday gift—lay in her lap.

Hannah didn't answer. The girl in Duras's story was pathetic and sad. It wasn't so different from the other novels, but right now Hannah couldn't bear it.

"You didn't touch the dinner," James said. "What else is in there?"

Hannah handed James her tote bag. He pulled out the wasabi beans. "I forgot how much you loved these." He needed to make small talk. Hannah understood. "You were really small when you started eating spicy things." This was true. In Paris Hannah sometimes went to Tang Frères for snacks and sauces. Once she put garlic chili sauce on eggs cocotte, and Monique chided her in horror. She ate it; she wished it had tasted better.

In Gwangju, they rented a sedan and began their journey toward Hadong. It was Christmas Eve. They'd flown the red-eye and were exhausted, but they were on a mission.

Hannah slept fitfully while James drove. James pulled over to the side of the road, opened his map, and nudged Hannah awake. They'd been driving a long time, and they were lost. "Do you see a little road that leads into Umulkol?" She studied the map. "I think so. It's hard to tell."

James reached into his briefcase and pulled out pages, the relevant section of the will. "'A Chinese parasol tree.' Shit, I meant to bring a picture. 'A melon patch . . .'"

"It's so desolate," Hannah said. She'd envisioned swaths of swaying yellow; it was an image she couldn't account for, but there it was.

"I guess winter wasn't in the plan."

They drove farther on, both growing discouraged. James peered through the windshield and drove slowly; Hannah shifted her eyes between the passenger's side and the map. Suddenly, "There," Hannah said, pointing. James looked up, followed her finger. "That has to be it."

"Why does that 'have to be it'?"

Hannah hesitated. She wanted to say, *Because of the way it hovers above the field, all alone. Because look how ancient and out of place it is, and the way the tips of the branches catch the light, like diamonds.* She said, "Because it's the only one there."

James reversed and drove down the road they'd just passed. He was trying to get closer to the tree but never quite arriving. Then suddenly he braked hard and stopped. "Check it out. Those are definitely not melons."

It took a moment for Hannah to see; James had always had better eyesight. Not far from the base of the tree, a series of dirt mounds dotted the land. Next to each mound, a large hole. "They're building something here, look." Bags of cement, lumber piled on pallets. James sighed. "This isn't what they wanted."

"So now what?"

"I don't know. I was hoping this was it. That we could just get it done and head back to the city." They'd planned to spend a night in Gwangju, then take the train to Seoul in the morning. Christmas morning. Grace and the children were already there.

"We can't just lug these all over the country." Hannah's eyes flashed to James's backpack, which held the two bronze urns.

"Lemme think. There's a place. I don't know if I can remember. We'll have to drive around. Maybe go on foot. I think when I see it, I'll recognize it."

"It?"

James bit his lip. He was uncertain but hopeful. A little desperate.

"Okay," Hannah said. "I'll drive, then. You look."

They found their way to the old village. The first time down the center road, they drove past it, but then Hannah looped around again. "It's somewhere here," James said. Daylight was waning. Just as Hannah switched on the headlights, James shouted, "Here!" Hannah pulled over and parked, just shy of a ditch.

"Careful getting out," she said. She reached into her duffel bag, found the knitted poncho and pulled it over her head.

The great stump was covered in moss, the path barely discernible beneath the overgrowth. James kicked the stump's edge. "We don't have a flashlight."

"How long will it take?"

"I don't know. Depends how far in we go. Do you remember this?"

Hannah shook her head, frustrated. How could she?

James looked around, his foot up on the stump like an explorer. "Well, let's hurry then. While we can still see."

They walked briskly, nearly jogging. James led and carried the backpack. The path was clear, well-worn, but they had to watch for overgrown roots pushing up. Hannah tripped once and nearly fell; James caught her by the elbow. At one point James stopped to rest and Hannah bypassed him. "C'mon," she said. Her certainty and determination mounted without reason. Mounted because they were breathing hard and racing the sun. "We have to hurry. We have to get there."

They got there—to a ridge, high above the village. "This is it," James said. Smiling, like a boy who'd just captured the flag. "This must be it."

Hannah took in the crisp mountain air. Hands on hips, shoulders back. Her fingers and toes were cold. The poncho was soft and tightly woven and kept the rest of her warm. She felt strong and winded at the same time—lungs tight, blood pumping, Hannah scanned the horizon, and the village houses below. Grimacing, she said, "I don't know." She was all quivering senses now, an animal in the wild, hunting. "I think we should keep going. This way. Just a little farther."

James gave her a curious look. "It's getting dark."

"I know. But it's clear out, look, you can see the moon. I'll bet there will be stars. We'll find our way back."

They continued along the ridge. The smell of pines was sweet and sharp. Then Hannah veered away, into the forest. It was barely a path but for a clump of yellowing burdock root that caught her eye. The ground was hard. Farther on, it became soft, supple, where the dense forest opened up and noon daylight had earlier penetrated. Darkness clicked down. Gauzy night clouds obscured the moon; if it had shone, Hannah would not have seen. She was listening. To her blood pulsing in unison with the earth's. She stopped, and James too. They stood in the center of a clearing. A grove of black pines towered; a fresh, dry layer of needles, moist layers below. Hannah's feet sunk into the live wet earth.

James caught his breath, bent over. He looked up at Hannah. He said, "Are we ready?"

Her breath was white; her eyes wide open. The moon would make her entrance through the treetops in just a moment; Hannah could feel it.

"Hannah?" James held a brass urn in each hand.

Hannah beheld her brother and remembered something he'd told her, what the police found: under the blankets, Soon-mi and Chong-ho holding hands.

Hannah reached out toward James, and he laid one of the urns in her two palms. She held it.

Flesh, hair, bones, blood. Heart. Essential substance. Never again to be contained. Hannah bent down, placed the urn beside her. With one hand, she cleared away a patch of needles. With the other, she felt for a soft spot, then dug down, plunging her hand as deep as it would go.

Hannah lifted her hand in a fist and squeezed the soil until it was warm in her palm.

"Yeah. Okay," she said. "Ready."

4.

December 25, 1992

Dear Mr. Lee,

I don't write many letters, so I hope these words don't sound strange. It's hard to write more than a few words before they start to seem like someone else's. That's probably why I've always written postcards. It's my job these days to help someone write words that belong to other people—real people with made-up voices—and that somehow makes more sense to me. I think real voices stay mostly silent, and inside.

This piece of paper is not very large, so I won't write more than can fit. You asked me what I think is important. This piece of paper is important: it belonged to my father, and he wanted me to have it. I guess I mean he thought it was important, and so now I do as well; even though it will take some time to really understand.

In your letter what seemed most important to me was the very ending. It was like hearing a silent, inside voice. It was like the ending to a story, a long story written over a long time, and it made me sad for you, and sad for your father. I never knew my grandparents, and your words made me feel a little sad about that, too.

But the sadness was like a gift, something I felt in my actual heart—like when the muscle is working so hard it pushes against the space that's holding it. It pushes and pushes, and it hurts, but you also know it's getting larger and stronger.

My opinion is that the only way for you to have that gift for yourself is to find your father. And then say to him those words that you wrote. I'm not sure, but I have a feeling it's never really too late.

I've been thinking about what to say to my father, and my mother, the next time I visit them; maybe I would try to explain this new word I learned, sankofa. It has something to do with going back to find something, but it's also about going forward. It reminds me of backstroking.

I am running out of space. Also, my baby niece is asleep in her crib next to me, and it's Christmas morning, and she is starting to wake up and cry. (Watching her sleep gives me that heart-hurting feeling too, though I'm not sure why.) I will finish by telling you that this piece of paper, and what I am enclosing with it, is also meant as a gift. Please take the soil in your hand and squeeze it tight until it is moist and warm.

Je suis votre bien-aimée,

Hannah Lee

5.

Their flights arrived within two hours of each other, so Charles waited for Veda at the gate. "You look good, girl," Charles said. Something was different about her, even Rhea would remark on it later that night: *You better get ready, Charles; your angel's ready to fly.* Veda let Charles give her a big bear hug and ruffle her hair, but it was as if she knew he needed to.

In the taxi Charles didn't start in with the questions; Rhea would know better what to ask and how to ask it. He was just glad to see Veda, safe and sound. The hardest thing about his work now was knowing what was out there while Veda went off on her own, into the jaws of the beast.

Dinner was ready, and they gathered round like old times. Rhea had made Hoppin' John, even though it was five days after New Year's. Marcus brought out two beers, and Veda asked could she have one, too. Marcus joked that it looked like someone went off and learned how to have a good time. Veda turned up her nose and said Yes, she had *thoroughly* enjoyed her trip. Her joke made them all laugh, but Charles sensed she was holding back, hamming it up to deflect. He caught Rhea's eye and knew he was right.

They ate, and Rhea told a story about the neighbor's uppity grandson slipping on the ice while shoveling (screamed *bloody murder*, and wearing those *fancy* leather-soled shoes) that had them all in stitches. Then the conversation turned to Veda and college, and Veda said, "So I was thinking of maybe getting an apartment." There was a hushed beat in which they could almost hear Charles's smile turn downward. He said, "Well, let's see about that." But they all knew he'd help her, of course he would, whatever she needed. What had Veda ever asked for, until now; and what did he expect, he wasn't hardly home anyway.

There were some things needed fixing around the house, but otherwise all was the same. In the morning Charles woke early and went for a run: there'd been snow, but today was warmer, the ground mostly slush. He ran on the street, where the plows had come through. In his mind, he made To-Do lists: have a beer with

Dennis, sit down with a realtor (Rhea agreed, they should see what the house is worth), figure out that money (time, finally, to get in touch with Alice), apartment hunting with Veda (close by, at least). He had a meeting set for later in the week with Bart and a guy named Jones, who would talk Charles through the training schedule for Tier 1—strictly exploratory. Then Bart would take him to lunch and say, "Go play golf for a week. Or sit on a cruise ship."

Despite himself, Charles recognized the New Year was a turning point. Small changes converging. Rhea had started going gray, even white around the temples.

Five miles felt good—his knees solid, lungs clear. A little creak in the ankles, which was nothing new. When he got home, he heard stirrings in the kitchen, Rhea or Marcus making coffee, but the house was still mostly quiet. He bent over and caught his breath, then headed up for a shower. From the landing he noticed something in the parlor: a stack of picture frames, face down, on the end table. Just then, Rhea came down the hall.

"You were up early; it's a mess out there. Look at you." She pointed to Charles's track pants, splattered with mud.

"What's this?" Charles stepped down and moved toward the parlor.

Rhea put her hand up and pointed to his filthy sneakers. Charles slipped off the shoes while Rhea went to get the frames. She sat down on the divan with them in her lap, and Charles joined her. He couldn't remember if they'd ever sat together like this in this room.

"I don't know," she said. "It just seemed . . . crowded in here. One day I realized there were certain ones that just made me sad, and others that made me mad." She handed the frames to him; there were three. The first was a school portrait, Rhea in the second or third grade. She had one big front tooth and a big gap. Her braids were neat and tight but there was a ribbon missing from one of them. Charles laughed. "Oh you laugh, sure. But you probably don't remember *this*." Rhea pointed to a mark below the left eye, a faint red smudge Charles had never noticed before. "You musta been a year old, two at the most. Mama was a misery those years. I didn't

know how bad she was until later, when I told Marcus stories. At
the time, she was just Mama, and we were just living with it. She got
better. She was better when you got older. But those coupla years
. . ." Rhea's voice got shaky, and she dabbed the corner of her eye
with a knuckle. "There was nothing could please her. And Lord
knows I tried." Charles looked more closely at the red smudge; he
could see now the traces of gritty powder trying to cover it up.

"She was never so easy," Charles said quietly.

"Well, that's true," Rhea said. "Not after Frank." Rhea took the
frame and laid it aside. The next one surprised Charles; it barely
looked familiar. Four boys in suits, the smallest one still an infant
and sitting in the lap of one of the boys. It seemed impossible that
it was him. "I found this one in Nona's things, 'bout fifteen years
ago. We'd just lost Bobby; Derrick's parole had been denied; some
woman was calling the house screaming about Carl. I understood
why she'd taken it down. Last year I put it back up, though. Those
boys were boys once. Mostly I was cleaning up after them, but they
kept trouble away; told the other boys to leave me be. Things weren't
so easy around here, but out on the streets, I knew I was safe." She
handed the frame to Charles. "Maybe you didn't even notice when
it went back up. I know y'all weren't close, but anyway; I think you
should have it."

Charles took it and nodded. His hands were still moist from his
run. He wiped them on his pants.

"Now this one," Rhea said. The last photo was the smallest. "I
framed this one myself. Probably I took it, too. I was about to put
it up, but then I thought, especially since V is talkin 'bout finding
a place of her own, and since"—she looked around the room—"all
this'll be coming down soon enough. I thought she might like it."

Charles stared at the photo. He was sure he'd never seen it before.

"There aren't many of these," Rhea said. "This may be the only
one." She wasn't scolding, just stating the fact.

It was a photo of Charles holding baby Benny, who was still
wearing the blue cap from the hospital. The photo was taken from
behind Charles's shoulder; it didn't show his face.

"I think it's a fine idea," Charles said. "She'll appreciate it."

"You'll give it to her, then?"

"Sure," Charles said, stacking it on top of the other. "I will."

Charles took a long, hot shower. He went through his list again and thought about whether he really wanted to keep the meeting with Jones and Bart. He let the hot water run over him a little longer. Charles thought about what Rhea had said, about Essie's misery, after Frank. And he thought about one more thing to add to his list: check the PO Box. It could wait, though; if he kept the meeting with Jones, he'd be near there anyway.

He got dressed and smelled breakfast cooking. Voices and laughter floated upstairs with the smells. How comfortable the three of them were together. It was their family reunion. He was starving, but he thought he'd wait a few minutes, let them have their time. Charles stood upstairs in the hallway and listened. The laughter brought him both comfort and unease—like he was lucky to be getting away with something.

He noticed now that the door to the boy's room was cracked open. That was odd. Had it been open last night? He looked through the crack, then pushed the door and stepped in. Everything was the same. The room stayed mostly unused, unentered. Charles hadn't been in the room for a long time. At some point he'd cleaned it out, took a trunk load to the Goodwill. It was basically for storage now, and he'd forgotten what he kept in here. Until now.

Charles walked to the closet and slid open the door. He looked up to the shelf. There was nothing there. He stared at the empty space. Maybe he'd remembered wrong. No: he was sure—

"Here." Veda's voice startled Charles from behind. He'd been standing there longer than he realized and hadn't heard her coming upstairs. She stood in the doorway, holding out the metal lunchbox. "I just don't think it should stay in here. I think—" she paused. "I think if you want it, you should keep it."

Charles stood frozen. He gaped—or felt like he was—at his daughter. His eyes moved to the lunchbox, then back to Veda. She was calm. In her expression he saw gravity. Charles was speechless.

He still didn't move, so Veda did. She stepped forward and held out the lunchbox. He took it. His face softened into a smile. He was sure it was the wrong note, the wrong reaction—pride, gratitude— but he couldn't help it. It was what he felt.

In her other hand, Veda had been holding something else—a small padded envelope. She held this out, too. "Rhea said this came yesterday. I guess some of your stuff still comes here." Again she surprised him: he'd never considered she noticed these things—his mail, its comings and goings.

Charles took the envelope.

"Breakfast is getting cold!" Rhea called from downstairs.

Veda turned to leave. Charles said, "V." She looked over her shoulder. "We'll find you a nice place. Your own place." She nodded. "Not too far away, though."

Veda smiled and looked at the floor. "Okay."

"Tell Rhea I'll be down."

Veda nodded again. She closed the door behind her.

Charles sat on the bed. He laid the envelope down and glared at it with suspicion. Then he took the lunchbox into his lap and opened it.

The contents stared up at him. A quiet laugh, just a puff of air, escaped him, and he shook his head. It was too much. The boy had done this. Carefully, tidily. It wasn't like him. But then, Charles hadn't known the boy at all. Who he really was. Why he did this. Maybe that was why Charles had kept the lunchbox. He hadn't considered *why* when he put it on the shelf back then; he just did it. That was what it was like in the days and months after.

Charles sat with the open lunchbox another moment. He did not touch anything. But he thought of the small picture frame, the one Rhea meant for Veda, and he resolved to place it inside. It would just fit. Charles realized he did not want Veda to have it: he knew the expression on his face, the one hidden from the camera, and it wasn't anything he wanted Veda to have, seen or unseen. It was his picture, the only one; he would keep it. Maybe Rhea hadn't meant it for Veda after all.

They were waiting for him downstairs. Charles picked up the padded envelope. What was this: a Korea postmark, the familiar Korean characters for AIRMAIL. Did it have to do with the money? His name was written in cursive, the letters lean and continuous. No return address.

He tore it open and unfolded the piece of paper inside. He read *Dear Mr. Lee,* and he scanned to the end.

"These pancakes aren't gonna wait forever! Marcus is gunning for seconds."

Charles exhaled. He held the letter in his hand and let his eyes settle on *Hannah Lee.*

Then he reached into the envelope and pulled out a small plastic bag, the handles tied in a knot. He opened it to find a Ziploc bag inside. He pulled open the seal and held the inner bag up to his nose. The contents smelled of cool, bitter earth. Charles closed his eyes. The bitterness was tinged with sweet: it was a peculiar, particular smell. He could almost taste it, like a strong tea made from early fruit.

He heard plates stacking and a chair screeching away from the table. There wouldn't be many more breakfasts at home with Veda. Charles opened his eyes and straightened his back. He resealed the bags, folded the paper, put everything back in the envelope. It would wait for later, and that was all right. It was too much for now. He'd been waiting this long. He realized it now, that he'd been waiting for Hannah, all this time; and he would wait some more. *Dear Mr. Lee.* Charles smiled at that.

He stood and carried the things that Veda had brought to him back to his room, and he laid them on the dresser with the two picture frames. Then he went downstairs to breakfast.

The pancakes were still warm and delicious, and Marcus poured coffee. They sat and heard more about Veda's travels—Josephine's castle and the boy from Miami, pilsners and cheeses and Las Ramblas on New Year's Eve. Charles listened, even as his mind wandered: he saw words he'd scanned moments before—*going back, going forward; Please take the soil in your hand.*

And there were the words Hannah Lee had written at the end just before her name—*Je suis votre bien-aimée*—the meaning of which Charles would be sure to learn but that maybe, he thought, he already knew.

Epilogue

2004–2005

This year she brought a trucker hat and an Usher CD. Five years ago it was a Will Smith *Men in Black* action figure and a mood ring. He would be twenty-six years old. Each time she went, Veda tried to think of what he'd like, things he'd think were cool. It was harder to actually envision him as a grown adult, but it made her smile to try.

She'd asked both Charles and Alice to join her. Her fiancé was a social worker and had encouraged her to ask them. To go to the grave, for once, together. Twenty years now. *A real commemoration.* But Charles was on assignment, out there, somewhere—Karachi, or Bahrain, or who knew. He wouldn't be back until after Christmas, at the earliest. Alice was evasive but didn't say no; until the last minute, when she called to say that the celebration for the new women's cooperative headquarters in Tirúa had been scheduled for September. Laila would be in Santiago setting up the weavers' storefront, so Alice needed to stay put.

Did Veda want to come for the opening? She was, after all, the major donor. It was an awkward invitation, and Veda had only to remember her first and last visit—eleven years ago after her father had solved the mystery of the inheritance—to form her answer. On that visit, which was even worse than she'd feared, Veda saw her mother living in a slum, Laila's bottles and pills evidently destroying their life. Things were much better now, and Veda had had some part in that: sometimes money helped. It helped Laila get clean. It helped them reclaim the house they'd lost, a pretty orange bungalow with a tin roof. Veda didn't have to think hard about transferring the money from her bank account to Alice's: it was Alice who had cared for the old woman anyway. Veda didn't want a stranger's half-witted charity, didn't need it. Alice did.

The fiancé frowned sympathetically at Veda as she spoke on the phone. Well, she'd tried. It was something. He would come with her to the gravesite, for consolation, and she was grateful.

Alice was lying. She traveled to New Hampshire in August. Her stepmother had called—this in itself was alarming—threatening to leave Alice's father, whose mind had been fading, slowly at first, then seemingly all at once. When Alice arrived she found Cheryl in sweatpants, shouting at a shrunken, unshaven Nick Sr., *I'm Cheryl, I'm your wife, you ungrateful sonofabitch.* Apparently he had been calling her by other names, none of which was Alice's mother's.

Alice stayed three weeks. She cleaned the house and fed her father, who recognized her once or twice. It was somehow not difficult for her to treat him like a child. Cheryl took long, hot baths, went to lunch with her Right to Life friends, and pulled herself together. One night after Nick Sr. was in bed, they sat on the porch, and Alice offered Cheryl a cigarette. Cheryl took a drag, then went inside and brought out her husband's most expensive bourbon. They sat together and smoked, and passed the bottle until it was finished.

Alice changed her return flight to Santiago, departing instead from DC. Then she rented a car. She had not planned it this way, although maybe she knew it all along. She drove eleven hours straight and went to the grave, alone. The hat and the CD were still there. She smiled and laughed. The laughter became sobs.

Yes, that's right, that's what he would have liked.

He was real, a real boy, not a phantom.

She never really knew him.

Charles was home in January to finally meet the boy from Miami—no longer a boy, soon to be his son-in-law—who seemed to make his daughter so happy. Rhea told him it was one of those romantic stories: a fluke run-in at a record store, after ten years.

Rhea and Marcus had in the end kept the house on Kenyon Street. Veda and the fiancé lived in Adams Morgan, and Charles kept a place in Arlington. They all gathered at the house, and before dinner they sat in the parlor, which the four of them had repainted—a cool mint green that Veda had chosen—and Rhea and Marcus had refurnished. They now sat in the room often and enjoyed it.

The fiancé said: *Mr. Lee, I understand you met your father some years ago for the first time.* He wasn't exactly tactless, or if he was, he knew it. Veda glanced at him sideways, but it was more a look of complicity than reproach.

Charles said, *Yes, that's true.*

I admire that, the fiancé said. *In my work, it can take years and years of therapy before someone is able to take that sort of risk.*

Well, I suppose it took me years and years of something.

Frank did well for himself, as it turned out, Rhea said. *Isn't that right, Charles?*

I suppose so. Africa agreed with him. Until it didn't. They were silent a moment. Frank had died five years before, in a boating accident. There was suspicion that his new wife was a gold digger and had gotten her cousin to sabotage the boat, but Charles found no evidence of this.

We were hoping to visit sometime. Take a trip to Dakar. Sooner than later. Veda and the fiancé looked at each other and squeezed each other's hands.

The company is performing in Burkina Faso this summer, Veda said, *so the timing is perfect.* She was the assistant to the director of a modern dance company.

You should do that, Charles said. He meant it, but everyone went silent for some reason. Rhea cleared her throat. Something unsaid began thickening in the room.

The boy was nice. He loved Veda, Charles could tell. Did she love him? He hoped so. He hoped she wasn't with him just to feel safe.

But he shook off the thought. Safe didn't have to be a four-letter word. The fiancé continued talking—he and Marcus, it turned out, both played the guitar—then refused another beer, said something about "solidarity" with Veda for the next seven months that Charles only half-caught.

The unsaid would be said soon enough—joyfully, expectantly—but for now, Charles's mind drifted back, literally drifted to the shores of West Africa—where, five months before, in August, he'd stood with his hand visored over his eyes, scanning the vast green-blue, looking, looking. Where was she? He couldn't see her. She'd swum out, strong and graceful as he remembered. He'd watched the long arc of her arms before they cut through the rippling waves, but then his vision had passed beyond her to the horizon. The high-noon sun was a perfect yolk, and it warmed his blood. When Charles closed his eyes, he heard the weedy voice of old Bart Sheridan in his ear, saying, *Well it's about time*—his response when Charles told him he was taking off, two weeks, for vacation. No ulterior mission, no names or addresses or police records to track down. *I'll clear it with Jones, don't worry about it*, Bart had said. Charles hadn't worried about it. He knew something about timing by now, and it *was* about time.

Twenty years.

Vacation, not exactly. He'd written to her, and she'd said yes. *Dear Charles: Yes, I will meet you there.* She had not been back to the ocean in all these years.

Charles stepped forward, from warm dry sand into cool wet sea. His feet sank down as the current pulled and the tide ebbed. He scanned again, squinted. Where was she, where was she. He waited. Waited.

There she is.

Acknowledgments

Throughout the course of this novel's making, many gifted and very busy people said Yes, without hesitation, when they could just as easily have said no. I am deeply grateful to:

Tricia Khleif, Gillian Linden, Erin Ehsani, Lisa Peet, Alice Quinn, Amy Williams, Sharon Denson, and the late James Salter, for providing invaluable feedback on drafts at various stages, along with much-needed encouragement.

My agent, Emma Patterson—pillar of calm, empathy, and positivity; tough and firm in all the right ways.

Dallas Hudgens and the Relegation Books team: Lauren Cerand, Steven Bauer, Jules Hucke, Zach Dodson, Nikki Hall, Mark McCoy, and Jeff Waxman. Thank you for believing in this book; for your passion, patience, and focus throughout the process, and for so palpably investing your talents and resources in me.

Robin Holland, for your friendship, and for the generosity with which you've shared your amazing ability to see and render beauty.

Ted Hughes for imparting knowledge about camptowns in Korea, and Saretta Morgan for talking me through the basics of military procedures and culture.

My colleagues at Skidmore College for your thoughtful support of many kinds.

The MacDowell Colony for the crucial month that launched me into this book, and Alison Gazarek and Eric Dieffenbach for making DIY residencies possible when I most needed them.

Bob Gray and Martha Wiseman for strategy sessions wrapped in beautiful meals and much kindness.

My mother, Wooza Chung, for family stories that feed my imagination, and for modeling a true survivor's spirit—ever expanding and evolving.

Paloma Woo and Esther Woo for showing me anew what family is and can be.

In addition, thanks to Max Magee and the gang at *The Millions* for taking me in and keeping me on through all these years. Ilsa Brink and Jane Hong for working with me to create and launch my new online home. Thanks to Kim Church, Caitlin Hamilton Summie, Shannon Cain, Deanna Fei, Bridgett M. Davis, Nayomi Munaweera, Sanaë Lemoine; and to the *Bloom* community for the privilege of learning from your wisdom.

There are too many people to thank for helping me sustain the creative life, always seemingly on the brink of extinction in one way or another: these are my *bien-aimés*, kin and non-kin, whom I thank for your companionship as we all kick down (in times of weariness, kick *at*) the walls of the damn box we didn't create or choose.

Thank you, finally, to John C. Woo, partner and love, who inspires and aggravates and nourishes and hassles me like no one else; and who thus reminds me every day what really matters, and what really doesn't. The adventure continues: what's next?